MURDER IN MIDTOWN

Books by Liz Freeland

MURDER IN GREENWICH VILLAGE

MURDER IN MIDTOWN

Published by Kensington Publishing Corporation

MURDER IN MIDTOWN

LIZ FREELAND

KENSINGTON BOOKS
www.kensingtonbooks.com

To the extent that the image or images on the cover of this book depict a person or persons, such person or persons are merely models, and are not intended to portray any character or characters featured in the book.

KENSINGTON BOOKS are published by

Kensington Publishing Corp.
119 West 40th Street
New York, NY 10018

All Kensington titles, imprints, and distributed lines are available at special quantity discounts for bulk purchases for sales promotion, premiums, fund-raising, educational, or institutional use.

Special book excerpts or customized printings can also be created to fit specific needs. For details, write or phone the office of the Kensington Sales Manager: Kensington Publishing Corp., 119 West 40th Street, New York, NY 10018. Attn. Sales Department. Phone: 1-800-221-2647.

ISBN-13: 978-1-4967-1427-5 (ebook)
ISBN-10: 1-4967-1427-X (ebook)
Kensington Electronic Edition: April 2019

ISBN-13: 978-1-4967-1426-8
ISBN-10: 1-4967-1426-1
First Kensington Trade Paperback Edition: April 2019

10 9 8 7 6 5 4 3 2 1

Printed in the United States of America

Murder
in
Midtown

CHAPTER 1

October 1913

2. How would you aid a police officer in making the arrest of one or more violent criminals?

My forehead broke out in a dewy film of panic. Ever since this past summer when I'd found myself in the middle of a murder investigation, I'd envisioned myself as a policewoman in the New York Police Department. In my dreams, I would rise quickly through the ranks by dint of hard work, bravery, and cleverness to become a detective. I set my mind on taking the police civil service exam and studied every night after my workday as secretary at the publisher Van Hooten and McChesney. I also set aside Sunday afternoons, as well as any other moment I could sneak a few glances at my well-thumbed pamphlet of New York City's municipal ordinances. I was nothing if not determined.

Yet here I was, taking the long-awaited test, and my cleverness had deserted me at Question 2.

Where to begin? The question was so broad as to render it ludicrous. *One or more* could mean anything from a single thief to a rioting mob. Were these hypothetical criminals armed? That would make a difference. And what was this police officer doing? I imagined a square-jawed hero in blue taking on a knife-wielding gang. Conversely, I conjured up a novice as weak-kneed and untested as I would be cowering behind the closest solid object between him and the malefactors.

Being bogged down with possibilities might be the opposite of drawing a blank, but it was just as lethal to a test taker. Never mind that I actually had aided a male police officer in the arrest of a violent criminal. Even Detective Frank Muldoon, not my biggest booster, had admitted—eventually—that a seasoned policeman couldn't have played his part in taking down the killer any better than I had done. But a civil service exam wasn't the best place to spin tales of my past derring-do or to crow about my triumph over Detective Muldoon's reactionary attitudes regarding women in law enforcement.

During all my months of preparation for this moment, I'd assumed I was exceptional. An original. Yet the sound of a hundred pencils scritching against paper filled the hall, and all those pencils were pushed by the hands of women with the same dream. The majority of them looked to be in their early twenties like me, although a smattering were a bit longer in the tooth. Judging from appearances, they came from all walks of life: hard-looking, severe women; young women who might have worked at the five-and-dime; a few whose rough clothing and crude shawls gave them the air of being fresh off the boat; even one or two who were so well dressed that I wondered if they'd mistaken this for the entrance exam for Bryn Mawr.

The young woman next to me possessed the bearing of a debutante and had set out this morning in a frock of winter white topped with a ridiculous hat festooned with ribbons, wooden berries, and imitation songbirds around its brim. In order not to soil the silk with pencil lead, she'd removed her right elbow-length glove and draped it over the back of her chair. Yet even she scribbled away, undaunted by Question 2.

What kind of policewoman would I make if I couldn't even face down the exam with the fortitude of this pampered Miss Vanderbilt type? Giving myself a mental shake, I resumed writing. My background is German, not Irish, but what flowed from my pencil onto that test paper was 100 percent genuine blarney. I outlined my intention to assist the stalwart, competent male policeman by offering an extra pair of hands, or my feet to act as his Mercury to fetch help from other stalwart, competent male policemen. I emphasized that my most important duty would be to follow the policeman's orders with alacrity. On and on I wrote, until I filled the required space with my tidiest Palmer method script.

Of the approximately 10,500 officers and detectives the New York Police Department employed, around seventy were female. At most, perhaps ten or fifteen of us in this room would be offered an assignment on a probationary basis. As I handed in my test paper, my odds of attaining one of these sought-after openings seemed slim at best. What did I have that any of these other hundred women didn't?

"When will we hear back?" I asked the sergeant at the front of the room.

He took my papers, tossed them without a glance on top of the stack at his elbow, and then leveled his cold-eyed stare on me. His scowl and gruff manner conveyed how far beneath his dignity he considered proctoring women's exams to be. "After they're graded."

"How long will that be?" I asked. "Weeks? Months?"

"It takes as long as it takes."

A wiseacre remark about the brisk efficiency of the NYPD died before it reached my lips. Something told me Sergeant Doom wouldn't be appreciative.

As I headed for the exit, I debated what to do next. Return to work? I still had my publishing job, thank heavens. But in our flat, my roommate, Callie, would be getting ready for rehearsal, and she'd be curious how the exam went. The urge to commiserate proved too strong to resist. Besides, no one at the office was expecting me. Last night before going home, I'd slipped a note under Guy Van Hooten's office door telling him I had a tooth that needed seeing to and wouldn't be in this morning. Normally I would have informed Mr. McChesney, since Guy was rarely in mornings, but Mr. McChesney was home sick yesterday and I wasn't sure he'd be in today.

I hadn't wanted to proclaim my law enforcement ambitions to anyone at work, and now I was glad I'd held my tongue. If my worst fears about the test results were realized, at least I wouldn't have to confess my disappointment to more than a small circle of confidantes.

I was mentally mapping out my route from the Centre Street headquarters back to Greenwich Village when I froze in surprise at the top of the beaux arts building's granite steps. The dark figure of Detective Frank Muldoon strode toward me, his severe expression making him look like a bird of prey homing in on some unfortunate little mammal. In this case, the mammal was me. Even stranger was the sight of Callie practically skipping at his heels to keep pace with him. The pair created a study in contrasts. He was in gray and black from fedora to shoe leather. She was blonde, with eyes the color of cornflowers, and wore a fitted dress of dusky rose. One tapered, gloved hand clutched at a gold wool cape and the other at a splendid velour hat trimmed with an egret feather.

Apologies bubbled out of Callie even before the two reached me. "I'm sorry—I had to tell him," she called out. "He just showed up and was asking all about what you were up to. Then he started making all sorts of accusations against you, and—"

Muldoon bristled. "I haven't accused her of anything . . ."

The word *yet* hung unspoken in the crisp air.

"Insinuated, then." Callie's frantic gaze was warning me, but of what I had no idea. "He was insinuating like crazy, Louise."

They were stopped now, and the full force of Muldoon's glower zeroed in on me. I was ninety-nine percent certain I hadn't committed a crime, but in the sights of that hawkish gaze even Saint Peter might have squirmed a little.

"What's happened?" I asked him.

He answered with another question. "What are you doing here, Louise?"

As if he didn't know. "Taking the civil service exam to become a policewoman." The look of irritation and disdain on his face riled me. "I told you my intentions last summer."

"I didn't think you'd follow through with the preposterous idea."

Preposterous, the man said. To the woman who'd saved his bacon, professionally speaking, not four months ago. "Evidently it's a good thing I did decide to take the exam this morning, since I need an alibi for . . ." I tilted my head. "What is it I'm supposed to have done?"

Before he could respond, Callie blurted out the news. "Your boss—he's dead."

That took my breath. Ogden McChesney was an old hypochondriac, but no one had suspected he was really at death's door. "Poor Aunt Irene," I said. "She'll be heartbroken. Mr. McChesney was one of her oldest friends—"

"Not Mr. McChesney," Callie said. "It was the young one."

"*Guy*?" That didn't seem possible. Guy Van Hooten, scion of the firm, was just over thirty. He wasn't in the pink—too many late nights, too much booze—but he certainly couldn't have dropped dead from stress or overwork. Indolence was his watchword. Some weeks he never even showed his face in the office.

Heaven knows he wasn't my favorite person in the world, but I'd never wished him ill. At least, not a fatal kind of ill. "How did he die?"

Muldoon's mouth flattened to a grim line. "We aren't sure."

"It was a fire," said Callie, in full town crier mode now. "The Van Hooten and McChesney building burned down, and Guy was found inside. Detective Muldoon here told me all that's left of your office is ashes."

The shock of my place of work's burning to the ground—perhaps sending my safe job up in flames along with it—would take time to absorb. Right now the startling news of Guy's death still gripped me. "When did this happen?"

"This morning," he said.

I tried to knit this together. Detective Muldoon was chasing down absent employees after a fire. Fires broke out all the time in the city. But a young, healthy man not being able to exit a burning building before the conflagration consumed him? That did seem suspicious.

"You'd better come back with me to Thirty-eighth Street," he said in a more kindly tone.

Maybe my test taking had convinced him I didn't kill my boss. But from the set of his jaw, I was now certain a murderer was what he was hunting. And I was inclined to agree. I could count on the fingers of one hand the times I'd seen Guy drag himself into work before noon. What else would account for his being at the office bright and early on a Thursday morning, apart from murder?

If Callie had come with us, she would have seen that Van Hooten and McChesney wasn't quite reduced to ashes. More of a blackened brick shell. But Callie still had her chorus rehearsal for an upcoming musical comedy, *Broadway Frolics,* to attend, so I accompanied Muldoon to my old workplace without her.

"Isn't this a little out of your territory?" I asked him as we approached Thirty-eighth Street. Last summer he'd been working out of my local precinct, in Greenwich Village.

"The Twenty-first Precinct's short-handed at the moment. Downtown keeps assigning detectives for special task forces, which ends up reshuffling us all."

I was going to respond, but at that moment we rounded the corner of Thirty-eighth and I saw the damage. A lump formed in my throat. It was one thing to be told my office had burned down, but quite another to view the smoking remains of where I'd spent so many hours. Van Hooten and McChesney's building on East Thirty-eighth had never been distinctive. In recent years the three-story brick edifice had lived in the shadow of newer buildings that had mushroomed on either side. Yet seeing its charred orifices exhaling tendrils of smoke filled me with a sadness I hadn't anticipated. A few glimpses through the broken windows hinted at the devastation inside. I wasn't sure I wanted to see more.

Guy Van Hooten had died in there. I was still struggling to accept that horror as I lifted my skirts and picked my way across wet sidewalks strewn with tiny bits of blackened debris. Policemen canvassed bystanders and neighboring houses to find out if they'd noticed anything suspicious earlier that morning. A bright red motorized fire truck, at least twenty feet long, still blocked the street traffic. Facing it were three horses standing abreast harnessed to an older, smaller engine. The old and the new, muzzle to fender. Firemen were reeling in the hose of the smaller vehicle, while other of their brethren milled nearby ready to douse any lingering flame. Overall, men in uniform were only slightly outnumbered by neighbors and gawkers.

Muldoon broke away from me to confer with police officers, so I drifted over to where my coworkers were huddled together in their coats and hats. The people from the offices upstairs congregated near the next building over. Jackson Beasley, with whom I shared the front office on the first floor, stood off to one side by himself, his black bowler crushed low on his bald head. He always held himself slightly aloof.

"It's about time you got here," Timothy Banks, our copy editor, told me. He was bundled in a long coat and his blue-and-white striped, slightly moth-eaten Columbia University scarf.

Next to him was Bob Sanders, our accountant. Slight, mousy, and nervous, he seemed an odd office mate for Timothy, a tall, jovial type, but they got along well. It was odder still that of the two, Bob was the family man and Timothy the perpetual bachelor. Jackson occasionally referred to them as Bob Cratchit and Tiny Tim, partly, I thought, out of envy of their friendship.

Bob glanced sidewise at me through his thick glasses and gave me a nudge. "We were beginning to suspect *you* burned the place down."

You aren't the only ones. I looked over at Muldoon conferring with a fellow detective. Why hadn't he simply sent an officer to my flat to question me? He hadn't needed to go himself. Maybe he'd wanted the satisfaction of snapping the handcuffs on me if I'd looked obviously guilty.

"Has anyone learned more about what happened?" I asked.

"There was one lady who was walking her dog early this morning," Bob said. "Guess she lives in one of the apartment buildings. Timothy's seen her before. She said she saw a strange man lurking around the building this morning in an old brown overcoat and a blue plaid scarf."

"Or maybe green plaid," Timothy said, with a slight roll of his eyes. "She's not sure."

"Brown coat, plaid scarf," I repeated. "That's it?"

"Said he was medium height." Bob's mouth twitched into a frown. "Or maybe tall but hunching over."

Timothy shook his head. "That old bat doesn't know what she's talking about. She's the crazy woman who yelled at me one day for stopping to pet her poodle. She was afraid I was going to kidnap it."

"Oh, her." I'd had my own encounters with the crazy poodle lady. Once, she'd accused me of stealing a potted aspidistra from off her windowsill. Not the most reliable of witnesses. "Has anyone been inside?"

Timothy shook his head. "The firemen won't allow it. The building's unstable. Part of the stairwell collapsed, and so did a section of the roof."

"The books are probably all gone, too," Bob said.

I guessed he meant the financial books, though I didn't suppose the other kind survived the conflagration, either.

Timothy nodded. "It's all gone."

As if to punctuate that thought, a loud crack followed by a crash sounded from inside the burned building. Shouts erupted. Two men were inside and came running out, followed by a cloud of smoke and debris huffing out the door and windows. "The staircase!" someone shouted, and firemen surged forward with a hose as spectators moved back.

During the hubbub, I drifted over to Jackson, who wasted no time filling me in on the morning's gruesome details. "Guy was hunched over his desk when the firemen found him, his body burned all over." He lifted his hat and wiped a handkerchief over the broad expanse of his brow, which, thanks to his receding hairline, seemed to account for almost half the acreage of his head.

"How awful," I said.

In a drawl that eight years spent on and off north of the Mason-Dixon line had not eradicated, he went on, "I had to identify him, which wasn't easy to do, I assure you. Guy was *a cinder.* And the smell . . ." He shivered. "Well, I'll spare you my description of that. You all don't have barbeque pits up here, anyway."

My stomach churned. Good thing I'd been too nervous to eat this morning.

"But the saddest part," he continued, "was that in death he was hunched over in a seated position—the very picture of a carbonized office drudge. Guy Van Hooten! Can you imagine it?"

Though they'd been college acquaintances in their Harvard days, Guy and Jackson were very different. Jackson was a worker bee, while Guy . . . wasn't. "Why was he here so early?" I wondered aloud. The only time I'd seen Guy in the office so early was one morning last summer when he'd stayed overnight at the office, drinking. Maybe that had been the case this morning, too.

"That was my very thought," Jackson said. "'It *can't* be he,' I told myself when the firemen informed me that there was a man in Guy's office. I was the first one here, you know, although a neighbor had already called the fire department. A few windows had broken—the heat, I guess—and smoke was pouring out of the place. I didn't go in, but I never dreamt there was anyone inside the building. Especially Guy. Otherwise I would've attempted to save him."

The claim struck me as more boastful than true, but who doesn't dream of acting heroically? Especially when the danger of actually being called upon to do so has passed. "It must have been awful for you."

"Yes, it was. And you know what was peculiar?" He didn't bother to wait for my response. "I thought for a moment that the person trapped in the building was *you*."

"Me?"

"Who else ever arrives at work before I do?"

"Not this morning." *Luckily,* I didn't need to add.

He nodded. "How's your tooth?"

"Fine." My lie about the dentist had slipped my mind. Now I felt almost guilty for this morning's absence. It was doubtful I could have done anything to prevent the building going up in flames, but who knew? At least if I'd been where I was supposed to be, I could've seen what Guy was up to. Why hadn't he been able to escape the fire?

Jackson seemed to sense the direction of my thoughts. "Didn't you say you found Guy once at his desk that way last summer?"

I nodded. "He'd had an argument with Mr. McChesney and spent the night drinking."

"I'm sure that's what happened this morning. Man was too drunk to get out. Maybe he never even knew the building was on fire."

A new thought distracted me. "Has anyone told Mr. McChesney what's happened?"

"I sent Oliver uptown to his flat with a note not long after the fire trucks arrived. I didn't want to leave the premises. Someone associated with the firm needed to be on the spot, and since I'm the senior employee . . ."

He wasn't, though. Jackson was our editor, but he'd only been hired last year. Others had been there far longer. Bob, for instance. "It seems odd that Mr. McChesney's not here."

"Only if you assume Oliver delivered the message straightaway."

Oliver, our office boy, had a knack for turning the simplest errand into an hours-long excursion. But Mr. McChesney might not have been at home. Or he might have been too ill to get out of bed.

My mind returned to this morning and all the unanswered questions. "You saw no one else when you arrived?"

Jackson shook his head. "Only neighbors. Some of them were watching from the sidewalk when I arrived. I didn't dare step inside—I touched the front door, but the knob scorched me. The place was already an inferno. Three fire trucks came, and policemen, and neighbors gathered on the sidewalk, some with their valuables. One woman carried an oil painting in one hand and clutched the case holding the family silver in the other. It took over an hour with two hoses going full blast to get the blaze under control. And by then the street had been cut off and was jammed with people gawking as if they were watching a spectacular at the Hippodrome. Revolting, if you want my opinion."

Now there were just soaked sidewalks, soot, a dwindling crowd, and a sickly, smoky stench.

"You must be exhausted," I said.

"I am," he admitted. "But we can't leave, can we?"

I didn't see why not. We obviously weren't going to get work done today . . . or perhaps ever again. At least not here. "Did the police tell us to stay?"

"No, but we can't just abandon the building, can we, without making an attempt to salvage things?"

My gaze swung back to the smoking ruin. Paper. Our work was all paper. What could there possibly be to salvage? The building had burned for two hours. The piles of books and manuscripts stacked on every surface had probably created a nice kindling for the fire. The effect of the blaze, followed by the flood from the fire hoses, on the office machinery and furniture was probably disastrous, too. "That might be a lost cause."

"Shouldn't we try to go in and see if there's *anything* we can retrieve?" he asked.

"No one's going into that building today except authorized city employees," Muldoon said.

His voice startled me. I hadn't noticed him hovering. "Is it dangerous?" I asked.

"The roof is going to collapse. What's left of it."

Jackson gulped. "Come to think of it, I'm not sure I want to sacrifice my life for office furnishings."

Scorched ones, at that. "I doubt there would be much to rescue."

Jackson shook his head. "The poor authors."

The chances of a manuscript surviving the conflagration were almost nil. Authors from all over the country sent us their books, mostly typed, but some still handwritten. Who knew if, in their eagerness to send off their masterpiece, those authors had made the effort to produce a copy. Though I carefully logged the manuscripts in a ledger book on my desk, that logbook probably hadn't survived the flames, either. In which case it would be impossible even to inform the authors of their misfortune. Dozens of dreams might have gone up in smoke this morning.

Muldoon was thinking about authors, too. "How many writers did Guy Van Hooten work with?"

Jackson and I exchanged a look. "Working with authors wasn't Guy's strong suit," he said.

"What *was* his strong suit?" Muldoon asked.

"The name Van Hooten." The man was dead and I shouldn't speak ill of him, but how could the police figure out what had happened to him if they didn't hear the unvarnished truth?

"Guy showed scant interest in the books we published and the actual work that went into producing them," Jackson explained.

"He did enjoy taking one or two of the authors out for drinks, though." I was thinking specifically of Ford Fitzsimmons. The time I'd found Guy drunk at his desk one morning, he'd passed out reading Ford's manuscript. After that he considered Ford his literary discovery and befriended him. I strongly suspected Ford had tried to have me pushed in front of an El train, but I'd never been able to prove it. Push or no push, Ford's book was due out in the spring . . . if there was still a Van Hooten and McChesney to publish it.

"I'll need the names of those authors, and of any other associates you can recall that Guy had interacted with recently," Muldoon said.

Jackson gaped at the detective. "You can't think an author set fire to the building."

That caught the attention of Timothy and Bob. They moved toward us. "You mean it was *arson*?"

Muldoon kept his expression neutral. "We can't rule anything out at this stage. Have there been any employees fired recently?"

"No," I said, at the same time Bob replied, "Jacob Cohen."

Jacob, a few office boys back, had been slightly before my time. According to Jackson, he'd been the most inefficient, surly office boy in New York City until Mr. McChesney had fired him while Guy was on Christmas vacation. I'd heard all this just last week, when Jacob resurfaced at the office to talk to Guy. Everyone had been relieved that Oliver was there to guard against Jacob's being hired back.

Had Jacob been so aggrieved that he set fire to the building? I frowned, trying to remember what had happened the week before. "Last Wednesday, Jacob Cohen came by the office, and he and Guy spoke for half an hour. The door was closed, but I could hear their voices raised at times."

Muldoon pulled a small notebook and pencil from his coat pocket. "Did you hear what they were arguing about?"

"I only caught a few snatches of words—something about a promise."

"Jacob probably assumed Guy would give him his old job back," Jackson said.

"But he wasn't rehired?" Muldoon asked.

"No, we have an office boy, Oliver," I said. "No business as small as ours needs two office boys."

"Jacob's getting long in the tooth for that job, anyway," Timothy said. "He's probably seventeen or eighteen now."

"He was never good at it to begin with," Bob added, before scanning the group anxiously. Clearly, he didn't like to malign anyone.

Timothy backed him up. "It was always puzzling that he lasted as long as he did."

Muldoon chewed over the information and then turned back to me. "So you heard them arguing behind the closed door. Were either of them angry when they came out of Guy's office?"

That was the odd part. "They seemed to part like old chums, with Guy slapping Jacob on the back. And Guy had me clear away the whiskey glasses and cigars in the ashtray on his desk."

"Guy Van Hooten and a fired office boy had been smoking cigars and drinking?"

"That's how it appeared."

Jackson clucked. "That was Guy. When he showed up at all, the office was just an extension of his club. The types of people he associated with weren't always the most upstanding, either."

"What kind of people?" Muldoon pressed.

Jackson arched a brow at me. "You didn't tell Detective Muldoon about Mr. Cain?"

"She hasn't told me anything more than what you've heard here," Muldoon said impatiently. "*You* didn't tell me about Mr. Cain, either, when I spoke to you earlier. I assume you're talking about Leonard Cain?"

"Yes, sir," Jackson said.

Muldoon's face darkened, and he stared at me as if I'd been associating with criminals. Evidently I had, but certainly not intentionally. "Mr. Cain came by the office several times," I explained. "I didn't know he was notorious. Is he?"

Skepticism, then a hint of astonishment, flashed across Muldoon's features. My question caused a ripple of surprise in the others, too. I shifted uneasily. My becoming a detective struck me as more far-fetched than ever. I'd clearly missed a basic clue concerning Leonard Cain. "All I know is that he owns a supper club," I said.

"Among other enterprises." Muldoon's expression conveyed that these enterprises weren't on the up-and-up. "What was his business with Guy Van Hooten?"

"I assumed they were friends. That's how Guy Van Hooten always greeted him—like an old pal."

"Whiskey and cigars?" Muldoon asked.

"Sometimes."

I should have guessed Leonard Cain was disreputable. He dressed like a dandy even though he looked and spoke like a longshoreman. It was embarrassing how naïve I could still be at the ripe old age of twenty-one. I blamed Altoona. Maybe there had been sleazy supper clubs, gambling dens, and houses of ill repute back in my Pennsylvania hometown, but I hadn't ever seen them.

"How often did Mr. Cain come around the office?" Muldoon asked.

I tried to remember. "Not too often—"

"All the time," Jackson said at the same time.

"Maybe once a month," I said.

Jackson shrugged as if once per month was frequent to receive personal visits at the office. Come to think of it, no one had ever visited Jackson. "Cain came by last night, didn't he, Louise?"

In fact, Leonard Cain had still been there when I went home. Guy and Cain were the only ones left in the building then. I could have been the last person to see Guy alive, aside from Leonard Cain and his killer . . . who might have been one and the same.

"I'll have a talk with Mr. Cain," Muldoon said.

Frustration surged through me. I wished I could be a fly on the wall while he made his investigation. But I wasn't a detective—not even a policewoman—and who knew if I ever would be?

Whether I'd have a job at all after today was starting to look unlikely. If Mr. McChesney decided to let us all go, I'd have to find another position lickety-split. I certainly wasn't going back to Altoona.

I couldn't worry too much about myself, though, when so many were in the same boat, if not worse off. Timothy was gazing at the building again, bereft. And poor Bob. Worry lines etched his face. He and his wife had young boys, twins, and one of them was sickly. Now he faced the prospect of being out of work. And who knew what worries Jackson had. He'd always been tight-lipped about his private life.

I turned to the latter. "Will you be all right, Jackson?"

He looked surprised, and a little uncomfortable, that I would ask. "Of course. I've put a little by for a rainy day." A laugh snorted out of him. "Or a fiery one."

I acknowledged his threadbare stab at humor with a weak smile.

His shoulders straightened. "I've never had trouble finding work. The world needs capable editors, and Harvard men rarely go begging for jobs."

He was full of himself, but I supposed it was good he was showing some pluck. "What about Oliver, and Sandy?" Sandy Novotny, our one-man sales force, charged with convincing buyers across the northeast that they should keep our meager backlist alive, was on the road in Boston. The thought of business made my head ache. There were still orders to fulfill—but our attic and basement areas had been most of our storage. And what would happen to the books in mid-production?

I looked up and saw Ogden McChesney standing before the wreckage of the firm he and Guy's father had given life to over thirty years ago. His lanky frame was bowed in grief, like a man walking into a strong gust. One hand was buried deep in his black overcoat, the other was leaning on his walking stick. I doubted the tears in his eyes were from the smoke.

Forgetting Jackson, Muldoon, and the others, I hurried over to him.

"Oh, Mr. McChesney! Isn't this awful?" I didn't know what else to say. His expression was so mournful.

"I'm just so glad you weren't hurt, or anyone else . . . besides Guy, of course." His face darkened. "How in the world could this have happened? That poor boy . . ."

Guy Van Hooten had been thirty at least, but he was still a boy to Mr. McChesney.

"I'm so sorry," I said.

He thumped his stick on the sooty pavement in anguish. "Why didn't he escape the fire? Where was he?"

"In his office—at his desk."

He shook his head. "Right on the first floor. Dear God! But then surely he had time—do you think he was drunk?"

"It's a possibility. But the police seem to suspect that someone set the fire on purpose."

The idea struck Mr. McChesney like a body blow. For a moment he was speechless, then questions reeled out of him. "Why would they think that? Whom do they suspect?"

"They aren't telling us much."

He glanced at the officers nearby, then at the flame-licked bricks of his old building. He sighed. "I'll have to speak to Guy's mother. Poor Edith. This will be an unbearable sorrow to her. Thank heavens she still has Hugh."

I knew little of Hugh Van Hooten, Guy's brother. "Apparently he takes even less interest in the family business than Guy did."

"That was by design. Cyrus Van Hooten didn't want two sons squabbling over the family business, and Hugh developed other interests. Or perhaps he was interested in other things because Cyrus made it clear to the lad that he wasn't going to inherit the publishing house. It was only ever a sideline for Cyrus, you know—a gentleman's business. An office to go to when he wasn't at his club. Hugh understood that and never seemed to mind that the firm was destined to be Guy's. Hugh's a promising young man, though you can't always tell it by looking at him. Very bright. An aviator."

Before I could ask more about Hugh, the others gathered round Mr. McChesney to voice their sympathy. He received them with grave nods.

"I'm not sure yet what this tragedy will mean for Van Hooten and McChesney," he announced. "I need to speak to the firemen and the police, but the building seems like a hopeless case. You can all go home, of course. I can pay you for two weeks, but after that . . ."

Jackson frowned. "*All* of us? Surely—"

"No, not all." Mr. McChesney turned to Bob. "We should get together, Bob, and see where we are in terms of finances, and how many orders we have outstanding."

"But the financial books are gone," Bob said. "Surely . . ."

"I've kept some records at home," he said with a long look at the accountant. "If you could come to my place sometime soon, we can go over them together."

"Yes, of course." Bob's expression was anxious, but that was nothing new. If anxiety ever came to life as a man, it would look like Bob.

Mr. McChesney's sad gaze took in the rest of us. "I'll send word when a decision about the future of Van Hooten and McChesney has been reached." He touched my arm. "Louise, make sure we have all their addresses."

The glum expressions all around said it all. We expected to receive our two weeks' pay and then notice that we were free to consider other employment.

"Louise Faulk! Is there a Louise Faulk here?"

The piercing voice calling my name came from a youth of about twelve. I gestured to him and he hurried over to me.

"Message for ya," he said, holding out an envelope.

I took it and tipped him five cents for his trouble, which the scamp seemed to think was no kind of tip at all.

The note inside was from my aunt Irene.

> *Louise,*
>
> *I've heard about the fire! Walter and I climbed to the roof to see the smoke. Is the building a complete loss? You must come to me as soon as you are finished there and fill me in on the details. Is Ogden with you? He will be heartbroken, poor man.*
>
> *Do not forget to stop by before you go home. I have a proposition for you.*
>
> *Aunt Irene*
>
> *P.S.—If you see Ogden, please give him my love and tell him that he must come by, too.*

"It's from Aunt Irene." I showed Mr. McChesney the paper.

He scanned it. "Dearest Irene." For the first time since he'd arrived, a smile trembled on his lips. He and my aunt were old friends. It was for her sake that he had offered me a job. "I'd like to go with you to see her," he said, "but I must speak to this detective first. Then I need to visit the Van Hootens and give Edith my condolences."

"Oh, of course," I said.

To my surprise, he grabbed both my arms as if he was suddenly afraid that I would leave him. "Come with me, Louise."

"To the Van Hootens?" The family house was uptown, I knew, near Central Park. Beautiful as the area was, I tried to refrain from going up there. One of those rarified addresses was tattooed in my mind, and I'd discovered that indulging the habit of visiting it became as dangerous as the lure of an opium den on an addict. And yet part of me burned with curiosity to see the Van Hooten family manse and to learn if I could why Guy was at the office so early this morning.

I glanced over at Muldoon, who had his eye on Mr. McChesney. Someone had obviously told him who the older man was, and I could see suspicion in his gaze. "I'll stay with you," I said, feeling protective of my remaining boss. Detectives had to suspect everyone, I knew, but Mr. McChesney was not a criminal. Unfortunately, I'd seen last summer how police could treat an innocent man.

But that was only half the reason I wanted to stay with Mr. McChesney. I also wanted to meet the Van Hootens. A condolence call on Guy's family might be a first step toward figuring out who'd set that fire, and why.

CHAPTER 2

The Van Hooten house, a four-story mass of gray stone in the French Empire style, was located one expansive mansion over from Central Park, on Sixty-seventh Street. Carvings of shells, women's faces, or floral flourishes embellished every cornice, ledge, and colonnette. Iron fencing enclosed both the entrance and several outsized, geometrically pruned shrubs that lined the front like sentinels. Ten months in New York had taught me what status went with possessing greenery.

Mr. McChesney expelled a long breath before pushing the doorbell, which was embedded in a brass lion's head that itself was a miniature of the knocker on the door.

"I never dreamed . . ." He leaned heavily on his stick. "Never *dreamed.*"

It wasn't the first time this morning he'd said this, or something similar. "No one could have dreamed all this would happen," I said.

The door swung open and a grave-looking butler appeared. It wasn't just that his demeanor was somber; his ghostly pallor gave him the look of a man who was fading away. His head bowed in acknowledgment of Mr. McChesney.

"This is a sad day, Pinter," Mr. McChesney said.

"A very sad day," the butler agreed in a whispery soft voice. If he ever lost his butlering job, he'd make an excellent undertaker.

"Is Edith in?" Mr. McChesney asked.

"Mrs. Van Hooten is not receiving visitors, sir, but I'm certain she will want to speak with you." Pinter flicked an uncomfortable glance toward me. *But not the interloper,* those pale gray eyes said.

"This is Miss Faulk," Mr. McChesney explained. "She was Guy's secretary."

After a pointed hesitation, the butler stepped back. With that, I passed into another world, one where family houses boasted rotundas, stained glass windows worthy of minor cathedrals, and chandeliers the size of automobiles. Every surface around me glistened, from the marble beneath my feet to the wood moldings overhead and along the impressive staircase, which appeared to be carved with scenes of some ancient battle. Imagine parading past the Peloponnesian war every time you forgot something upstairs.

Pinter took our coats and left us waiting next to a reproduction of Bernini's statue of Hades and Persephone. At least, I assumed it was a reproduction. Both the violence of their pose in the silent luxury of the front hall and the ostentatious extravagance of the piece were disconcerting.

"Did Van Hooten and McChesney pay for all this?" I whispered.

Mr. McChesney coughed. "*All this* paid for Van Hooten and McChesney. Cyrus had the money, and married into wealth. Oil. The publishing business was never more than a place to park himself while his wife's money accrued interest. He didn't take the book business too seriously. An attitude he passed on to Guy, unfortunately."

Double doors parted in one motion like raptor wings taking flight. Pinter held them for us. "This way, please."

On a deep green velvet Queen Anne sofa perched Mrs. Van Hooten, regal and swathed in black from head to toe. Her gown was high necked, out of which her firm jaw and chin poked out like a dagger. Her pale blue eyes had a metallic glint, emphasized by white-silver hair. Her head was crowned by a mantilla-style comb to which a flowing black length of lace was attached. Either she'd had mourning clothes at the ready or she'd never stopped wearing black for her late husband. From the woman's stony demeanor, I suspected the latter. She looked like someone who hadn't smiled for a very long time. A fire blazed in the cavernous fireplace, but the room still felt frigid.

"Edith." Mr. McChesney rushed forward, but once he reached her he stopped short, overcome with emotion.

She squeezed his outstretched hand. "So good of you to come to me, Ogden." She flicked a cool glance at me.

Mr. McChesney didn't notice. His eyes were filled with tears, and his voice rasped out, "I had to tell you how sorry I am. So very sorry. It's heartbreaking."

"Tell me what happened to my poor boy." She searched his face and gestured to the empty space next to her, beckoning him. "The police told us so little, I'm still bewildered. Thank heavens Hugh was still here when they came by. He said he was going to Thirty-eighth Street to find out more. Did you not see him?"

"We must have just missed each other," Mr. McChesney said, seating himself next to her.

"The officer who came by said Guy died in the fire. How is that possible?"

"I know very little myself. Just that Guy was found in his office, at his desk."

"I *always* told him he worked too hard," Mrs. Van Hooten said. " 'You mustn't overdo,' I counseled him. Now not heeding my advice has cost him his life."

She thought overwork had led to Guy's death?

To his credit, Mr. McChesney managed not to choke, but my own gulp of incredulity did not go unnoticed. Mrs. Van Hooten's steely gaze swept my way for the second time, and the temperature in the room dropped from chilly to arctic. It was as if Mrs. Van Hooten and the fireplace were canceling each other out.

"I don't recognize your young companion, Ogden."

I stepped forward. "My name is Louise Faulk, ma'am. I was your son's secretary."

She gave me a more thorough up-and-down look and then glanced at Mr. McChesney for confirmation. "This isn't the type of girl Guy would have hired."

She knew her son that well, at least.

"I took Louise on last winter," he said. "She's Irene Livingston Green's niece."

"Is she." Mrs. Van Hooten's expression conveyed exactly what she thought of my pedigree. Being a famous authoress's niece rescued me from being beneath her notice, but only by a degree.

I was left standing. "I'm so sorry for your loss, Mrs. Van Hooten."

"It's a loss for the world," she said. "Guy, I always said, had enormous potential. Everyone speaks of Hugh as the brilliant one, but I never thought so. Guy . . ." Her voice trailed off in mournful silence.

I struggled to find something to say. "The office will be a very different place without him," I managed, forgetting that the office was no more.

Mrs. Van Hooten lifted a black-bordered handkerchief to prevent a tear from showing the bad taste of actually spilling over. "My son was a wonderful man to work for, I've no doubt. Always a kind thought and a helping hand toward the little people. Of course, I warned him against careless altruism. He never heeded that advice, either."

I actually could have reassured her on that score—I doubted Guy had possessed a charitable bone in his body—but I held my tongue, following Mr. McChesney's example. Mrs. Van Hooten was more than happy to interpret our silence as respectful, sensible agreement.

Moments stretched, with only the muted crackling of the fire and the relentless movement of a grandfather clock's pendulum making any sound. Mr. McChesney had fallen into a funk, and Mrs. Van Hooten fixed her gaze on the Turkish carpet. I shifted impatiently. I wasn't there, to be honest, out of respect so much as curiosity.

Uninvited, I dropped into the nearest stiff-backed chair. "Mrs. Van Hooten, we were a little surprised that Guy was the first person at the office this morning. He usually . . . makes a later appearance." When he showed up at all. Last summer the office had taken bets on how long one of his extended absences would last. "Did he happen to mention why he left so early today?"

Her eyes widened—though whether more in shock at the audacity of my having made myself comfortable or at my probing question, it was hard to tell. I'd caught her off guard, enough so that an answer sputtered out of her. "When would he have mentioned such a thing to me? It's been many years since my sons have required a nanny, and I never served that role."

No, she wouldn't have. Edith Van Hooten would have been the type of mother who reigned supreme in her parlor while a nanny presented two boys scrubbed within an inch of their lives and togged out in well-pressed suits. She would have expected and received a kiss on the cheek from both, smiled impatiently at their childish babbling for five minutes until she was bored, and then waved them away until their bedtimes.

The scorn that filled me was followed by a chaser of discomfort. How could I condemn her? Not a year ago, I'd sacrificed everything so that a child could be brought up in just these circumstances.

The lady was blinking at me. "Well?" she asked impatiently.

Focus, Louise. "I thought perhaps if you had seen Guy this morning, he might've mentioned whether he was meeting anyone at the office."

"If he had, surely there would have been *two* people found in the fire."

I bit my lip. The important thing with someone like Edith Van Hooten was not to seem as if I was interrogating her. She wouldn't stand for that—especially not from a mere female secretary.

"He didn't mention anything to me, young woman." She sniffed. "Of course, I never come down before ten."

My gaze finally caught Mr. McChesney's. He must have read my thoughts. "So you don't know what time he left?" he asked.

"I do not."

"Do you know if he slept here at all last night?"

The question rushed out before I could stop it, and it immediately hit the forbidding stone wall that was Mrs. Van Hooten's thin-lipped scowl. "Are you insinuating that my son was a reprobate?"

Now that you mention it. . . .

Mr. McChesney squeezed her hand. "Louise was only asking because . . . well . . ." His eyes filled with panic as he groped for words. Footsteps sounded in the marble hallway, and hearing them, he visibly welcomed the prospect of being interrupted. "Is this Hugh?"

The doors opened again. Hugh Van Hooten was brown haired and brown eyed like his brother, but there the resemblance ended. Hugh was tall and angular, while Guy had been more compact, buffed, and polished. My late boss would never have let his hair flop in his eyes, or have worn a brown tweed coat that made him look like a stage actor's impersonation of a professor. With what appeared to be an oil stain on his jacket sleeve, no less.

He rushed toward Mr. McChesney and didn't even stop at a handshake, but jerked the older man up to his feet for an embrace. "So good of you to come see Mother," Hugh said, gripping the man's forearms.

"I'm so sorry, my boy." Mr. McChesney was on the verge of losing his composure again.

Hugh acknowledged his words with a sober nod. Then he glanced over at me.

"This is Louise Faulk," Mr. McChesney said. "Guy's secretary."

Hugh greeted me with a warmer expression than his mother had. "Kind of you to come, Miss Faulk. I've been to the building. The fire inspector told me it'll have to be demolished. God only knows what will become of the business."

"Time enough to consider all that in the coming days." Mr. McChesney's mouth turned down. "But I'm not optimistic."

Hugh looked down at me. "Hard luck for you and your colleagues."

"What does that matter when Guy is dead?" Mrs. Van Hooten's eyes flashed. "What kind of people would be concerned for their own self-interest at a time like this?"

People who'd worked with Guy. None of us had loved him. Still, it galled me to think that the woman could consider us all completely heartless. "Please don't think that way, Mrs. Van Hooten. We all considered Guy"—my brain searched frantically for a complimentary word—"unforgettable."

"So true." Did I detect something in Hugh's eyes just then, in the instant that he turned from me to his mother? "*Unforgettable*. That is the perfect description of Guy, wouldn't you agree, Mother?"

Her lips tightened again, and that handkerchief returned to the bridge of her nose.

Mr. McChesney stood, and I followed his example. "I'll leave you now, Edith," he said, "but please send for me if there's the slightest service I can perform for you. I'll be thinking of you constantly, my dear."

"Cyrus always insisted you were a good man." Her words left the impression that this had been a point of debate between the couple.

"Rest here, Mother," Hugh said. "I'll see them to the door." He spoke as if she had been making a motion to see us out herself, which she had not.

In the hallway, Hugh closed the double doors, motioned us a few steps toward the Persephone statue, and lowered his voice. "Does either of you have a guess where my fool of a brother was last night?"

It wasn't until he asked that question that it struck me what a strain it had been humoring Mrs. Van Hooten's delusion that Guy was a responsible man who had ever considered the needs of anyone besides himself.

"Guy didn't sleep here?" I asked.

"As far as I know, he hasn't been home since yesterday morning."

Mr. McChesney nodded. "Then perhaps he wasn't early to work, after all."

Hugh snorted. "Guy was never early in his life, except in managing to get himself born before me."

"Then he might never have left the office after I saw him last night," I said. Or he might have left for a short time, perhaps with Leonard Cain, and returned.

Mr. McChesney's face set in a puzzled frown. "What would he have been doing there all that time?"

"Passed out drunk at his desk?" Hugh guessed. He seemed to know his brother.

"Why didn't he come back here, or go to a hotel?" I wondered.

"The very question those damned police detectives will be asking," Hugh said. "I talked to two of them while I was at Thirty-eighth Street, but I'm sure they'll descend on the house again soon enough. That's why I came back so quickly. I need to prepare Mother to put off all inquiries in no uncertain terms. No doubt she'll agree. Guy's always been her angelic boy. If there's evidence to the contrary, she'll want it contained."

His words baffled me. "Why wouldn't you want the police to look into the matter?"

For the first time, the Van Hooten haughtiness showed in Hugh's expression. "Why would a family wish vermin to invade their home?"

He was comparing the police to vermin? "There's a chance an arsonist killed your brother. Don't you want to find out who it was?"

He raked a hand through his unruly hair. "Guy is dead. Heaven only knows what he was involved in, or what happened this morning. It won't do the family any good to be bothered by a police investigation and have the lurid details of his life dragged through the damned newspapers."

"Are there lurid details to be found?" I asked.

"Surely not," Mr. McChesney said, adding in a lower voice, "not *too* lurid."

"Hopefully the evidence of whatever Guy was involved in burned with the fire." Hugh dug his hands in his pockets. "My brother was never good at cleaning up his own messes—but I'd rather the mess was kept from spreading, if at all possible. My mother is old, and frailer than she appears, and Guy was her favorite son."

Mr. McChesney stared with strange intensity at Persephone's shapely calf. "The police can be so invasive. And then there's the coroner . . ."

"I'll have a word with Ardolph Kline about that," Hugh said.

When our last mayor had died at sea in August, Ardolph Kline, President of the Board of Aldermen, became Acting Mayor of New York until an election could be held. It startled me that a man with grease stains on his sleeves could toss out his name so casually. "You know Acting Mayor Kline?"

"He was at Phillips Andover with my father. I'm sure he'll put a stop to any coroner business if I ask him to. Letting Guy's body be subjected to further degradation and having his private life poked into by the police, as well as by the journalists who follow them like buzzards, will serve no purpose."

"If a relative of mine died, I'd want to know why," I said.

Hugh stared down his long nose at me. "If a relative of yours died in a fire, it wouldn't sell newspapers, would it? Also, you wouldn't have a fledgling business at risk, with investors who'd bolt at the first whisper of impropriety or scandal."

"Are you saying you care more for your business than—"

Mr. McChesney took my arm and squeezed it strongly enough to cut off my circulation as well as my words. "Time for us to go, Louise." He held out a hand to Hugh. "We promised to pay a visit to Louise's aunt, and we've intruded on your grief too long already. Take care, my boy."

"Certainly. Pinter will see you out."

Hugh left us to return to his mother, while Mr. McChesney and I waited for our coats. After the butler shooed us out the door, I couldn't help grumbling my displeasure. "Why did you stop me? Didn't you hear him? He cares more about his investors than justice."

"These people possess great wealth and even greater pride. Part of what maintains both is guarding their privacy from the prying eyes of the public."

The reverence in his tone for "these people" sickened me. Of course, Mr. McChesney had been on the receiving end of the Van Hooten largesse. His company had been founded on it. But they weren't a different, superior species, however they might consider themselves to be. Just remembering Hugh's words made my blood boil. Despite the oil stains on his jacket, he was Edith Van Hooten's son through and through. A chip off the old battle-ax.

"Everyone has pride," I said. "But the world will descend into chaos if people can just run around burning down buildings and killing one another with impunity."

At the sidewalk, we saw two men pass through a gaggle of journalists and then come toward us—Muldoon and another detective. Muldoon almost stumbled when he saw me standing there, which gave me a jolt of satisfaction. There was something delicious in catching him off guard. It made him seem almost human.

Mr. McChesney acknowledged the two men with a nod. "Detectives."

"What are you doing here, Louise?" Muldoon asked.

"Paying a condolence call on the family," I said. "And you?"

"We need to ask questions," Muldoon said.

Knowing what a stone wall he was rushing headlong into almost made me feel sorry for the man. At that very moment, Hugh was no doubt coaching his mother to say nothing. Or maybe he was putting in that call to Acting Mayor Kline. Given how Mrs. Van Hooten and Hugh had seized up at my gentle inquiries, I could well imagine the chilly reception a police detective's questions would receive inside that opulent manse.

"Good luck." I smiled at Muldoon and trilled a goodbye with my gloved fingers.

Aunt Irene nearly tackled her servant Walter in her impatience to answer the door when we arrived. Held back by a silver circlet decorated with citrines, her curls drooped in afternoon limpness, which gave me an indication of how long it had been since she sent me her message. My rumbling stomach was another hint. I hadn't eaten anything today.

"I was expecting you at least an hour ago," she said. "What's happened? I've been so upset I've canceled the usual Thursday night soirée. Walter's been telephoning to let people know."

She was so eager to get news out of us that she worked against her own interests, talking nineteen to the dozen and blocking our path inside. Mr. McChesney, a gentleman, was not given to gossiping in doorways.

Walter rescued us. "Excuse me." He mimicked a breaststroke past his employer. "Only one of us is being paid to answer the door, and it's not the one in the tiara."

Aunt Irene let out a puff of irritation, but dutifully stepped back with a flick of her pleated skirt of raw silk. She had two regular servants, and both of them often treated her more like an exasperating relative than an employer.

In the vestibule I unbuttoned my coat and explained what had delayed us. "Guy Van Hooten died this morning. Mr. McChesney wanted to call on his mother."

Aunt Irene had only heard about the fire, not about Guy Van Hooten's death. She didn't know him, of course, except from what Mr. McChesney and I had told her. Nevertheless, she looked almost as dazed as Mr. McChesney as she took her seat on the couch between Dickens and Trollope. The two old toy spaniels, plump and snoring, were the only inmates of the house who hadn't bestirred themselves at the sound of our arrival. Watchdogs they were not.

A pot of hot tea and a plate of finger sandwiches were brought in straightaway. The cook, Bernice, must have been hovering at the kitchen's swinging door like a racehorse at the starting gate. I couldn't have been more grateful.

My aunt didn't even wait for the tea to be poured to exhort us to tell her more. "How could it have happened? And how is poor Mrs. Van Hooten bearing up?"

In fairness to my aunt, she was no ghoul, nor an idle gossip. The goings-on of her friends and acquaintances were always listened to with sympathy and understanding, and she was not stingy with advice when it was called for. Her generosity had helped not only me, but also friends and even friends of friends.

She was, however, a writer, and like any good chronicler of human nature, she soaked up details like a sponge. Her avidity for news, I reckoned, was roughly eighty percent humanitarian and twenty percent mercenary.

I laid out what facts we knew. The entire telling didn't take much longer than the duration of the devouring of two egg-salad sandwiches—that's how paltry my knowledge of what had happened actually was.

My aunt leaned back, her face thoughtful as she absently petted the dogs who sat on either side of her like bookends, both awake now and leaning toward the sandwich tray in quivery longing.

"Died at his desk," she wondered aloud. "I've often thought that's how I'll be found when I meet my maker. Not that I'm in any hurry, heaven knows." She let out a nervous chuckle and glanced ceilingward. "At least, I *hope* heaven knows."

Depositing my teacup on the piecrust table at my side, I scooted forward on my chair. "But Guy was the last person I'd expect to die in the traces. Wouldn't you agree, Mr. McChesney?"

A second passed before my boss registered that I was talking to him. "Oh, yes. The very last."

"Especially first thing in the morning." I told Aunt Irene about Guy's lax work habits and also what Hugh Van Hooten had told us concerning his brother's absence from the family house last night.

"Is it known when the fire began?" she asked.

"It had to be before eight in the morning," I said. "That's when the first witness on the street saw smoke. A few minutes before, a woman walking her poodle noticed a hunched man on the street in a brown overcoat and a plaid scarf."

"That's not a peculiar sight in midtown," Mr. McChesney piped up.

"She described him as lurking." Of course, the poodle woman was, to put it kindly, eccentric. I wasn't sure how reliable the police would consider her testimony to be.

My aunt steepled her fingers. "Even if a young man was inebriated last night, he should have been sober enough to escape a fire this morning."

"He might have died from breathing the smoke before he reached consciousness," I said.

"Or perhaps the arsonist knocked him out before setting the fire," Aunt Irene suggested.

I frowned. "The firemen didn't say positively that the fire *was* arson. . . ."

Mr. McChesney lifted his head. "They didn't, did they?"

"But they must suspect. Why else would it have started?" Aunt Irene asked.

"Why do buildings all over town catch fire?" In the papers I read about the fire department putting out blazes every day. "Carelessness, usually."

"Guy Van Hooten was alone in the building, you said." Aunt Irene poured herself some more tea. "Do the firemen know if he was careless with the gas or with matches?"

"We've heard nothing," Mr. McChesney said. "And there was

so much damage. Perhaps we'll never find out the cause of the fire."

That possibility bothered me most. Was there anything worse than not knowing? The question reminded me of Hugh Van Hooten. "Guy's brother told us his family will resist any efforts by the coroner to do an autopsy," I told Aunt Irene. "He said they won't help with the investigation in any way."

"How odd." Her eyes narrowed in thought as she lifted her teacup to her lips.

"Autopsies are hideous and surely not necessary in this case," Mr. McChesney said. "The poor fellow died in a fire. By all accounts, it was a grisly death. Pardon me for speaking of it, but it's the truth. No family like the Van Hootens would willingly put up with such a desecration of a family member."

"But if the death was murder, and the autopsy would help discover who killed their beloved son and brother?" Aunt Irene asked.

Had Guy been a beloved brother to Hugh, though? Hugh had seemed more annoyed than mournful at his brother's death. *Guy was never early in his life, except in managing to get himself born before me.* If that didn't show bitterness . . .

"It was all an accident," Mr. McChesney said, rolling through the events in his mind again. "Tragic. The fire . . . no matter how it started . . . and then poor Guy. I for one can see the family's point of view. Guy's gone. No police investigation will change that."

"But don't *you* want to know the truth?" Aunt Irene asked him. "It was your business."

"If the family refuses to cooperate with a police investigation, there's nothing I can do."

My aunt swung toward me. "The police aren't the only ones who can investigate, are they, Louise?"

This past summer, I'd conducted an investigation of my own to clear my friend Otto of the murder of my roommate's cousin, which had taken place in our flat. My success had led me to think I could find a place in the NYPD. But in that case, the murder had been bound up in the lives of my own friends, not an old New York society family hell-bent on guarding its privacy.

"You're quite at leisure now," my aunt reminded me.

That was another problem. "I need to find a job. I can't live off Callie."

"You already have a job." She smiled. "I'm giving you one."

Salvation! Didn't I mention Aunt Irene was a generous soul? "What do you need me to do?"

"Type." At my confusion, she held out her hands. "Look at them. Quite useless against that beast of a Remington. Arthritis. Bernice wraps them in hot towels every afternoon. It's the damp cold that worsens the problem, Dr. Lazenby says. So it would be such a help to me if you could be my typist until the spring. If that's agreeable to you?"

I would have kissed her if it hadn't required knocking over Dickens to do it. "Of course I'll help you. You didn't need to wait for a fire to ask me."

"Perhaps the fire was all your aunt's doing," Mr. McChesney said. "The whole conflagration was just a ploy to free you up."

My aunt laughed but quickly sobered again. "I've seen Louise type—grateful as I am for her help, her skill's not enough to murder for."

Murder. It was still so hard to believe that someone would have killed Guy. I'd never liked him myself, but men like him always struck me as the kind of people nothing bad ever happened to. No matter how irresponsible or profligate he was, Guy's vaunted position in life was meant to inoculate him from the evils and dangers the hoi polloi were subject to.

But it hadn't. And my aunt was right. Something inside me burned to discover what—and who—had brought about his early death.

"Come here in the mornings and type my pages," my aunt said, "and in the afternoons, you can look into that fire—and what Guy Van Hooten was up to—for Ogden."

Mr. McChesney's eyes grew large. "For me?"

"You want to get to the bottom of whatever happened to your business, don't you?" she asked. "You said yourself that the Van Hootens will stonewall the police. In one way, I can't say as I blame them—my few experiences with policemen have revealed them to be blunderers, more often than not. But Louise is very astute, and dogged once she sets her mind on something. She'll find out what happened. I'll refund all the money you pay her if she doesn't."

She expected Mr. McChesney to pay me? He and I both must have mugged our surprise like actors in a moving picture. "You can't expect a girl to waste her afternoons for no pay at all. Admit it, Ogden," Aunt Irene admonished. "If I, a poor working woman, can give her money to type for me, surely you can fork over five dollars per day for her to risk life and limb to hunt down an arsonist-murderer on your behalf."

I gulped. The prospect of being five dollars per day richer was as sweet as a song to my ears, but I hadn't considered the task she was setting before me in such stark terms. Risking life and limb? Hunting down a murderer?

Mr. McChesney scratched his chin. "Yes, but you *need* a typist, while I never had any intention— "

"No intention of finding out what kind of fiend burned down the business you spent a lifetime building and which killed your partner?" She glared at him imperiously. "If that's true, you're not the Ogden Cornelius McChesney I thought I knew."

To be honest, the Mr. McChesney I knew *was* the type of passive man who would allow himself to accept the investigation of the proper authorities, no matter how slipshod or halfhearted. He was not a forceful man, or daring. He hadn't even wanted to put his neck out to discover new authors, or branch out in unfamiliar sales territories. The mere suggestion of beginning a mail-order business had once sent him home ill for a week. Gumption wasn't his strong suit.

Nevertheless, something in my aunt's thundering pronouncement made my former boss sit up straighter. He had loved her once, and she had refused him, twice, calling him an old fool. He'd probably wondered if he'd ever have the chance to prove himself to her. Now a gauntlet had been thrown down, and to my surprise, cautious, ulcerous Ogden McChesney took up the challenge.

"Three dollars per day would be more in line with my budget," he said. "I was hoping to retire soon, you know, Irene. And Louise isn't a real detective, is she?"

Aunt Irene swiveled toward me. So did the dogs. "Well, Louise, what do you think? Is this acceptable to you?"

The sound had to be coming from a phonograph, and the only one of those in the building was in our flat. Callie was home.

I hurtled up the stairs, eager to fill her in on everything that had happened during the day even as I became more puzzled by the exotic, undulating pulse of the music issuing from our apartment. I pushed through the door, slightly winded, and sucked in my breath. Callie was not alone. In fact, she and a man were entwined together so intimately that they were as close to mimicking the act of carnal love as it was possible to without having an actual bed beneath them. The man—handsome, yet a stranger to me—leaned over Callie, who was practically dipped into a backbend. This required considerable strength on the man's part and impressive flexibility from both Callie and her foundation garments.

"Another reason to be grateful for the no-bone corset," I observed.

Still almost upside down, Callie's face broke into a smile. "Louise!" she called over the music. Noticing me backing away to give them some privacy, she laughed and whacked her partner playfully on the shoulder. "Let me up, Teddy. We're shocking my roommate."

Teddy, whom I had been hearing about for weeks but had not yet met in the flesh, complied.

"I didn't mean to interrupt," I said, still poised to flee.

Callie lunged for the phonograph to turn down the volume. "Stop blushing, Louise. It wasn't lovemaking you interrupted. Just the tango."

"*That* was a tango?" I'd heard of it—the whole country was hearing about it—but hadn't yet seen it performed. It and other so-called lewd dances like the turkey trot were being debated and banned in other cities. Boston, for one. I understood the controversy a little better now.

"I was just teaching Teddy. Isn't it fun?" she asked him.

"I'll say." Children in candy stores were blasé compared to the eagerness he displayed.

"I'll have to teach you, too," Callie told me.

"I need to do a few months of limbering exercises first." Even then I wasn't sure I'd ever be comfortable being that intimate with a dance partner. "I'm not quite tango-ready."

"Oh!" An idea suddenly occurred to Callie. "You two don't know each other yet, do you? Louise Faulk, Teddy Newland."

We smiled at each other in greeting. Teddy was a type I'd only encountered in novels and in Manhattan—a young man about town for whom the chief concern wasn't work but how to spend all the money he was receiving from his rich father. Some, like Guy Van Hooten, found ersatz employment. Others idled away their days drifting from one club to the next. Life for these rarified creatures was all yachts, tailors, and tangos.

And chorus girls. Teddy was an investor in the show Callie was about to open in. I'd assumed he looked upon chorus girls as a sort of entertaining dividend, but the sinister vision I'd conjured up from weeks of Callie telling me about him was immediately shattered by Teddy himself. I'd imagined a wolf. In reality, he was more a golden puppy dog with a dapper mustache, and the look he gave Callie was one of unabashed adoration.

He wasn't so lost in her charms that he forgot his manners, however. "Here, let me help you." He reached for the box Bernice had sent me home with.

"What did you bring?" Callie asked.

"Sandwiches and coconut cake."

Rapture overcame her. "There's dinner taken care of."

Teddy's face collapsed into a pout. "I wanted to take you to Delmonico's."

"Once you've tasted this coconut cake, you'll forget all about Delmonico's," Callie assured him. "Besides, I can't leave Louise tonight. Not after all that she's been through."

Teddy regarded me with furrowed brow and then blinked, remembering. "Of course. That fire in midtown this morning. Callie was telling me about it earlier. Your office?"

"Yes."

He clucked in sympathy, while Callie took my arm and guided me over to our most comfortable chair. "Was it as awful as Detective Muldoon said it was?" she asked.

I collapsed into the well-worn upholstery, shocked at how bone-weary I felt. I hadn't realized it until just that moment. "The building's a burnt shell. After the firemen put the blaze out, policemen canvassed the neighborhood to find out if anyone had witnessed anything suspicious."

"It was arson, then?" Teddy asked.

"That's what the police seem to assume. Arson, possibly with intent to murder."

Callie, who had gone to the kitchenette to begin arranging the delicacies I'd brought home, poked her head back into the room to admonish Teddy, "I told you a man died."

"Oh, yes," he said, clearly having forgotten. "Dreadful." He sank onto our lumpy sofa and swung a leg, fidgeting. "Know the man well, did you?"

"He was my boss."

"Ah." He blew out a breath, at a loss for what else to say. I doubt he had much experience with either fires or bosses.

Rather than dwell on what had been preoccupying my mind all day long, I tried to remember something of what Callie had told me about Teddy Newland. He was an investor in her show, but he was also interested in racehorses and airplanes. I struggled to find a conversation starter on either of those topics.

It was obvious from his facial contortions that he was straining as hard as I was. "Dead, you say," he murmured. "That's hard lines for the poor fellow. Death is so . . . final."

I agreed that it was.

"Older man, I suppose?" he asked.

"No, quite young still. Just past thirty."

"Good Lord." Teddy sat up straighter. "*I'm* almost thirty."

His alarm was clear: If one thirty-year-old man could be caught in a fire, who was to say that we all wouldn't be engulfed in flames soon?

"You probably don't have many enemies, though," I pointed out.

"Your boss had enemies?"

I'd said too much. Blabbing about a case that I was being paid to look into wasn't politic or discreet. I had a lot to learn.

Hoping to correct my blunder, I waved a hand tiredly. "Oh, you know how office colleagues gossip." Teddy probably knew nothing of the kind. The only office he'd ever stepped foot in most likely belonged to the attorney who handled his family trust. "In any event, you'll learn more from reading the afternoon papers than from me. The journalist buzzards were already descending on the Van Hooten house this afternoon."

My words, meant to dispel interest, produced the exact opposite effect. His eyes blinked wide open and he gripped the seat at his sides as if to brace himself against a zephyr whipping through the apartment. "The Van Hootens? This place where you worked... was it by any chance Van Hooten and McChesney?"

I nodded.

"And your boss was Guy Van Hooten?"

"Yes."

"Dear God!" He bolted to his feet. "Guy gone?"

Callie rushed in from the kitchenette, balancing a tray of sandwiches. "You knew Callie's boss?"

"Know him?" He rounded on her, spluttering at her almost accusingly, "Why didn't you tell me Guy was dead?"

"I did," she said. "That is, I told you Louise's boss had died."

"But I didn't know who that was." He was rushing for the door now, grabbing hat and coat off the rack in our hallway. First, he snatched my hat by mistake, which didn't fit, obviously. In replacing it and taking his own, he nearly tipped over the hall tree.

Callie trailed after him. "You're leaving?"

"Of course," he said, finally triumphing in his scuffle with the coat rack. "I need to go uptown and call on the Van Hootens. At once. Poor Hugh! Guy was his brother."

Callie paled. "Oh no."

Teddy flew out the door, and in the next instant hurried back to kiss her cheek and grab a sandwich off her tray. Then he was off again at a gallop. Callie and I stood staring at each other in amazement until we heard the front door slamming behind him two floors below.

"Teddy knows Hugh Van Hooten?" Hugh, distracted of appearance but sharp of mind and tongue, did not strike me as a likely candidate for bosom friend to the man I'd just met.

Callie dropped into the seat Teddy had just vacated. "They attended Exeter together."

That explained it. School ties were the glue that bonded wealthy men in this town.

"Teddy has money invested in Hugh's business, too." She bit

into a sandwich. "Hugh's infected Teddy with his enthusiasm about planes. He's some kind of aeronautical genius. Next to him, someday the Wright Brothers will seem what a man doing duck calls is to Caruso."

Callie tended to be overly enthusiastic about her friends' talents and abilities. Not that I was complaining, since I was, after all, one of them. If I were to take up street cleaning, she'd declare that no one in a white coat in the entire city scooped waste as well as her roommate.

"What's Hugh like?" I was being a little cagey here, withholding my own first impression of the man. But I had my investigator hat on, and I didn't want to influence Callie's opinion.

Her brow pillowed as she considered her answer. "I've only met him a couple of times. He's handsome, although the first time I saw him he was so messy I mistook him for one of those socialists. When I said as much to Teddy, he laughed and told me he wasn't a socialist, only a mechanic. Well, he did have oil beneath his nails, so I assumed he was there as someone's chauffeur, which caused some embarrassment when we left the club and all got into a car. I asked Hugh why he wasn't driving. Once that was straightened out, I found him a little blunt but pleasant enough, dirty nails and all. He even laughed at my mistake, can you imagine?"

"Guy wouldn't have found it amusing to be mistaken for a chauffeur."

"Well, that's about all I know of Hugh, except that he has an aerodrôme somewhere in New Jersey where he tinkers with planes. And that Teddy has given him money to work on some kind of aeronautical invention that's going to be the biggest thing since cornflakes. It's thrilling, isn't it? Teddy promised to teach me to fly someday. Wouldn't you like to soar like a bird?"

I shuddered. One thing in life that terrified me was heights. "The only birds I envy are penguins at the aquarium—they have a cushy life on solid ground with a clean, shark-free pool to splash around in."

"Teddy told me Hugh says that soon we'll all be flying around as casually as we take taxis now."

Heaven help us. "Did Hugh ever mention Guy?"

"Even if he did, I doubt I would've put it together. I never knew

Hugh's last name until tonight. He was just Hugh, or Old Hugh, or sometimes Hoots." She frowned. "I might've guessed from Hoots who he was, but for all I knew it had to do with owls or something."

Callie's knowing Hugh was a piece of luck for me. She was a point of connection with the Van Hooten family, no matter how casual. Perhaps through her I'd manage to talk to him again and learn more about Guy's life.

"Why all the questions about Hugh?" Her gaze sharpened. "What are you up to?"

I told her what had happened at my aunt's, and how I was charged to find out who, if anyone, had started the fire at the office.

Callie sat back and regarded me with amazement. "So you're going to be your own one-woman police force."

"I might have to be." I'd almost forgotten the exam that morning, but now I related how badly I thought I'd done and how crowded the room had been with hopeful candidates.

She waved a hand, dismissing my pessimism. "I bet you did better than any of those other women. Look at you—you're already detecting and you don't even have a badge yet."

"I doubt that would endear me to the brass. It surely didn't to Detective Muldoon. You should have caught the look on his face when he saw me leaving the Van Hooten house today."

"I can just imagine. He nearly scared the daylights out of me when he pounded on the door this morning. I worried he was going to drag you off to the hoosegow."

"It's too bad he's involved in the investigation of Guy Van Hooten's death," I said.

"Why? You might be able to get good information out of him. He knows you."

"Knows me enough to mistrust me. I'd just as easily get information from that plate of sandwiches."

"You need to turn a little charm on him," she suggested.

That brought a laugh—both at the idea of that glowering bear being bedazzled by feminine wiles, and that *I* would be the one performing the role of bedazzler.

"You could be as alluring as a siren if you chose to be," Callie said.

"If I were to send out a come-hither signal, I don't think Frank Muldoon would be the one I'd want to receive it."

"But that's the beauty of knowing your powers." She smiled. "You can lure whichever target you choose. Perhaps one day that will be Muldoon . . . or perhaps there'll be someone else."

Please, God, let there be someone else. In any case, I wasn't in any hurry to have a romance in my life. There was too much I wanted to accomplish on my own without the added worry of being the pillar supporting a man's daily cares. Anyway, what man would be interested in a policewoman, or a disappointed want-to-be policewoman turned typist-investigator? More troubling still, I wasn't sure many men would want me how I was—damaged goods, my aunt Sonja in Altoona had ungraciously called me—and to find out I would have to explain my past to a potential romantic partner. The prospect of doing so was a good dousing of ice water on any romantic dreams I might harbor.

Callie, unaware of the tempest she'd set off in my mind, jumped to her feet again and scurried back to the phonograph. She restarted the tango record.

"Here." She beckoned me with open arms.

I groaned. "Didn't you dance enough at rehearsals today?"

"That was hours ago." She tugged me up on my feet. "Let me teach you. It's so much fun."

I'd been a diligent, if not particularly gifted, student at Miss Nestor's Dancing School in Altoona, where I'd become proficient in polkas, two-steps, and waltzes. Prim Miss Nestor would have fainted if she could have seen me now. Callie, playing the man, gripped me in a tight embrace and pushed me around the room, her forehead locked on mine with such a serious expression of concentration that I couldn't help giggling.

"You're not trying," she said. "Think about passion."

My experiences of passion weren't the best. I did try to imagine how it would be if I were in the strong arms of Detective Muldoon, staring close range into his brooding dark eyes. How it would be if they were fixed at me in desire instead of irritation, as was usually the case. My imagination worked well enough that I was able to throw myself into the moment and follow Callie even as she dipped me into a backward swoop. Suddenly I found myself closer to the floor than I was comfortable with.

"What the Sam Hill?"

At the unexpected exclamation, Callie and I both turned toward the door, where Wally, our landlady's troll-like son, was staring open-mouthed at us.

"I never expected that you girls were that way!" he said.

"What way?" Callie asked in a cool voice.

His lip curled. "You know. *That* way."

"Oh, yes," Callie said. "Louise and I have been *this way* forever."

Apparently she had hit upon the only thing that would repulse the repulsive Wally, because he backed away from the door as if what we had was catching. "I only was going to tell you to keep the racket down."

His footsteps thundered down the stairs.

Two things happened at once: Callie began to laugh, and my stockinged foot slipped on the wood floor, upsetting my precarious balance. I dropped to the floor, which only made Callie whoop harder. When my friend Otto discovered us moments later, we were both wheezing with laughter.

"What's going on?" he called out over the music. "I was almost crushed coming up the stairs by that moose Wally."

"I told him"—Callie fanned a hand in front of her face, trying to sober up—"that Louise and I were lesbians."

Otto's face screwed up. "What?" He scooted over to the phonograph player and turned down the volume. "What'd you do that for?"

"Because he gives me the willies."

"You'll be lucky if you aren't evicted."

"And luckier if we are," I said.

"The tango doesn't involve falling to the floor, does it?" Otto said, giving me a hand up.

On my feet again, I rubbed my bruised hip. "Not usually."

"I'm sorry," Callie said. "I didn't mean to drop you. Only that oaf looked so comical."

"He did."

We started laughing again.

"Good glory," Otto said, put out. "I came rushing over because I heard Van Hooten and McChesney burned to the ground, and that someone had died. I was worried sick—only to find you two dancing and laughing without a care in the world." He froze, as if a lightning bolt had struck his cerebral cortex. "That sounds like a song, doesn't it?"

Otto, a butcher's assistant-turned-songsmith, was always trying to dream up the next Tin Pan Alley sensation. One tune he'd written this past summer had sold surprisingly well, although the fact that his name was connected to a famous murder case could have accounted for at least some of its popularity. He wasn't Chauncey Olcott by a long stretch, but he wasn't writing home to beg for money, either.

" 'Dancing with No Care in the World,' " he said, trying it out as he took a small notebook and pen out of his breast pocket. "No . . ."

" 'Dancing with My Clumsy Roommate,' " I suggested.

A fringed throw pillow sailed through the air at me from Callie's direction. "Who was the one who fell on her caboose?"

"I slipped. *You* were supposed to be leading."

Otto brightened and scribbled away. " 'My cares took a tumble, and I danced away.' This might be even better than my 'Income Tax Rag.' "

"Tell me that's not your latest," I said.

"Why not? Folks love songs ripped straight from the headlines." His brows drew together. "Maybe I should make it the 'Income Tax Tango,' though. What do you think?"

"I'm not sure the ratification of a tax act will make people pop on their dancing shoes," I said. The prospect of the government taking a one percent cut off our wages didn't fill us with joy.

"You're right." He frowned. "How about 'The Sixteenth Amendment Blues'?"

Callie and I shook our heads.

Otto looked away and his gaze fastened on the table. "Is that coconut cake?"

Five minutes later we were all settled in seats with plates of cake balanced on our laps. "I need to save a piece for Teddy," Callie said.

Otto's mood sank at the mention of the name. Five months ago he'd come to New York to profess undying love for me, but changed his mind almost as soon as he'd laid eyes on my roommate. I couldn't blame him—and I certainly wasn't jealous. Otto and I had been friends since we were kids, and I hoped we always would be. As a friend to both, however, I couldn't help worrying. Callie was young, pretty, and talented, and she seemed no more ready to settle on one man than a hummingbird was to hang around one flower when a whole garden awaited it. And so tenderhearted Otto had discovered that he was yesterday's daisy.

"Why would Teddy know anything about Bernice's coconut cake?" he asked.

"He left just before you arrived."

"Oh." He sagged a little more in his chair.

"Don't worry," I told him, "if you want more coconut cake, you can come with me to Aunt Irene's house party next week and Bernice will stuff you full of it."

A cake shortage wasn't the real issue, yet the prospect of an evening at my aunt's cheered him somewhat. Otto was a favorite there.

"But what about the fire, Louise?" he asked. "I hope you weren't in any danger."

I gave him a rundown of my day, from the police exam right down to falling on my rump when he came into the apartment.

When I finished, he sat slack-jawed with incredulity. "Have you gone stark stirring mad? You shouldn't get involved in another murder. Last time you almost got yourself killed."

"But we cleared your name," I pointed out.

"Exactly," he said. "Last summer there was a life at stake—mine—so it made sense for you to risk life and limb. But to put yourself in danger for money?" He shook his head. "I don't like it."

"But what about Teddy?" Callie asked. "He's such good friends with Hugh—and maybe the person who wanted Guy dead will go after Hugh next. And then Teddy might be in danger, too."

"I'd worry more about those airplanes Teddy buzzes around in than murderers," I said.

Callie shook her head. "Teddy says he won't give up flying, so there's no getting rid of *that* risk. But if you could manage to catch the Van Hooten killer, Louise, that would at least eliminate one possible danger."

Otto laughed mirthlessly. "By all means, let's all devote our lives to keeping Teddy Newland from harm. I'll apply to medical school so I can find the cure for the common cold so Teddy'll never have to catch one."

Callie glared at him. "Oh, are medical schools clamoring for songwriter applicants?"

"There's no point in arguing," I said before their sniping could escalate. "I've promised to look into the fire for Mr. McChesney, and I intend to follow through whether it benefits Teddy or not."

Otto stabbed at his cake.

"You can't let Teddy know what I'm up to," I warned Callie.

"Why not?" she asked.

"I can't risk the Van Hootens finding out that I'm looking into Guy's death. They'll clam up around me just as they will for the police."

Callie's eyes narrowed. "How are you going to manage to be around the Van Hootens, anyway?" she asked. "You were Guy's secretary. I doubt you'll be receiving many invitations into their social circle."

"Mr. McChesney is close to the family. And now I've got another connection—Teddy."

Callie studied me; then her eyes brightened. "Oh—I see. We'll *both* be secretly investigating." I'd worried that she wouldn't want me to involve her in this scheme, but from her tone you might have pictured her rubbing her hands together in gleeful anticipation. She was in.

Otto groaned. "Here we go again."

Callie took his empty plate and patted him on the head. "Never fear. Maybe you'll get another hit song out of it."

Even that possibility failed to lift his gloom. "Let's hope it's not a funeral dirge."

Chapter 4

That evening I stayed home worrying I'd tackled something beyond my abilities. True, I'd succeeded in ferreting out a murderer last summer. But perhaps I'd just been lucky—if nearly being pitched off the top of the Woolworth Building could be construed as luck.

I reviewed what little I knew: On Wednesday night, Guy had stayed late at work, and the last person with whom he was seen was Leonard Cain. Cain was reputed to be a shady character, maybe even a gangster. But did he have reason to murder Guy?

From what I'd heard today, Jackson knew more about Cain than I did. He'd known Guy better, too. Before I interviewed anyone about Guy's death, it would be worthwhile to ask Jackson some questions. I was eager to get started, but my mornings now belonged to Aunt Irene.

At nine o'clock sharp the next morning, I presented myself at my aunt's, knowing she wouldn't be up to greet me. She wrote late into the night and rarely stirred from her bedroom before eleven. Walter escorted me up to her office, where a small stack of handwritten papers lay waiting for me next to the hulking Remington. On the top was a note penned in Aunt Irene's angular hand.

Louise,
If you have any difficulty deciphering these pages, apply to Walter. He's accustomed to my chicken scratch. Bernice has been told to keep you watered and fed. Don't let them boss you.
Irene
P.S.—I've been giving the matter some thought, and I really think you should begin your investigation by interviewing the coworkers who were closest to Guy Van Hooten. But we can talk more later!

Of course she'd decided I should talk to the coworkers closest to Guy. She'd probably come to that conclusion in half the time it had taken me.

I sat down to work. Irene Livingston Green, née Irma Mayer of Altoona, Pennsylvania, had made her name writing stories of girls whose stalwart hearts and plucky personalities saw them through all the romantic difficulty their picturesque small towns could heap upon their pretty heads. These paragons of virtue usually had flowery names that appeared in the title, like *Myrtle in Springtime* and *Violet in the Shade.* Looking forward to a cheerful respite from fiery death and gangsters, I cranked a blank white page onto the platen. Centering the title—I was never the best at that—I typed:

THE CURTAIN FALLS

Hmm. No flowery name. Maybe she was going for a change of pace.

The first paragraph reassured me—the heroine's name was Lily, and even though she resided in New York City, not a small town, she was peppy and outgoing. In the scene, she and her roommate, Clarice, were returning from a party, discussing a handsome, brooding playwright they'd just met and bantering over Lily's tendency to borrow Clarice's clothes without permission. That last detail brought a smile. Aunt Irene had pinched my predilection for borrowing Callie's clothes.

I clacked along, wondering whether Lily or Clarice would end up with the playwright. My money was on Clarice, since she was an aspiring actress. I had to redo one page because I noticed I'd typed *b* for *v* a few times, so that Clarice was scolding Lily for borrowing her *kid globes* without permission. As my aunt had said, I was far from a flawless typist, but the time passed pleasantly enough. The novel's familiar setting diverted me. Lily and Clarice even lived in Greenwich Village, as Callie and I did, in a building similar to ours. In fact, the fictional pair were strikingly similar to Callie and me.

My fingers paused over the keys.

After a quick rap, the door swung open and Walter came in bearing a tray for me. At least, I assumed it was Walter. When I looked up, a bearded, pot-bellied man was placing the tray on Aunt Irene's rolltop desk. A tremor of alarm passed quickly, and I smiled to myself and focused an intent gaze on the page in the typewriter. "Thank you," I said.

He stepped back and cleared his throat. I didn't look up from my work.

The air twitched with impatience. "Is there anything else you'll be wantin', miss?"

The unexpected, ludicrous Irish brogue shredded my composure. In my best leprechaun, I answered back, "Aye, how about a wee verse of 'Molly Malone'?"

Walter, beneath his thick makeup and beard, scowled but steadfastly refused to break character. "What's so funny, I'd like to know."

I whooped. "Would you now?"

Giving up, he tore off a hank of beard. "The accent was what gave me away, wasn't it?" He slapped the fake hair against his palm. "I shouldn't have attempted it. It's been years since I appeared in *The Countess Cathleen*. Was it too much?"

"A wee tooch." Noting the slope of his shoulders, I made myself stop laughing. Walter, an ex-actor, prided himself on his mastery of disguises. "Don't be discouraged. I knew it was you because—well, who else would bring me a tray of food?"

For the first time, I glanced down at the tray's contents. A boiled egg in a cup, a piece of toast, and half a glass of milk. Bernice, who whipped up mouthwatering creations in Aunt Irene's kitchen every day, wasn't above telegraphing her mood through her culinary offerings. That egg and dry toast might as well have been a twenty-foot electrified billboard flashing her displeasure.

From Walter's next words, I judged rightly. "Bernice is just anxious about our being involved in the investigation, which she thinks will bring trouble. You know what a doom and gloomer she is."

"Cassandra of the kitchen," I agreed.

"I, on the other hand, am willing to assist you in any way possible. After our success last summer, I'm sure we'll be able to find the coward who burned down Mr. McChesney's building."

Last summer, Walter—in disguise—had delivered a message for me at a key moment, so I couldn't object to his use of the word *we.* God knows I might need all the help I could get in the days to come.

Luckily for my stomach, I remembered I'd agreed to meet Otto for an early lunch. I finished typing the pages Aunt Irene had left and scribbled a note for her, which I placed on the newly typed stack.

Back in August, returning from a visit home to Altoona, Otto had discovered a sausage stand in the bustling area outside of Pennsylvania Station. The hulking granite and marble exterior of the station sprawled over nine midtown acres, and on the surrounding streets, passengers encountered merchants catering to their needs, from reading material and toiletries, children's toys, hats and stockings, and most of all, food. Food carts parked along the sidewalks released half a dozen mingling aromas. There, Otto had found Ziggy's.

Around noon every day except Sundays, a steady stream of regulars queued up for the best bratwurst in town, and the most affordable. The only drawback was there was nowhere to eat once Ziggy handed over your wax paper–wrapped bundle of heaven, unless you were bound for a Pullman car. Otherwise you could eat standing on the sidewalk, commandeer one of the benches in the station, or claim a spot on the steps of the new post office across the street.

A queue had already formed at Ziggy's when I arrived, and I spotted Otto in it, last in line but one. That one, a dark man of medium height, looked vaguely familiar, but it was his richness that struck me first. His coat, brown cashmere with a fur collar, seemed a bit much even on a brisk autumn day. Even swells were willing to battle the elements and the lowbrow mob to claim a bratwurst on a bun.

As I slipped in beside Otto, the man behind let out a sound of annoyance and spoke in a slightly nasal voice. "You're cutting in line, girlie."

"I'm with this man," I told him, indicating Otto, whose face had gone as white as the post office granite. He tugged at my sleeve, a silent request to back away from the confrontation, but just because a man wore a coat that probably cost more than I earned in a whole year didn't mean he had the right to play the big cheese in the bratwurst line.

"Are you going to eat, or just watch him?" Mr. Rich asked.

"Of course I'm going to eat." My stomach was growling at the aroma of the smoke coming off Ziggy's coals. "But you see, my friend here was going to buy for both of us whether I came to stand beside him or not, so I assure you that you won't miss out on my account."

The man's lips turned down, but his dark eyes glittered in amusement. "Just assure my stomach that Ziggy won't hand you his last brat."

"Oh, for pity's sake," I said. "I've never heard such a baby." Especially from a man whose lapel, I now noticed, boasted a diamond pin whose worth would probably buy a ten-cent lunch for every person within shouting distance.

"Louise . . ." Poor Otto looked like he was going to faint.

I wasn't about to let the perturbed man off the hook. "Wouldn't you expect a girl to stand beside you if you promised to pay for her lunch? Or, like a sultan, do you prefer your women to stay ten paces behind?"

The man laughed. "You're giving me ideas."

Otto, unable to contain himself, scolded me. "Louise, this is Al Jolson."

I gaped, and the man's face broke into a colossal smile. Al Jolson was Broadway's sensation of the moment. *The Honeymoon Express* was the first Broadway show Otto and I had attended together, and Otto had spent the rest of the summer mimicking him singing "The

Spaniard That Blighted My Life." I felt foolish not to have spotted him right away. In my defense, our tickets were in the balcony's back of beyond, so I hadn't seen the man up close. And who would have expected a luminary of the Great White Way to be queuing up for sausage on a bun?

"This is quite a coincidence," I said, recovering from shock. "I'm standing between two famous songsters."

Otto writhed. "Louise . . ."

Jolson smiled warily and pointed a gloved finger at Otto. "Who—this kid?"

His skepticism brought out the promoter in me. "*This kid* wrote the song hit of the summer."

"The song hit of the summer was 'You Made Me Love You' by yours truly."

Mr. Jolson didn't suffer for lack of ego.

"Okay, but you must have heard 'My Tootsie from Altoona,' " I said.

His gaze fastened on Otto. "Wait a second—don't tell me." He concentrated and then snapped his gloved fingers. "Otto Klemper. That's the name, isn't it?"

Otto hadn't looked so amazed since we were ten and a man at the county fair had guessed his weight. He reached out his hand. "It's an honor to meet you, Mr. Jolson."

"It's Al to my friends and colleagues."

Otto's face turned fuchsia. "Gosh, I can't believe you would've heard of me."

"I always know the competition, kid. That song of yours was a pip. Written any more?"

"Plenty," Otto said. "Right now I'm working on a nifty novelty about the income tax."

Jolson laughed. "I'd like to hear it sometime."

I might have initiated the conversation, but I was out of it now. I edged ahead of them, keeping our place in line while they talked. Or, rather, while Jolson talked and Otto stared at him worshipfully as though he could absorb every syllable that fell from the great man's mouth. When we finally got to the front of the line, Jolson insisted on paying for all of our lunches. From Ziggy's eagerness and the amount of kraut he piled on our buns, Jolson must have been both a regular there and a big tipper. He wouldn't stay and eat with us, though.

"Gotta eat on the hoof today. But you come find me when you have something to play for me, kid."

Long after he'd walked away in a jaunty swagger, Otto stared after him. I worried his bratwurst would slip out of his hand and we'd end up at the back of the line again.

"That was Al Jolson," he said in wonder.

"Uh-huh." The air was nippy, and I looked longingly toward Penn Station. "Do you want to find a place inside?" Sometimes the cops would oust loiterers in the passenger waiting area, but maybe if we ate fast . . .

Otto remained planted where he was, in a daze. "How can I eat the bratwurst Al Jolson bought for me?"

"Would you rather have it bronzed?"

I managed to maneuver him to the post office steps. In the sun it wasn't so chilly, and I liked sitting there amid those colossal stone buildings. It was like a postal Parthenon.

"Do you think he meant it, about me playing my song for him?"

"Seemed to." I bit into my roll, savoring my first bite.

Otto followed suit, and for a moment we chewed silently, letting the flavors fill us with a shared nostalgia for the world we'd left behind. I wasn't homesick, but on occasion my thoughts were fleet-winged swallows, returning me to Altoona. That city was my past, my childhood, the only world I'd known until my falling out with my aunt Sonja after I'd been assaulted by one of her boarders and ended up pregnant. There are times when you hope people will rise above expectations. Aunt Sonja didn't. She'd blamed me and worried about what her friends and neighbors would say about her, the aunt who'd raised me. The only help she gave me was finding a home where I could have the baby and place it for adoption. I hadn't seen or heard from her in well over a year.

Otto brought me out of my brooding. "Mr. Jolson seems like a stand-up guy, doesn't he? Imagine him inviting me to play him a song. Why would he go out of his way to be so nice to me?"

"Because he's an entertainer, and you might be able to provide him with material."

"Oh." From the look on his face, you'd think he'd just discovered Santa didn't scooch down everyone's chimney on Christmas morning.

"Doesn't mean he's not a nice man," I pointed out. "Even the most talented people don't rise to the top of their professions without keeping an eye out for themselves."

"I guess you're right," said Otto, who didn't have a calculating bone in his body. Sometimes I worried this town would eat him alive.

"Finish your food." I gave him a playful nudge with my shoe. "I can't sit out here in the cold all day. I'm a newly fledged private investigator with places to go."

"Where are you going?"

I told him Jackson's address, on Sixty-fifth near Amsterdam Avenue.

He frowned. "That's San Juan Hill."

He wasn't telling me anything I didn't know. One thing I'd learned backward and forward for the police exam was the geography of New York City. Jackson's neighborhood had earned its name from the many skirmishes there between the local population and the majority Irish police. "So?"

"That's a colored neighborhood," he said.

"Won't they allow me in?" I joked. "Strange, Jackson Beasley lives there and I can't think how *he* manages to get in and out of his apartment if they don't."

"Jackson's a man."

"And I'm an adult, and it's the middle of the afternoon. I'll be as safe there as I am in Greenwich Village."

"Maybe I should go with you."

I laughed. "Some career as a detective I'm going to have if I have to haul a songwriter along for protection all the time." Despite the bravado, I appreciated his offer. Having someone in this city who'd known me for so long and cared about me was a comfort. Even if I did keep a few secrets from him, I never doubted that I could turn to him if I was in trouble. "Believe me, if I need an escort, I'll let you know."

I didn't regret turning down Otto's offer. Jackson's block held several run-down buildings, but nothing I wasn't used to seeing in pockets all over New York. Small children newly forced into their scratchy woolens played hopscotch and kick the can. I weaved around them. Women and some men loitered on stoops, conversing and tracking my progress down the sidewalk. I hurried toward the address I'd written down when Mr. McChesney asked me to create a list of employee addresses after the fire.

During the months we'd worked together, I'd never visualized Jackson's residence. Why would I? But now that I was face-to-face with the plain brownstone façade flanked by larger, unkempt buildings on both sides, I wondered why Jackson with his Southern gentleman pretensions would have settled here. There were better affordable neighborhoods, surely.

He lived on the second floor, but as I crossed the foyer to the staircase, something scampered in front of my feet. By the time my stopped heart started beating again, the mouse had already disappeared. I darted up the stairs.

Within moments of my knock at the flat on the second-floor landing, an attractive dark-skinned woman opened the door. Her hair was pulled back in an elaborate braid that curled into a crown at the top of her head. She also wore a fringe. Her dress was navy blue, simple but of good-quality linen, and set off by a red-and-purple patterned shawl. Next to her, in my own workaday shirtwaist and skirt, covered by a rather plain navy-blue coat, I felt a little dull.

"Is this Jackson Beasley's residence?"

The housekeeper gave me a cool up-and-down. "Yes, it is."

"Well, is Jackson—Mr. Beasley—in? I work with him at Van Hooten and McChesney. Worked, I should say."

The gaze narrowed. "Louise?"

"Yes," I said, surprised.

An internal struggle showed in her eyes. "He's not here. He went out."

"And you don't know where?"

"No."

"Then I'll leave a message for him, if I may."

Reaching for the clasp on my shoulder bag, I cast a longing glance past the housekeeper into the apartment. She didn't take the hint and ask me in, so I dug around in my satchel until I located a scrap of paper and a pencil. Then, bracing the paper against the wall, I began writing.

"Wouldn't it be easier to tell me the message?" the woman asked.

"I suppose so," I said as I continued to write, "but I need to write down the places where he can reach me."

"I'll remember if you tell me."

Too late. I'd written down my address and Aunt Irene's, and even added Aunt Irene's telephone number, just in case. Our building didn't have a telephone, something Callie complained to Wally about incessantly. She'd been making noises about wanting to move somewhere "less prehistoric" at the end of the year. Now I worried my financial situation would be too precarious to afford a move.

"Here you are." I handed the page of scrawled information to the woman, taking the opportunity as she glanced down at it to peer into the room again. From what I could see, Jackson's apartment was amply furnished with pieces that were pretty, if clearly second-hand. Bookcases full to brimming looked tidy and orderly, lace antimacassars draped the backs of chairs and the brown velveteen sofa, and a large vase of chrysanthemums sat atop an embroidered runner down the compact dining table. The room looked almost feminine, and neat as a pin. No signs of mice up here, at least.

I glanced back. The housekeeper frowned at my open snooping.

"Lovely room," I said. "You obviously keep it famously."

Her lips compressed into a tight, impatient expression. She probably had things to do.

I turned to leave.

"He's very upset about what happened yesterday," she said, stopping me. "The fire, I mean."

I was surprised she'd heard about it. "We all are."

She edged into the hallway. "Is it true Mr. McChesney will close the business now? I mean, forever?"

Odd question for a housekeeper to ask. "I don't know. I'm afraid so."

Her face registered disappointment. And anxiety. Perhaps she was worried about Jackson not being able to afford her anymore.

"I'm sure Jackson will find a new job soon," I said. "He's practically been running Van Hooten and McChesney since he started working there."

She nodded. "That's what he's always grumbling about. That, and how he gets no credit for most of that work."

I supposed it was true. No one really acknowledged how Jackson had kept Van Hooten and McChesney going. No one there truly liked Jackson. Part of the reason for this was that no one could esteem Jackson as highly as he himself did. Evidently he even boasted about his work to the maid.

"Please tell him to leave me a message at any of those places, and as soon as possible."

"All right," she said, already retreating back into the apartment.

The woman could have taken a few lessons in door answering from Walter. My aunt's butler had his quirks, but even at his iciest he managed to say please and thank you and address visitors courteously.

Distracted by the oddity of Jackson's domestic, I was barely looking as I edged past a man at the building's outer door. Then he spoke to me.

"Louise?"

I froze. *That voice.* It terrified me more than the mouse had. The corridor was dim, with only a sliver of light coming through the partially opened door. I looked up into the face of Ford Fitzsimmons, a writer I'd discovered last summer who had subsequently tried to kill me by arranging for me to be pushed off a platform into the path of the oncoming train. Unfortunately, I'd been unable to prove it, and Ford was still free to roam the city and follow me into dark hallways.

I reacted as I always did now when I was within any proximity of Ford. I braced myself against something sturdy. In this case it was the frame of the door I wanted to escape through. What was he doing here? Jackson had edited his book, but I'd never heard that the two of them socialized.

Had he been following me?

I hadn't considered Ford as a possible culprit in the arson—frankly, I tried not to think about Ford at all. But he had a history of duplicity, attempted homicide, and general vileness. Maybe he'd been displeased about the way Van Hooten and McChesney had treated his book so far. But it hadn't even been published, and thanks to Guy's favoritism he'd received the largest advance of any new author we'd acquired during my tenure there.

I made myself look at him. His brown tweed coat was new and of better quality than the clothes he'd worn last summer. A plaid scarf was wound loosely about his neck. The hall was dark, but the scarf looked green. Or blue.

Just what the poodle lady had described the arsonist wearing.

"Why are you here?" I asked.

"I heard about the fire. Poor Guy. By God, it's terrible." The disturbance he felt showed in his blue, blue eyes. In fact, he was so shaken that he'd evidently run out of his house without his hat. He raked a hand through his thick wheat-blond hair. "What will happen to my book?"

So that was the crux of his panic.

It was a legitimate question, even if it took a selfish bastard to ask it after his colleague had died. I doubted Mr. McChesney had yet to take serious stock of what was to be done with the books in production. He was still in shock.

I tried to recall what little I knew of the progress of Ford's manuscript. Jackson and Ford had worked on a revision of it, I knew. "Have you given Jackson your second draft yet?"

"Weeks ago," he said.

"Then perhaps he's finished editing it."

"Wonderful—but where is it? Did it go up in flames? That's what I want to know."

I tried to keep my expression neutral—not an easy feat when I was sending up prayers to the Gods of Fire for Ford's manuscript to have been reduced to ash.

"Didn't you make a copy?" I asked unnecessarily. His feverish panic told the tale.

"I retyped the damn thing and handed it to Jackson with my own hands. Why the hell would I have needed a damned copy?"

In case of a damned fire.

He looked into my face and growled, "Oh, what am I asking you for? You're just the secretary. It's Jackson I need to talk to."

"He's not home."

The whole time we'd been standing there, Ford's body, though paused to talk to me, had seemed to be merely in suspended animation, still pointing in the direction of the stairs. Now he slumped a little and faced me. "Where is he?"

"Out, was all his housekeeper told me," I said.

A notion sparked in his eyes. "Do you think the housekeeper would let me hunt for my book? Maybe Jackson took it home to work on it and it escaped the fire."

"I doubt it. She didn't even let me through the front door."

He smirked. "I can be persuasive with ladies."

At one time that smile of his had charmed me. Now everything about the man gave me skin crawlies. Attempted homicide will do that to a budding relationship.

"How did you get Jackson's address?" I asked him.

"I asked McChesney. *He's* in the directory."

I drew back. "You went to Mr. McChesney's house?"

"This is my livelihood at stake, Louise. My life. Years of work."

He was right. My sympathy for all the authors affected by the fire resurged—except for Ford. In his case, I was definitely rooting for the fire. I also wondered if this could all be an act, a carefully planned smokescreen of frenzy to hide his culpability. I glanced again at the scarf. I wouldn't put it past Ford. I wouldn't put anything past him . . . except what motive would he have to set fire to his own publisher? The panic he showed argued against it.

"If I see Jackson, I'll tell him you're looking for him," I said.

"Sure you will."

I smiled. "Always a pleasure, Mr. Fitzsimmons."

He growled something to me as I pushed out the door.

I left the house, quickening my pace as I retraced my path toward Broadway. The denizens of San Juan Hill didn't make me nervous, but turning my back on Ford Fitzsimmons did. The man, a man I'd once dreamed of making my protégé and possibly something even more personal, was a viper.

Instead of heading downtown, I kept going toward Central Park West, where Mr. McChesney lived. I was curious to find out exactly what Ford had said to him.

CHAPTER 5

"Oh, Louise, it's you." Mr. McChesney's bloodshot eyes stared at me through the sliver of the door he'd cracked open.

"May I come in for a moment?"

Rather than assenting verbally, he opened the door the rest of the way and retreated into the entrance hall.

I followed. "Where's Mrs. Carey?"

Mrs. Carey had been working for Mr. McChesney forever—or at least as long as Aunt Irene could remember. As an infrequent visitor here, I'd only encountered the woman a few times, but she was unforgettable. She looked as if God had formed her the way children shape snowmen, by stacking spheres on top of one another. She had a perfectly round torso and on that her round head seemed to be plopped directly on her shoulders. Two dark eyes animated her face, and her gray hair was twisted into the crowning orb on the top of her head. But for all her roundness, she wasn't soft. More like a dragon guarding the gates. Why hadn't she answered the door?

"Oh, I . . ." He gestured in a wave that mimicked sending her away. "I couldn't stand her fussing."

Why she might have fussed was obvious. Mr. McChesney needed tending to. He was dressed in what appeared to be yesterday's wrinkled clothes, and though it was afternoon, he hadn't shaved and was still padding about in slippers. His sallow skin made me wonder if he'd slept at all since the fire, or eaten.

"Aren't you feeling well?" I asked.

"I'm sick—sick in my bones, sick at heart. I'm an old man, and now I have no business. And yet, I'm lucky. To think of poor Guy!"

His body shook in a dry heave of grief. I unpinned my hat, unlooped my bag from over my shoulder, and opened the entry closet door to place them on the shelf there. A cap and scarf already lay there—a gray-and-blue plaid scarf. I thought again of the poodle lady's description of the suspected arsonist. A plaid scarf wasn't much of a clue. Ford had worn one, and here was another. Probably half the men in Manhattan owned plaid scarves and brown coats.

I closed the closet and turned my attention back to Mr. McChesney. Of course the tragedy had hit him hard. I felt a pang of guilt for having forgotten him. Only the fluke of having run into Ford had brought me here. "Let me make you something," I said.

"Oh, I don't know . . ."

"Tea, at least." I went to the kitchen. While waiting for a kettle of water to boil, I checked Mrs. Carey's larder. That economical woman didn't keep much extra on hand, but I found some bread and a bit of cheese. I cut these up and also sliced an apple from a bowl on the counter. By the time the tea had steeped, I'd put together an appetizing snack. But when I took it to Mr. McChesney in his sitting room, he held the teacup as if the only point of it was to warm his hands.

I sat opposite him. The only light emanated from a standing lamp topped with an amber shade. The dark green drapes, drawn tightly, looked almost black in the dimness, and the heavy mahogany furniture didn't brighten things up any. Mr. McChesney didn't speak. The silence became uncomfortable.

"I ran into Ford at Jackson's," I said.

"So he did go there. Poor fellow. I knew Jackson would have bad news for him."

"You did?"

"That manuscript was given to Timothy to copy edit." He

frowned at me. "Didn't you know? I'm surprised. You always seem to have a keen eye on everything that goes on at the office." He put his cup down. "*Went* on, I should say."

"That must've slipped past me." Much had slipped past me in recent weeks, when the police exam had been my focus. A pointless distraction, I feared now.

"I'm sure Jackson told me he was done with it." Mr. McChesney sniffed. "Of course, it should have been Guy's project, since Guy had discovered the book."

Actually, *I* had discovered it and passed it on to Guy, to my everlasting regret. But how was I to know the author would attempt to have me flattened by a train?

"I never thought much of the book myself," he continued. "Too newfangled. But I'm sorry for the boy now. Sorry for all the authors. And poor Guy." He shook his head.

"Did Ford seem happy with the way his book was treated by Van Hooten and McChesney?" I asked.

"He certainly wasn't happy to have his manuscript reduced to a cinder."

"I meant before the fire. He didn't have a grudge against the firm, did he?"

His face crumpled in thought. "Jackson told me he was displeased with the change in the book's title. But even the most fanatical author wouldn't consider killing an editor over a title change." He frowned at me. "Have a bit of this apple, Louise. You must be hungry."

I wasn't, but perhaps if I munched a little, Mr. McChesney would be inclined to eat something himself. The fruit was crunchy and sweet, with just the right amount of tartness—a perfect fall apple. "Have you seen the police today?" I asked.

"No." The power of suggestion failed. He drummed his fingers on his knees, completely indifferent to the food.

"I wonder if they've discovered anything new," I said.

"What does it matter if they have or haven't? Guy's dead, and my future's ruined. And the future of so many, like that poor man Fitzsimmons."

"Don't waste your tears on him."

He might not have heard me. His gaze was focused inward. "If only my life had been different, things might not look so hopeless now. If, for instance, I had married." He glanced at me. "Did your aunt ever mention that I proposed to her?"

Only about a hundred times.

"Not that I would want to live off your aunt's money, mind you. But perhaps if I'd married I wouldn't feel so . . . discouraged." He frowned at me. "It's a terrible thing to end up alone, Louise, and not to have a soul to share the buffeting life can deal you."

I'd felt enough buffets already to understand what he meant. Yet I couldn't see marriage as a mere life raft to clamber onto merely to ride out life's storms, and I was certain Aunt Irene wouldn't feel flattered to be anyone's raft, either. "You aren't alone. You have friends, Mr. McChesney. My aunt is concerned for you—so are we all."

His lips attempted a smile. "I must seem selfish to you, and a terrible mope. How is your inquiry getting on?"

"That's why I'm here, to ask you about Ford."

"To ask if I think he burned the business down? Heavens no. I would hate to blame an author."

"So would I—if he didn't do it." I took a sip of tea. "Today I went to Jackson's house to ask him about Guy's dealings with Leonard Cain. Do you know anything about that?"

"Cain." He drew the name out, giving it the sinister sound it deserved. "Now there's a villain."

"You know him?"

"I've encountered him once or twice—an unpleasant fellow—but I don't know him."

"So he was only a friend of Guy's?"

"I'm not even certain they were friends. I wouldn't like to think so, at least."

"Cain came to the office on more than one occasion to see Guy. I left them talking together Wednesday night."

"I wonder what about?" Frowning, he reached for a piece of bread and bit into it. Success.

"I've heard some of Cain's business is unsavory."

He chewed this over some more before declaring, "By thunder, you may be right." His eyes narrowed as he swallowed. "Leonard Cain. A very bad man. *He* might have killed Guy, certainly."

"Why?"

He shrugged. "For money? All young men rack up debts these days. Guy certainly could have. And Edith Van Hooten, fond as I am of her, is not the kind of lady who would bail out her son without strong words and remonstrances. Perhaps for that reason, he might have put off paying Cain what he owed him. If there was anything Guy hated, it was being lectured."

He preferred to be menaced by gangsters rather than be given a stern talking-to by his mother?

"If Cain were found guilty, it would be a good thing all around," he continued. "Shady characters like that shouldn't be allowed to do business in this city."

From what I'd heard and read, men like Leonard Cain had personified business in the city for the last fifty years or so. Though the current Republican mayor and other progressive reformers had Tammany Hall on the ropes, the forces that had backed the Democratic machine at the corrupt epicenter of the city were still alive and kicking. Graft and bribery hadn't disappeared. Businessmen like Cain thrived because politicians, policemen, and functionaries and bureaucrats of all stripes could be bought.

A ringing in the hallway caused us both to jump. Mr. McChesney straightened, his posture rigid.

"That's your telephone," I said.

"I fear it's to do with the fire." He remained in his chair.

"Would you like me to answer it?"

"If you wish."

I was already on my feet. Going to the trouble and expense of installing phone service only to let it ring unanswered struck me as absurd. Plus, the call might be from the police, perhaps even Muldoon. I was curious to find out if there were any new developments in the case.

In the hallway I snatched up the receiver of the candlestick phone. "McChesney residence," I said, a little breathless.

"Good heavens, Louise—don't tell me you've taken up domestic service, too. Aren't two jobs keeping you busy enough?"

Aunt Irene's voice made me smile. "I came by to talk to Mr. McChesney about something, and Mrs. Carey isn't here. I don't think he's feeling well. He's taking it all very hard."

"Poor man. I'll have him to supper tonight. That usually cheers him up."

"He could use a meal. Would you like to speak to him?"

"Yes, but first I have a message for you." Her laugh sounded tinny over the line. "I feel like an exchange operator. A man telephoned here for you. A Mr. Jackson?"

"Jackson Beasley?" I guessed.

"That's it. A very nice-sounding man—his voice had a Southern lilt. He seemed like a proper gentleman, like Mr. Beauregard in *Violet in the Shade*. He asked me to tell you that he would be at the Horn & Hardart on Broadway and Forty-sixth between three and four thirty, and that you could meet him there."

I pivoted to check the hall clock behind me. It was close to three already. "I'd better scoot."

She lowered her voice. "Is this part of the investigation, or should I scold you for being an automat floozy?"

"Jackson is a coworker," I assured her. "I need to speak to him about Guy Van Hooten and Leonard Cain."

"Be careful, sugar bun."

"I doubt much harm can come to me in an automat."

"I'm not so sure. The only time I went there I bit into a Kaiser roll so stale it nearly cracked my tooth."

"I'll just have coffee," I promised.

I called Mr. McChesney to the telephone and hurried out to meet Jackson.

At noontime, the Broadway Horn & Hardart, that mechanized food palace for the proletariat, could resemble a reenactment of the sacking of Rome. At this time, later in the afternoon, there was relative calm among the smattering of tired shoppers, loners, and discouraged actors bucking up their spirits after a long day warming the benches in producers' outer offices.

Jackson was already seated at a two-person table when I arrived. An empty plate and a cup of coffee lay in front of him. I paid my nickel and watched the brass dolphin spout chicory brew into my cup.

Immediately after I sat opposite him, I could tell that coffee wasn't all Jackson had been drinking this afternoon. Dark stubble ran along his jaw. His eyes were red, and cigarette butts piled in the ashtray at his elbow.

I settled myself across from him. "Thank you for telephoning my aunt."

"I assumed it must be urgent if you hunted me down to my lair," he drawled. "Seems I've had a few visitors today."

"I saw Ford at your apartment. I guess your housekeeper told you about that, too."

For a moment he didn't speak.

"Is something wrong?" I asked.

His lips flattened. "I can't imagine what Ford wants."

"He wants to know what's become of his novel."

"Another casualty of the fire, I imagine."

"So you didn't have a copy at home?"

"If I kept copies of everyone's books at home I'd soon run out of room to sleep—unless I made a mattress of manuscripts." The idea amused him. "Is that what you came here for? To find out what became of young Fitzsimmons's magnum opus? I didn't think you cared for the man."

"I don't. Actually, I wanted to ask about Guy. Specifically, what you know about Guy and Leonard Cain?"

He grunted and lit another cigarette. "What's the point of talking about it now? Guy's gone. Ashes to ashes . . ."

I shouldn't have been surprised that Guy's death had hit him hard. When Callie's cousin Ethel had been murdered in our apartment, it felt as if my world had been upended—and there had been no love lost between Ethel and me. Seeing someone cut down in the prime of life was profoundly disturbing. Guy's death hadn't affected me as strongly as Ethel's, but I'd been immediately plunged into the why of it, which helped. Also, I hadn't seen Guy's body, as poor Jackson had.

"What's the use of any of it? A damn waste," he said on an exhaled cloud of smoke.

"Mr. McChesney wants me to find out if Guy was involved in anything that led to the fire and his death."

"You? Why?"

The incredulity in his voice annoyed me. "I helped solve the murder of my roommate's cousin."

"Did you?" His big dome of a forehead lined in thought. "All I remember is that you accused Ford Fitzsimmons of trying to kill you." He shook his head. "Madness."

"The police wouldn't have found the real killer without my help." How Muldoon would have howled at my arrogance. I added, as if the detective were actually listening, "At least, it would have taken them much longer."

"Hmm." Jackson's expression conveyed more than a dollop of skepticism. "And so Mr. McChesney wants you to find out who committed the arson."

"And also to find out if it was intended to be murder."

He drew back. "You mean the fire was set deliberately to kill Guy?"

"That seemed to be what the police were thinking yesterday."

"Well, then, why not just let the police handle it? Better all around—and safer for you."

"I'm not worried about my safety." Not as much as everyone else seemed to be. "And the police are going to have a hard time with this one. The Van Hootens don't want an investigation at all."

"Afraid of what'll come crawling out once the log's kicked over," he drawled.

"What did Guy have to hide?" I asked.

"All the vices of the rich and young. Gambling, drinking, women . . ."

I stopped him. "Women? What women?"

"He didn't confide in me much. If I were you, I'd concentrate on the gambling."

I sat up straighter. "That's why I wanted to ask you about Leonard Cain. He was still at the office when I left Wednesday night."

Jackson thought for a moment. "Guy did tell me that he'd been going regularly to one of Cain's clubs—the Omnium, I think it was—and getting into a bit of a fix there."

"What kind of a fix?"

He laughed. "I worry about this investigation of yours, Louise.

What kind do you think? Gambling debts. The Omnium has an infamous back room, although it might actually be upstairs or in the basement, for all I know. I've never been there. Wherever it's hidden, it's got a roulette wheel with Guy's name on it. He mentioned playing roulette more than once."

I thought about Wednesday night, when I was covering my typewriter and preparing to leave work. Guy and Cain were shut up in his office and I had no idea when either would leave. I didn't particularly want to barge in to tell Guy I had a dentist appointment the next morning, so I wrote the note about my next morning's absence and went to slip it under the door. As I bent down, I heard Cain say, "I'm here to settle up, Van Hooten." At the time, his tone hadn't struck me as threatening, but now that expression, *settle up,* sounded more sinister.

"Do you know anything about Leonard Cain himself?"

Jackson leveled a stare at me. "The first thing you should know is that Mr. Cain isn't a man you should tangle with, or accuse without proof. In the South we call them big dogs. A big dog's jaws are always dangerous, even if he seems tame and friendly."

"But if Cain had a debt to collect, that might be a motive for murder. And he was the last one to see Guy." I told him about "settling up."

"That's worrying, but if I had a nickel for every person I'd heard Guy have words with I could empty out this entire automat," Jackson said.

"Who else argued with him?"

"Well, *I* did from time to time."

"At work," I said dismissively. "Colleagues have differences. That's normal."

"True." He scratched his stubbly chin. "What about that brother of his? The younger, smarter, yet less-favored Hugh. He came to the office a few weeks ago."

"I didn't see him."

"It was late. They were holed up in Guy's office, going at each other like two tomcats."

"Why?"

"I didn't have my ear to the keyhole," he said.

"But you said they were going at each other. Arguing, not actually fighting, I assume."

"Oh yes. Shouting, not hitting."

"Then you must have heard something."

Jackson hesitated. I could read the conflict he was having over repeating what he'd heard. Telling tales out of school. He swallowed down the dregs of his cup. "I didn't listen on purpose. But Hugh had looked livid before he went into Guy's office, and their voices sounded angry, even though the door muffled their words. I remember one thing clearly, though, and that was something Guy said. He shouted, 'Would you kill our mother?' "

I frowned. "I assume it wasn't meant literally."

"At the time, I took it to mean that Hugh was threatening to do something that would make their mother unhappy to the point of apoplexy."

Such as killing Guy? No, surely not. They wouldn't have been discussing that. But maybe Hugh had threatened to do something that would hurt Guy.

"The argument might have meant nothing, for all its ferocity," Jackson said. "Siblings squabble, and the intensity of it can sometimes seem fiercer to outsiders than it does to the participants themselves."

Would you kill our mother?

That Guy had spoken those words made Jackson's telling seem more credible to me. Mrs. Van Hooten had doted on Guy. Hugh was second in birth order and second in her heart. And whatever Mr. McChesney said, Hugh's not receiving any stake in the family publishing business had to have stung a little. It had been a slight. He certainly hadn't spoken of Guy with any great love, just hours after his brother's death.

What did Hugh know about Guy that would have killed their mother if she had found out about it? Something about the gambling debt he owed to Leonard Cain?

"When did you overhear this?" I asked.

"Three weeks ago?" He shrugged. "I couldn't say for sure."

"Recently, then." I tapped my fingers against my coffee cup. Could anything about that sibling argument have led to Guy's death? It still seemed more likely that Leonard Cain was behind the fire. Perhaps because I'd seen Cain talking to Guy with my own eyes.

I pushed my coffee away. Every guess was a wild guess at this point, but talking to Jackson had confirmed my hunches. "Thank you for calling me back so quickly," I said.

"I got back to the house not too long after you left. Miriam said that your business sounded urgent."

"Miriam, your housekeeper?"

He flinched. After checking that no other automat patrons were within earshot, he said, "Miriam's my wife."

Heat flushed my cheeks. I stared at him for several seconds before I could speak. "Your *wife*? I didn't know you were married. You never mentioned . . ."

"My colored wife?" His lips turned down. "No, not to many, I don't."

The memory of how I'd spoken to her, how I'd assumed she was the maid, filled me with shame. "I'm so sorry. She must have thought me very rude. I treated her like a housekeeper."

"She's used to it."

Yes, with a husband who claimed her only under duress, I could see how she might be. Was she the reason we were meeting here, not at his home?

"Miriam's kind, and intelligent," he said defensively. "Maybe the smartest woman I've ever known. Yet my family will have nothing to do with her. Or me, now. That's why we moved here. We lost everything. We've learned to be careful."

"Surely, now that you're here . . ."

His lips twisted into a sneer. "Do you really think here is so different?" He stubbed out his cigarette. "Well, you're young. I used to think the best of people, too. People I'd known all my life, whose hearts I would have sworn were no different than mine. During one summer break during my college years I tutored children in my hometown in Latin. Miriam was one of my students." He shook his head. "Do you know, I had friends criticize me for accepting her as a pupil? Said I was wasting my time, as if I were teaching a dog tricks. But Miriam was my best student—it was a pleasure to talk to her about Ovid and Virgil."

"You fell in love over the classics."

He smiled, and for a moment he seemed less like Jackson and more like a man a woman might actually find appealing. "Not just at first. My hopes really were those of a teacher for a promising student. But then after I graduated from Harvard and came home, I discovered her mother had died and she'd been forced to take work laundering to help support her younger brothers and sisters. But she still carried her Ovid with her. I think that's what made me love her first."

His smile was short-lived. "When it all came out, I learned very quickly who my friends were. They fell away like autumn leaves against the first brisk wind. From my family I received nothing but ultimatums and even threats to turn us in to the authorities. But by then there was a baby on the way and my back was up. Of course there was no question of our marrying in Alabama. We might both have ended up in jail, but I wasn't going to abandon Miriam."

I detected something in his voice—a hint of regret. Did he wish now he had capitulated to his family's demands?

"Because of rumors, I'd already lost my job at a paper down there. The owner was part of the white-hooded crowd. So we came north, and set up house together for the first time. But not long after, our baby, the sweetest baby girl you ever saw, was born with a bad heart. She died after three days."

I felt sick. "I'm so sorry."

"We were heartbroken, and alone in our heartbreak. My father wrote me that the baby's death was a blessing—a *blessing.* Miriam's people told her that it was a punishment. Everybody had God tugging our tragedy from both directions."

"How awful. I'm so sorry for all you both went through. But you mustn't think Mr. McChesney would have fired you if he'd known about Miriam. Guy, either."

"Maybe not. But being cast out by your own people can make you lose faith in the goodness of your fellow man."

I stared down at my hands, remembering my uncles putting me on a train fifteen months ago. Aunt Sonja hadn't come to the station. I'd spied tears in my uncles' eyes, but neither of them had argued that I shouldn't leave Altoona. And none of them had written me since that day.

I'd felt shaken. Abandoned. When I'd come here, I'd created a new family—my aunt Irene, Callie, and Otto. Yet not one of them had I told about the boy I'd given birth to. I was no more trusting of people than Jackson.

"You've gone silent, Louise."

I gave myself a shake. "I was only thinking."

His lips flattened. "I've seen other people 'thinking' after I've told them about Miriam."

"That's not what I meant."

"Don't worry," he said, "we were never friends, were we? I won't think the worse of you if we never speak again."

I drew up, torn between compassion and anger. "You don't know me, and I'm fairly certain you're selling some others short, as well. You didn't need to keep Miriam a secret from anyone at Van Hooten and McChesney."

He sighed. "Yes, well, there's no point in worrying about any of this now, is there? There is no more Van Hooten and McChesney."

"There might be."

"Don't be naïve. You think Ogden McChesney is the type to rally after a setback like this one? He was barely muddling along the way things were. It was the Van Hooten money that started the firm and kept it going. I'm sure that Hugh and his mother are thrilled to be done with the publishing business now."

I feared he was correct.

"I'm happy to be done with it, too," he said.

"With what?"

"The business, my job, Van Hootens—all of it. I'm looking forward to starting fresh. Why not?" He breathed out wearily. "I've done it before."

Despite his words, his defiance, depression clung to him. I didn't want to leave him on such a defeatist note. "I hope you're not going to cut all ties to Van Hooten and McChesney. I'll be curious where you go next, and I hope we can be friends. I'd like to know Miriam, too."

"Time will tell," was all he said, unconvinced.

I stood, said goodbye, and left. Jackson half rose, but he didn't make a move to leave. When I crossed the street, he was sitting there still, watching me through the window with that long stare of his. I'd meant what I said about wanting to know Miriam, but I could tell he didn't believe me. He'd heard those words before.

Chapter 6

A door slammed and I sat up, bleary-eyed, as quick, light footsteps came from the doorway.

"Guess what I found out, Louise."

Callie had been gone when I'd arrived home exhausted from an afternoon spent running around midtown. I'd lain down on the sofa and listened to an impromptu concert given downstairs by a few of the Bleecker Blowers, back from their upstate trip. I must have nodded off somewhere in the middle of "Fascination."

Callie took no notice that she was addressing a half-asleep person. She tossed herself into the chair and hugged a fringed pillow. "I finally managed to get Teddy talking about something other than airplanes. Well, almost. It was still all about Hugh Van Hooten."

Hugh's name set off my mental alarm clock. "What about Hugh?"

She studied me. "Your hair's all bumpy. Were you asleep?"

"I'm awake now." I brushed a hand over my hair and rearranged a few pins as I glanced at the mantel clock over the bricked fireplace. It was six o'clock. "What are you doing home?"

Callie's rehearsal schedule seemed relentless. The show was set to open Thanksgiving week, and they were scheduled for an out-of-town tryout in Philadelphia first.

"Most of us got a four-hour dinner break. Annette, the leading lady, can't carry a tune to save her life, and the director's starting to panic. I don't know what he thinks he can do with her during dinner to solve that problem, unless he's got a Frankenstein lab set up backstage and intends to do experiments with her and some canaries."

I laughed. "It's a break for you, anyway. Do you want something to eat?"

"Not really. I had a big lunch with Teddy, which is a break for *you*. Here's what he told me over a filet of sole: Guy owed money to Leonard Cain."

"Oh." I'd leaned forward to hear the big news, but now I sank back again. What was left of my afternoon after leaving Jackson had been spent looking into Guy's financial situation. He was not only in arrears at his club, he personally owed money to several members for card game losses and also to the old man who worked as the club's concierge, from whom he had borrowed cab fare. Additionally, I discovered he had failed to pay a bill to one tailor and a jeweler near the office. This was probably the tip of the iceberg. "I'd already figured out that Guy had money problems."

Callie kicked off her shoes and then tucked her feet under her. "If you're going to send me out snooping, you need to keep me up to date. I feel bad enough wheedling information out of Teddy. If it's going to be old news, I'd just as soon skip it. Anyway, these weren't small money problems. Hugh let slip to Teddy that Guy had asked him for an enormous sum—several thousand dollars."

"Did Hugh give him anything?"

"Teddy doesn't know. Hugh was saying that to give him the money, they would have to stop work on the project they're working on—some sort of stabilizer for mounting photography equipment on airplanes. But Teddy says the work at the air park has gone on without a hitch, so Hugh couldn't have given all his cash to Guy."

Would you kill our mother? Guy had asked Hugh. Would Edith Van Hooten have been upset to learn that her son had racked up debt? The family wasn't living in genteel poverty. Surely even a few thousand dollars, a sum that would ruin most people, wouldn't have caused more than a few tremors in the Van Hooten family finances.

"I wonder what Guy wanted that large a sum for," I said. To pay off his club dues and tailors, or something else?

"At the aerodrome one day, Hugh was in a stew and told Teddy that Guy had finally gone too far. He said the way Guy was gambling at the Omnium Club and carrying on, there might not be a Van Hooten Aeronautics before long."

The Omnium, Cain's club. That man's name set off all kinds of alarm bells. But if Hugh was worried that the family money keeping his airplane business afloat would be diverted to pay for Guy's excesses, that would give Hugh a strong motive for murder. Though wouldn't burning down another family enterprise, the publishing house, be counterproductive?

Unless the building was heavily insured. I needed to look into that.

"Hugh also told Teddy he should be happy to have sisters, and Teddy agreed he liked sisters because girls are so much jollier." Callie smiled. "Isn't that sweet?"

"Did Hugh think it was sweet?"

"Hugh said, 'You think girls can't cause a family trouble? That's all you know!'" She shook her head. "That's what's so puzzling about Hugh. One moment he's nice and friendly—Old Hoots—and then he gets in a mood. That's what Teddy says, at least."

Teddy didn't strike me as the brightest bulb on the marquee, yet what he said about Hugh's personality lined up with what I'd observed the one time I'd met him. "I wonder if Hugh could have killed his brother."

"That's what Teddy said we *shouldn't* think."

I froze. "You didn't let on to Teddy that we were investigating the murder, did you?"

"I'm not that dippy," Callie said. "I just asked him, like I was curious and the idea occurred to me. I *can* act, you know."

I hoped she'd done some Laurette Taylor–caliber acting.

"Anyway, Teddy insisted Hugh wouldn't swat a fly," she said. "Teddy might have his faults, but he's a good judge of character."

"How well do you really know him?"

She crossed her arms. "I've known him for two months, which is more like two years with some people. Teddy's an open book—unlike others I could mention."

She meant me. Callie was my closest female friend, yet there were things I hadn't been able to bring myself to tell her. "Everyone has secrets."

"Not Teddy. Or if he does, it's something like having broken a neighbor's window with a baseball when he was nine."

For a moment, I thought about what we let our friends see, and what we didn't. "Maybe Hugh Van Hooten is adept at masking the Mr. Hyde side of his personality. I don't suppose you could arrange it so I could talk to him?"

"I might someday, but right now Teddy said Hugh's sticking close to home. He's even planning to skip the aerodrome on Sunday to stay with his mother."

"Currying favor with the matriarch," I said.

Callie leveled a shaming stare at me. "The poor woman's just lost her son. If Hugh *weren't* staying close by her, you'd be calling him a monster."

She was right. "I'm seeing everything through a lens of suspicion." It wasn't hard to guess why. "I bumped into Ford Fitzsimmons today."

Her eyes widened. "Oh no."

"He's just as egotistical as ever. He'd heard about the fire and was worried his book was lost. The man cornered me in a hallway and for a moment I thought *he* might have been Guy's murderer. But he wouldn't have wanted Van Hooten and McChesney to burn down, so it doesn't fit, unfortunately."

"It's only unfortunate if you have your heart set on Ford's being a murderer."

"There's no one I'd rather see in Sing Sing."

"Well, you're still in one piece, so perhaps he's mended his ways."

I was still in one piece, but my reaction to Ford reminded me of something important. If I let personal prejudices cloud my judgment, I'd never get anywhere. The point of conflict in all the stories about Guy's last days was the question of money. Guy was in debt. The most likely person he owed a large debt to was Leonard Cain, the person Guy had last been seen with. Somehow, I needed to find out why Cain had visited Guy Wednesday night.

So what was I waiting for? I stood up and headed for my bedroom.

Callie tagged after me. "What's the matter?"

"Nothing. I need to go out."

"Now?" Callie asked as I threw open my wardrobe and cast a critical eye over my two evening dresses.

"Neither seems right," I said, frustrated.

"Right for where?"

"The Omnium Club."

Her face collapsed into a grave frown. "You need to watch your step around Leonard Cain, Louise. My friend Flossie in the chorus said that a fella she was stepping out with had a cousin who worked for a guy who was bumped off by some of Cain's men."

The word of a girl of a fella of a cousin was thin testimony, but the seriousness in Callie's voice convinced me she believed Flossie's tale.

"Why would Cain have killed the man?" I asked.

Callie shrugged. "Business, was all Flossie knew."

"How was he killed?"

"By a gunman late at night outside his apartment." She let that sink in for a moment and said, "I'm telling you, Cain is dangerous. Flossie said there was another associate of Cain's who died the same way."

Worry rippled through me, but I steeled myself. "If a little Broadway chorus hearsay puts me off, I shouldn't be investigating at all. I'm looking into a suspected murder. The culprit isn't going to be a Boy Scout."

"But you will be careful, won't you?"

"Of course. I'm always careful." Callie's raised brows compelled me to add, "Almost always."

She eyed me steadily. "The Omnium's hardly a place a single girl can waltz into unaccompanied, you know. We might persuade Teddy to be your escort, but it's such short notice."

I shook my head. "How would we ask him without letting on that I was investigating Guy's murder?"

"But you can't just walk into the lion's den by yourself. You'll have to dig up somebody."

"I don't have to dig. I've already got him."

* * *

Callie devoted what was left of her break to dolling me up for the Omnium. "You might as well look good on your big night out." Under her breath, she added, "Seeing how it might be your last."

She was full of grim humor as she looked me over with a mouthful of pins she'd just removed after tacking up the hem of one of her dresses that she was loaning me. And what a dress it was. A fitted top of ivory lace overlaid a silk messaline dress of pale green. The lace sleeves extended to three-quarter length, where Callie's best evening gloves took over.

"That color brings out the green in your eyes." She poked the last of the pins into her pincushion, a little pewter dog with a green velvet pad on its back. "You might as well keep the dress. It's always made me look like a corpse. Which reminds me . . . is this what you'd like to be laid out in when Cain finishes with you?"

Apprehension gripped me. In borrowed finery, tottering on unfamiliar heels, I felt like an imposter. "Do you think I'll stick out at the Omnium?"

"I was only joking," she said. "Just because you're not used to dressing up to the nines doesn't mean you'll be conspicuous. And you certainly don't look like a detective."

Fidgety, I glanced at the mantel clock. "It's getting late."

"That's why they call them nightclubs." She put her hands on her hips. "We need to find you something to carry. You can't walk into the swellest spot in town with that saddlebag of yours looped over your shoulder."

She finished me off with a little black velvet bag—wholly impractical for carrying anything more than a key and some powder. To these I added a pencil for taking notes. Habit.

The effect of Callie's handiwork was clear in Otto's eyes when he showed up. "Louise! You look so glamorous, I hardly recognized you."

Despite their reflection on my usual less-than-glamorous appearance, the words bucked me up. "Just what I wanted to hear."

"No, no, no." Callie practically vibrated in frustration. "You should look this beautiful all the time, because you are." She frowned, adding, "At least you are until you start walking. Make sure you don't clump."

I gave her my solemn oath to float like a fairy. Then I hugged her. "Thanks."

Her return hug segued into a readjustment of a few hairpins. "An artist's work is never done," she muttered.

Otto turned his hat brim in his hands. "We'd better go." He'd heeded my instructions to look smart. His hair was parted in the center and pomaded back sleekly enough to suit a magazine ad. He wore his dark coat dressed up with a red scarf. The creases of his best suit peeked above his black shoes, which had an extra shine on them. "I've got a cab downstairs."

We all trundled out and piled into the cab's single seat. On the way uptown, Otto regaled Callie with the story of our meeting with Al Jolson. This morning seemed years ago to me now.

We dropped Callie off at her theater before continuing on.

"Have fun, you two," she said in parting. "Watch out for gunmen."

Otto looked alarmed. "What did she mean?"

I slid farther over on the seat. "Oh, you know Callie's sense of humor." Unless I wanted to lose my escort, now wasn't the best time to tell him about the Cain method of removing inconvenient people.

No one could accuse the Omnium of hiding its light under a bushel. The name was spelled out in electric bulbs above the columned entrance, where a uniformed doorman stood to greet guests. Or perhaps to keep them out. The closer I got to the man after Otto helped me out of the cab, the more I suspected the latter. He was well over six feet, with bristly red hair peeking out between his collar and his hat. His neck was as thick as a tree trunk, and beneath that livery were muscles like a carnie strongman's.

"Reservation?" he growled at Otto.

"I wasn't aware we needed one," I said. Callie would have told me if we did.

The giant flicked a glance at me, then addressed Otto again. "Been here before, bub?"

Otto's Adam's apple hurdled over his starched collar. "No, sir."

Sirring the doorman would get us nowhere. The man probably wanted money—more money than Otto and I had on us if we wanted to pay the bill when we were done. I hooked my hand through the crook of Otto's arm and tried to strike an imperious tone. "We're meeting a friend of ours here. Al Jolson."

I squeezed Otto's elbow, hoping he'd follow my lead. After an audible gulp, he did. "Is, um, Al here yet?"

The man squinted, sizing us up again. "No, he ain't."

There was nothing to do but brazen it out. I turned to Otto. "What time did he say he'd meet us?"

"Eleven?" he squeaked.

"He's probably still at the Winter Garden, then." I smiled at the doorman. "I'm sure it'll be all right if we wait inside, won't it? Al wouldn't like to see us shivering out here on the sidewalk."

Grudgingly, the redheaded ox opened the door.

Entering the Omnium was like stepping into another universe. A short entrance passage, where we offered up our outer things to an attendant, opened onto a colossal room. Modern chandeliers hung from the high, gold-painted ceiling. A black-lacquered bar stretched the length of the end of the room. The jet surface was nearly as reflective as the long beveled mirror behind tuxedoed barmen. Above the bar an overhang served as a mezzanine level with more tables overlooking the other tables below, which were arranged around a dance floor. I felt I'd entered a theater where the patrons were the performers. People stared at the dancers on the floor, customers at the bar and other tables. Even Otto and I drew attention, until we were rightly sized up as neither famous nor distinctive.

I had a hard time not gaping all around me. The high walls of the club were decorated in the style of Greek pottery—with elongated black figures playing sports, gowned women striking elegant poses, and horses drawing chariots. All the figures were three times life size and limned against a sunset-orange background. Four lacquered support pillars also took up the motif, with the bottom half of each carved in the figure of a spear-carrying guard.

The sheer frivolous opulence of it all dazzled me. I only snapped out of my awe when I noticed Otto taking it in with the same open-mouthed wonder. The officious maître d' whose job it was to show us to our table was already halfway across the room. I nudged Otto and we hurried to catch up.

The table he led us to was so close to the swinging kitchen door that I had to spring out of its way when a waiter burst through bearing a tray. For a moment, the clanking of pots almost drowned out the sound of the band playing "My Melancholy Baby." Clearly, the maître d' had sized us up as insignificant people.

I frowned pointedly at the table and then drew my shoulders back. "This won't do. We'll wait for our party at the bar until a better table comes free."

The maître d' stood his ground. "There might not be a better one."

"We're waiting for our friend, Al Jolson," Otto piped up.

"Mr. Jolson?" The man's expression was more skeptical than impressed, but the way he said the name confirmed that Jolson was a regular here.

I took Otto's arm. "Mr. Klemper, a songwriter, is an associate of Mr. Jolson. Al has commissioned a piece from him."

"About the income tax," Otto said.

The man considered our words as a waiter carrying used glasses banged through the swinging door. It hit one of the chairs at our table on the rebound. The maître d' frowned, obviously weighing the demands of two nobodies against the possibility of offending a famous patron. "I'll see what I can do. Follow me."

He marched us back through the crowd to the bar, where he indicated two seats to us and rapped to get the attention of the nearest bartender. "The first round for this pair's on the house, Bill."

"Gee, thanks!" Otto exclaimed.

I gave him a sharp nudge with my foot. "Thank you very much," I said with what I hoped was sophisticated reserve.

We maneuvered ourselves onto the high seats. Otto leaned in to me. "What was that all about?"

"The table was too far back," I explained in a lowered voice. I could never have seen Leonard Cain from a tiny table by the kitchen.

"What'll you have?" the bartender asked.

I didn't drink liquor often, even at my aunt's weekly soirées. I said the first drink that came into my head, which was something I'd heard Callie mention and always wanted to try. "Two champagne cocktails."

When the bartender pushed them toward us, Otto and I eyed our glasses warily.

"Looks like ginger ale with a maraschino cherry, doesn't it?" he whispered.

"Your Altoona's showing."

"Thanks for letting me know." He touched his glass to mine. "*Prost.*"

We drank and both fought to maintain smiles as the bitter bubbly hit our taste buds. "Definitely not ginger ale," Otto gasped.

After a few sips, though, I understood the appeal of the stuff. We polished off our glasses and ordered seconds.

"Is Mr. Cain here tonight?" I asked the bartender.

"He's here most nights." The bald man had a craggy face and a voice that sounded like Brooklyn.

I scanned the room. "I don't see him."

"What you see ain't the whole club."

Of course. Jackson had told me that the Omnium had a back room, where the gambling took place. I looked around for a secret passage that would lead to this famous gaming den, but I didn't see a door other than the ones leading to the kitchen and the powder room. The bar didn't allow the best vantage point of the club. The dance floor would be better.

"We should dance," I told Otto.

He drained his champagne. The stuff was growing on him, too. "I thought you'd never ask." He hopped off his stool, lit up with enthusiasm. Lit up, period.

Otto wasn't the best dancer in the world, but with two champagne cocktails in him what he lacked in skill he more than made up for in exuberance. We joined the dance mid-waltz, and when the next number began, I recognized the rhythms of the tango. I started to head back to our champagne, but Otto held me fast. "We can do this."

The champagne really must have hit him hard. "Are you serious?"

"For Callie," he said, and pulled me close.

Heeding sanity, many people had exited the dance floor, so it was a thinner, braver crew we joined in the dance of seduction. Otto surprised me. His movements might have shown more recklessness than skill, but it was a decent effort. His forehead hovered near mine, his eyes full of champagne-induced intensity. Other patrons were watching us, making it harder for me to scan the club for nefarious characters or secret doors, which had been my reason for dancing in the first place. At one point, Otto lowered me in a dramatic dip, and I could see the gallery above the bar. Behind the patrons, there was a door. And at the door, a dark man stood in evening clothes, beefy arms crossed, watching us. When I came up again, I stumbled slightly.

"Ow!" Otto whispered. "That was my foot."

"I found it," I whispered.

"My toe? I'll say you did."

"The private room." I jerked my chin upward. "That's Leonard Cain."

Otto followed my gaze. His tango almost stalled out.

I mashed his foot again, this time on purpose. "Don't stare."

Following my own advice wasn't easy. Out of the side of my eye I tracked Cain as he walked past several of the mezzanine tables. A waiter stepped out of his path, almost bowing in deference. The gesture went unacknowledged. Then Cain disappeared from my sight. Was he coming downstairs?

Happily, the song finally ended, and the tables surrounding the dance floor burst into applause. Otto and I smiled and acknowledged them.

"We need to get back to the bar," I said, sotto voce.

"It's your circus, Mr. Ringling."

It was, and I needed to think fast. Otto's champagne spirits might prove a handicap while I talked to Cain. An idea occurred to me, which bounded forward into a plan when I caught sight of Cain heading toward the bar area.

"Get me some cigarettes?" I asked Otto.

"You don't smoke."

"I do when I'm in a nightclub." He still balked, but I gave him a nudge. "Please? I'll order more champagne."

He snapped his fingers. "Okeydoke."

He flitted off in search of a cigarette vendor while I hurried back to our seats at the bar. I ordered more drinks and picked up the barely touched one I'd left behind, just in the nick of time. Turning quickly, I stepped off my stool just at the right moment to bump into the nightclub owner and spill my drink on his jacket and Callie's skirt.

"Oh dear!" I exclaimed. "How clumsy of me."

The instant after the collision, Cain glared at the champagne dripping down his lapel and off his sleeve. Then the glare transferred to my face.

"Fool!" he said, reaching for his handkerchief.

I snatched a napkin from the bar and tried to help to mop up the damage, ignoring my skirt. I hoped Callie meant what she said about giving me the dress. I dabbed at Cain's chest to get his attention, which I did. His hand reached for my wrist. The lascivious curiosity burning in his gaze made my skin crawl.

I stepped back instinctively, and the interest in his eyes turned to vague recognition, and suspicion.

"Say, don't I know you?"

Despite my revulsion, I tried to keep up a little flirtatiousness. "There's no reason you should remember someone like me, Mr. Cain. I was Guy Van Hooten's secretary . . . until yesterday, that is." I sighed. "Such a tragedy."

"Right. So much of a tragedy that you had to come out dancing." He eyed the place next to me. "I assume that man I saw you tangoing with is your escort."

I hinted at a smile. "I don't like to wallow in sorrow all by myself."

"Wise girl. I doubt Van Hooten would have spent long mourning if you'd burned up instead of him."

"Heaven forbid." I swooned my way back onto the chair, covered my eyes with my hand, and sniffled.

"Hey, now. When I saw you at Van Hooten's office, I took you for a sensible girl. No reason to fall apart now."

"But there is. I've lost my job. And now the police are asking questions."

He seemed amused even as his lips remained pressed in an even line. "Did *you* set fire to the building?"

"Of course not."

"Then why worry?"

"You know how the police are. Full of suspicions. They seem to think that the fire might have been set on purpose to murder Guy."

"The police." He sniffed in contempt. "Bunch of clods." He rapped on the bar, indicating he wanted a drink. The unspoken command was obeyed so promptly, the bartender might have set a pouring speed record. Cain downed what looked like a shot of whiskey. "Don't get me wrong. The boys in blue have their uses. You just have to know how to handle them."

"I was sure you must know all about the police," I said, doing my best eyelash-batting. "They certainly seem very interested in *you*."

His dark brows drew together. "Whaddaya mean?"

"Oh, nothing. Only they asked so many questions."

"What kind of questions?"

"Well, like what you were doing there Wednesday night—Guy's last night—and what you talked about, and did you seem angry. That sort of thing." I sipped from the champagne glass. "They seemed very interested in what I overheard."

He leaned against the bar, eyes narrowing. "What exactly did you overhear?"

"Gosh, almost nothing. Honestly." I blinked at him. "Just that one remark about how you were there to settle a score or something."

His face darkened. "And you said it that way? That kind of language lands people in the chair."

"I hope not. Still, what *were* you there to settle, Mr. Cain?"

"What is this, an interrogation?"

"No, but naturally I'm curious what I should tell the police next time they question me. What I overheard might have sounded a little sinister, but I'm sure there's a simple explanation behind it."

"It's none of your business."

"Exactly what I told the police—it was just no business of mine. I'm a secretary, not a snoop. Of course I'd exonerate you if I could, but when I know so little about what occurred that night, how could I possibly be able to tell anything other than the bald, incriminating facts?"

"Incriminating? Baloney."

"You were the last person to see Guy alive, for all we know. And if you were there to squeeze a debt out of Guy, and he wasn't able to pay up . . ."

He glared at me, and it was hard not to shrink back from the menace in those eyes. "You've got your facts mixed up, girlie. *I* was the one who owed *him*. Three thousand dollars."

Despite my attempt to be cool and detached, my mouth dropped open. "Three thousand!" An incredible sum. To me, at least. "That's a lot of money."

"Guy said he needed a lot. He certainly wasn't getting it from those moldy books he peddled, and his old lady's purse strings were knotted tight."

"If you owed it to him, why wouldn't you have paid him before he left the club?"

"Because he didn't win it here. Not that there's gambling here, understand?"

I understood perfectly. "Then where did the money come from?"

"I'd convinced Guy that I was on to a sure business deal, so he gave me some money to invest for him."

"Invest in what?"

"Business." His eyes narrowed, and I decided that perhaps it was best not to press him on that particular subject right then. "When it paid off like I said it would, I handed him the dough like any honest partner would. End of story."

"You handed three thousand dollars to Guy the night before last?"

"That's right."

"Then what happened to all that money?"

"Same thing that happened to everything else in that building, I imagine. It went up in flames." His lips twisted. "If I'd waited to pay him the next day, I'd be three thou richer."

"You paid him in cash?"

"I do most of my business that way."

Had Cain been carrying three thousand dollars in cash the night I'd seen him? I had no idea. It was such an exorbitant sum, I imagined wheelbarrows would be needed to transport it. Or at least a briefcase.

He read the question in my face and his impatient smile became a glower. "What's your game, sister?"

"I'm just curious where that three thousand dollars was. I didn't see you bring it in."

He leaned in. The whiskey reek of his breath and the even sharper bite of pine aftershave turned my stomach. This was not a good man. When he held my arm, the gesture was meant to be threatening. "And you know what three thousand looks like, do you? Don't make me laugh. If you've seen more than a few sawbucks at once, I'd be surprised. You're a secretary in borrowed duds, and the way you're asking questions is going to land you in more trouble than you can handle."

Otto finally appeared, brandishing cigarettes. His pace faltered and then sped up when he noticed the expression on my face. "What are you saying to her?"

Cain scowled at him.

I shrugged Cain's hand away. "This is my escort, Otto Klemper. Otto—Leonard Cain."

Instinct told Otto that this wasn't the kind of introduction that required a handshake. His voice was higher when he spoke, but I admired his bravery. "It sounded as if you were threatening Louise, Mr. Cain."

"Louise, is it?" He eyed me with a sneer. "She didn't give me her name. Just asked a lot of questions."

"And got a lot of questionable answers for my trouble," I said.

"Sorry you didn't like them. The truth was all I had on such short notice."

"The truth?" I shook my head. "I might not have seen three thousand dollars all in one place before, but I doubt it's easy to conceal. You weren't carrying a case."

"I wasn't concealing anything," he growled, "it's just that you weren't looking. So don't go running to the cops making out that I lied about anything, because I didn't."

"Louise wouldn't make something up," Otto said. "She's very honest."

"I don't know what she is." His insolent gaze swept up and down my body.

I suppressed a shiver. "I'm just a person who wants to know the truth. An honest citizen. Maybe you don't know many of those."

Cain lifted his arm. For a moment I thought he was going to slap me, but instead his fingers snapped so loudly that nearby tables turned to stare. Almost immediately, our friend the doorman was at his shoulder.

"Red, reacquaint these two with the street."

"You're kicking us out?" Otto asked.

"But I haven't finished talking to you," I said.

Cain snorted. "You've finished, little lady. And if you ever come here again, I just might call the police myself and tell them about a secretary coming around asking a lot of questions that sound like a lead-up to a shakedown."

"That's a lie," Otto said.

"Red, get rid of them."

Red clamped a paw around my arm and grabbed the scruff of Otto's collar with the other and propelled us toward the front door. My first nightclub outing, and I was being given the bum's rush.

"What till my friend Al Jolson hears about this!" Otto said, practically shaking a fist at Cain.

He smirked. "If you're a friend of Jolie's, then I'm the pope."

People laughed, and both our faces reddened. In short order, we were shoved out the front door. Our coats and Otto's hat were tossed out after us.

Against the cold breeze that had blown up since we'd gone inside, we pulled our coats around us.

Otto was hopping mad. "That man is a toad!"

I agreed. "But I suspect he really was telling me the truth. If he'd wanted to lie, why would he have mentioned the three thousand dollars at all?"

"Who cares? He insulted us! I've a good mind to go back in there and—"

Remembering Flossie's stories of the killings, I pulled Otto away from the door. "Never mind. Let's just go home." Strange, but a part of me felt elated. I'd wrangled useful information out of Cain. Not a bad night's work, really. "This time I'll spring for the cab."

"*You?*" Granted, I never paid cab fare if there was a streetcar, train, or subway available, but he was looking at me as if I weren't in my right mind.

"It's all right," I said. "I'm getting paid well."

Otto was on his way to flag down a taxicab when his hat was caught by a gust and flew off his head. He scampered after it into the street and was almost run down by a car roughly the length of a whale that pulled up to the curb. A chauffeur hopped out and when he opened the passenger door, a man in shiny shoes and a top hat emerged. He watched Otto capture his hat and smash it right down to his ears so it couldn't escape. A familiar smile broke out over his face.

"Hey, kid!"

Otto's eyes, now even with his hat brim, popped open. "Mr. Jolson?"

The star rushed over and pumped Otto's hand as if they were old pals. His smile even included me. "Say, what're you kids doing at this dump?"

"Getting kicked out." I told him I'd accidentally spilled a drink on Leonard Cain . . . but omitted the rest of the story.

Jolson thought this was hilarious. He hooked one arm around me and the other around Otto. "You kiddos better come in and have a drink with Jolie. I'll clear this right up. If Lenny's still sore, I'll give him some tickets to the show."

Otto protested, but there was no overcoming our host's enthusiasm. Not that I wanted to. Cain had as good as called us liars in front of the entire club. Vindication would be sweet.

The look on Red's face as he opened the door for Jolson and us was priceless, and so was Cain's when Otto and I strolled in next to the celebrity he'd just denied we could possibly know.

I bowed my head to him as we were shown to the best table in the place. "Lovely to see you again, Your Holiness."

CHAPTER 7

Lily and Clarice entered their cramped but imaginatively decorated flat in a gay mood. The weekend had been everything they had hoped, and now their spirits were dancing with memories of flirtatious glances and confidences exchanged in stolen moments of privacy.

The only damper was Clarice's cousin, Myrtle, who would surely scold them for coming in so late. They both hushed their voices and looked around guiltily as they came inside, slipping off their shoes to make less noise. "Perhaps she's already asleep," Lily suggested, noting that the only light in the apartment was a glow emanating from Myrtle's bedroom. "She must have nodded off with the lamp on."

Clarice tiptoed away to check on her cousin while Lily made her way toward the kitchen. A cup of cocoa was just what they both needed. They could sip it on the fire escape and talk over their conquests.

No sooner had she lit the burner for the saucepan than a blood-curdling scream rent the air. Clarice! Lily ran back out to the hallway and discovered her friend frozen in the doorway, illuminated softly by the bedside lamp. Her hands lifted to her lips in stunned disbelief. "It's Myrtle!" she ejaculated in horror, nodding her pretty blond head toward the bed, upon which Myrtle lay facedown, a butcher knife protruding from between her bony spinster shoulder blades. "She's dead!"

Not just dead, Lily thought. Murdered.

My hands froze over the Remington's keys. It wasn't just that the scene was a radical departure from anything my aunt had ever written before. With the exception of a few minor details, this scene replicated almost exactly what had happened to Callie and me last summer when we'd returned home from a party at Aunt Irene's and discovered Callie's visiting cousin Ethel murdered in her bed.

The memory of that night had lost none of its power to unnerve me. I swayed in my chair, reliving those awful moments. I'd never seen so much blood before, and hoped never to again. And now the gruesome tragedy was being turned into a novel.

At that moment, my aunt ducked her head in the door. When she saw me, she scooted inside, pulling a chair close to the typing table. "What do you think?"

"It seems strangely familiar."

"Nonsense—I've only used a few aspects of last summer's events."

"It's very close."

"But you can't think any of the characters are recognizable. I changed up so much. Did it give you gooseflesh?"

"Yes," I answered in all honesty.

She leaned back, pleased. "This could be a new beginning for me."

Despite my personal misgivings, I didn't want to discourage my aunt. This book might be a turning point for her, and if it felt a little like exploiting Ethel's death . . . well, she wasn't the first. The newspapers had made hay of the story for a month, and Otto's song had received a boost in sales, and I supposed I even owed my new-found career, such as it was, to having tried to solve the mystery of who killed Ethel.

"It's very different from anything you've done," I said. "I was surprised. Even the name of the poor woman."

Aunt Irene clasped her hands together. "Myrtle—so you noticed."

Myrtle in Springtime was the name of my aunt's first and most popular book. Van Hooten and McChesney had published it, which is how she met Mr. McChesney.

"I felt it would be symbolic of what I'm doing."

Murdering Myrtle. I nodded, understanding. "It seems rather a shame to kill off your best-selling heroine, even symbolically. What about Fern, or Violet?"

She laughed. "Oh, Myrtle had her day, but she doesn't bring in much now. I don't mind killing her off. She's had a good life."

I frowned. I'd been under the impression that *Myrtle in Springtime* was still doing well. Maybe I was mistaken, but it turned my thoughts back to the investigation. "I'm curious about the finances of Van Hooten and McChesney."

"Why?"

I gave her a quick rundown of all that had happened yesterday, ending with, "Leonard Cain mentioned that Guy couldn't count on getting any money out of Van Hooten and McChesney. Do you think that was true?"

My aunt didn't look me in the eye. "I'm not in a position to know anything about it."

"He also mentioned that Edith Van Hooten was very tight-fisted."

"Wouldn't surprise me a bit. Widows sometimes are. They're getting their hands on the purse strings for the first time. Many become open-handed when that happens, but others might become paranoid about money, and apt to be miserly."

"According to Cain, she took the miserly route."

My aunt frowned. "Is Mr. Cain the type of man whose word you trust?"

"Not exactly . . . but then again, I didn't feel he was telling me outright lies. Anyway, Mrs. Van Hooten could be the biggest skinflint in the world, but it would still be difficult to imagine her holding back money from Guy. He was the sun at the center of her solar system."

"Her firstborn son." My aunt sighed. "I suppose neither you nor I can fully understand that bond."

Beneath the typing table, my leg began to vibrate. I could understand better than Aunt Irene knew. This was what came of keeping secrets.

I pushed away from the table and stood. "Would you mind if I left a little early today? I wanted to visit Mr. McChesney."

"It's sweet of you to worry about him," my aunt said. "He seemed so downcast when he was here last night. Even Bernice's excellent lamb stew didn't cheer him."

"He's lost everything."

"But that's just the attitude I was telling him not to take. There will be insurance money."

"How much?" It was one of the things I'd wanted to ask Mr. McChesney about.

"I've no idea," she said. "I'm not sure he does, either, for all his tooth gnashing over that business. He should be glad to be rid of it. For years it's done nothing but aggravate his ulcer."

True. "Yet I think in his own way he loves the publishing business."

"What did Wilde say—'Each man kills the thing he loves'?" Aunt Irene shook her head. "It should be the opposite. The thing we love is almost inevitably what does us in."

Mrs. Carey was back. Her round, stern face greeted me at Mr. McChesney's door. "He's in," she said in answer to my question, "but you'll have a wait to see him. He's with the doctor."

I frowned. "Mr. McChesney sent for the doctor?"

She puffed up. "*I* sent for the doctor when I came in and discovered what a state he was in. And the house—no doctor for *that,* of course, but me."

"I'll wait." She looked as if she were going to argue. "Aunt Irene will want me to find out what's wrong. She's worried about him."

My aunt's name softened her a little. "Just as you please," she said, letting me pass. She closed the door, took my coat, and marched ahead of me. "He told me Miss Livingston Green tried to get some food in him. I don't know what he means, sending me away and then starving himself." She stopped at the parlor door and opened it. "You can wait here, but you'll have company."

"Thank you, I—"

My steps froze in the doorway. Muldoon, sitting in the velvet upholstered wing chair, sprang up at the sight of me. I hadn't been expecting this meeting, and from the momentary, flustered look in his eye, he hadn't, either.

I moved toward him. "Please sit down," I said. "I've been looking forward to collapsing into a chair myself. I couldn't get a seat on the cross-town bus." An unsettling nervousness fluttered inside as I drew closer.

He remained standing until I sat on the sofa. Though Mrs. Carey had pulled back the drapes, the sun barely seemed to penetrate the gloom of the heavy furnishings and forest-green walls.

Muldoon tapped his hands on his knees. "I'm glad you're here. I needed to speak to you about something serious."

Oh dear. Now that I looked more closely, the deep furrows of his brow revealed themselves. So did the hard glint in his eye. What could I have done to set him off? "Did you?" I kept my voice bright.

"Perhaps this isn't the place to—"

"Yes, it's gloomy here, isn't it?" I interrupted, to waylay whatever unpleasant line of conversation he'd been about to take up. "You should come to my aunt's sometime. Not long ago she was wondering if she would ever see you again at one of her Thursday night parties." I'd been wondering, too. He'd come to one during the summer after the case of Ethel's murder had concluded, but he'd never repeated the visit.

"I don't have much time for that sort of thing."

"That's unfortunate."

"Not that I didn't find it very pleasant, seeing you there," he added quickly.

"There are always so many different people at her house. It's a marvelous opportunity to see the passing parade of Manhattan."

"That's not exactly what I meant. I see plenty of the passing parade in my job."

I tilted my head. "Are you here to interview Mr. McChesney?"

"I'd hoped to. The doctor had just arrived when I got here." He took out his watch and frowned. "Twenty minutes ago."

"Were you going to ask him anything in particular?" Surely the police were looking into the insurance angle, too.

He lowered his voice. "Louise, I need to—"

The door swung open and Mrs. Carey reappeared and addressed us both. "The doctor says no visitors. You'll both have to move along."

Muldoon protested. "I only need to speak to him for a few minutes."

"You'd find the conversation one-sided," a thin voice said. In the doorway stood a gray-bearded man clutching a medical bag. "I just gave my patient a sleeping draught."

I could read an unspoken curse in Muldoon's expression. He'd come all the way uptown for nothing.

We tramped back out into the hall and shrugged on our coats. I debated whether I'd prefer to flee before Muldoon could deliver whatever lecture he'd been building up to, or endure his talking-to so I could find out details I needed for the investigation.

Outside the apartment building, he settled the question for me by stopping me before I could flee. "Where are you going?"

"Back to my aunt's."

"I'll walk you across the park."

I hadn't intended to walk, but Muldoon took hold of my arm and soon we were crossing Central Park West. Normally a man taking a lady's arm to cross a boulevard was a gentlemanly gesture, but Muldoon's grip on my sleeve gave me a taste of what it must feel like for criminals he dragged off to the paddy wagon. His irritation as he spoke confirmed that this was not going to be a pleasurable stroll through the park.

"What the hell are you playing at, Louise?"

I jerked my arm free. "What gives you the right to talk to me like that?"

"Excuse me," he said, but only after muttering something worse than *hell* under his breath. "I forgot I was speaking to prim Louise

Faulk, secretary, and not the girl who goes to nightclubs to confront a character notorious for illegal gambling and God knows what else and gets herself booted out on her rear."

"How did you find out about that?"

"Do you think the NYPD is so incompetent that we didn't note that Cain was the last man seen with Guy Van Hooten? Could it really be surprising to you that we would plant a man in his club to watch him?"

Heat crept up my neck and into my face. To be perfectly honest, it never *had* occurred to me that the police would be doing exactly what I was doing. I could just imagine what a spectacle Otto and I had made of ourselves, being dragged out by that big lummox Red. That must have caused a few guffaws when it was mentioned at headquarters.

"How did the officer know it was me?" I asked.

"You're not exactly a stranger among the detectives."

Not after last summer, he meant. "No, I suppose not."

His voice rose again. "Have you lost your mind? Do you know what kind of man Cain is?"

"I've heard stories of executions. Very nasty."

His face went slack. "You knew, yet you went there and got into a tussle with the man?"

Now that was just wrong. "I didn't *tussle* with him. I spilled a drink on purpose—just to catch his attention. After that we merely talked."

"About what?"

"About why he had visited Guy Wednesday evening. I'd heard that Guy owed Cain money. Cain insists that it was just the opposite. He says he paid Guy three thousand dollars on some sort of investment. And I doubt it was a regular investment like stocks and bonds."

Muldoon blinked slowly. "You don't say."

I frowned. "Sarcasm doesn't suit you. And it's poor thanks for my having shared my findings. You could at least sound appreciative."

"I'll sound appreciative the moment you tell me you'll give up whatever it is you're doing and leave the detective work to the police."

"I'm sorry, I can't oblige you. I'm being paid to look into the fire."

"By whom?"

"Mr. McChesney. I promised him and Aunt Irene that I would try to find out who set the fire."

He shook his head. "Your aunt should know better. She ought to be protecting you."

Despite being one of the younger detectives in a police force in one of the most modern cities in the world, Frank Muldoon remained a reactionary creature at heart. All around us the twentieth century pulsed, throbbed, and hooted, but he was still chugging along with quaint ideas of how proper young ladies should behave.

"Keep your nose out of this one," he continued, not giving me time to speak. "Oh, I know what you're going to say about solving the murder last summer, but there's a world of difference between that crime and this one. Last summer's murder was a personal matter. This looks like a professional killing. It's much more dangerous."

"So you really think Cain did it," I said.

"I won't dignify your so-called investigation with either a yes or no. Stay out of it, Louise."

The poor man. He might as well have been talking to the trees we were passing. Quite beautiful trees they were, too, in their burnished autumn finery. We'd already walked as far as the new *Maine* memorial near Columbus Circle. It was impossible not to stare at the bright gilded figure in her seashell chariot at the top of the pylon.

I nodded at the statue. "Did you read the papers? She was fashioned from the melted-down metal recovered from the *Maine* itself."

He tilted his head, interested in spite of himself.

A battleship had been turned into art. Tragedy into inspiration. I felt a little like Columbia urging on her hippocampi. No matter what Muldoon said, I would drive forward.

"Cain wasn't responsible for Guy's death," I said.

His eyes narrowed. "What led you to that conclusion?"

"Logic. Fire's not his style. When Cain kills a man, he sends an ape with a gun to kill them. He wouldn't show up in person at the victim's place of work and then set a fire. Also, why would he have waited until the next morning to burn the building down? It doesn't add up."

His jaw clamped shut, and we walked a ways in silence. I slid a sidewise glance at him. Muldoon didn't wear a uniform, but he walked with military-erect posture. Why didn't he speak? He rarely missed an opening to argue with me.

"Well?" I asked, growing uncomfortable with the silence. "You have to admit that fire isn't the most efficient way to assassinate someone."

He stopped and turned to me. "Look, I shouldn't say a word to you about this. The only reason I'm telling you anything is so you'll realize how deadly serious this situation is."

I leaned forward, my curiosity growing.

"The coroner doesn't think fire killed Guy Van Hooten."

"The coroner?" I asked. "I thought the Van Hootens were against an autopsy."

"Mistakes are sometimes made." He kept his face a blank, but he couldn't hide that glint in his eye that told me that occasionally mistakes were made on purpose. "The Van Hootens are friends of Acting Mayor Kline, but the coroner is our captain's cousin. Guy Van Hooten's lungs had no smoke in them."

It took me a moment to make sense of that grisly statement. "Then . . . Guy didn't inhale any of the smoke."

"That's right."

"So he was dead when the fire started."

"You didn't hear that from me. In fact, you didn't hear it at all."

My mind was attempting to cycle through possibilities. "What killed him, then?" Flossie's story about Cain was still fresh in my mind. "A bullet?"

"No—there was no bullet wound."

"A blow?"

"The body was very damaged, but the coroner didn't see any fractures on his skull."

"Strangulation?"

"We're less sure of that. Because of the condition of his tissue, bruising around the neck was impossible to detect. But the coroner noticed a burning inside his mouth, on his tongue. We'd seen that in another case. That's why he went ahead and did a few tests."

"What did you suspect?"

"Poison. The coroner found evidence of cyanide. The lining of Guy's stomach was dark."

How awful. I bit my lip. "I suppose I'd rather be poisoned than burned to death."

"Cyanide kills quickly if enough is given, but it's still no picnic," he said. "After talking to the coroner, I went back to Thirty-eighth Street. There were peculiar stains on the floor by the desk—evidence of some liquid that had dried and burned in the heat. Possibly . . . well, vomit."

I almost smiled at his hesitation to say the word in front of me. As if my sensibilities were too delicate to hear about bodily fluids. "Is that what you were going to discuss with Mr. McChesney this morning? I suppose you'll need to check alibis again, depending on when Guy died."

He frowned. "The coroner still can't be very specific. It might have been anytime during the night. Your colleagues seem to be a predictable bunch. Most of them claim to have gone home after work and stayed in until leaving again for the office the next morning. They all sing the same song, except for Sandy Novotny."

"Sandy's our salesman. He was in Boston Wednesday night." Wasn't he?

"And he has a telegram sent to his wife that night to prove it."

I released a breath. Not that I suspected Sandy, but his being out of town did put him in a dodgy position.

"I wanted to hear McChesney's account of his whereabouts again," Muldoon continued, "but I suppose that will have to wait. I need your promise that you won't divulge police findings to possible suspects, Louise. I told you all this in confidence."

His voice dropped, and when I looked into his steady gaze, I felt the crazy, unfamiliar inclination to do what he asked. I heard myself saying, "I won't say anything to Mr. McChesney."

"Good girl."

My jaw clenched at the words, the verbal equivalent of a dismissive pat on the head. *But I don't promise not to tell Aunt Irene.* Or anyone else, for that matter.

Back at my aunt's house, I wasted no time filling her in on all that I'd learned.

"Poison!" she exclaimed.

As far as I was concerned, it was another reason not to believe Cain was at the bottom of Guy's death. Administering poison to Guy while he was at his office desk would have required more cunning than Cain and his henchmen possessed. They were bullet men.

Who did I know with cunning? Ford leapt to mind—but he had no motive for killing Guy. In fact, he had every incentive to keep Guy alive.

A throat cleared. I'd forgotten Walter was standing by the door. Aunt Irene looked up at him with interest. "What is it, Walter?"

"If you don't mind my interjecting an opinion . . ."

"If I minded, I would go mad. You always give your opinions anyway."

He nodded. "It seems clear to me what kind of culprit we should be looking for, if it's a matter of poison."

I didn't understand. "What kind?"

My aunt's breath caught. "The female kind. Poison is the woman's weapon."

Walter's head bobbed. "To find the killer, the French have a phrase for you: *Cherchez la femme.*"

Aunt Irene looked pleased. "You're exactly right, Walter. Find the woman who had a reason to kill Guy Van Hooten and we'll have our poisoner."

CHAPTER 8

There was one big problem with the *cherchez la femme* directive my aunt had given me: I'd never personally heard of or seen any lady connected to Guy. I considered asking Callie to use her Teddy connection to find out if Hugh knew of Guy's having had a liaison with any particular girl. But with Callie now wholly consumed in rehearsals, it wasn't fair to keep pestering her to help me in my investigation.

Of the people I knew, Jackson would be the one most able to help me. I went to the candy store down the block, where there was a telephone the owner allowed us to use. When I attempted to call Jackson, the operator informed me his address no longer had service.

An hour later I arrived at his flat carrying a bouquet of chrysanthemums I'd picked up at a flower vendor on Broadway. I hoped it would be a little compensation to Miriam—a very little—for my lack of friendliness the last time I'd been there.

But when she opened the door and I greeted her with an overly bright, "Hello, Mrs. Beasley," her face tensed warily.

She turned and called into the room. "Someone to see you." To me, she said, "Come in," and stepped back a pace.

"I did come to see Jackson," I began awkwardly, "but I was hoping to be able to chat a little with you, too."

"I'm fixing lunch."

"Oh, well." At a loss, I held out the flowers. "I brought you these."

"Flowers?" Jackson boomed from behind us. "Trying to woo my wife away from me, are you, Louise?"

His eyes had that glassy look again. I was relieved he still seemed to be grooming himself, unlike Mr. McChesney, but he'd clearly been drinking and it wasn't even noon yet.

"I'll take care of this," he told Miriam.

One of her lips curled sourly at being dismissed, but she left us.

I was offended for her, and also for myself at this not-so-subtle hint that my visit was unwelcome. "I tried to call," I said. "They told me you no longer have telephone service."

"I had it taken out, at least until I find another job. Economizing, you know."

"I understand."

His flat stare fixed on me. "Well, you'd best come in and sit down."

"Thank you." He pointed me to one of two matching armchairs facing each other by the unlit fireplace and settled into the other himself.

"I assume this is about your investigation." He smiled. "From secretary to Sherlock Holmes in a petticoat in one short week."

His soft drawl didn't disguise the belittling intent of his words. "Yes, it's about Guy," I said. "Do you know if he had any lady friends?"

"A man in Guy's position never lacked for female attention. Didn't even matter how he treated them. Women are fools."

My instinct was to answer his misogyny by going full-on suffragette, but I reminded myself that I was here to gather information, not to proselytize. "How did he treat them?"

"Who?"

"These ladies you were speaking of."

"Negligently, I imagine. The same way he approached everything in life."

He imagined. I needed more than musings. "Do you know any of their names?"

"Good heavens. This was back in college—a decade ago."

"I was hoping you would know something about his recent life."

He frowned at me. "You saw how it was, Louise. We worked in the same office. Did Guy confide in you?"

"I was only his secretary," I said, gambling that feeding Jackson's ego might enhance his memory. "He would be much more apt to open up to you—a male colleague, his equal."

He shifted, and looked at his hands as if weighing whether to reveal more. "As it happens, he did tell me once that there was a particular girl he took an interest in."

I inched forward on the chair. "Who?"

"I never met her. I doubt any of his friends did, either. According to him, she wasn't the type he could take home to mother."

"Why did he tell you about her?"

"I suppose he wanted to unburden himself to someone who might understand a little about it." He drew up. "That's why I can't tell you much more. I didn't encourage him comparing my situation to his tawdry affair."

"Then it was an affair?"

"Oh, certainly."

That might account for Guy's needing to approach his brother for money and then investing in Cain's "business." Perhaps it also explained where the three thousand dollars went. "When did he tell you this?"

"Months and months ago." He squinted at the ceiling in thought. "Last spring?"

"What happened to her?" I wondered aloud.

"Same thing that happens to most women of her kind. He probably tired of her, and that was the end of it. Life isn't a fairy tale."

"No," I agreed.

He stood. "I'm sorry I can't tell you more."

He was halfway to the door by the time I got to my feet. "Maybe you can come again some time when we're more at leisure to entertain," he said.

I murmured something to the effect that this sounded nice. Actually, it sounded like a brush-off. Still, I couldn't complain. I'd dropped in without warning, and he'd given me a tiny tidbit of information. Guy had had a mistress.

"Did Guy mention what kind of personality this woman had?" I couldn't help asking even as he hustled me out.

Hand on the doorknob, he looked down at me. "What do you mean?"

"Well, for instance, perhaps this woman had a temper."

Jackson laughed. "Is there a woman in the world who doesn't?"

He was right. Neither sex had a monopoly on temper. Pushed far enough, anyone could reach a boiling point.

It had been cold and cloudy when I left Greenwich Village, but now the sun was shining. By the time I walked to Mr. McChesney's flat, I felt I was baking inside my coat, and I took off my hat as soon as I was in the foyer of my old boss's building. When I looked up, the birdcage elevator was coming down, with Bob Sanders, the accountant, inside. It seemed apropos, since Bob had always reminded me of a nervous bird.

He tilted his head in surprise when he stepped out and saw me, and shifted the coat he was carrying to his other arm, covering something he was already clutching there.

"I didn't expect to run into you here," he said in his light, rushed voice.

"I tried to visit yesterday, but Mr. McChesney was with the doctor."

His smile disappeared. "He's taking it all very hard, and I'm afraid my visit didn't raise his spirits any. I counseled him to declare bankruptcy—a liberty, I know, and perhaps not my place, but no one knows better than I how the company's barely been scraping by these past years. I thought perhaps he'd welcome encouragement to lay down the burden of keeping the business going."

"He'd consider bankruptcy a blow." Yet what other choice was there?

"I shouldn't have distressed him, poor man."

"Did you go over the books with him?"

His body stilled. "What books? The books burned in the fire."

"Mr. McChesney said he kept a few records here at his flat. I thought he asked you to look at them."

His eyebrows twitched. I kept my gaze trained away from whatever was under his coat, and yet both of us seemed focused on it without looking. Bob was always such a bundle of nerves, it was hard to discern if this was him being sneaky or just normal Bob awkwardness.

"He didn't have them after all," he said.

"Did the police take them?"

"Mr. McChesney didn't say." He shifted his weight. "He told me that you're . . . well, that you're looking into the fire?"

"Informally. In fact, you might be of some help to me. Did you know the woman Guy was seeing?"

His eyes behind their round frames grew big. "Me? No, of course not." He chuckled lightly. "Guy and I didn't exactly travel in the same social circles."

"You never heard him mention a woman's name?"

"No, no, I didn't. He made some lascivious remarks about the Dolly Sisters once, and I told him I didn't appreciate that kind of talk. But I don't think he ever got closer to the Dolly Sisters than first-row orchestra seats."

"Have you started looking for a new job?"

"Yes, I have a family, you know. Children." With his free hand, he poked his spectacles back up to the bridge of his nose. "Needs must."

"How are they?"

"Middling. My little boy has a bit of a cough. Colder weather setting in usually causes problems."

It had to be a strain. "I'm sure you'll find something soon. You were always so valuable to Van Hooten and McChesney."

"It's kind of you to say so." He aimed an anxious look toward the door. "I really should go. I'm late for an appointment. I'm sure I'll see you at the funeral."

"Yes." Guy's funeral was two days away, on Wednesday. "I'll be there."

We said goodbye, and he darted toward the door.

Knowing Bob had just left made me more sympathetic to Mrs. Carey's huff when she answered the door. "How's a man supposed to get rest when there's people coming and going all the time?"

"I don't mean to be a nuisance," I said, "but I wanted to check on Mr. McChesney."

"I was just going to bring him a tray. I expect he'll want me to bring you something, too."

"Oh, you don't have to—"

"Yes, I do, or else *he* won't eat, and then I shouldn't have bothered myself at all."

"Well . . . thank you, that would be nice. I am a little hungry."

"Then you should've just said so to begin with." She jerked her chin in the direction of the parlor door. "You can show yourself in."

I knocked lightly and opened the door. Mr. McChesney was sitting in the chair Muldoon had occupied the day before. A lap robe lay over his legs, and he held a thick book.

"Don't get up," I said, hurrying in and sitting before he could upset himself.

"You just missed Bob," he said.

I explained that I'd spoken to him and expected to see him again at the funeral. The mention of Guy's service distressed my old boss. "I'm not sure I'll make it."

He did look frail. Despite Mrs. Carey's ministrations, he was thinner and grayer than the last time I'd seen him.

"I was supposed to be a pallbearer," he said, "but I've asked Bob to stand in for me. He agreed to."

"I hope you'll feel better by Wednesday."

Mrs. Carey came in and set tea and sandwiches in front of us. "He'll be stronger if he eats and rests."

When she was gone, I picked up a sandwich with a thin slice of ham in it. "Did you ever know any of Guy's lady friends?" I asked.

He shook his head. "Guy didn't confide in me. He and I weren't on social terms in the way his father and I were."

I tried not to show my disappointment.

"Why?" His face crumpled in worry. "Was there some girl—a fiancée, perhaps? I'd hate to think of a poor girl left brokenhearted."

"It's an idea that Aunt Irene had. She thinks a woman's at the bottom of it all."

"A woman? Surely not. What a monstrous idea."

It was true that murders were more often committed by men, but I wasn't going to rule out the fairer sex. "I've met one murderess and saw her work firsthand."

He put his uneaten sandwich back on the plate. "You've seen

too much of what's evil in this city. It was wrong of me to ask you to look into this matter."

"It wasn't you, it was Aunt Irene. You know I would do anything she asked, short of committing murder myself."

"Why did Irene suggest you look for a woman?"

Muldoon had told me to keep the information about the poison under my hat. I'd blurted the news to Aunt Irene right away, but Muldoon wasn't interviewing Aunt Irene and wasn't likely to know or care if I'd spilled the secret to her.

"Jackson mentioned Guy had a particular woman friend," I said, fabricating a plausible lie off the cuff, "but he didn't know her name. Aunt Irene thinks I should search for her."

He nodded, distracted. "How is Jackson?"

"He seemed a bit demoralized. He needs to find a new position quickly."

That news made him look very depressed. "Poor man. Of course I'll give him a glowing reference."

"I'm sure that would help." Worried I was tiring out my old boss, I stood. "I should go. Please take care of yourself. Aunt Irene will want you to dine again with her soon."

"I hope I'll feel up to it. I'm not the brightest company at the moment."

"I've worn you out. I meant to ask you about insurance, but that can wait till the next time I see you."

His brows drew together. "You too?"

I didn't understand.

"That detective was here earlier. Wanted to see my fire insurance policy."

"Do you have it?" I asked, unable to hide my eagerness.

He shook his head. "Bob wanted to see it, too—but the policy was at the office. I can't remember the dollar amount of the policy, or the exact details. Cyrus took it out. The people at First New York will know all about it." He gave his head a self-deprecating shake. "Some businessman I am! I hope the sum will be sufficient to cover the outstanding debt."

My morning's efforts left me little wiser than I'd been when I set out. For the next two days, I struggled. In the mornings I went to Aunt Irene's and typed up what seemed almost like my autobiography. In the afternoons, I tried to track down more of my old coworkers to see if they knew anything of this mysterious woman of Guy's that Jackson had mentioned. The two I found, Timothy and Sandy, knew nothing. Both said I should ask Jackson.

It felt as if I'd hit a brick wall.

Calvary Church near Gramercy Park was only half full when I arrived on Wednesday morning, but I took an inconspicuous place near the back so I could observe who came in. Singly or in twos, mourners arrived and walked down the long aisle of the austere old church. Not that the dark wood and stained glass didn't have a Gothic splendor, but I'd expected the church of the Astors, Vanderbilts, and Roosevelts to be more ornate, if not gilded to its vaulted ceiling. Yet this backdrop made the stylish mourners stand out in high relief. Men and women paraded through the nave in fur coats and hats of dyed black fox, rabbit, and mink, and velvet and cashmere. The women wore wide-brimmed hats in the latest style, extravagantly plumed and netted.

The Van Hooten and McChesney contingent joined me, except for Bob, who was with the pallbearers. From my vantage, I was able to observe all the mourners, taking special care to see if there was a young woman who seemed especially distressed. But the females present were all frustratingly dry-eyed and stoic. If there was a scorned mistress in the pews, I couldn't spot her. I did see faces from the society pages, politicians, and well-heeled Van Hooten friends. Teddy was there, though he didn't notice me. Finally, Mayor Kline entered, gray-bearded and distinguished, with Edith Van Hooten on his arm. A long black veil covered her face. Behind them walked Hugh Van Hooten, cleaned, polished and pressed for this sad day, and behind him was Mr. McChesney in a black Prince Albert coat and leaning heavily on his cane. His pale, drawn face worried me.

The service began, and though I glanced in the prayer book held by Sandy, standing next to me, I had trouble voicing the responses. A lump had risen in my throat when they had marched in with Guy's casket. The hollow sadness that took hold of me wasn't just for Guy, though. One of my clearest early memories was attending the funeral of my parents, who'd died within a week of each other when I was seven, of typhus, which they'd caught living in cramped quarters on the wrong side of the tracks. Aunt Sonja never forgot that her sister had married down, or that I—and her sister's untimely death—was the result. I'd been scrubbed within an inch of my life for that funeral, the day I'd moved in with her. If she could have, she would have soaked me in bleach.

Someone came in late. I twisted back to see a blonde—an older woman, and plump, unlikely mistress material—squeeze into a pew near the door, next to Frank Muldoon. He was seated in the back pew across the aisle, his purpose there probably the same as mine, to observe. Our gazes held a moment and his brow quirked up, and though I'd felt on the verge of tears moments before, it was all I could do to hide a smile.

Unfortunately, or fortunately, it was then that the priest boomed out the words of the Book of Common Prayer that always chilled me. *"Man that is born of a woman hath but a short time to live, and is full of misery. He cometh up, and is cut down, like a flower."*

Had Guy's life been full of misery? He'd had every advantage—family, wealth, position. And yet he'd been cut down, as the liturgy warned, and far too young.

After the service, we filtered out, many gathering on the corner of Twenty-first and Park. As I congregated with my former coworkers, I kept an eye out for Muldoon, but he must have slipped out before me. Probably on his way to the cemetery. He'd been at Ethel's burial last summer when he was investigating her death. Mr. McChesney and Bob were also going to see Guy to his final resting place.

Sandy, Jackson, and Timothy stood near me. Even Oliver, our office boy, had shown up, which surprised me. Another surprise was his appearance. He seemed to have grown up since just last week. I knew boys in their teen years underwent phenomenal growth spurts, but what made the difference with Oliver were his clothes and his bearing. He was wearing a nice dark coat, polished shoes, and a new felt fedora instead of his old floppy cap.

"Big turnout for Guy," Jackson observed, looking down Park Avenue as mourners exiting the church were reabsorbed into the busy sidewalks.

"Full house," Sandy agreed. "Guy would be pleased."

Oliver laughed. "Doubt he cares about that now."

Jackson scowled at him, as he used to do at the office. "It's a comfort for the family."

"I was surprised there weren't more ladies at the service," I said. "You'd think Guy would have left a few broken hearts in his wake."

Despite my carefully neutral tone, I caught Timothy and Sandy exchanging a wondering glance. No doubt they thought it odd that I was speculating on the women our late boss had left behind when I'd just tracked them down yesterday to ask about Guy's women friends. To them it probably seemed I had a weird fixation.

"Say what you will about Guy," Sandy said, "the man wasn't a skirt chaser."

Oliver laughed again. "That's all *you* know."

Jackson squinted at him. "Don't speak ill of the dead."

"Even if it's true?" Oliver asked.

"Especially if it's true," Jackson said. "We're outside a church, for pity's sake."

Frustration rose in me, especially when our group began to disperse. I kept my eye on Oliver as we all promised to keep in touch, and when he headed uptown, I caught up with him.

"You don't mind if I walk with you a ways, do you?" I asked.

"It's a free country, toots."

Unlike the others, I never minded Oliver's cheekiness. His boyishness reminded me of my young cousins I'd lived with back in Altoona. "You're looking smart," I said. "Have you found a new job?"

"Nah, not yet. I got an interview, though."

"Where?"

"Wall Street. I figure that this time I should go where the tycoons are."

"I wish you luck. If I can be any help, with a reference or anything like that . . ."

His brows formed a V of puzzlement. "Do people ask secretaries for references?"

I let the question pass. "Something you said earlier made me curious. About Guy and women?"

"Sure," he said. "I knew Guy was keeping a girl."

"How?"

"I saw her."

My feet stopped moving. "Where?"

"He had me chase over to her apartment a few times when he wanted to send her something. Always acted very casual-like about it. I think he might've broken it off with her, though, 'cause I never saw her after June." He pushed back the brim of his hat, concentrating. "Or maybe July?"

"Did you actually see this woman?"

"Sure. A few times."

"What did she look like?"

"I guess she was pretty enough, but you'd think a fellow like Guy'd want a flashier doll than her. She was just kind of ordinary. Brown hair, brown eyes. Good figure, though."

"What was her name?"

"Cowan. *M. Cowan* was the name on her door. 'Course, I never really talked to her. She'd just open the door, take what I'd brought, and shut it. Gave me the feeling Guy'd told her not to speak to me." He looked into my face. "You ever meet her?"

"I don't think so," I said.

"Then what are you asking all the questions for?" He studied my face. "You ain't jealous, are you?"

The question gave me a jolt. "Of course not. I just could have sworn I'd heard Guy mention a girl's name once." He had, that morning during the summer when I'd found him drunk at his desk. "It started with M. Minna or something. Do you remember the address?"

"Not exactly, but I can tell you where it was. A blue house on Thirty-fourth between Second and Third. It's above a restaurant. North side of the street. You can't miss it. She was on the third floor."

"Oliver!" I felt like hugging him. I *did* hug him. "You're a wonder."

"No need to get squishy." He squirmed away. "It's not dignified behavior for an older woman."

We parted company and I wasted no time going to Thirty-fourth Street. As Oliver predicted, the house wasn't difficult to spot. The four-story building was blue-painted brick with white stone eyebrows above the windows, which made it stand out like a flower among weeds among its neighboring brownstone buildings.

The Hungarian restaurant at the ground floor had a faded red, green, and white awning over the door. At the windows of the residences above, window boxes lay fallow except for a few wilting asters. The building's door was open, but a thin woman in a pinafore apron sweeping the foyer blocked my path to the stairs.

"Who're you here for?" The authority in her voice made me think she was the landlady of the premises, not a domestic. But my instincts had been wrong about that before.

"I'm looking for Miss Cowan."

"You're four months too late. She left last summer."

I tried not to show my disappointment. "Did she leave a forwarding address?"

"How would she have done that? She snuck out like a thief in the night. Not that she ever stole anything from me." Her lips turned down. "But I was glad to see the back of her just the same."

"Why?"

Her eyes narrowed on my black clothes. "You look like a nice girl, so I'll only say this—she wasn't respectable. If I'd known she wasn't, I never would've rented to her when she came to look at the place last fall. But she dressed real fine, had the money, and swore her *husband,* a traveling man, would be able to keep up the rent."

"Did you ever see her husband?"

"Sure. He was in and out all the time—nice-looking fella. Dressed like a swell and bought her nice things. My guess his 'traveling' was mostly from uptown to here. There was a younger fella, too, that used to come see her, but he didn't look so nice. Barely more than a boy, he was. But if there was anyone else actually living in those rooms besides Myrna Cowan, I'm the Queen of Sheba."

"Myrna." *That* was the name I'd heard Guy say last summer in his stupor.

"Late in the spring, the fighting started between her and her man. The other tenants complained, so of course I had to say something. Then it became clear she was in the family way. I felt sorry for her, of course, but what could I do? My Charlie and I argued about it for a week, but before we could tell her she had to go, she disappeared. Left an awful lot of nice things behind her, too." She added quickly, " 'Course, we had to sell them to cover the amount she owed us for leaving so sudden-like."

I was willing to bet selling Myrna Cowan's belongings reaped more than what the couple was owed.

A picture of what had happened to Myrna started to take shape. She and Guy had found this apartment conveniently located close to Van Hooten and McChesney. She'd lived there and Guy had visited. Then, when she'd become pregnant, the troubles had begun.

But why had she vanished? And where?

"I hope she isn't a relation of yours," the iron-haired woman said, shaking her head. "But I guess it happens in the best of families, morals being what they are these days. Like my Charlie always says, once people started having phonographs in the house, it was a downhill plunge for any kind of decency. When I was young, we didn't live for pleasure all the time."

"I can believe it." Before the woman could react, I thanked her for her help and left.

My search for Myrna Cowan started that very afternoon. I began with the business directory and made calls from Aunt Irene's flat, looking for a Cowan family with a missing daughter named Myrna. Unfortunately for me, if such a family existed, they were not listed.

There was always the possibility that Myrna had come from out of town. Or that she was using an assumed name.

I went back to my coworkers with the specific name, but no one had heard of Myrna Cowan. Guy had kept his secret well hidden from all of us except Oliver.

By the end of the week, I was no closer to finding the mysterious Myrna. Callie's company was leaving for Philadelphia on Sunday evening. I accompanied her to Grand Central, and Teddy met us there to see her off. I stepped back to give the two some privacy, even though Teddy was going to follow her there later. Since he had a stake in the show, he would go down for the opening and stay in Philadelphia during most of its out-of-town run.

"Break a leg," I told Callie when the train whistle warned of her imminent departure.

She kissed me on the cheek. "Don't let the flat go to ruin while I'm gone. No champagne sprees without me." She'd loved the story of Otto and me at the Omnium.

I laughed. "I promise."

After the train pulled out, Teddy offered to take me home in his car. I'd been walking all over town in my Myrna Cowan quest and was too tired to refuse. We spoke a little about Guy's funeral.

"Poor Hugh," he said. "I've never seen him so cut up. He's been out of sorts all week."

Curious. "I got the sense from him that he and Guy weren't close."

"They weren't. But he's been having a devil of a time with the camera mount he's been working on."

"Oh." I probably sagged in disappointment, like a ghoul. As if I *wanted* the man to be guilty of fratricide. "He wants to take pictures from airplanes?" It seemed silly. "Is there much demand for that?"

"Well, not now, of course," Teddy said, shifting after a turn. "But just think of the possibilities for cartographers. Not to mention the military uses it could have."

I frowned. The idea of military men buzzing over our heads had never occurred to me.

"But I don't think it's only the mount that's upset him," Teddy said.

"Why?"

"First, there's no reason for it to. You see, he's mostly got the bolting mechanism worked out, and the rest is just a stabilization issue. A camera has to be still while planes, given aerodynamics, naturally move, which means that—"

I had to interrupt him. "What else would Hugh be worried about?"

His face went blank for a moment; then he said, "Oh! I don't know. There was some fellow at the aerodrome who nettled him the other day. *That* was odd."

"Who?"

"Short man, with close-cropped curly hair. The name Hugh called him was Cohen."

Cohen. "Not Cain?"

"Oh no. It was Cohen, I'm fairly certain of that. I think he was Jewish."

"A young man?"

Teddy nodded. "Very. If he was even eighteen, I'd be surprised."

"Jacob Cohen." It had to be. Strange. He'd visited Guy at the office the week before the fire. "He was at the air park in New Jersey? Was this after the funeral or before?"

Teddy frowned in thought. He looked almost pained. "Just before. Do you know this Jacob Cohen person?"

"He was our office boy. Mr. McChesney fired him."

"He and Hugh had a big dustup. Hugh practically had him dragged out of the hangar. 'Don't come around here bothering me with this again,' he said. Or something very like it. I couldn't make heads or tails out of it at the time, but if he's who you say, maybe it was to do with some money Van Hooten and McChesney owed him."

No. Jacob would have gone to Mr. McChesney for that, and he would have done so months ago, after he was fired.

There was only one reason Jacob Cohen would have gone to Hugh—some business between him and Guy that was left unfinished.

Chapter 9

Mr. McChesney knew where Jacob Cohen had found work after leaving Van Hooten and McChesney, but for a moment on Monday afternoon it seemed touch-and-go whether I would be able to get the information from him.

"He's too sick to see anyone," Mrs. Carey told me at the door.

"I only need to speak to him for a moment," I said. "It's very important."

She wouldn't budge. Mr. McChesney had caught a chill at the burial and was in a weak condition. The doctor had ordered him to rest undisturbed, and she was going to carry out that order.

In the end, she conveyed the question about Jacob Cohen from me and came back with a slip of paper. *DeVaux's Fur Warehouse, West 20s,* was all it said. No other greeting, no signature. But I recognized his writing, so I knew it was from him. Strange.

Still, it was the information I needed. I only hoped Jacob still worked at this place. I thanked Mrs. Carey and hurried downtown.

After asking around, I was directed to Twenty-ninth Street. Several furriers plied their wares there, and a few other clothing makers seemed to be migrating up to the area, as well. A great wheeled garment cart nearly ran me down. Inside DeVaux's, I looked around in wonder at racks and racks of all different kinds of fur. It seemed as if the world had been picked clean of any mammal with a pelt.

The manager I chased down had little patience for my questions. "Cohen works nights," he said, barely noting my presence over the top of his spectacles. The clipboard he clasped to his chest seemed as much a part of his uniform as the suit on his back, the measuring tape around his neck, and the fat red pencil snugged over his ear.

"Do you know where I could find him now?"

"Who're you with?" The eyes behind those glasses were guarded. "The city? He's over sixteen."

"I know."

"I don't have any trouble with my people. It's all legal here. Ask anybody."

"I'm not from the city. This is a personal matter."

The sides of his mouth curved down. "I got no time for personal."

"I just need to know where he lives."

"Like I said—"

"Please, sir," I blurted out, surprised to hear the desperate quaver in my voice. I didn't relish coming back to this place at night. "It's a grave matter."

The impatience in his gaze turned to impatience mixed with pity. "Get yourself mixed up in something, did you? Doesn't surprise me these days, the way you young people racket around. In my day, parents didn't put up with nonsense. You'd be out on the streets."

As if putting children out on the streets was a solution to young people racketing around.

I swallowed any argument, though, and attempted a weak, pleading smile. Oliver Twist, bowl upraised. "Please. It would mean so much."

He relented. "Go see Herb. He's got everybody's address. Tell him I said it was okay."

After more cajoling, the man called Herb opened a file drawer and dug out a card with Jacob Cohen's address on Orchard Street written on it. He stood over me, meaty arms crossed, as I copied the information. "Nothing down there's worth the trip," he said.

"How would you know?" He didn't even know why I wanted to speak to Jacob.

"I grew up off Delancey, till the city showed up to take my brother and me to the orphanage. The orphanage was hell, but even hell was better than the tenements."

What could I say? I didn't choose Jacob Cohen's residence. "Thanks for the address."

He shook his head. "You'll see."

When I emerged from the subway on Delancey and turned onto Orchard Street, I started to have an inkling of what Herb had been trying to tell me. My progress was immediately slowed by the swarm of humanity in front of me. The street was lined with peddlers and pushcarts, and around them crowded women laden with baskets and bags, checking out wares. Young children darted here and there, most below school age, but some obvious truants. There were also dogs underfoot and various vehicles trying to push through the jumble. As far as my eye could see, five- and six-story residences towered above the street like a cavern, their balconies and fire escapes full either of discarded furniture and other unneeded household goods, or people themselves. Old people, young children, and mothers grabbing a moment of rest from their unceasing labor all looked down on the crowd below.

I threaded my way toward the buildings on the north side of the street and found 145 Orchard Street, which had a leather goods store at ground level. A plump man in a patched coat was leaning against the resident entrance, chewing on an unlit cigar. He sized me up. "Cohens are up one flight in the back."

I was astonished. "How did you know who I was looking for?"

"The only ones like you who come around are the charity ladies, nurses, or ladies to see the Cohens. You don't look like the first two."

He said it like a compliment, but I wasn't sure. "Thank you for the information."

He spat. "Think nothing of it."

The day was bright, but I never would have known it from the building's interior. No light penetrated the dim hallway except through the filthy glass of the side panels along the doorway, one of which had broken and was partially boarded over. The stench of the place I'd experienced before but never so intensely—it was the smell of poverty, of too many bodies crushed together too closely, and right away I nearly tripped over one of them. A little girl holding a stuffed sock that had been made up to resemble a doll. She gaped up at me wordlessly even as I hopped away from her with an apology.

Other children weren't so silent. The wails of two different babies pierced the air, coming from somewhere above, and three children were making a Luna Park fun ride of the stairwell's rickety banister, with two sliding down while the third tried to knock them off with a broom. They paid as little attention to me as they did to the fussing baby perched on a basket on one of the stairs.

I scooted past them all and hurried up to knock at what I hoped was the right door, eager to have this interview over with and be gone. If Jacob Cohen worked nights, surely he would sleep during the day. Which meant he would be at home, but he probably wouldn't appreciate the interruption. Although the man outside had indicated that many women visited the Cohens. Belatedly, I began to wonder why, and to worry.

Steps approached from inside, and the door swung open abruptly. The woman before me wasn't who I'd expected to find here. She was around my age, tall, and pretty. Dark eyes looked down at me from a heart-shaped face. If her complexion seemed a little sallow, it might have just been the poor lighting, or the effects of living in this place. Why *was* she living here? She didn't look poor. Her dress was simple but beautifully tailored in navy-blue brilliantine. It set off her slim figure to perfection. She was far too young to be Jacob's mother, and I doubted Jacob was married. Yet there was a baby in a crib behind her. Was she a sister, a cousin?

"May I help you?" she asked.

"I'm looking for Jacob Cohen."

Her expression tensed, and her demeanor became less welcoming. "Why?"

"I need to speak with him. I work—worked—at Van Hooten and McChesney."

I hoped the name of the company would earn me an entrée. I was mistaken. Her full lips turned down in a scowl. "Jacob doesn't work there."

"Maybe you haven't heard. Guy Van Hooten died the week before last."

Her grip on the edge of the door grew tighter, as if she were depending on that claw hold to keep her upright. "That's nothing to do with us."

"If I could just come in for a few moments . . ."

Behind her, the baby cried, and she turned instinctively toward it, leaving the door unguarded. I seized the opportunity to step inside.

It was a small room, perhaps ten by ten square, and every inch seemed occupied. A stove stood at one end, flanked by a drop-leaf table on one side and a rocking chair on the other. Opposite the stove was another table with a sewing machine on it. A dressmaker's form stood nearby with a half-finished dress on it. A cabinet held supplies needed for the dressmakers' trade—fabric folded neatly on shelves, with nooks for thread, pins, and various notions. The remaining wall space was a network of hooks and shelves containing all the necessities of life—toiletries and brushes, canned goods, towels and rags, keepsakes, candles, crockery for grease and flour, and a brand-new teddy bear.

I was admiring the work in progress on the dressmaker's form when the woman turned back to me with the baby in her arms. Seeing me on this side of her threshold obviously annoyed her. The baby was several months old and wore a white gown that was probably nicer than the one I'd been christened in. The child looked plump and clean, as if it belonged in a different world.

"Is Jacob here, Mrs. Cohen?"

"*Miss* Cohen," she said. "Myrna. I'm Jacob's sister."

Myrna. The name hit me like a thunderclap. I hadn't made a connection between the names *Cowan* and *Cohen.* I'd come here to uncover why Jacob had been at Hugh's aerodrome. But following that lead had led me straight to a bigger puzzle: Myrna Cowan.

Her eyes narrowed, and I could tell she thought I was judging her for being both a miss and a mother. If only she knew.

"Jacob's not here, then?" I asked.

"No."

I stared at the baby. He was a perfect little dumpling, rosy-cheeked and with pale blue eyes. Pale blue eyes with a metallic glint. Edith Van Hooten's eyes in a cherub face.

Myrna caught me staring and turned slightly, shielding her child. "Who are you? What are you to Jacob?" Her hostile gaze swept over me again. "You can't be his girl. You're not his type. And that's no insult to you, believe me."

I wasn't quite sure how to proceed. Myrna was wary of me already. I gestured at the dressmaker's form. "That's a beautiful dress, and I'm assuming you made what you have on. You do fine work."

"I get by."

"In a better part of town, you could do a whale of a business."

"Do you know about the dressmaker's trade, Miss"—she twisted her lips—"I still don't know who you are."

"Louise Faulk."

"Jacob never mentioned you."

"Our days at Van Hooten and McChesney didn't overlap, but he's visited the office. I was Guy Van Hooten's secretary."

She tightened her hold on her baby, who let out a gurgle. "Why are you here, really?"

"I thought, since you're a seamstress—"

"Don't lie. You aren't a customer." She took in my dress with a single dismissive sweep of her eyes. "You don't care about clothes. That's a dress off the discount rack at B. Altman's, I'd put money on it." She sniffed. "Small wonder they couldn't sell it. The blue-and-tan stripe looks like a mattress cover."

The dress had cost me $7.95. That's what came of taking Callie's advice to add variety to my wardrobe. I always went wrong when I ventured away from plain skirts and white shirtwaists. My usual day wear might be boring, but at least nobody told me I looked like a mattress.

She continued to eye me suspiciously. "What's the real reason you're here?"

"I heard Jacob had gone to see Hugh Van Hooten at his air park. I wanted to talk to him about it."

"I would rather not speak about that." She lifted her chin. "I don't even want to think about that family."

"But aren't they . . ." I nodded at the baby. "Guy was the child's father, wasn't he?"

If I'd assaulted her, she couldn't have reacted more vehemently. She stepped back, glaring. "I want you to leave." She turned and put the baby in its crib, the nicest piece of furniture in the room.

"Am I wrong?" I asked.

She straightened up from putting the baby down, her hard glare still in place. "I don't know you, and I don't like a stranger coming in and poking her nose where it doesn't belong. Guy is dead. The baby is mine."

"I didn't mean to be nosy," I said. "I really was just looking for Jacob, but then I realized you must be someone I'd heard of. Myrna Cowan."

A shadow fell across her face. "That was the name Guy said I should use."

"Why?"

"Why do you think?" She shook her head in disgust. "I guess he thought the landlady wouldn't rent to a Jew. Or maybe he just wanted to forget what I was when he was with me."

"That's terrible."

"Yes, it was. And my going along with it was terrible, too. But you see, I was in love. I would have called myself anything he wanted me to. He promised me so much—you wouldn't believe the life I was going to have as Guy Van Hooten's wife. Like him, I also thought if I became Myrna Cowan long enough he would forget I was a Cohen."

"But he didn't," I guessed.

"That was the part of me he would never forget."

"But he did promise you would be his wife?"

"Oh yes. And the most foolish thing is that I believed him. At least in the beginning. He was full of promises about my becoming Mrs. Van Hooten, just as soon as he could prepare his mama for the shock of having a Jewish daughter-in-law. He never thought we'd fool *her*. In the meantime, he gave me gifts to string me along. Foolish, extravagant things—furnishings, clothes, jewelry . . ."

That explained his need for money, the debts. And now most of the gifts had enriched the landlord and his wife.

"I was at your flat."

"On Thirty-fourth Street?" Wistfulness filled her eyes.

"It was so close to the office, but I never knew."

"And yet he was probably at the flat more often than at the office." She smiled. "I used to wonder how he could possibly be making a living, but he seemed to have enough to pay my rent, and buy my clothes, and trinkets." She pushed the cuff up from her wrist, revealing a pearl bracelet. "He gave me things like this—pawned now, most of it. Then he gave me that sewing machine." She eyed it mournfully. "That was at the end. A rich man who intended me to be his wife wouldn't buy me a sewing machine. It was his way of assuaging his guilt, you see. I was working for a seamstress when we met. He was giving me a means to support myself again." She looked at the bassinet. "Me and his son."

A son. How could Guy not have wanted to be a part of his son's life?

You're a hypocrite, Louise. I had abandoned a son, too.

"The baby tore it for him," Myrna said. "He knew he'd never be able to present that lady dragon he called a mother with a Jewish grandchild. He was a coward. And when he realized that I knew he was a coward, he abandoned me."

"I'm sorry." I didn't know what else to say.

"That's why I haven't shed a tear over his death. Not one tear." Her expression was so pained, so tight, I wanted to cry for her. But I knew the tears were there, waiting for a day that would sneak up on her. "I cried when I left that flat. I cried when I held our baby in my arms. But I won't cry now. For me, Guy Van Hooten died the day he told me it was over."

Guy was dead, yes. But her baby was still a Van Hooten and lived in a tenement. "You have Guy's son. His flesh and blood. Surely now your religion would be irrelevant to the family."

"To the Van Hootens?" A bitter laugh erupted from her. "It matters more to them than if I'd been walking the streets. Which his mother probably would assume I had been if she knew of me."

"She doesn't know she has a grandchild?"

"No, and if I have my way, she'll never know."

I tried to piece it all together. "Then why did Jacob go see Hugh?"

She reddened. "Jacob's a fool. He came up with the bright idea to beg money from Hugh on his own. For all the good it did him. All he got for his trouble was insults. Hugh said we couldn't be sure if the baby was Guy's."

"That's despicable."

"That's what Van Hootens are. I tell you, I'll sell my body before I'll accept a nickel from any of them. My baby's name is Noah Cohen, *Cohen,* and the father's name on the birth certificate is 'unknown.' There's less shame in that than carrying the name of a family that uses women the way Guy used me."

"Wasn't Jacob angry with Guy?"

"He always believed Guy would come around, even after I moved out of the apartment and came here to have the baby."

I surveyed the crowded flat again. "Does Jacob live here now?"

"He keeps things here, but he mostly stays with friends. Our father died last year, in a place near here, where we grew up. I'm all the family Jacob has now, but he hates the baby's crying. I know Jacob's young to be independent, but he's always been headstrong. I don't have the energy to mother him and Noah both."

"But why do you stay here?"

She fixed me with a proud stare. "I won't be here forever. I'm saving my pennies. I've got a bank account, and I'm putting money by for Noah. He'll have things, and he'll get the best education I can give him."

"The Van Hootens could give him those things now. If you'd just show them the baby—"

"I won't beg for their charity. Guy abandoned me, and Hugh Van Hooten as good as called me a liar. I don't need them. Someday Noah Cohen will be a man the world looks up to, and then the Van Hootens will be sorry they turned their backs on him."

"Edith Van Hooten can't turn her back on a child whose existence she's unaware of," I argued. "The Van Hooten wealth could help you find a decent place to live."

Her eyes flashed. "Anywhere's decent where I don't feel beholden to people who think they're too good for me. Maybe you can't understand what it's like to be treated like garbage, to be put out on the street when you've been used up. How could you?" Her gaze swept up and down my person again, and her contempt felt almost like a physical rebuff. "I suppose you're a thoroughly *decent* person. In fact, you should get out of here before my shame rubs off on you."

I wasn't going to pour out my own sob story to prove my hard luck bona fides. "I wish I could help," I said simply.

She wasn't having any of my sympathy. "Do you think I'm such a fool that I haven't pieced together why you came here? You're wondering if I or Jacob had some part in that fire. That's really why you wanted to talk to Jacob, isn't it?"

"It was, initially," I admitted.

"The police spoke to Jacob already. If they thought he'd done it, he'd be in jail by now."

But the police didn't know about his sister's relationship to Guy, I bet. Or his visiting Hugh Van Hooten. Hugh probably wouldn't have wanted to mention that connection to the police, either.

"Jacob's no arsonist," she continued. "What would be in it for him to harm Guy, a man he idolized? And *I* certainly didn't set fire to Van Hooten and McChesney, if that's what you're thinking. I won't cry, but I'm sorry Guy died. I don't know why he was in that place when it caught fire, or why he didn't get out in time. Was he drunk?"

I recalled Muldoon's warning not to say too much. "Something like that."

"Poor fool." Her eyes brightened with moisture, but only for a moment. She shook her head and glared at me. "You can take your nosy questions and leave now. You won't find a firebug here."

"I'm sorry if I disturbed you."

"Just do me a favor," she said. "Forget you ever saw me."

I doubted I could do that. Myrna Cohen wasn't a person you could forget. Guy hadn't. He'd said her name, longingly, in a drunken delirium last summer. And the money Guy had been desperate to lay hands on . . . had it just been to pay down his usual debts, or could it have been for his son? If he'd known the conditions the baby was living in—and surely Jacob had told him—he might have felt the need to help was urgent. Urgent enough to go into some kind of business deal with a man like Leonard Cain.

I took one last look around the place. The shelves were crammed full, but a yellow box with red lettering drew my eye. *Bromley's Rat Killer.* A skull and crossbones appeared at the bottom of the box.

"Do you have a problem with rats?" I asked.

"We did," Myrna said. "I got rid of them."

Chapter 10

On the way home, a witch stopped me in my tracks in front of a hardware store on Bowery. The owners had attired a coat rack in a black dress and cape, fashioned a head out of a flour sack draped over the top, drawn on a scary face, and topped it off with a pointy black hat. Halloween was a few days away, and the witch triggered a pang of nostalgia in me. I'd outgrown the days of dressing up and tramping through the neighborhood years ago, but I'd always enjoyed carving pumpkins with my cousins, Aunt Sonja's boys, helping them with their disguises, and sending them out to create whatever mayhem grammar school goblins were capable of. I would miss that.

Household items spilled out onto the sidewalk from the mouth of the store, everything from boxes of screws and nails to lanterns, mops, and axes, all marked with inexpertly painted price signs. I went inside and found a clerk hidden in the crowded shop. Along the walls, packed, musty shelves ranged to the ceiling, and the floor was an obstacle course of everything from piles of cement mix to a bathtub. Bicycles hung from ceiling beams. When I told the clerk what I wanted, he swung a ladder over and clambered up to retrieve a box of Bromley's Rat Killer off a high shelf. It looked identical to the one I'd seen at Myrna Cohen's. Underneath the skull and crossbones was written: *Danger: poison. Potassium cyanide.*

"Thank you." I handed back the box.

"You don't want it?" he asked, confused.

"No, I just needed to see what was in it. I don't have rats."

"It'll kill other things, too," he assured me.

"It might have already."

My suspicions had been running amok since I spotted that box of poison at Myrna Cohen's. She was certainly bitter toward the Van Hootens—but bitter enough to poison Guy? He was the lover who'd spurned her, yet I could have sworn I'd also discerned regret and a lingering kernel of love for him in her eyes.

Jacob Cohen could also have visited the office that night before the fire and killed Guy. It would have been easy for him to slip something into Guy's drink. But according to Myrna, Jacob admired Guy. And would he have shaken down Hugh after he'd just killed his brother? That would have taken a boy with a special kind of gall.

Then there was the matter of the three thousand dollars, which surely Guy's killer had taken. Jacob and Myrna Cohen weren't living like people sitting on top of that tidy sum. Although she'd mentioned "putting money by" for the baby . . .

When I got back to my building, the Bleecker Blowers were playing "Meet Me Tonight in Dreamland." As I climbed up the stairs, I sensed someone watching me. Sure enough, Wally's beady eyes were staring up at me. Not that there was anything to see except my ankles. Callie and I had long since realized we had to gather our skirts in one hand. Being hobbled was a small price to pay to deprive the creepy landlady's son a peek at our drawers.

Today, though, I welcomed an encounter with The Troll. "Wally—just who I needed to talk to."

He flinched. "Me?"

I backtracked down to the foyer. "Do you have any Bromley's Rat Killer?"

His head tilted. "You got rats in your apartment?"

"No."

"Then what do you want rat poison for?"

"I'm just curious if you have it." I considered for a moment. "Though I suppose it doesn't necessarily have to be Bromley's. Any rat poison would probably do."

"You just said you don't have rats."

"We don't. I'm just curious."

"About rats?"

"No—about keeping rat poison. Specifically, any poison containing cyanide."

He scratched his head, setting off a small avalanche of dandruff. "I got something in the basement. I ain't sure what's in it, though."

"Is it in a yellow box with red lettering?"

"Maybe. You want to come down and take a look for yourself?"

Not even for the sake of the investigation would I set foot in Wally's basement lair. I gathered my skirts again. "I'll take your word for it."

He edged closer. "Callie ain't been around lately. She leave you?"

"She's in Philadelphia."

His head turned in a considering way, like a fat lizard. "That business with you two—that was a gag, right?" He lowered his voice. "I didn't tell Ma."

"Thank you for that, Wally," I said gravely, avoiding the question. Then I turned and continued upstairs, my mind focused on cyanide again. The rat poison had seemed like a damning clue when I'd seen it on the shelf in Myrna Cohen's flat. But how many households in New York City had an identical box?

The next morning before going to Aunt Irene's I swung by our police precinct, Muldoon's base of operations, but he wasn't there. Rafferty, the officer I spoke to, recognized me from the previous summer. "What'll you be wanting with Muldoon? Helping him solve another case?" He winked.

"This outfit needs all the help it can get, doesn't it?"

When he finished laughing, he answered, "I'll tell Muldoon you said that, Miss Faulk."

The week progressed, though, and I didn't hear from him. I began to wonder if ignoring me was his way of signaling that I should stay out of his investigation. Wednesday evening, I went back to the fur warehouse to talk to Jacob Cohen. He was not happy to see me.

"What did you want to get my sister all stirred up for?" He led me out by a loading dock so he could smoke. "She was already mad at me for talking to Hugh Van Hooten."

"Why did you?"

He looked at me as if I were crazy. "Are you kiddin'? You saw the dump she's living in. Myrna oughta have something for the kid. Guy'd want her to."

"He didn't help her after the baby was born."

"He sent that crib. I bet he would've sent more, too, if he hadna died. Last time I talked to him, he seemed real cut up about how everything happened. I don't think he was gonna tell his mother about Myrna, but he might've forked over some more dough eventually."

"You said he seemed cut up? About what, specifically?"

He shrugged. "About Myrna, I guess. That's why when I first heard about Guy being dead, I thought . . ."

"Thought what?" I prompted.

"Well, that he might've done it himself."

"Suicide?"

"Maybe not even on purpose. But you know . . . like maybe too much to drink and a cigarette? My old man got drunk like that once and nearly burned our place down. It was a dump anyway, like Myrna's place now. I can't stand it there. She harps on me 'cause she thinks I'm like Guy. But Guy was the greatest. He took me to the horse races a few times. That's more than my old man ever did."

"You really liked him."

"Sure. It wasn't his fault I got fired, it was that old man's. And as for Myrna . . ." He tossed his cigarette end down and mashed it under his heel. For a moment, I could see a struggle going on in him, between wanting to stand up for his sister and remaining faithful to his hero. "Well, I don't understand all that love stuff. Six months ago, she was walking on clouds. Now she jumps down my throat if I even say his name. But I don't think he was as bad as Myrna says. Some people just take longer to do the right thing, you know?"

I nodded. If Guy hadn't run out of time, maybe there would have been a happier ending for the couple eventually. But it was pointless to dwell on might-have-beens now. What I extrapolated from my visit with Jacob was that he was second only to Edith Van Hooten in his admiration of Guy and was unlikely to have caused him harm.

I made little progress on anything besides my aunt's book, which would have been more gripping had I not known how it was going to turn out. Her pages took me right back to the shocking events of the summer and highlighted the difference between then and now. After Ethel's murder in June, events had unfolded rapidly. Now I was discovering that clues and suspects weren't always going to appear as quickly as I needed them to. By Thursday, all I'd accomplished in my investigating was to prove by way of an informal survey of everyone I met that almost anyone in Manhattan could have provided the rat poison to murder Guy.

I did toy a bit with Jacob's suicide theory. Suicide didn't quite square up with the Guy I'd known. He was always looking forward to the next throw of the dice. Yet, given the unhappy circumstances—money worries, and the rupture with the woman who'd had the son he was too craven to acknowledge as his own—it didn't seem far-fetched that the man might have taken his own life.

Thursday evening, as usual, my aunt's friends, friends of friends, and even passing acquaintances of friends of friends descended on the house on Fifty-third Street to talk, drink, and eat finger food prepared by Bernice. I'd expected attendance to fall off as the weather grew cooler, but just the opposite happened. Manhattan's population shrank during the summer as anyone who could afford to fled the concrete oven that was the city. Now, with autumn in full swing, the whole world seemed to be here. Those who didn't have theater tickets or other activities planned could always fall back on Aunt Irene's Thursday nights.

Otto loved going. My aunt treated him like a nephew, and Bernice took special care to attempt to fatten him up with the choicest of the delicacies she'd prepared for the evening. Mostly, though, he camped out on the piano stool and entertained whoever wanted to hear him play. When he wasn't showing off his own creations, he played hits of the day and old parlor classics. He knew how to please.

Lacking any show-offy talent, I tended to my aunt's guests who found themselves ill at ease and out of the swim. Ideally I would herd my misfits back into conversational huddles, but often I just listened. I met some interesting people this way. Also crackpots.

That night a struggling violinist and frustrated socialist-Utopian with a heavy Eastern European accent was schooling me on the upcoming revolution. According to Mr. Popescu, the world was on the verge of a grand return to its pastoral roots. The industrial age, choking on all the soot it had belched out for half a century, would grind to a halt and we city dwellers would have to skitter out of our urban burrows to join our country-dwelling brethren. A new generation of peasants would tear down New York City brick by brick and return it to its natural state of farms and simple fisherfolk.

"Will we give it back to the Indians?" I asked. "Or will we return to a system of patroons and peasants?"

He scowled at me. "This time humanity will get it right. There will be true equality in the distribution of land. Every man will have his share of acreage."

Just my luck that as soon as I found a city I loved, Communists would come tear it down.

As I listened to this nightmarish Utopian forecast, my gaze began to stray. When I caught sight of Muldoon entering the room, it was hard to contain my relief. I flagged him over.

Mr. Popescu flicked his glance that way, too, annoyed my attention had wandered.

"Would this new forty acres and a mule scheme benefit every woman, too?" I asked him.

He pursed his lips at my naïveté. "Woman will return to her natural state. You will be able to put aside your typewriters and walk away from your switchboards."

"Back to babies and butter churns? No thanks."

He shook his head. "That is the problem. You are so far from how nature intended you to be that you no longer recognize what a woman should be."

Muldoon had threaded his way over, and I tackled him the way a person on a ledge would grab for a rope to climb back to safety. Or in this case, to sanity. I took his arm and pulled him to my side.

"This is Detective Muldoon of the New York Police Department," I said, introducing the men. "Mr. Popescu believes civilization in New York will collapse soon and Manhattan will become farmland again. I'm not sure what will happen to the police force."

The Romanian's face soured. "The masses will police themselves. When all men are truly equal, there will be no crime."

I patted Muldoon's arm. "I'm afraid you'll be unemployed, Detective. Better start saving up for a plow."

He tried not to smile, but our mirth at Popescu's expense must have come through. The man scowled at us. "Some who are shackled are afraid to throw off their chains!" He turned on his heel to leave us, then pivoted back, took half the sandwiches off my tray, and huffed away.

"I hope he's wrong," I said. "I finally cracked forty words per minute on my aunt's Remington. I'd hate to think it was all for nothing."

"You came by the precinct earlier this week." Muldoon's face tensed as if he were expecting something unpleasant. "Did you have news?"

"If I had, it would be old news by now. It was nothing earth-shattering, luckily." To be honest, I'd mostly gone by to see if *he* had news.

His eyebrows rose. He still didn't like my playing detective, although it hardly felt like playing now that it was consuming my life. "Really? Haven't blown the case wide open yet?"

I bristled at the sarcasm. "I was going to tell you something, but now I don't think I will."

That look of dread returned. "Go ahead."

It would have served him right if I kept all my information to myself. Trouble was, I was hoping for a few tidbits in exchange. I swallowed my pride. "I'm beginning to wonder if Guy Van Hooten killed himself."

Silence stretched. His gaze remained fastened on me. "*That's* your big news?"

"I never said I had news. It's a theory, that's all."

He sighed, almost as if he weren't terribly interested in talking about Guy Van Hooten's death. What else was there to talk about? "What brought you to this conclusion?"

He sounded so skeptical, I didn't want to admit that the idea had been given to me by a seventeen-year-old. I took a breath. "First, he was in debt. He also had personal problems."

"What kind of personal problems?"

I shrugged. "A woman, of course. A star-crossed lover situation."

"Mm-hmm." He couldn't have looked less impressed.

"So you don't credit my suicide theory?"

"You believe Guy poisoned himself and then . . . what? Set the building on fire during his last gasps of life?"

I'd considered that thorny problem. "Maybe the fire was just an accident. He could have set out a candle that burned down and only caught fire later."

Muldoon didn't look convinced.

"Or he fell unconscious while he had a cigarette burning," I said.

"So he committed suicide and then accidentally, coincidentally, the building caught fire."

"There's no arguing with a closed mind," I said.

"I didn't come to argue. Anyway, I wouldn't waste my time worrying about Guy's death anymore if I were you. We're following a different lead, and we might be close to an arrest."

I was bird dog alert. "Who?"

"I can't tell you. Even if I wanted to—I can't."

"Then you *do* want to tell me?"

He groaned. "Louise . . ."

"I could get you a piece of cake from the kitchen," I said. "Bernice's coconut cake."

"Bribing an officer," he joked. "Shame on you."

"Just a hint?"

"No, sorry."

I sighed. "I never get what I want out of you."

"I could say the same."

"Well, thank goodness for that. You're probably just like Mr. Popescu. You'd be happiest if I went back to Altoona and churned butter or something. That's not going to happen."

"You don't know me as well as you think." The faintly teasing tone he'd been using was gone. "And I'm not sure if what you think you want will bring you the joy you expect it to."

"I wouldn't worry my head over that possibility if I were you. I don't."

"That's why I worry."

He left me to pay his respects to Aunt Irene. My aunt pulled him down onto the sofa next to her, and for the next twenty minutes, Muldoon sat with a lap dog panting on his knee and listened patiently to her questions. No doubt Aunt Irene wanted details to make Detective Mulligan in her book more authentic.

Muldoon left before I could talk to him in private again, and I kicked myself for that. He had news about the case. *A different lead,* he'd said. I should have tried harder to wheedle it out of him. Callie would have. Why couldn't I be wilier?

As Otto and I cabbed downtown after the house party broke up, Muldoon loomed in my thoughts. Why had he shown up tonight? He'd been at my aunt's before, of course, and perhaps he thought it would be the easiest place to find me. Certainly it was a little more impersonal than seeking me out at my flat. He had strong feelings about unmarried men and women visiting alone together—his sense of propriety seemed to have been set in cement sometime during the McKinley administration. Yet I recalled now that his shoes had been freshly polished, his suit coat brushed, and his hair combed perfectly. His manner had seemed expectant, yet when I told him what I'd wanted to say, he'd appeared disappointed. Did he think that I'd merely been paying a social call when I sought him out at the precinct?

Would he have considered a social call from me a good thing?

"Louise?"

I turned to look at Otto. The cab had stopped. I was home.

Otto got out with me. "You don't have to come up," I told him.

But it was dark, and he worried about my being alone in the apartment while Callie was gone. He didn't trust Wally, with good reason.

Sure enough, Wally was right there as I came in. He frowned at Otto. "I guess some fellas don't know when they're licked."

Otto frowned. "What's that supposed to mean?"

"Never mind," I muttered. "What did you want, Wally?"

"Letter for ya." He held out an envelope.

I went toward him to take it, but he drew it back at the last moment. His fleshy face smirked at my exasperation.

"You should have put that under her door," Otto told him. "Landlords aren't supposed to interfere with the mail."

Wally's eyes narrowed on me. "I was gonna shove it under your door, till I noticed the return address—it's from the police. So I was asking myself, what would the police want with Louise Faulk now? What's she done? Maybe I oughta tell Ma about it. She's about fed up with all the police trouble you two have brought down on our house."

Our sin was having a houseguest who was killed in our flat last summer, but ever since then Wally and his mother had treated us as if we were scarlet women. I was glad Callie wasn't here now to see the speculation in Wally's eyes.

I snatched the envelope from his hands. I could hardly wait to open it—though of course I wasn't going to do so in front of him.

"My correspondence is none of your business. And I assure you nothing in this letter would supply you any blackmail material, so you can crawl back into your lair now."

Otto and I went upstairs. When we were out of earshot, he asked, "Is that what I think it is?"

I nodded. We let ourselves in and I headed for the kitchen. "Aren't you going to open it?" Otto asked.

"I'm going to make cocoa. Wouldn't you like some?"

"Sure, but . . ." He stared at the envelope, which I'd dropped on the table. "How can you stand not to tear it open and find out what it says?"

I was itching to tear it open, in fact. And yet as long as the envelope remained closed, my dreams were still alive and my future as a policewoman remained a real possibility. The moment I opened it, I'd have to bow to the wisdom of the NYPD. And in all probability, I'd need to start pounding the pavement to get another secretarial position.

"For Pete's sake," Otto said, "if you don't open the letter, I will."

"All right. Go ahead."

His eyes bugged. "You really mean it?"

"You'll be my good-luck charm."

He took the single sheet out, unfolded it, and read. As his eyes scanned the lines, his face paled.

"What?" I ordered myself not to burst into tears if it was bad news. Dream or no dream, it was only a job. I'd just have to find something else to do with my life.

He held out the sheet of paper, his face breaking into a grin. "Wait till we tell Callie she's going to be living with a cop."

CHAPTER 11

The letter was real enough. It bore the raised seal of the NYPD and the signature of the Police Commissioner, Rhinelander Waldo. But Otto, just skimming it, had missed an important detail. Although I had passed the exam, I was instructed to report to downtown headquarters on Friday morning for an interview with a Captain Percival Smith. Friday was tomorrow, which meant that from the time of my receiving the note, my interview was only twelve hours away.

I should have passed the time resting up, but I could no more sleep than I could have flapped my arms and soared across the Atlantic Ocean.

After a few unrewarding hours of tossing and turning, I got up, took a long bath, and dressed in my favorite work clothes. White shirtwaist, not a lot of frills. A buff-colored skirt with very little in the way of ornament except for a pleat in back. My jacket was a brown herringbone pattern, fitted but not too tight. Brown hat with a not-too-outlandishly-wide brim decorated with a matching satin band and a few jaunty feathers.

Callie always said I would probably march down the aisle on my wedding day looking like a votes-for-women protester, which I took as a compliment. Of course, if this had been *her* interview, she would have worn some fantastic creation copied from the latest sketches out of Paris, and probably charmed Captain Smith right out of his garters. But I'd learned the hard way that "to thine own self be true" was doubly important for taste in clothes. If I wore anything too fine, I'd trip over my hem or spend the whole interview twitching in discomfort.

As I marched into Captain Smith's office, my head high but my heart thumping, I was glad I hadn't worn any confining garments. I might have passed out. Surely the department would want me, I told myself, trying to exude confidence.

The captain, who looked to be in his sixties, with spectacles perched on a beaky nose, iron-gray hair, and a full mustache, was absorbed in studying a folder. I stopped across the desk from him and suppressed the urge to salute. *You're not an officer yet, Louise.* He didn't invite me to sit down, so I remained standing at awkward quasi-military attention. A minute ticked by with no acknowledgment. I leaned forward to peek at what he was reading.

"You're hovering," he snapped, still not looking up.

I stepped back. "Excuse me, sir."

He scanned the lines on the page in front of him. "Do you always hover, Miss Faulk?"

"No, sir."

"Bad habit," he said.

"Yes, sir."

"Why don't you sit down instead of looming there over me."

"Thank you, sir." I dropped into the armless leather-seated chair provided. Another minute ticked by before Captain Smith glanced up from his file to inspect me. The gray eyes behind the spectacles blinked wide open. "Good God, you're a girl."

Since he'd already called me Miss Faulk, I assumed he was referring to my age rather than my sex. "I'm twenty-one."

He sniffed at that. "Twenty-one is a dangerous age. You think you're an adult, but you're still a young idiot."

Saying "Yes, sir" to that pronouncement didn't strike me as wise, so I held my tongue.

"Mind you," he continued, "I'm talking about twenty-one-year-old *men*. With girls, who knows? Some say women are smarter, but that's a lot of flapdoodle. In my experience, females always seem to be giggling." His eyes narrowed on me. "Do you giggle?"

"Rarely, sir."

"Good." He went back to inspecting the folder. "This says you were involved in a police investigation over the summer."

"The Ethel Gail murder."

A sigh huffed out of him. "Now why were you mixed up in that? Murder's not the type of thing decent girls should be involved with. Don't you have any sense?"

"Ethel Gail was my roommate's cousin. She was staying with us when she was murdered."

"Well, I suppose that's some excuse." He looked down again, threading his pencil between his fingers like a magician about to perform a trick with a coin. "You did very well on the test." His tone was lugubrious, as if my high score were bad news.

"Really?" I barely stopped myself from leaning forward to try to see the file.

"You scored the second highest grade on the exam of the women who've taken it."

Second? I puffed up.

His brows drew together. "Mind you, the test isn't everything. We're looking for women officers of good character." He eyed me closely. "Do you have a good moral character?"

I swallowed. "I believe so."

"You believe? You can't give a straight yes or no?"

"I-I'm not sure what you mean."

"I mean do you have any bad habits? Is there anything in your personal history that would reflect badly on yourself or the New York Police Department if it were to come to light?"

Without a doubt, most men, including Captain Smith, would consider having had a baby out of wedlock to be a stain on my reputation. That hadn't been my fault, but there was no way I could tell Captain Smith about having been raped by a traveling salesman. I'd never confessed what had happened to my closest friends, not even to Callie or Aunt Irene. When I'd told Aunt Sonja, she'd banished me from her home. I certainly wasn't going to bank on the captain being more understanding toward my misfortune than the woman who'd raised me.

Besides, who would ever find out? Especially in the police. Yes, the baby I had given birth to had been adopted by a couple who lived in town, and I occasionally strolled by their house on Eightieth Street in hopes of catching a glimpse of little Calvin Longworth, now ten months old. But no one else in the world knew of my relationship to him but me and the home for unwed girls that had arranged the adoption. Even *I* wasn't supposed to know about the Longworths—I'd only found out because I'm nosy and stole a look at my paperwork.

Captain Smith hitched his breath impatiently. "Well? Why don't you say something? Do you have anything to hide?"

"No, sir."

No one would ever know. I'd make sure of it.

He cleared his throat, and an adenoidal sound came out of him. "Good. Glad to hear it. Nothing worse than having an officer bring scandal down on the force."

"I will never do that."

"To be honest, Miss Faulk, your folder raises flags."

I was shocked. How could that be? "What flags?"

"That murder business. And you're a single girl, yet you don't live at home with your parents."

"My parents are both dead. I was raised by an aunt and uncle. I have another aunt here, which is why I moved to New York City."

That wasn't entirely untrue.

"But now you're living practically on your own, getting mixed up in murders. We prefer girls from good families, not independent troublemakers."

"I've never made trouble," I said, adding, "knowingly."

"Hmm." He emitted that nasal sound again. "But then we have your score. Second highest. Hard to argue with that. And to top it off, there's this letter of recommendation from Detective Frank Muldoon."

It was a good thing I was sitting down, because my body felt rubbery. Muldoon had written a letter on my behalf? I couldn't imagine what it said. He'd only ever tried to talk me out of applying to join the force.

"Is it a good letter?" I asked, honestly uncertain.

"Oh, it's a humdinger. Detective Muldoon goes on for two pages about your intelligence, tenacity, and valor. Now how does a woman manage to show valor?"

"I lured Ethel Gail's killer to the top of the Woolworth Building."

"And that worked out, did it?"

Surely he'd heard. "Perhaps Detective Muldoon failed to mention that I was nearly pitched off the top floor. But the killer was apprehended."

He skimmed the letter again. "No, that's here, too." He shook his head. "Sounds like a lot of tomfoolery to me, and it would have served you right if you'd gotten yourself killed. But you lived, so I suppose you do have some claim to valor."

"Thank you."

He slapped the folder shut with a sigh of exasperation and finality. "All right, Miss Faulk, I'm recommending you to the board for the position of probationary police officer, starting the week after next."

I couldn't believe I'd heard correctly. "You mean . . . I have the job?"

He glowered at me. "What do you think? That I'm such a dumb cluck that I'd waste the commission's time recommending someone for a job who shouldn't have it?"

"No, sir. Thank you, Captain Smith."

"Mind you, the probationary period is a trial. You may be fired for any infraction for three months, so mind yourself. There's no room for showboating antics in the NYPD. Especially not from a woman. Remember that."

"I will." *And I'll ignore it, as I see fit.* "What about training?"

He frowned. "Training for what?"

What did he think? "Police work."

"What training do you need?" His voice turned brittle with impatience. "You show up and follow orders. Will that be a difficulty for you, Miss Faulk?"

"No, sir."

"Good. You're to report to the Thirtieth Street Station a week from Monday, nine-thirty p.m., for the night shift." He tossed my folder into a tray and reached for another. "Dismissed."

Thirtieth Street. A week from Monday. Nine-thirty p.m. I wanted to write it all down so I wouldn't forget, so I could prove to myself that I wasn't dreaming. Tears threatened. *I've done it!*

All at once, however, a worry popped into my head. "What about uniforms?"

He scowled at me. "You're responsible for those."

"But where do I find them?"

"Do I strike you as an expert on women's clothes?"

"I was just curious—"

"Don't be curious. Show up for your job and do what you're told."

"Yes, sir," I said. "Thank you."

I backed out much as I'd heard one was supposed to exit the presence of a royal personage, and didn't breathe easier until I was outside the building. My mind was reeling. I was a police officer. Or I would be in a week. And most puzzling of all—that letter. When had Muldoon written a recommendation? And why? I certainly hadn't asked him to. Knowing his feelings, I wouldn't have dared. And yet he had done it all on his own. And the letter had been glowing enough to overcome the perceived negatives of my application.

Puzzlement over Muldoon's letter was just one of the feelings fluttering in me. *Second highest score on the exam.* I was going to be a policewoman. My life wasn't going to be just typing and making coffee. I would be a part of a brotherhood, and a smaller sisterhood, of people trying to maintain order in this big, messy metropolis. I would belong to that fraternity, that family, and to this city.

I couldn't wait to tell Aunt Irene. And I needed to inform Mr. McChesney that I wouldn't be able to look into the fire anymore. The NYPD wouldn't want its officers doing paid detective work on the side. I wasn't making much progress, anyway. Muldoon had intimated that the police were close to cracking the case, and had hinted it was an angle I hadn't even considered. I'd let my colleagues handle it now.

My colleagues!

I floated in a general uptown direction toward my aunt's house, barely noticing what streets I was on. It was a miracle I wasn't run over.

My thoughts swung back around to Muldoon's visit to my aunt's house the previous night. His behavior now struck me in a whole new light. Could he have known about the exam results? *Of course.* Something like that was bound to have filtered down to him. That's why he'd asked if I had any news to tell him. He'd probably assumed that I'd received the letter already.

And to think, I'd taken in his nice clothes and spit-and-polished appearance and entertained the notion that he might have had a personal reason for being there. As if he'd ever tried to win my good opinion.

His writing that letter confounded me, though. He'd made it clear he didn't think I should be a policewoman. And yet he'd helped me anyway.

In return for his generosity, I decided to tell him everything I knew about Guy Van Hooten's death. True, I'd discovered nothing conclusive. But I was willing to bet he didn't know about Myrna. She would have mentioned speaking to the police. And my mind kept returning to Jacob and Hugh, and Hugh's refusal to do anything for Myrna's baby. And how, the morning Guy's body was discovered, Hugh hadn't seemed at all cut up.

Something about Hugh Van Hooten rubbed me the wrong way. Here was a man who obviously disliked his brother—or at least held him in contempt—and hadn't even mourned his passing on the very morning his death was discovered. Nor had he seemed surprised, as far as I could remember. Of course, I hadn't been there the moment he found out about Guy, but only hours later, after he'd been to the ruins of the building. Yet wouldn't any normal brother have seemed more visibly shaken after viewing that ashen rubble?

Myrna had told me that the Van Hootens wouldn't accept Guy's natural son, and Jacob's fruitless visit to the air park indicated that Hugh didn't intend to give his illegitimate nephew any assistance. Of course not. Hugh's life revolved around his aeronautical adventures, and those weren't cheap. A new young Van Hooten could eat into his inheritance, especially if old Edith Van Hooten decided to recognize the child and began doting on the baby the way she had on Guy.

Given how well connected the Van Hootens were, I was willing to bet the police weren't looking closely at Guy's brother. Maybe if I told Muldoon about Jacob visiting Hugh at the air park, that would convince him the Van Hootens deserved closer scrutiny.

When I arrived at Aunt Irene's she was out visiting a friend, so I went to the kitchen to scrounge lunch and announce my big news.

Walter was overjoyed. "You'll wind up police commissioner," he predicted.

"That's for civilians," I said, unable to hold back a dismissive sniff.

Bernice was less impressed. She hung back at the stove, hand on her wooden spoon the size of a billy club, and eyed me over a pot of soup. "What kind of a job is the police for a girl like you?"

"A good one," I said.

Walter stuck up for me. "She's already doing the work of a real detective. This'll make it official."

Bernice gave the pot several vigorous stirs. "Official?" She shook her head. "I remember her almost being killed while doing her so-called detective work last summer. This'll make her putting her life at risk official, too. Or maybe she'll just get herself in the police business the way some do, and she'll harass honest folks, or accept money for looking the other way while letting the not-so-honest people do their worst."

I swallowed back indignation. "All policemen aren't corrupt."

"There's enough dishonest ones to make you wonder where the good ones are, or why they put up with the bad apples." Her gaze cut through the steam to pierce me. "Which kind will you be, I wonder?"

Walter sputtered. "How can you ask that? It's outrageous."

"She doesn't know the first thing she's getting herself into. She got a notion in her head, like the notion of a girl to take to the stage."

"Callie 'took to the stage,' as you call it," I pointed out, "and she's a success."

"Today she might be a success," Bernice said. "There's others who don't last at it."

No names had been mentioned, but Bernice's arrow hit the bull's-eye. Beet-red blotches appeared in Walter's cheeks. "I played Shakespeare," he said, trembling with indignation and wounded pride. "*Hamlet*. For eight months."

I happened to know he played a gravedigger in *Hamlet* in his company's tour of the Midwest, and maybe Bernice knew that, too, because she kept shaking her head. Walter looked as if he would brain her with the nearest convenient skillet.

For the sake of domestic harmony, I attempted to veer the conversation away from thespians and back to my job. "What about Detective Muldoon?" Bernice had met Muldoon, and because he'd declared her chicken sandwiches the best he'd ever had, he was always mentioned in the most glowing terms in the kitchen. "*He's* honest." With my gaze, I dared her to challenge that assessment.

"Mr. Muldoon can look after himself. Can you?"

"The New York Police Department wouldn't be offering me a position if they didn't think I could." I drew up to my full height. "I made the second highest score on the exam."

Bernice ladled up pea soup into a waiting bowl and plopped it in front of me. " 'Pride goeth before the fall.' Now sit down and eat."

I felt like a child. "I prefer my sermons on Sunday," I grumbled, though I sat down obediently. "I hope Aunt Irene's happier for me than you are."

"She will be," Bernice said. "But that won't make her righter than I am."

I ate the soup—my stomach was too rumbly for me to flounce out of the room as I wanted to. But Bernice and I didn't speak any more on the subject. She was always such a killjoy. She'd hinted that she'd had trouble with the police in her past. Small wonder that she was prejudiced against my chosen profession.

Of course, newspapers were also full of negative stories about cops. Scandal sold papers. That didn't mean all cops were crooked.

When I was done, I went upstairs to the office. Might as well type some pages.

After a few minutes, Aunt Irene, in a cloud of silk and fringe, fluttered in. She enveloped me in a gardenia-scented hug and then held me at arm's length. "Well! You've done it. What a sensation. My own niece, a policewoman. Sugar bun, I'm bursting with pride." She winked. "Or is that Officer Sugar Bun."

"I wanted to be the one to tell you."

"Walter couldn't help himself. I knew something was up the moment he met me at the door. Once I started questioning him, it was only a matter of seconds before I squeezed it out of him."

"Maybe you should be the detective."

Her response gratified me. I preened in her admiration for a few minutes—my second-place exam finish might just have happened to come up in the conversation—and then attempted to strike a more humble note.

"Of course I'll be a probationer for three months." That reminded me of Captain Smith's warning. "And I'm afraid I have to disappoint you."

The folds of her face flattened. "Why?"

"First, I won't be able to type for you. I'm going to be working the night shift, at least at first, so mornings might be a problem."

"Oh, don't worry about that. I'll just hire someone else."

She didn't seem at all unhappy at that prospect, either. I thought of a few of my more egregious typing errors. Small wonder.

"Also," I said, "I'll need to tell Mr. McChesney I can't continue to look into Guy's death."

My aunt blinked at me in surprise. "You've found out who caused the fire?"

"No. That is, I'm not certain." I frowned. "Not certain at all, in fact."

I gave her a rundown of all that had happened with Myrna, and my suspicions about Hugh.

"Then I don't see how you can just give up the case," she said.

"I can't run with the hare and hunt with the hounds. Being a policewoman and pursuing my own investigation wouldn't be right. The police are looking into Guy's death, and my doing so on my own makes it seem as if I have no confidence in their efforts."

"Well, do you?" Aunt Irene asked.

A light knock and a hitched throat turned our attention to the doorway, where Walter stood looking more butlery and somber than usual. "Detective Muldoon is downstairs," he said.

My glance met Aunt Irene's. For a moment it seemed almost as if by talking about my investigation we'd conjured him up.

My aunt recovered herself faster than I. "Well, show him up. What's the matter with you, Walter? Frank Muldoon is a friend here."

Walter didn't move. "I believe he's come in the capacity of a policeman. He asked to see Miss Louise. He seems very serious."

"Then we'll just have to try to cheer him up."

"Yes, ma'am."

That *ma'am* more than anything made Aunt Irene and I look at each other in bewilderment when Walter left. His formality shook us.

"When *isn't* Detective Muldoon serious?" I said.

She flapped a handkerchief, fanning herself. "Perhaps he wants to have a little tête-à-tête with you. I thought you two seemed chummy last night."

"Not at all," I said.

"Nevertheless, I'll leave you alone." She took a step toward the door.

"No, please." I grabbed the fringe of her sleeve. "Stay."

Why did worry suddenly grip me? Walter's manner had made it seem as if Muldoon had come to arrest me. Also, being faced with Muldoon so soon after I'd learned about the letter he'd written on my behalf caused my stomach to twist up. I'd known I was going to have to thank him, but all at once being beholden to him felt awkward.

When Walter ushered him through the door, Muldoon looked as anxious as I felt. He still wore his overcoat and had held on to his hat, as if he anticipated making a speedy exit.

Aunt Irene sailed forth to greet him. "How good of you to stop by, Detective. I was just telling Louise that I needed to see to something downstairs. I'll have Bernice send up some tea. Or would you rather have coffee?"

The more effusive she was, the deeper the lines to the side of his mouth became. They were like dimples of doom. "Thanks, but I can't stop long. Maybe I shouldn't even be here, but I was close and thought someone from Van Hooten and McChesney should know before news about Ogden McChesney becomes public."

Aunt Irene tottered. Her hand reached to the lace at the top of her neckline. "Ogden? Is he"—she gulped—"dead?"

Muldoon shook his head. "No, ma'am. We've arrested him for arson and are also holding him for the murder of Guy Van Hooten."

He waited for our response. None came. I'd drawn even with my aunt, and now I hooked my arm through hers. We stood holding each other up, both dumbfounded.

He continued. "We suspected him initially, of course, because there was a fire insurance policy. And then the witness of that morning identified Mr. McChesney as the man she'd seen."

"Is *this* the new angle you were telling me about last night?" I asked.

Aunt Irene pivoted toward me. "You never said the police suspected Ogden."

"I didn't know," I said. "He told me the police were investigating a new angle. I had no idea they were going to take a flying leap into the absurd."

"The witness placed McChesney at the scene," Muldoon said, "moving furtively, dressed in a coat and scarf found at his house."

My face heated. I had seen that scarf. I'd dismissed it because I just couldn't imagine Ogden McChesney doing such a thing. I still couldn't. It was unthinkable. "Your so-called witness is a cranky old lady who believes everyone looks suspicious. And no wonder. Half the men in Manhattan have plaid scarves and brown coats."

Muldoon held up a hand. "Before you say anything more, I should tell you that Ogden McChesney has confessed."

The pressure on my arm increased as Aunt Irene swayed toward me. "How could he confess?" Her voice was faint. "Why would he have burned down his own building?"

"The most common motive in the world," Muldoon said. "Money."

There had to be some mistake. "He's covering up for someone," I said.

Muldoon shook his head. "I'm afraid not. With Guy's death, Ogden McChesney became the sole beneficiary of the fire insurance policy covering Van Hooten and McChesney. This was laid out very clearly in the policy—in the event of one partner's death, the policy was paid out to the surviving partner. When we interviewed him at his home, McChesney admitted he had everything to gain by burning down the building. He seemed relieved to confess."

"Did he confess to killing Guy, too?" That I would never believe.

A shadow slanted across Muldoon's face. "No, but that's not surprising. Murder's a much more serious charge than arson."

Murder could be a death sentence. The electric chair. I felt sick.

"Where is Ogden now?" my aunt asked.

"He was taken downtown for questioning." He fidgeted with his hat. "I won't lie to you. With that confession, he will be booked on a charge of murder."

Aunt Irene was striding toward the door. "I've got to telephone Abe Faber." Her lawyer. She turned before leaving the room, aiming a withering scowl at Muldoon. "I thought you were cleverer than this, Detective. Ogden McChesney might be many things—an old fool, first and foremost—but he is most definitely not a murderer."

I wanted to applaud her steadfastness. And yet . . . the memory of my most recent encounters with Mr. McChesney scratched at the back of my mind. His moodiness, his disheveled appearance, the hypochondria. Barricading himself in his room after Guy's funeral. In retrospect, he'd acted like a guilty man. My heart all but acquitted him, but my brain was struggling harder to dismiss the charges.

"I'm sorry about this, Louise," Muldoon said when we were alone.

"If you'd only mentioned Mr. McChesney's name to me last night, I could have told you how muddle-headed your thinking was," I said.

"We have his confession."

And by what means had they squeezed it out of him? Bernice's jaundiced view of the force leapt to my mind, and squared up with a few of my own observations from watching them operate last summer. They had brutalized my upstairs neighbor, and they also probably would have kept Otto behind bars until he confessed if not for my aunt's intervention in sending Abe Faber to free him. I wasn't blind to all that. Policemen weren't angels.

Yet Mr. McChesney had been acting guilty.

But guilty of murder? No.

"Mr. McChesney has been paying me to look into the arson," I said. "Why would he do that if he'd set the fire himself?"

"Maybe he didn't think much of your investigative skill."

I reddened, both at his tactlessness and the memory of something Mr. McChesney had said when my aunt was convincing him to hire me. *Louise isn't a real detective, is she?* No, he probably hadn't thought I would be successful. And Muldoon didn't have much more faith in me. It was maddening. "Last summer—"

He help up his hands, palms forward. "I know, I know. Last summer you were the incredible sleuth."

If only I were half a foot taller so I could look down my nose at him. "Watch your sarcasm, Detective. You might be surprised to hear that we'll soon be working for the same organization."

"I knew that already. That's why I came here last night. I expected you would have already received the news. When I figured out that you hadn't, it sort of threw me."

"So you came last night to congratulate me."

"Yes, congratulations." The word carried all the cheer of a man swallowing a toad.

My thank-you was likewise subdued. My elation had evaporated. "Smith told me you had written a letter in support of my application."

"Don't thank me for that. You might even be sorry I wrote it someday."

"People can look back and be sorry about all sorts of things," I said. "But applying to join the police was my choice, and you helped me, and I'm grateful."

His gaze was almost mournful. "You've made some peculiar choices, Louise. Some force is driving you that I can't understand. I worry that what happened last summer set off something inside you."

"No, it was before that," I said, forgetting myself. What was I doing? I fumbled for a way to derail my confession. I had never told Muldoon I'd been raped. Or that I'd given the baby away. I couldn't imagine that I ever would.

"I've always been a crusader," I said.

"Then you'll meet nothing but frustration as a policewoman. The job isn't what you think. Justice doesn't always win. I've got murders I've never solved, and each one haunts me. The sadness clings to you. If you want to be a crusader, go work with orphans, or lend your energy to some civic cause. It's not too late for you to change your mind."

"Why did you write the letter at all? You obviously don't believe women belong on the force."

"There's a place for some women in the force," he allowed.

"But not me." Anger stirred in me again. "You think that I'll get bored or disgusted after a few weeks and decide to go back to secretarial work. Well, you'll either be disappointed or astonished. I'm going to make a success of this."

"That won't astonish me in the least," he said.

The man was maddening. "First you write a letter recommending me, clearly against your better judgment. Then you tell me I'll regret ever applying to be a policewoman. And now you're saying that you won't be surprised if I'm successful in the job. I don't understand you."

"I think you'll be grand at whatever you set your mind to," he said. "That's why I wrote the letter."

"Then you admit I have some sense. That last summer wasn't just a lucky guess."

"Of course."

I drew closer to him. "Then listen to me now. I don't know why Mr. McChesney confessed, I only know he didn't do it. Perhaps he set the fire, but he certainly didn't murder Guy. There has to be some mistake. It's Hugh Van Hooten you need to look at."

"Why? What would he stand to gain by murdering his brother?"

Did it necessarily have to be about gain? "They were brothers, and they weren't close. Haven't you ever heard of Cain and Abel?"

"I didn't detect hatred in Hugh's tone when he spoke about Guy."

"He must have been laying it on thick for you, then. He had only contempt for Guy."

"Contempt, sure." Muldoon gave his chin a contemplative scratch, as if he thought contempt was just a normal reaction to Guy Van Hooten.

"And as it happens, Hugh *did* have a motive for killing Guy."

And out it all came. I told him about Myrna, and the baby, and Jacob's visit to the air park. I laid out the overheard conversations, and Guy's puzzling *Would you kill our mother?* I even revealed my unscientific sampling of households with rat poison.

The telling took a while. Muldoon let me go on until I finally ran down like a windup toy in need of a few sharp key turns.

"And that's not even mentioning the three thousand dollars Leonard Cain said he gave Guy that night," I added at the end. "Where did all that money go?"

"Up in smoke."

"And Guy just happened to be killed after receiving such a large sum?"

"We aren't sure of the exact time of his death. He might have done anything after Cain paid him. Maybe he lived long enough to post the money to the Cohens."

"I wouldn't live in a tenement if I had three thousand dollars, would you?"

He looked contemplative, but then shook his head. "It doesn't matter about the money. Or the baby. Or the rat poison. We have a confession given freely and willingly."

I was still skeptical of that confession. And why was Muldoon so quick to convict Mr. McChesney of Guy's murder? "Won't you even look into Hugh?"

"The taxpayers don't thank us for poking into the lives of citizens when we already have a suspect who's confessed in custody."

"That confession can't be real."

"I know, I know. You don't believe McChesney's confession, but you've got a head full of bees when it comes to everyone else. Theories buzzing like crazy."

I crossed my arms and said nothing. I could argue the point till I was hoarse, I realized, and it wouldn't change the fact that Mr. McChesney was behind bars. For the moment.

My silence put Muldoon off balance.

"I'm sorry to be the bearer of bad news." He fiddled with his hat again. "You do realize I came here as a friend?"

I nodded, barely. I wasn't feeling very friendly toward him at the moment, even if he had written that letter.

Discouragement tugged at his mouth. "We always seem to get off on the wrong foot."

"Because you keep arresting my friends."

"I should go." He didn't move, though. "I expect we'll be seeing each other again soon."

"I expect we will."

He looked as if he wanted to say more, but gave up. "I'll show myself out."

When he was gone, I collapsed onto Aunt Irene's reading chaise and frowned at the glass-fronted bookcases. How were we going to get Mr. McChesney out of this tangle?

Or was he—horrible thought—guilty?

Aunt Irene bustled back into the room. "Get up, chicken. You're going downtown."

"Did you get a hold of Mr. Faber?" I asked.

"Yes, Abe's on his way to try to extract Ogden from the grips of the law. And now you need to pop your hat on and grab a pad and pencil. You're going to be Abe's assistant today. He'll be waiting for you."

"What does Mr. Faber say to that?"

"I can't give you a direct quote, but I recognize cursing even when it's in Hebrew."

I was eager to go, although I wasn't sure I was the right person for this particular job. "Wouldn't you rather go see Mr. McChesney yourself?"

She waved me toward the door. "I would just become an emotional mess and fly apart. Probably say something in the drama of the moment that I'd regret." She took out her handkerchief and blew her nose. I worried she'd fly apart right before my eyes, but in the next moment she straightened and aimed her most commanding gaze at me. "I'm trusting you to prove this is all balderdash, Louise."

A shot of panic froze me. Not that I believed Mr. McChesney was capable of cold-blooded murder. But his behavior had been suspicious. And he had admitted to setting the fire. The fire he'd said he would pay me to look into . . .

Aunt Irene's eyes narrowed at my hesitation. "He's innocent of that murder," she repeated. "You knew it the moment that Mr. Muldoon told us." Her expression soured. "Detective." She looked as if she wanted to spit. "He doesn't deserve the title. And to think how I welcomed him in my home and thought him so fascinating. You'll be a much better detective than that sorry excuse for an investigator."

"I won't be a police detective, you know. Not for a long while." *Maybe never.*

"Nonsense. The captains or whoever's in charge at those precincts will see your worth. You'll prove it by freeing Ogden."

My aunt wasn't just expressing her confidence that I would succeed, I realized. She was commanding me to succeed.

Chapter 12

Jefferson Market Courthouse, where Mr. Faber had instructed me to meet him, wasn't far from my flat. I'd even been inside it once before. As the El rushed toward that fantastical Gothic clock tower, I tried to imagine poor Mr. McChesney among the criminals housed there awaiting trial or sentencing. It didn't seem possible. And what if I failed to find proof of his innocence and he ended up being sent to the penitentiary forever with the most hardened men? It would be the end of him. That would break Aunt Irene's heart.

Mr. Faber, who had helped get Otto released from police custody last summer, met me at the building's entrance. "I really don't see the necessity of your coming, Miss Faulk." He stood a few inches taller than my five foot five, and was dressed impeccably in a dark suit, black coat, and bowler hat. He carried a handled leather case, which he gave to me with a smile. "But I trust your aunt's instincts, and as you're here you may as well act the part."

I took the case from him, dipping a little against its weight. "What's in here?"

"The law is a weighty matter," he joked without smiling.

Inside, we were ricocheted between a series of clerks and officers who asked us the same questions. Names. Who were we here to see. Purpose of visit. Without fail, my presence with Faber drew extra scrutiny. I might have been the first female legal assistant anyone had ever seen in New York City, which made me stand up a little taller. I took my trailblazing seriously, even if it was bogus.

Finally, we were led into a private room, bare but for several hard chairs and a wood table whose surface was a devarnished network of scratches. The walls stood blank except for a framed reproduction of a painting of grim, long-nosed Peter Stuyvesant on one wall and a photograph of William Howard Taft hanging crookedly on another. Wilson had been elected a year ago, but evidently the gears of government turned slowly even when it came to picture replacement.

At last, the door opened and Mr. McChesney was escorted in by not one but two guards. He wore a brown suit, wrinkled, but it was his own. I don't know why I took any comfort from that detail when his thin wrists were manacled. I knew the reason for the handcuffs, of course. My upstairs neighbor, Max, had escaped from custody from this place last summer and hadn't been seen since.

Abe Faber and I stood. At the sight of me, Mr. McChesney seemed shocked, and not pleasantly. "Louise! What was your aunt thinking, allowing you to come to this place?"

"I'm here as Mr. Faber's assistant," I said.

The lawyer turned to the guard closest to Mr. McChesney. "Surely I may speak to my client without handcuffs."

The guards exchanged glances and then looked at Mr. McChesney, obviously sizing up their elderly suspect as harmless.

The handcuffs were unlocked, and the two guards withdrew to the hallway. When the door closed behind them, Mr. Faber gestured to the table. "Let's sit down and talk this through."

He spoke as if he were addressing a wayward child, not a man who stood accused of murder. Yet his gentle tone had a calming effect on Mr. McChesney, who seated himself across from us.

"There's really nothing to say," he said. "I've already explained everything to the detectives."

Mr. Faber's lips flattened into a grim line. "Well, *I* have plenty to say, and the first and most important thing is that you should talk as little as possible to the police."

"What am I to do if they ask me questions? I have nothing to hide." He hung his head. "Not anymore."

"From what I've heard, you've already given them enough information to send you to the electric chair."

"I deserve no better. Believe me, no threat of punishment could torment me more than what I've already been through."

His words made that knot in my insides tighten. I knew he'd confessed, but his verifying that confession chipped a crack in my heart. I reached out my hand to his. "Then you did start the fire?"

He looked surprised that I would ask. "Didn't the police tell you?"

"Detective Muldoon said you'd confessed, but Aunt Irene and I hoped that there was some circumstance . . . that you were covering for someone, perhaps."

He cast his eyes at the table, where someone had scratched a tic-tac-toe. "Poor Irene. I've let her down."

I pitied him, but I couldn't help feeling incensed, too. "You lied to me. You hired me to look into the fire that you had set. And then you suggested that Leonard Cain might have been the culprit."

"I know. I was in shock. I didn't want to believe I was responsible for poor Guy's horrible death. And Cain is a bad man, isn't he? Cravenly, I thought that if he took the blame, I might wriggle free. I can't tell you how sorry I am, Louise. Grievously sorry."

Mr. Faber cleared his throat. "Before we tread the path of sorrow, let's get the facts straight. You set the fire that resulted in your building burning down, just as you told the police?"

Mr. McChesney held his hands together on the table in front of him, almost as if they were still cuffed. "I did."

"And the woman who identified you as the suspicious character on the street before the fire—she was correct? She saw you?"

"I suppose so, though I didn't notice her. But I was wearing my old brown coat and a plaid scarf, as she said."

"And you burned down the building so you could claim the money from the fire insurance policy of which you were the sole beneficiary once Guy Van Hooten was no longer alive?"

"Yes, but I didn't know I'd be the sole beneficiary. That is, I must have known when Cyrus took out the policy that only the surviving partner would benefit, but I'd forgotten about that clause. Because Guy was so young! Who knew he would die? I just wanted to get out from under the business, which was sinking." He turned to me. "You've spoken to Bob. Didn't he tell you how the land lay, money-wise?"

"He said the business was barely scraping by," I told Faber. "But, Mr. McChesney, this doesn't help you."

"I don't want to be helped!" he burst out. "I acted selfishly. My doctor told me I needed a better climate and less stress. For months I've sat up nights dreaming of California. Sunshine and warmth, and no Van Hooten and McChesney to fret me twenty-four hours a day. I asked Guy to buy me out, but of course he laughed at that."

Faber held up a hand. "There—that's just the type of thing you shouldn't say to the police."

"But I already have," Mr. McChesney said. "And why not? I didn't kill Guy—I didn't mean to, at any rate. I never liked the boy, but I never wished him ill, much less dead." His gaze, growing frantic, sought out mine. "You believe that, don't you?"

"Of course. But what do you mean, you 'didn't mean to kill Guy'?"

"Just this: I never dreamed he was in that building . . . never. His office wasn't open. I didn't even check inside. I just assumed, given the early hour and the fact that the place was so silent . . . No one would have dreamed that Guy, of all people, would be there. Would they, Louise?"

"Everyone was surprised, but—"

He interrupted, practically frantic now. "I could barely make my legs support me that morning when I came back to Thirty-eighth Street. And then when we went to see Edith . . ." He buried his head in his hands, guilt consuming him. "Facing her was the hardest of all."

" 'I never dreamed,' you said," I reminded him. "You repeated it several times that morning. You didn't think he'd be there. That was what you meant, wasn't it?"

His head bobbed. "If only I'd checked that blasted door! Why didn't I?"

Mr. Faber's eyes narrowed on me. "Your memory of those words—'I never dreamed,' etc.—could prove useful. You'd swear to that in court?"

"I won't need to. This is—"

"I don't want Louise testifying," Mr. McChesney broke in. "I don't want a trial at all. If only I could forget it all—but I can't. Every moment of that morning after I started the damn fire was a horror. Like a horrible dream, and I couldn't wake up. I'm still living that nightmare, night and day. It's no more than I deserve. Whether I intended to or not, I killed Guy."

"No, you didn't," I said.

"If you didn't know he was there, you didn't kill him," Mr. Faber said. "So stop even thinking you did. We need to prove that Guy Van Hooten was asleep, or drunk, at the time. It was an accident—the death, if not the fire."

"Wait." I was astonished. "Detective Muldoon, one of the detectives on the case, told me that Guy was poisoned." Aunt Irene hadn't told him? Worse, the police obviously hadn't divulged this information to either Mr. McChesney or Abe Faber. "There's evidence Guy was dead before the fire started."

Faber dropped his pencil.

"Poisoned?" Mr. McChesney repeated. "Who would have wanted to poison Guy?"

Who wouldn't? I almost said aloud, but now was not the time for levity. I couldn't help remembering Muldoon asking me not to tell about the poison. Had the police intended to keep it secret from everyone unless they needed to divulge the information for a conviction?

"Poor Guy." Mr. McChesney shook his head. "If the police think the fire didn't kill him, why charge me? I had no reason to poison him."

"You just told us the man wouldn't buy you out of the business you were eager to sell," Faber reminded him.

Mr. McChesney sagged in his chair. "But I know nothing of poisons."

Faber looked at me. "Did the detective mention the specific poison involved?"

"Cyanide. It's in rat poison."

The attorney made a note. "Very common."

Mr. McChesney thought about that. "The building had mice once, years ago. We might have used poison then."

"*Do not* volunteer that information to the police," Faber said to him. "If they want to connect that particular poison to Van Hooten and McChesney, make them dig for it." He swiveled toward me. "What else do you know that the police might not have mentioned?"

I laid out all I'd learned. Mr. Faber seemed especially worried about the three thousand dollars, which suggested a money motive. Mr. McChesney swore he knew nothing about the money.

I added, "And the police certainly haven't found it in Mr. McChesney's home or bank account, or they would have mentioned it." It would have been damning evidence.

Abe Faber put his pencil down. "You're a dark horse, Miss Faulk. Perhaps my law office *could* use you."

"I'm bespoke," I said. "As far as my career's concerned."

"Pity." Faber sighed before turning back to his client. "We need to make the case that you meant no bodily harm to anyone."

But my old boss, worrying a nail, was in no mood to exonerate himself. "I burned down a building. The fireman I spoke to at the scene said the fire could easily have spread to surrounding buildings if their ladder company hadn't arrive in time. I might have killed dozens."

"You didn't kill anyone," Faber reminded him. "And the firemen did arrive in time."

"But I didn't know they would," Mr. McChesney insisted, growing more morose. "I won't make excuses. I'm guilty. If only I could convince myself I weren't!"

He buried his head in his hands again. The sound of his sob shivered through me. Seeing someone I'd known as nothing less than kind and benevolent suffering such torrents of guilt shook me. Even if Faber managed to save him from the electric chair, what then? Ogden McChesney had dug himself into a trench of guilt. Now, even when presented with evidence that he wasn't a murderer, he couldn't believe his own innocence.

A short time later, we left him in custody, cuffed again and shuffling off to God only knew what kind of cell, bowed with depression. Mr. Faber and I walked out of the building into the dying daylight. Even the New York air tasted fresh after being in the jail. It contained the essential element of freedom.

A train clacked by overhead on Sixth Avenue. When it had passed and the noise receded, I said, "It's hopeless, isn't it?"

Faber drew back. "Hopeless? Never! I'm surprised at you, Miss Faulk. I thought you had pluck."

I waved toward the courthouse. "But he will go to jail for arson."

"Oh yes. Up to five years, I expect. It's a shame, but that confession will be difficult, if not impossible, to overcome."

"But he doesn't want to overcome it. That's what frightens me. He feels guilty even for Guy's murder, which he didn't commit. But he isn't the type of man who will be able to shrug off the guilt he's been carrying. He's a broken soul."

"Ah! I see now why you're distressed." He leaned toward me. "You're new to this world, Miss Faulk. Believe me, I've dealt with all sorts. Men suicidal with guilt and grief. Men who have killed their wives, who swindled their friends, who, in short, have committed the worst felonies and indecencies. They all have one thing in common."

"What?"

"Resilience. Whatever their sentence, and however just or unjust they consider it, all jailbirds start to look at the blue sky beyond the prison bars. The guiltiest dream of parole, that second chance. Even the confessed murderer on death row hopes for pardon. Believe me, at some point, Ogden McChesney's thoughts will wend once again toward California. And perhaps when he's freed he'll have a few years left of his life to go there. It's my job to make sure that the state's electric chair doesn't cut off his chances to make that transcontinental journey."

I wanted to believe what he said, but I remained doubtful. I'd never seen a man so distraught.

"You'll still help him?" Mr. Faber asked me.

I thought of Aunt Irene, and how grieved she would be if the situation were hopeless. For her sake, I needed to adopt a little of Mr. Faber's cynical optimism. "Of course," I said.

But even as I accepted Mr. Faber's answering smile, I writhed a little at my duplicity. I'd said I wouldn't run with the hare and hunt with the hounds. Yet here I was, almost a policewoman, vowing to aid the criminal defense.

Finding out who killed Guy wasn't all that I needed to accomplish in the week before I started my new job. Aunt Irene's book wasn't finished yet, and I didn't want to leave her without any help. Friday afternoon, I hit upon an idea for killing two birds with one stone. I ran the idea past Aunt Irene and she agreed with me, so on Saturday morning I got up, dressed, and went to see Jackson Beasley.

Miriam didn't answer the door this time. Jackson did. He held a newspaper in his hand, opened to an article about Ogden McChesney, publisher, being held in custody for arson and the murder of his business partner. Every paper I'd seen at corner stands or in the hands of newsboys had at least one article about Mr. McChesney. The headlines were full of fire puns—PUBLISHER SCORCHES PARTNER, that sort of thing—but I didn't get a close look at what particular rag Jackson had picked up.

He slapped the paper by way of greeting. "Did you know about this?"

I nodded.

"I couldn't believe my eyes." He beckoned me in, then closed the door. "That old hypochondriac—a murderer!"

"He's not, though."

He pointed to the newspaper. "It sounds as if the police are fairly certain. And to think I actually felt sorry for him at the funeral, when he looked so frail. The old faker."

"He's terribly remorseful about the fire—"

Jackson snorted. "I'm sure he is, now that he's been caught."

"But he swears he had nothing to do with Guy's death."

He shook his head and sank into his usual chair. He gestured for me to take one nearby. "What are you doing here? Shouldn't your little investigation be at an end?"

Letting the dig pass, I sat. "I came to see your wife. I have a proposition for her."

His brows rose at that. "Unfortunately, she's not here. She's at work—cleaning houses." That last was added bitterly, as if he found his wife's doing menial labor an affront to his dignity. "Latin doesn't pay bills."

"Can she type?" I asked.

He frowned. "Yes, very ably."

"Good. My aunt is in need of a typist. I was doing it for her, but I have a new job."

"Bully for you. Another publisher?"

"The New York Police Department. I'm going to be a policewoman."

His astonishment was almost comical. "A policewoman? You?"

"Why not?"

He couldn't come up with an answer. "Well, well. I suppose I should congratulate you. And now Miriam will have a chance to start something new, as well. I wish it were that easy for me. Guy was my connection in this city, even if he treated me more like a lackey than an equal most of the time." He sighed. "And now even that small connection's been cut, thanks to McChesney's infernal greed. Murdering a man for money!"

"But he didn't."

"Oh, I know. You were a pet of his and can't bring yourself to believe it."

"Yes, there was fire insurance money . . . but if all he'd wanted was money he would have taken the three thousand dollars and not set fire to the building at all." I was thinking as I spoke, turning the scenario over in my mind.

"Three thousand dollars?" Jackson blinked at me. "What three thousand dollars?"

"That's the amount Leonard Cain paid to Guy when he visited the office that last night. The police haven't found it in Mr. McChesney's accounts, or in their search of his house."

"Three thousand dollars," Jackson repeated. "Guy had *three thousand dollars* when he died?"

"If Leonard Cain can be believed. Granted, that's a big if."

"Guy borrowed five dollars from me the week he died." He sputtered at the perceived effrontery. "I gave it to him. I thought he was broke."

"He was short of funds—at least until Cain paid him the money."

"You mean the money was right there in the office?" Jackson asked, still trying to believe it.

I nodded. "Mr. McChesney says he didn't know about the money. The police assume it burned in the fire. Maybe it did."

Jackson bleated out a laugh. "Expensive kindling."

I couldn't think of anything more to say on the subject. I stood. "When Miriam comes back, will you have her call my aunt? If she's interested in the job, that is. I'm sure my aunt will pay her generously, and she can start as soon as she wants."

"Certainly."

"You still have my aunt's number?"

"Somewhere," he said, absently.

From my satchel, I retrieved a pen and paper and wrote the number down again. I handed it to him.

Jackson insisted on seeing me out. "Do you think Guy hid the money after Cain gave it to him?" he asked as we went down the stairs.

"Impossible to say. The police don't know what time that night he was killed. So perhaps he had time to stow the money somewhere. He might have repaid a debt to someone, or even given it away. We might never know."

"Three thousand dollars."

I sympathized with his fixation on the money. To a struggling man, the idea of three thousand dollars slipping out of the world, benefitting no one, was unbearable. Cruel, almost. Like a beggar watching a restaurant throw uneaten meals into a rubbish bin.

As he opened the front door to let me out on the stoop, a man's angry shout drew our attention.

"Beasley!"

Jackson released a groan of dread.

Brandishing a newspaper, Ford Fitzsimmons steamed toward us full-tilt. "You rotten bastards!"

Jackson and I both recoiled. I hadn't expected to be sworn at in the street, even by a man who'd tried to kill me. Jackson, equally offended, made a weak protest that was soon overwhelmed by a spew of righteous anger.

"That fire was set on purpose," Ford said, as if we were responsible for it. "And who's going to pay? Who?"

"Get yourself under control, old fellow," Jackson replied.

His drawl just seemed to aggravate Ford's indignation. "Oh, yes—by all means, let's be gentlemen. It's a gentleman's world, isn't it? Handshakes and cigars—'and isn't it just too, too unfortunate that we've lost your life's work, Mr. Fitzsimmons. It showed *such* promise. What a shame.' You're all alike! No one cares about the writer, the artist."

From this tirade, I deduced that Jackson hadn't been able to lay hands on Ford's manuscript in progress.

"*I* didn't set fire to your manuscript," Jackson said.

"But your boss did. *Deliberately*. Same as if he'd taken my manuscript from my hands and put a match to it."

"He didn't burn down a building as a personal affront to you," Jackson said. "You're no worse off than you were. It's unfortunate that this happened, but think of it this way—you were given an advance for a book that was never published."

Ford cackled, almost maniacal. "Wonderful! I was paid two hundred dollars so you could destroy my book. Which I now have to try to create all over again—an impossible task. That's not what I had in mind when I signed the contract."

"It's not what any of us had in mind," Jackson assured him.

"I should sue!"

"Sue whom?" I asked. "Or what? Van Hooten and McChesney no longer exists."

Ford turned his disgusted gaze at me for the first time. "McChesney's a friend of yours, isn't he? Or a friend of that old bag aunt of yours. Well, let me tell you, I'll be at his trial and I'll whoop with glee when they send him to death row. Guy was an idiot, but by God, he never would have destroyed me the way that old man has."

I scowled at him. "Whooping with glee won't bring your manuscript back."

"No, but it will feel like justice."

"A man's life for a book," I said.

"That's right. And until I have that satisfaction, I intend to file suit against everyone in this town with the name McChesney or Van Hooten."

He stalked off in an undiminished blaze of fury.

Jackson shook his head. "He'd never believe it, but I'm sorry for him." He sighed. "It was a pretty good book, too."

A pretty good book. By a perfectly detestable man.

My next errand took me back to Myrna Cohen's. She opened the door a crack, saw me standing in the dark hallway, and immediately tried to push it closed again. I held it open with my palm. "I just want to speak to you."

"I'm done talking about Guy."

It was Hugh I was more curious about now, though. "This is a professional visit," I said. "I need something made."

She looked me over, trying to judge whether she could trust my word. Reluctance written all over her face, she stepped back. "A dress?"

"A policewoman's uniform."

Her expression became wary. "You said you were a secretary."

"I was. I've just been hired by the NYPD and I need a uniform. Could you make one? I have a picture." A very crude picture, sketched from the policewomen I'd seen downtown. I dug it out of my satchel and handed it to her.

Her brow crinkled as she studied the paper. The uniforms I'd seen were simple affairs: blue shirtwaists with brass buttons down the front and long sleeves ever so slightly puffed at the shoulders; a high white collar clasped at the neck. The blue skirt was cut in a simple A-line down to the ankle.

"Could you copy that?" I asked.

"You don't say what materials you want."

"It has to be dark blue."

"Blue is a color, not a fabric."

I remembered the navy blue dress Myrna had been wearing the last time I was here and told her I'd admired it. "Some fabric like that would be perfect, wouldn't it? And brass buttons. Nothing too outlandish."

She still looked doubtful.

"I need it within a week."

"I'm very busy."

I fished some money from my purse. Ten dollars. More than I'd paid for the last dress I'd bought, the one Myrna had said made me look like a mattress. When she hesitated, I added another two dollars. After all, I was asking her to procure the material. Not that she would have to go far. There were several fabric sellers on the street.

She snatched the money from my hands. "All right. You'll have it."

While Myrna took my measurements, I looked down at the baby lying in his crib, staring at the ceiling with those Edith Van Hooten eyes. The last time I'd seen Calvin Longworth, my son, he'd been about Noah's age—a little older, perhaps. But that had been months ago. I craved seeing him again, and touching his little booted foot as I touched Noah's now. But even as my heart hitched at the kick and the gummy smile the tickle earned, I wondered if seeing my own son would be worth the ache it would leave me with.

Myrna, almost smiling, watched me play with the baby.

I took a chance on bringing up the Van Hootens. "Did you ever know Hugh?"

Her mouth tightened. "Guy talked about his brother, but never fondly. He called him an old stick, or a lunatic."

The words were contradictory, but I'd seen at least two sides to Hugh's character myself. He'd seemed almost kind at first, then impossibly arrogant. "So you gathered there was some friction between the brothers."

"There was no love lost." She looped a tape measure around my waist. "Guy tried to avoid Hugh. Said Hugh was a show-off and always had been."

"How did he show off?"

"He made the best grades, won an award at his school. . . ."

Achievements, in other words. That *would* nettle Guy, a man who'd never put effort into anything.

"Hugh must have resented Guy for having inherited his father's business," I said.

"Who would've envied anyone that place?" She frowned at me. "Raise your arms."

As she measured my bust, I tried again. "Edith Van Hooten favored Guy. That must have annoyed Hugh."

"It annoyed Guy, too. He didn't ask to be the golden boy of the family."

She kept giving me motives for Guy to have killed Hugh, not the other way around.

"Did Hugh know about you before your brother went to see him?"

Myrna put the tape measure around my neck and scribbled down the number on a sheet of paper. "You ask a lot of questions. I told you, I don't want to think about that family."

"An innocent man has been charged with Guy's murder."

"What's that got to do with me? I don't know who killed Guy, or why, and I don't care." Her voice became strained. "Do you hear me? I don't care. A smart person stays out of business that the police are poking into."

That probably wasn't a bad credo, but it made me wonder.

She stepped back. "Why are you looking at me that way?" Her hands lifted to her lips. "My God, do you think *I* committed the murder? The father of my child?"

"No," I said. "I don't think you did it. And I'm not with the police yet. I only came here because Mr. McChesney is going to be tried for Guy's murder and I believe he's innocent."

"Yes, so you're looking to have them arrest someone else. Someone like me."

"But if you didn't do it, you have nothing to worry about."

She laughed. "Listen to yourself. You just told me that Mr. McChesney was innocent. Innocent people end up convicted for crimes they didn't commit. Especially poor people like me, who no one cares about." She pulled the twelve dollars out of her pocket and handed it to me. "I don't want your money. I don't want to be involved."

I didn't take it. "I'm not trying to connect you to the murder. I only wanted to know who else might have had a motive."

"I'm not going to point the finger at Hugh Van Hooten or anyone else. I know nothing." Her arm remained outstretched.

"Keep it," I said. "I still need the uniform, and you need the money. For Noah."

Her gaze strayed to the crib. Finally, she dropped her arm. "All right. I'll have your uniform by Friday."

Quick as she could, she showed me the door.

CHAPTER 13

On Sunday morning I was bounced awake.

"Get up, Louise! We're going to New Jersey."

At first I thought I must be dreaming. Callie was perched on my mattress, dressed in the strangest getup. It consisted of a white knit hat, a plum-colored scarf, and snow-white coveralls that tapered down to her ankles, where they gathered just below the tops of black leather lace-up ankle boots. A pair of goggles was strapped across her head at the hairline.

My head, muzzy from sleep, couldn't make sense of what I was seeing. "You're in Philadelphia," I argued at my hallucination.

She laughed. "No show on Sundays. I don't have to go back till tomorrow afternoon." She hugged her arms around her knees, deliriously happy. "Guess what? I got a line in the show. It's a pip. Gets a laugh every night before the second act curtain."

"That's terrific." I struggled up to sitting, propping pillows behind me. "So the show's going over well?"

"Well, our leading lady still can't sing, and the leading man can't remember his lines. Other than that . . ." She slapped at my calf. "Get out of this bed. We're going to catch the train in an hour to the air park. Teddy's going to give me a flying lesson today. What do you think of my new togs?"

She hopped off the bed and did a turn, arms outstretched, so I could admire her outfit. I'd never seen her in pants before, but I had to admit she wore them well. Her figure would have made a potato sack alluring. "Are you going to wear those on the train? We might be arrested."

"No, I'll change into this when I get there. Teddy swears the washroom at the aerodrome isn't too primitive."

"And Hugh will be there?"

"Of course. It's a glorious day—Indian summer. Teddy says it might be the last best flying day of the year." A little of her delirium disappeared. "That is, I assume you still want to talk to Hugh Van Hooten? I saw in the paper about Mr. McChesney's arrest. That must be awful for your aunt."

"He didn't do it," I said. "And yes, I do want to speak to Hugh."

"Do you think Hugh did it?" She wasn't smiling at all now. "That'd be awful. Teddy thinks Hugh hung the moon."

I didn't want to insult Teddy's judgment, so I shrugged noncommittally. "I think Hugh might tell me something more about what was going on in Guy's life. *If* I can get him to talk."

"If you can get him to talk about something besides airplanes, you mean."

A sharp knock sounded at the door. Callie turned, hands on hips. "Who's coming to see you on a Sunday morning?" Her eyes narrowed jokingly. "What've you been up to?"

I yawned and stretched. "Nonstop hedonism."

She laughed. "I leave town for one week . . ."

As she went to see who it was, I shrugged on my thick wool flannel robe. I wouldn't put it past Wally, if he'd heard Callie come in, to pay a morning call under some feeble pretext.

When I went out into the parlor, however, I found Otto and Callie standing face-to-face, gaping at each other. Not that either of them had much room to judge—although Callie's aviatrix clothes paled in comparison to Otto's bizarre outfit. He wore a light green tweed jacket and matching knickers, puffy at the knees. His vest was the same green plaid as the cap perched on his head. His calves were clad in argyle, his feet encased in brown-and-white spectator shoes so new they gave off a glare.

"I thought Halloween was already over," I joked.

Otto's new footwear let out a squeak as he turned to me. "There you are. I was hoping you'd come with me today."

"Is there a steamship leaving for the Scottish highlands?" I asked.

"Very funny. I'm going to Long Island to golf with Al Jolson."

I admit it. I was astonished. Sure, we'd had a drink with Jolson at the Omnium, but I never imagined he'd really reach out to Otto. "How did that come about?"

"Your success inspired me, Louise. After we opened that letter from the NYPD and discovered that your dream had come true, I said to myself, 'Darn it, Otto, why don't you show some of that kind of pluck?' So on Friday I went to the Winter Garden Theater, talked my way backstage, and played a song for Jolie."

"*Jolie*?" Callie was shaking her head, trying to keep up. "And what's this about a letter?" She looked at me, then gasped. "Did you hear back already?"

I nodded. "I start next week at the Thirtieth Street Station."

She rushed over, grabbed me, and spun me around. "For Pete's sake—when were you going to tell me?"

"I haven't had time."

"Thirtieth Street?" Otto frowned. "That's the Tenderloin. Is it safe?"

I laughed. "The police aren't needed in the nicest places."

"Someone must be patrolling Millionaires' Mile, making sure the Vanderbilts don't get robbed," he said. "Why can't you be one of those policemen?"

"Because I don't get to choose," I said. "I follow orders. With alacrity."

Callie spun on him. "Now what's this business about *Jolie*?"

He lifted his hands as if he was still trying to understand it himself. "I played Al a couple songs. He said there's a producer he wants to hear them who's got a place on Long Island with a private golf course where they go play on Sundays. So he asked me to come along."

Callie's glee at the prospect of her flying lesson faded. "A producer? Who?"

More squeaking as Otto bobbed on his heels. "Lee Shubert."

The color drained from her face. "You mean you're going to be hobnobbing with the biggest producer in New York and you came here to invite *Louise*? She doesn't know Lee Shubert from a lamppost."

"You were in Philadelphia," Otto said.

"I was, but I'm here now."

Worry seized me. I was losing her. "You aren't changing your mind, are you? Teddy promised you a flying lesson, remember? And it's my best chance to talk to Hugh."

"I know . . ." Callie dug her hands into her jumpsuit pockets. ". . . but Lee Shubert."

"You're already in a show," I reminded her.

"But what about next year?" She frowned. "Or next week. How long can a show run with a leading lady who sings like a cockatoo with a head cold?"

Desperation made me shameless. "Wouldn't Teddy be disappointed if you canceled today?"

The dilemma tormented her. "Life's so unfair. I spent eighteen years bored out of my mind on a farm, and now I have to choose between the Great White Way and soaring in the clouds." She looked up, then laughed at the expression on my face. "Oh, don't worry—I won't let you down. Though if it had just been Teddy . . ."

Otto sighed. "I guess it'll be just me and my golf club going to Long Island, then."

Callie and I swiveled toward him. "Golf *club*?"

I was no frequenter of fairways, but that didn't sound right.

"The man at the sports outfitter tried to sell me a whole bagful of clubs," Otto said, "but when I told him how much I could spend, he said I should just buy one. But it's a beaut."

"You've never played golf, have you?" Callie asked him.

A little of his confidence disappeared. "Not exactly."

"Not ever, you mean," I said.

"All right, never, if you want to nitpick," he said. "But the fellow who sold me my putter told me the game's a lead pipe cinch to learn." When Callie smiled, he said, "Easier than flying."

"At least you and your putter won't be hundreds of feet up in the air," I concurred.

My reminder of this chased all the regrets about Mr. Shubert from Callie's mind. "Up in the clouds. I can't wait!"

Even the prospect of being a spectator to Callie's first flying lesson made my skin go clammy. I took comfort in the fact that while she was aloft, I would be on solid ground, hopefully enticing Hugh Van Hooten to talk about the circumstances surrounding his brother's death.

The train ride was shorter than I'd expected, not far at all once we'd crossed the river. The most striking thing was how abruptly cityscape seemed to give way to a more rural setting, with picture-book small towns and fields between. Teddy met us at the Perth Amboy station in an open red Stutz touring car to drive us the rest of the way to the aerodrome.

It had been so long since I'd been out of the city, the miles of flat, tree-lined roads now seemed to me as exotic as arctic ice floes would have been, or the Alps. As we drove farther from the station, the houses started to appear lonelier, and water towers in the distance and the now-inescapable telephone poles were sometimes the only reminders of people.

The day was fine, a miraculously perfect Indian summer day. I perched on the backseat, head tilted back and squinting in the sun, and let my city-scarred lungs suck in clean country air with just a hint of salt. Birds wheeled overhead. Gulls. Though I couldn't see the ocean, we obviously hadn't traveled too far inland.

In front, Callie and Teddy were chattering away, and after we turned onto a narrower dirt road, they stopped the car and switched places. Five minutes of instruction later, the car lurched and chugged forward again.

"Isn't this exciting, Louise?" Callie called back to me over the sound of the engine. "I'm learning to drive, and in an hour or so I'll be learning to fly."

"Watch out!" Teddy warned.

Too late. The Stutz bounced across a rut in the road. Callie hooted as if we were on a ride at Coney Island. "At least in the air there won't be potholes."

"You can't fly today," Teddy said. "It's too soon."

Arguing ensued, until Teddy remembered there was another person in the car and turned back to me. "Besides, it would hurt

Louise's feelings to be left behind." He seemed surprised when I laughed.

"Anything over three stories gives Louise the vapors," Callie explained. "We ate on a roof garden last summer and she looked queasy the whole time."

He sent me a pitying look that he might have bestowed on a bedridden invalid. "How awful for you."

"I'm happily earthbound," I assured him. "I'll leave the skies to the birds and the—"

"Fools," Callie finished for me with a bright laugh. "You should try driving, then. Once you've learned, we can take the new Lincoln highway all the way to California. Wouldn't that be fun?"

"A Pullman berth would be more restful."

"Oh, trains are as old hat as covered wagons." She swerved to miss a darting hare; then when Teddy directed her to turn into a drive, she yanked the steering wheel so quickly that the car performed the maneuver on two wheels. Back on all fours, the Stutz sped toward an enormous building the size of four regular barns and came to a shuddering stop.

A sign over the cavernous door announced: VAN HOOTEN AERONAUTICS.

Teddy hopped out, running around the car to open doors for Callie and me. A couple of men in oil-stained coveralls came out to greet us. Their curious reactions told me all I needed to know about how often women visited here. Of course, between the food hamper we'd packed and Callie's Gladstone bag with her flying clothes, they might have been worried we were moving in.

The hangar was a gargantuan garage, mostly open front and back, letting in abundant light. Yet inside, fresh air fought a losing battle against fumes of oil, gas, and glue. Overhead, wooden ribs supported the high curved roof. What really drew my eye, though, were the airplanes. Four of them, all strikingly different, were parked inside. I'd seen drawings of airplanes and photographs, of course. I'd even watched one fly overhead back at home in Pennsylvania. In the air it had seemed small and faraway, a noisy gnat bothering the heavens. Up close, they were enormous, complex, and strangely vulnerable-looking constructions of canvas, metal, and wood, like modern mock-ups of prehistoric birds, with wings dozens of feet long. The bands beneath their canvas looked like veins beneath the thinnest skin.

Teddy grinned at me. "Beautiful, aren't they?"

"Which one's yours?" I asked.

He led us to one of the closest. The seats were aligned one in front of the other, encased in the body of the airplane that would serve as a sort of cocoon for the aviators from the shoulders down. The machine had a wood propeller at the front, and Teddy touched it as a horseman might a horse's muzzle as he described the specifications of this beast, rattling off incomprehensible information about tractor construction, engine cylinders, rudders, elevators, and stabilizers. I did understand "thirty-six-foot wingspan," and I stared up at the wings of the biplane, duly impressed. Our apartment didn't measure thirty-six feet side to side.

The plane had been painted white, with accents of crimson. Near the back were written the newly painted words *Gail Force*. Callie's last name was Gail.

Enraptured, Callie turned to me. "Isn't that wonderful? It's like having a steamship named after me."

Hopefully not like the *Titanic,* I thought.

She bounced off to get dressed.

"You'll be going up soon?" I asked Teddy. My stomach tightened at the idea of Callie up in the *Gail Force*.

"Just as soon as Callie's ready—but that might take a while. I need to teach her all about it, first. Don't worry, I'm not going to jump the gun."

That was somewhat reassuring. Callie might even tire of the lesson and lose a little of her flying mania in the face of a long lecture.

I stuck with Teddy until Callie appeared in her flying getup, which earned appreciative stares from all the men. Then the blocks were removed from behind Teddy's plane's wheels and the machine was pushed out of the enclosure. Before leaving me to take her lesson, Callie gave my hands a squeeze. "Don't worry, Louise. Teddy wouldn't dream of taking me up if it weren't perfectly safe."

I smiled, though of course what she'd said was ridiculous. My first real awareness of airplanes had come five years earlier when I'd read a newspaper account of a man who'd died flying in a plane with Orville Wright. Still, it would have been unhelpful to mention that incident to Callie when she was minutes from going up herself. Nothing I said would change her mind.

But as I watched her stride toward the plane, I backed away instinctively. "I can't look," I muttered.

"Then make yourself useful and hand me a wrench."

The command came from a long pair of legs braced on a workbench under a nearby plane. The voice had startled me; then I realized whom it belonged to. Hugh Van Hooten. I'd almost forgotten about him.

The wing he was wedged beneath belonged to a plane that looked much like Teddy's, only slightly larger—another two-seater "tractor" type. I'd learned from Teddy that a tractor was the kind that had the engine in front, pulling the machine forward, as opposed to pushers, which were locomoted from the rear. This plane looked very modern, from what I knew, which was still laughably little. The most notable thing about it was that it had a single wing jutting from both sides of the fuselage.

"How can that possibly fly?" I said. If I were going to be in an airplane, I'd want as many wings as possible.

"Well, at the moment it can't, but it might have a better chance to if you'll hand me that wrench I asked for."

Hugh's long-fingered hand pointed me toward a hefty metal toolbox, where I located the wrench. It was oily, and I carried it to him with my fingertips.

"Thanks." He tightened something out of my sight, gave a grunt of satisfaction, and scooted out from his uncomfortable seat. On his feet, he looked at me closely for the first time. *"You."* He didn't disguise his displeasure. "Teddy told me he was bringing some girls out today. He never mentioned that one of them would be the friend of the man who killed my brother."

"Mr. McChesney didn't do it."

Hugh's face tensed in disgust. "He confessed."

"Yes, but—"

"Can you imagine what learning about that did to my mother? To hear that her firstborn son—her dearest son—was murdered by his business associate, a man who had been one of my father's closest friends?"

"He didn't—"

"By God, you were even there that morning when he came to offer my mother condolences. Condolences!" His laugh was ragged, mirthless. "Very heartfelt, I'm sure."

When I could finally get a word in, I jumped at my chance. "He admits to starting the fire. Not to killing your brother."

"And what do *you* think killed him?"

"A detective told me that it was poison," I said. "Cyanide."

He looked up at me, his gaze more peevish. "Based on tests on my brother's badly burned body. Tests not approved by the family, by the way." He turned and headed back to his work area, climbed onto a stepladder, and bent over the plane's engine. He clearly considered the conversation over.

"Whether you approved or not doesn't alter the truth," I said. In fact, his not approving made me think Hugh Van Hooten knew all along that an autopsy would reveal something he didn't want the police to find. "Don't you want to know what killed Guy?"

"I'm not interested in the why so much as the who. And now I have a name."

"The wrong one."

"We're talking in circles, Miss—" He straightened and wiped his hands against his coveralls. "What do you call yourself again? I'm hopeless with names."

"Louise Faulk."

"Miss Faulk, if you don't mind, I have a lot to do. As you can imagine, this business with my brother has put me behindhand."

How could a man be so little interested in his brother's murder? If it were my brother, I didn't think I could concentrate on anything else. I would be obsessed. But Hugh already had an obsession—his airplane. My object was to jolt him out of it.

"Myrna Cohen," I said.

He stilled.

"I went to see her," I continued. "I also saw the baby. Guy's baby."

"And?" His voice was tight.

"I also learned about your encounter with Jacob Cohen when he came here asking you for money."

"None of this, Miss Faulk, is your business." He smiled, catching me off guard. "Is this how you intend to exonerate your boss?

By pointing the finger at the poor Cohens? Or is it me you want to implicate?"

"I only want to find out who is really guilty," I said.

"You can do better than the police?"

"You didn't sound very confident in the police before."

A mechanic hurried in. "Ready, Hoots?"

Hugh nodded, pulled a pair of leather gloves out of his back pockets, and put them on. "Be right there."

When the man was gone, he turned to me. "I admit I feel much more favorably toward the police now that they have a killer in custody."

"They have an arsonist in custody."

"And you trust McChesney's word that he didn't kill Guy? The man burned down his own business for money, and his partner in the bargain, whether or not it was premeditated, and then showed up at our home shedding crocodile tears over the whole affair. He even involved you in that last scene of his act. You were there! Doesn't the memory of that morning shake your confidence in that old man?"

Memories of that morning did make me uneasy. But I also remembered that Mr. McChesney had seemed distraught, and his sorrow had struck me as genuine. It still did. Hugh, on the other hand, had not exhibited one moment of sorrow at his brother's death.

I wasn't even sure I believed his outrage over Mr. McChesney. He was merely relieved that the police had a person in custody so he didn't have to think about it anymore... and didn't have to worry about becoming a suspect himself. I couldn't forget his saying that Guy was his mother's "dearest" son. There had to be a well of bitterness toward his sibling for those words to have slipped from his tongue so readily.

"I'd like to talk to you more about that morning," I said.

His dark look told me he was considering having me chucked off the premises. After a moment's thought, however, he said, "Then by all means, do. I wouldn't want to hamper your little investigation. But you'll have to talk to me as I work."

This was a better outcome than I'd hoped. "Very well."

He tilted his head. "As a matter of fact, you can help me. And if you do, then perhaps I can answer all your questions." He smiled. "A favor for a favor. Deal?"

Quid pro quo. I nodded eagerly and fell into step by him as he hurried to a wall of neatly arranged shelves and cubbies. The precise placement of items by size and type was my first insight into Hugh's mind. The neatness showed again how different he was from his brother, whose desk drawers had been indiscriminate clutter catchers.

He began pulling things out—a leather cap, then another, and two pairs of large, buglike goggles. He loaded those into my arms, then looked me up and down. "A duster coat, I think." Glancing at my feet, he added, "Your shoes are sturdy enough. I approve of girls in sensible boots."

As if I craved his good opinion of my sartorial choices. My retort, however, was cut off by the uneasiness thumping in my chest. A duster I could understand if I was going to be helping him. Also gloves. But the goggles . . .

I swallowed with effort. "What is it you want me to do?"

"Nothing difficult. I simply need a passenger."

I looked over his shoulder at the airplane he'd been working on. Though my stomach was twisting into pretzel knots at the very idea, I tried to keep my head and sized up the craft. *Could I do this?* While my guts said *no, no, no,* my head was saying, *Just hunker down and close your eyes.* How long could it last? I'd hung over a wall fifty-eight stories above the sidewalks of lower Manhattan and survived. Could a simple hop in an airplane be worse than that?

And there was Hugh's promise to consider. He'd agreed to talk with me about his brother's death if I helped him. Maybe this flight was a sort of test to see how trustworthy I was.

"All right." My voice sounded raspy, dry. I wobbled toward the airplane like a condemned prisoner walking the last mile. "Do I sit in front or back?"

"Neither. That plane's weeks away from her next test. Haven't got the motor quite right. We're taking a ride on *Beulah.*"

Beulah? "It sounds like a mule."

"Oh, she's a workhorse, all right," he answered breezily. He looped his arm through mine and steered me toward the doors at the back of the building. "*Beulah*'s our training plane. Solid little machine. Just had her wing repaired, but she should be running like a top now. If not, I guess this flight will show us, won't it?"

If not?

Outside, Teddy and Callie were in his airplane, which had been rolled a distance away from the hangar. Teddy was pointing at the controls. Callie, kneeling backward in her seat and bent over, was nodding. I tamped down the urge to run to her to say goodbye. But that was foolish. If I was going to do this, and I'd already said I would, I wasn't going to look like a ninny.

"This way," Hugh said, tugging me by the elbow.

He led me around the corner of the hangar. My feet stopped, and he overstepped me by a few paces before my stationary arm, which he still had a grip on, forced him to swing around.

"What is it?" he asked.

That's what I wanted to know. I pointed to the contraption in front of me. The machine looked as insubstantial as a child's plaything. Only this toy boasted biplane wings with an enormous span, a tail like a box kite, and long skids in front. Its weight rested on tires that might have been stolen off an old Schwinn. Wires crisscrossed between the various parts, holding it all together. It was as if a mad scientist had taken a kite, a bicycle, and a sled and tried to create a giant dragonfly.

Most alarming of all, there was no sturdy, barrel-like center of the plane with front and back seats. Instead, there were side-by-side places in front on the lower wing where two could perch with nothing but a bar below for the feet to brace on and two small poles on either side to hang on to.

"You expect me to go up in *that*?"

"Of course," he said. "Miss Faulk, meet *Beulah*."

Chapter 14

In the end, what gave me courage wasn't fear of looking like a fool in front of Hugh Van Hooten and his assistant. It wasn't even that *Beulah* was a biplane, not a mono-wing. That extra wing was cold comfort now. No, what bucked me up was the fact that I was a policewoman. Well, almost a policewoman. How could I stake any claim to bravery if I shrank from a ride in an airplane? I smashed the too-large cap on my head and pulled the goggles onto my forehead. I wasn't going to show myself up as a coward in front of Hugh Van Hooten.

"Ready when you are," I said in a voice completely at odds with the roiling in my stomach.

Did Hugh notice what my devil-may-care attitude was costing me? Probably not. He was circling the plane, giving it one last going-over. And thank heavens for that. The closer I came to *Beulah,* the more uncontrollable the shaking in my limbs became. The engine was mounted right out in the open, behind the seats, and upon closer inspection it seemed too small to power this crazy machine. Yet if it were bigger, and heavier, maybe the plane would never get off the ground.

How *did* planes get off the ground? It probably had to do with air currents and the elevators and stabilizers that Teddy had been droning on about. I was putting a lot of trust in Hugh, who, even if

I suspected him of having had a hand in his brother's murder, was supposed to be a brilliant aviator.

"Did you design the plane yourself?" I asked, trying to keep my voice steady.

He shook his head, not just to respond in the negative, but in pity and amazement at my ignorance. "You mean you can't even recognize a Wright design? This is a Model B, although I've made significant alterations."

"So you know better than the fathers of aviation?"

"Don't be a nincompoop. Anything can be improved. And in *Beulah's* case, modification was an absolute necessity. She had a smashup and busted her wing."

A smashup. My nerves were as tight as violin strings.

"She's all snug now, though." He bestowed a loving pat on her wing. "Hop on."

Easier said than done. At least for me. Callie's getup made sense now. To get onto the passenger seat, I had to pick my way through the spider's web of wires and also metal bars attaching the skids to the wings. My skirt, practical as it was, had not been designed for an aviatrix.

Seeing my difficulty, Hugh came up behind me and hoisted me over the first skid and then up onto the seat. I let out a gasp of surprise.

"There." He thumped me down on the seat like so much human cargo. "Put your gloves on and batten yourself down as best you can." He gestured at my clothes. "Tuck in, button up, and hang on."

The seat was actually more secure than it appeared. It had a back like a parlor chair, and was even upholstered in a deep green fabric. My feet rested on a bar in front, and two perpendicular poles jutted up on both sides of the seat. Overhead was the upper wing. It was like sitting on a veranda. A veranda that was about to zoom off toward the horizon.

I can't do this.

I can *do this.*

Hugh settled beside me, and moments later the motor came to life like a band saw behind my head. The deafening sound made my heart somersault. The whole machine was vibrating.

He turned to me and said something. There might as well have been a glass wall between us. My ears hadn't adjusted. He pointed to the goggles over his eyes and then pointed to mine, which were still perched at forehead level. I snapped them over my eyes.

The plane, aided by Hugh's friend and the roaring motor and whirring propellers behind us, lumbered into movement and then turned onto a wide pathway of well-worn grass.

Hugh turned to me, grinning.

Before I could examine the cold sensation those white foxlike teeth gave me, the plane lunged forward. Over ground that had looked perfectly flat moments before, every bump and rut registered. Just like a car, I told myself. But automobile engines didn't keen in your ear. In an automobile, I'd never had the feeling that I was rushing forward *against* the elements, against nature, against common sense. As the plane accelerated, pressure pushed me back against the seat. My hands gripped the poles for dear life. I was perched on the wing of an angry, noisy insect tilting at the air.

The plane ate the ground, but nothing seemed to be happening. I turned as we bumped past the *Gail Force*. Callie and Teddy gaped at us. Her hands were planted on her hips, and her expression was both astonished and annoyed. I wanted to lift my shoulders and shout, "This wasn't really my choice," but there was no chance. The machine lifted.

The disorienting lurch made me face forward. This had to be what a fledgling felt when it made its first flapping hop out of the nest into the void. My stomach jumped into my throat, then plunged again as the plane first dipped and then rose higher into the air.

Wind flattened me against the back of my seat. Cold wind. But there hadn't been a breeze at all this morning. It was all us, rushing cloudward—*we* were the wind, skimming forward and up as fast as a locomotive. Sickness and exhilaration battled in me. And terror. A line of trees loomed ahead. From the hangar, they'd seemed a mile away. Now they were dead close.

Though I had my feet firmly braced and a white-knuckle grip on the poles, my body was almost lifting from its seat in my urge to get over those trees. The plane careened toward the top of the canopy. At the very last minute, we tilted slightly up and skimmed over them, so close I could see veins on the golden leaves.

Relief nearly brought tears to my goggled eyes.

Hugh turned to me, a triumphant grin on his face. He leaned closer and yelled, "You think I killed him, don't you?"

I stared back, unable to find words.

He shook his head and turned his attention forward again. Maybe he thought I couldn't hear him.

I'd heard. He'd guessed correctly that I suspected him of being involved in his brother's death. My *little investigation,* he'd called it. This flight wasn't doing him a favor, I realized belatedly. There would be no quid pro quo. This was his way of terrorizing me.

He'd chosen his weapon well. My heart was lodged in my esophagus. I'd always scoffed at the idea of anyone dying of fright, but my heart's frantic beating had me preparing to meet my maker.

Before, when I'd seen an airplane flying, it had seemed to soar like a raptor, with the ease of a mechanized hawk wheeling overhead. But ease had nothing to do with this experience, it turned out. The plane lurched and dipped like a roller coaster.

Callie was wrong. The air did have potholes, and *Beulah* hit every last one of them.

Hugh's grin had disappeared. In profile I could see only a determined set to his jaw. *Determined to what?*

The plane banked, causing a new wave of clamminess and nausea. I squeezed my eyes closed until I felt the craft straighten out again; then I screwed up my courage and glanced down. We hummed above a boardwalk, then a beach. To the right, water lapped at the shore. The ocean. And ahead.

I blinked. Ahead were buildings. And more water. And then the skyscrapers of Manhattan. I'd just assumed Hugh would circle the plane back to the aerodrome. Instead, we were flying toward the city.

"What are you doing?" I screamed at him.

"Showing you the town!"

I'd seen the town—from the proper perspective of street level. I'd even seen it from fifty-eight stories high. The words "go back" were on the tip of my tongue, but the air gulped them down before they could get themselves said. Dear God. I was boneless with fear, but I was rapt.

Beulah followed the coast. More houses appeared below, and people. It was such a beautiful day, strollers and Sunday picnickers had been drawn to the beach. Now they were all looking up, shading their eyes, pointing as we streaked overhead. I looked down at them, sick with envy. Indian summer? Maybe on the ground. Up here, frigid air blew through my duster, my clothes, my bones. I longed to be back on earth instead of perched aloft, teeth chattering, nerves screaming like the unholy whine of the engine behind me.

We skimmed over a body of water; then there were houses below. Staten Island? Ahead was lower Manhattan. The Woolworth Building, of course, its tower like a cathedral that had overshot its base. And out in the harbor, the Statue of Liberty.

After we passed the tip of Staten Island, we flew over the Jersey piers and straight toward Lady Liberty, right by her torch. Crowds waved from the ground, as if we were part of a show. I only had a moment to look back at them all, wondering how I could send a distress signal, before Hugh banked right and we were headed back toward the southern tip of Manhattan. Toward my old friend the Woolworth Building.

Right toward it. My heartbeat thundered in panic. "Watch out!" I shrieked.

We shaved by so close I could see into the building's lantern tower, the place I'd almost died last summer.

Hugh didn't look at me. Only laughed.

He enjoyed terrifying me. And why not? If he did kill Guy, he had every reason now to wish me dead, too, a bothersome woman asking too many questions. It would be so easy for him—a simple matter of a violent dip, a firm shove. My crumpled body would be found on the pavement, or in a field, or just washed up on the shoreline. I could imagine the sensation in the press. WOMAN DROPS OUT OF AIRPLANE. And no one would imagine Hugh had done anything on purpose. Airplanes were inherently dangerous, and there would be no witnesses. Callie might wonder why I'd gone flying with Hugh, stealing her thunder, but she would never know what exactly had happened.

I would simply be erased. Hugh's worries would be over.

The streets of my much-loved adopted city blurred past below me, and each landmark I picked out caused a pang of longing. The elegant Singer Building . . . the Brooklyn Bridge . . . Jefferson Market's tower . . . the sharp narrow V of the Flatiron Building. I sighted the charred remnant of the space on Thirty-eighth where Van Hooten and McChesney had been. Hugh took us up to Central Park, banking left and flying past the great residential buildings. The Dakota. The Ansonia. With each wide boulevard we passed, I braced myself. *Will he do it here? Or will he wait until we're over water?*

What I wouldn't do to be safe in my apartment again, or at Aunt Irene's, or playing cards with Otto in his studio flat. A normal Sunday.

We crossed the Hudson, flying toward Hoboken. Now, I thought. I braced myself for that shove, rigid in my seat, hanging on so tight my hands ached. I wasn't going to make it easy for him.

But he didn't touch me. When my fears cleared enough for my senses to register the world around me again, Hugh was piloting us back to his air park. We were farther from the ocean than we'd been going in, but we were definitely flying back.

Landing was worse than taking off. The plane descended by a series of tummy-roiling drops; then, horrifyingly, the engine cut out and we careened toward the ground, rushing and straining in what felt like a death plunge. I closed my eyes again, held on, and shrieked out a final prayer.

And then it was over. The plane stopped vibrating, even if my bones didn't. I opened my eyes. We were far from the hangar.

I yanked off my goggles and slid off my seat to the ground. My body was noodle limp, but my nerves were still jumping. I tore off my cap and hurled it at Hugh. "You sadist!"

He raised his hands, feigning shock. "I just gave you the ride of a lifetime, and that's all you can say? That I'm a sadist?"

"Did you expect thanks? You deliberately tried to terrify me. Don't deny it."

He pushed his goggles to the top of his head. "I won't deny that I enjoyed watching you squirm. After all, didn't you come here to wring a confession from me that I'd killed my brother?"

"Why didn't you just tell me you were innocent? I thought you were going to toss me out of the plane."

He laughed. *Laughed.* "Maybe you'll think twice next time before you go bothering people with your harebrained suspicions."

"It's not harebrained to suspect those closest to Guy. People are rarely poisoned at random."

He shook his head. "If I were truly a mad killer, Miss Faulk, would you still be alive after that flight? I could have disposed of you easily."

"I'm aware of that."

"There's your answer, then. Not that you should need proof. I had nothing to gain by killing Guy."

"What about the baby? Myrna's baby is your mother's only grandchild. You don't see that as a threat to your inheritance?"

He ripped off his gloves. "Good God. You really do take me for some kind of monster."

"You told Jacob Cohen you couldn't be sure that the baby was Guy's."

His jaw dropped. "That's a damned lie. *I* tried to convince Guy to acknowledge the baby as his own. He wouldn't. And when Jacob Cohen came here after Guy died, I offered him money. My own money."

"Hush money?"

His face reddened. "Money for the baby's upkeep. But Jacob said the demented girl wouldn't accept it. She wants the Van Hooten name and everything that goes with it for her son, or nothing. That, of course, is not in my power. I told Jacob that my mother wouldn't believe the baby's paternity—perhaps that's why he said what he did. I don't like that fellow. I considered a scheme to pass money surreptitiously to Myrna through Jacob, but I worried bookies and con artists would see more of the money than that child would. For all the difference in their social status, he and Guy were peas in a pod."

So he'd offered money for the child's upkeep and Myrna didn't want it? She hadn't told me that. Of course, Hugh could be handing me a line, but everything he said rang true. Myrna was as stubbornly proud as he said, and Jacob, even according to the testimony of his own sister, was just as untrustworthy.

"It would be like Myrna to care more for the acknowledgment than the money," I admitted.

"The girl's an idiot." He tapped his gloves against his thigh. "First she was naïve enough to let Guy connive her into his bed, and when she found herself in trouble she clung to the notion that he would sweep her away to our mother's house, where she would be welcomed with open arms."

"You're certain your mother would shun her?"

"A penniless Jewess with an illegitimate child?" He sniffed. "Mother wouldn't even hire her as a maid."

Lovely people, the Van Hootens. "A Jewish woman who is the mother of your mother's first grandchild, and deserves as much respect as any debutante your mother might have picked out for Guy."

"You and I might think so, but my mother never would."

"So when you were at the office and argued with your brother . . ."

"You're a regular repository of tittle-tattle, aren't you?" Sighing, he explained, "When I heard about the Cohen girl through the grapevine, I thought Guy had behaved abominably. So yes, I argued with Guy, but he convinced me of the hopelessness of the case. Mother would not only not disapprove of the Cohen girl, the scandal of it would make her apoplectic."

Would you kill our mother?

That's what Guy had meant.

"Guy was Mother's favorite, and he was shameless in using her partiality to his advantage. But he knew her, and he was sure she would categorically reject this illegitimate child."

And Guy didn't have the moral courage to follow his own heart and go his own way.

I wondered if they both weren't selling Mrs. Van Hooten short, though. "That boy is your mother's own flesh and blood," I pointed out. "Her grandson. Perhaps she would want a living piece of Guy now."

"Even if the child was a reminder of her darling's indiscretions? An embarrassing public acknowledgement that her boy was less than perfect?" He twisted his gloves in his hands. "No, for once in his life, Guy was right. Mother would see the boy as a stain on the family. She will protect the Van Hooten name to her dying breath. Perhaps you don't understand how callous people can be when there's an old family's reputation at stake."

Lowly Faulks could be protective of their name, too. Aunt Sonja had sent me away partly because she was afraid my shame would taint her son's chances in life. The memory made anger rise in me. Why did shame have to come into it?

"Just a little more courage would solve a lot of life's problems," I said.

He frowned. "Courage?"

"Courage to face down so-called polite society, to ask better from people, and see if they might not rise above their prejudices."

For the first time since we landed, he looked more thoughtful than angry. "Look, I know nothing of my brother's publishing business. But if you truly believe Ogden McChesney didn't kill him, then what about Guy's other work associates? There must have been someone at work Guy irritated. He certainly had that effect on me."

"I'll look into it," I said.

Hugh regarded me for a moment, studying me as he might a map. Then he shook his head. "With you on the case, the criminal world must be all atremble."

Just when I'd almost forgiven him for scaring me half to death. I tossed up my hands. "Never mind getting me back to the hangar. I'd rather walk."

"No need." He nodded to something behind me.

A red car bumped down the field. With Callie driving, it looked like a whirlwind on wheels. The Stutz skidded to a stop not far away and was switched off with a gasp and a shudder. She hopped out, cap askew. Teddy was right on her heels.

"Louise, are you all right?" she called out. "Did you have trouble?"

"No, no trouble," Hugh answered, his mouth a grim line as he eyed Teddy.

"Then what's the big idea landing out here?" Teddy asked. "We saw you coming in, and then you disappeared over the hill."

"I just wanted to demonstrate a field landing to this friend of yours. Give her a taste of real flying."

Callie narrowed her eyes on me. "You could've knocked me over with a sneeze when I saw you taking off. What got into you?"

I shrugged. My knees still felt noodly beneath me, and I was so relieved to see her, I wasn't quite sure I trusted my voice.

"Louise is curious by nature," Hugh said. "Lucky she's not a cat."

"Did you and Teddy go up?" I managed to ask.

Callie turned toward Teddy, exasperated. "Someone's having engine trouble. All I did was spend an hour getting lectured and oily. And for this I gave up a chance to meet Lee Shubert!"

Teddy looked sheepish. "Maybe next time. But at least Louise got to fly. How was it?"

"A thrill." I avoided Hugh's gaze. "I'll never forget it."

CHAPTER 15

On Monday, Callie returned to Philadelphia for *Broadway Frolics'* week of tryouts. I rattled around the flat, wondering what to do next. I sat down to make a list of suspects in Guy's murder, but after an hour I was still staring at a blank page. In the afternoon, I headed uptown to my aunt's. Miriam had agreed to start work for her, and I was curious and a little apprehensive about how her first day had gone. I didn't actually have any idea how competent Miriam was, or how well she and my aunt would get along.

If the arrangement didn't work out, what then? Awkwardness all around. Perhaps I should have been there this morning to help Miriam settle in. I would miss having my aunt's to go to every day, and chumming around with Walter and even grumpy Bernice.

By the time I was knocking at the door, I'd decided that if things didn't work out with Miriam, I would simply find a way to squeeze in time to resume my typing duties for my aunt.

When I saw Aunt Irene, though, she could hardly contain herself. "Weren't you smart to send Miriam to me. What a marvel. You can't believe the amount of work she got done today—typed my pages, and actually gave me a few ideas for fixing problems that I hadn't noticed yet. Wonderful ideas! Of course, the prospect of revising threw me into a tizzy. She'll have to retype the whole book, I warned her. But Miriam said not to worry, it shouldn't take her but a week, and anyway what had been done was a little messy anyway."

My face froze in a rictus smile.

"*Not* that she was critical of you. Not at all. And what do you think—for her first day she brought us a sweet potato pie and insisted we all have a piece."

"Uh-oh." Bernice was never happy about sharing culinary glory. "How did that go over?"

"Bernice took one bite and burst into tears. Said it tasted exactly like the pie her grandmother used to make. I don't think I had ever seen her quite so emotional."

It sounded as if Miriam had made a hit. Despite my bruised pride, I was glad.

When Walter came in, I half expected him to join in the paean to Miriam. "She might be a good baker and typist," he assured me, "but I don't think she'll ever catch a criminal."

His loyalty made me smile. "Give her time." After typing up the fictionalized account of last summer's murder, Miriam would know as much about detective work as I did.

Tuesday brought me no closer to knowing how to restart my investigation, so I suggested an impromptu trip to Philadelphia to Otto. We left on Wednesday morning and attended Callie's show that night. I was eager to see it. If Callie was right about its dubious chances of success, I might not have the chance to go to the show on Broadway, since I would be working the night shift in a new job the week of the opening . . . and possible closing.

Broadway Frolics was a frothy toe-tapper of a musical comedy. Callie hadn't been kidding about the leading actress's voice, but even that didn't harm the show overmuch. The revelation to me was Callie herself. She really did get a laugh and applause for her single line. She was also a standout in the chorus, and it wasn't just pride in my friend that made me think so. By turns, she was graceful, sultry, and wonderfully comic. Otto and I could barely contain ourselves.

When she came out the stage door and saw us standing there, holding out our programs for her to sign, Callie nearly fell over. She laughed and hugged us.

"You tricksters—why didn't you tell me you were coming?"

"We wanted to surprise you."

She glanced around as if expecting someone else to join us. "Did Teddy plan this?"

Otto and I looked at each other.

"Teddy?" I repeated. "No, we did this on our own."

"Oh." Anxiety flashed through her eyes, but she shook it off. "I've been expecting him to come down, or call, or at least send a wire."

"Teddy hasn't been here?" I'd assumed he would be in Philadelphia for most of the out-of-town run of the show.

"He's probably busy with something," she said.

I nodded, but her words caused a ripple of worry. It was hard to imagine Teddy busy.

We went out and celebrated a bit too much, and stumbled back to our rooms at the Continental Hotel on Chestnut Street in the small hours. The next morning on the train back, both Otto and I were feeling the effects of last night's revelry. In the lounge car, we nursed coffees and headache powders. I was staring out the window when Otto kicked my leg under the table.

"What's the—"

A shadow fell over us. I looked up and Leonard Cain, a thick cigar clamped in his mouth, loomed over our table. "What are you two doing on this train."

He had a lot of crust. He might control the clientele of the Omnium Club, but he didn't own the Pennsylvania Railroad.

I was about to retort that it was none of his business, but Otto piped up, "Just coming back from seeing a show in Philly."

Cain twirled the cigar as he contemplated us through narrowed eyes. Then he sat down. "See, I'm a little curious because I was tipped off that the police were in my club the night you two were there. And then somebody tells me later that they recognized this one"—he jabbed a thumb at me—"from the papers last summer. That she worked with the police."

"I wasn't working with the police that night at the Omnium," I said. "I didn't even know they were there until later."

His dark brows rose. "How'd you find out?"

"I spoke to a detective." That sounded bad, so I added, "But he was just telling me to stay away from your club."

"And she has," Otto said. "We both have."

"And yet you just happened to be on this train the same time I am," he said. "Just coincidence."

"That's right," Otto croaked.

Cain paid no more attention to Otto than he would to a gnat. His dead-eyed stare was all for me. "You got nothing to do with the police now, I take it."

Otto and I looked at each other. "Not at the moment," I said.

Cain's voice lowered to a gravelly whisper. "If I ever find you sticking your nose into my business again, girlie, watch out. I don't care how many celebrities you know." He struck a match to light his cigar and glowered at Otto, who shrank in his seat. "That goes for you, too, songwriter."

He left the car in a billow of blue smoke. Otto and I locked glances. Neither of us seemed to be breathing. Beads of sweat had popped out on his brow. I felt clammy, as well.

"What was that all about?" I wondered.

"You can't let him know you're a policewoman, Louise. You heard him—he'll kill us."

"Why would he want to do that unless he had something to hide?"

"Who cares why? You heard his threats. I don't want to die—at least not till Al Jolson records one of my songs."

I laughed. "All right. I'll try to hold back my curiosity till then."

But thoughts of Cain consumed me all the way home and into the night. Had my gut instinct been right at the beginning? Cain was definitely hiding something if he felt threatened by just bumping into Otto and me on a train.

The next morning was chilly, with a pouring rain, and the headlines were all catastrophic. Storms across the Great Lakes had claimed over two hundred lives. Hard to believe just days before I had been sunning myself in an open car. In a gloomy frame of mind, I slogged my way down to Orchard Street to see how my uniform was coming along. Myrna had measured me so hurriedly, a fitting would probably be needed. With my umbrella open, I edged through the diminished pushcart crowds on the sidewalk, went up, and knocked at Myrna's. The door cracked open, a dark eye appeared, and then the door shut again.

I waited, perplexed, then knocked again. "Myrna, it's me. Louise Faulk."

A minute passed and then the door swung open. Myrna, blocking the threshold, thrust a paper bundle wrapped in twine out to me. "Here."

I took it from her. "Shouldn't I try it—"

"Just go," she said. "A police detective's been here. Said *someone* had told him about me and Jacob knowing Guy. Now they're watching my building."

The hallway was frigid and I was damp through, yet my cheeks blazed. "I didn't mean to—"

"I don't want you here."

The door shut and a key turned a lock from the inside.

Distressed, I tramped back down the stairs, past children who were seeing who could leap the most stairs down to the worn tiles of the ground floor hall. That wasn't going to end well.

"Be careful," I said.

A girl in a dirty smock stuck her tongue out at me. "We don't want you here!" she said, mimicking Myrna.

Outside, the rain was still coming down. While I was struggling to open my umbrella, a hand clamped down on my shoulder. *Cain,* instinct shouted. I whirled and nearly jabbed Muldoon's eye out with my umbrella's metal tip.

He hopped back in the nick of time. "Watch it with that thing."

I sagged against the wall behind me as I opened my umbrella. "What are you doing? You scared me half to death."

He had an umbrella, too, which made it hard to stand together on the narrow sidewalk without causing bodily harm to someone. With his free hand, he took my arm. "Come with me. We need to talk."

On Delancey Street, he indicated a bakery and we went in. Several small tables were pushed against the wall and front plate-glass window. While we unloaded our dripping things, Muldoon indicated that I should claim one of the empty tables. I stood until he returned from the counter with two steaming cups of tea and a cinnamon bun. "Best in town," he said.

It looked heavenly, and the yeasty smell of the baking bread all around us worked on me like a pacifier on a baby. I sat and cupped my hands around the thick china mug, absorbing the warmth through my palms. "If this is about Leonard Cain, I swear I didn't even know he was on the train," I warned Muldoon.

His face screwed up. "Leonard Cain?"

Okay, so maybe this *wasn't* about Cain. "How did you find me?" I asked.

"It wasn't easy. You weren't home last night."

"Otto and I went to Philadelphia." I explained about seeing Callie's show. "I didn't know I was supposed to check in with you before I left town."

"What happened with Cain?"

"Nothing. We met him on the return trip, and he made some vague threats. He seemed to think I was mixed up with the police."

"You are."

"Yes, well, I decided it wouldn't be wise to bring up my new job. Cain looked agitated about something. It makes me wonder if any of the story he gave of the night of Guy's murder was true."

Muldoon swallowed a slug of tea. "One of our men examining the evidence from the fire did find charred pieces of bank notes. One piece looked as if it might have been a fifty-dollar bill. But whether that money was brought by Cain, or belonged to someone else, who can say?"

Guy had been broke, though. And none of the rest of us would have left fifty dollars lying around. So that did provide minimal corroboration for Cain's story.

"What were you doing at Myrna's?" I asked Muldoon. "Were you the one who talked to her? She was very upset."

"I was just following up on what you told me."

That seemed like a victory of sorts. "I thought you were so sure Mr. McChesney killed Guy."

"I'm just looking at all the evidence. When you brought new information to me, I had to follow up."

"You must not be very satisfied with her answers if you've been watching her flat."

His brows jumped. "How did you know?"

"Myrna told me. I guess someone must have noticed a six-foot Irishman hanging around. Can't think why."

Scowling, he took a sip of tea.

I leaned forward. "Was it Myrna you wanted to talk about?"

"No, Hugh Van Hooten came to talk to me." He scratched his jaw. "Although talk is a mild word for what he was doing. The man wasn't happy, and neither would the brass be if they found out their newly minted policewoman had been riling up prominent citizens before she'd even shown up for her first day."

For some reason, I hadn't expected Hugh to run to the police about me. "I was only asking questions."

"What did you hope to accomplish?"

"Someone other than Mr. McChesney murdered Guy—you have to see that. You wouldn't have talked to Myrna if you didn't have doubts."

"I don't have many doubts. I just want to be thorough."

"You can't say the word *killer* and hold the image of Ogden McChesney in your head."

"Louise, he confessed."

"To setting his building on fire when Guy was already dead."

His lips turned down, but I didn't pause to wonder why.

"*You* were the one who told me about Guy's being poisoned," I pointed out.

"McChesney could have poisoned Guy and subsequently set the fire to cover his crime."

"But Guy wouldn't have been at the office in the morning when Mr. McChesney set the fire. He had to have been killed the night before, sometime after I left."

"So McChesney killed him the night before, after you left," Muldoon speculated. "He poisoned his partner and fled. Went home. Then he got himself into a stew over what he was going to do when Guy was found. So after a sleepless night, he decided to burn the building down around Guy."

I shook my head.

"He even confessed that his motivation was the insurance money, and according to the policy, he received more if Guy were dead." He looked at me pityingly. "A prosecutor will eat this up, Louise. It's an open-and-shut case."

"But he didn't do it."

"I understand why you want to believe that, but there's probable cause to believe that he did."

In frustration, I tapped my nails against my cup. "And my angering prominent citizens who might file complaints makes life sticky for you. Isn't that really why you wanted to talk to me?"

His lips twisted. "You'll be part of the force soon, heaven help you. You might as well learn now that politics are part of the job."

"You'd let a man be executed for murder because you don't want to upset the Van Hootens?"

"Logic points to his guilt."

Yet he'd followed my tip and had been looking at the Cohens. He wasn't as rigid in his belief in Mr. McChesney's guilt as he would like me to think. "And your gut?"

He shook his head. "Guts and heart make great fiction, but they aren't evidence."

I looped my bag around my shoulder, gathered my uniform bundle to my chest, and stood. "It might not be evidence, but my gut is telling me not to stop looking until I find the information that will prove Mr. McChesney isn't a killer."

"I'll be the first one to congratulate you if you find it."

I was skeptical of that, but I didn't want to argue. "Thanks for the tea." I started to go.

"Louise." He waited until I turned back to him. "Good luck on the new job next week. Chin up."

Given how I'd been received at Myrna's, I didn't have high hopes for my uniform. When I unwrapped the paper, however, I couldn't believe my eyes. The navy blue of the shirtwaist was of a lightweight challis that felt as soft as silk under my hands. The brass buttons she'd chosen were round, with a rosette stamped on them. She'd fashioned a white collar, as I'd asked, and included a brass clip with an inset lily on it. The skirt, of a light half-wool gabardine, was simple but had a few tucks that made it fit perfectly. They were the best-tailored garments I'd ever had made.

Even Callie, when she got back on Sunday, approved. What's more, she'd bought a hat that she claimed would look perfect with my uniform. The blue hat had navy-blue netting over a tan silk crown. Callie had dressed it up with two ruby plumes attached to the brim with a tuft of rabbit fur. It was nicer than any hat I owned.

"You can have it," she said when I tried it on. "I'll probably be too busy to do much running around these next weeks."

It seemed a peculiar thing to say. "Wearing a hat doesn't require a whirlwind social life." I frowned. "Is this about Teddy?" He hadn't been by, and she hadn't mentioned him.

"I don't want to talk about him," she said with a finality that made me drop the subject.

On Monday night, I dressed in my new uniform and Callie's hat and headed uptown.

The Thirtieth Street police station was relatively new and always a bit of a shock to stumble upon. Situated midway between Sixth and Seventh avenues, it resembled a medieval fortress of gray stone and orange brick, complete with crenellated turrets on the bottom half. I'd just so happened to walk by it several times in the past week, trying to imagine myself actually belonging there. Now I marched through the arched stone entrance between the green lights, brimming with nerves and pride. It was time to start living the life I'd dreamed of for months and months.

Once inside, it occurred to me that my dreams hadn't featured a precinct overseen by a desk sergeant whose pocked, ruddy, unsmiling face looked like hammered meat. Several police officers stood around, some obviously dealing with cases they'd brought in. A woman blocked my path, arguing with a uniformed officer who'd caught her boy stealing.

"How dare you call my Tommy a thief!" she blasted at the policeman.

"He swiped a watch from a peddler, bold as brass."

"Hogwash," growled a boy of around ten years in a slouch cap. Tommy, I presumed. "I found it on the sidewalk."

His mother rounded on him. "Shut your mouth, you!" Then she turned back to the officer and explained, "He found it on the sidewalk."

"I was gonna give it back," Tommy said.

His mother yanked his cap off his head and cuffed him with it across the ear. "I told you to keep quiet." She looked up at the sergeant but spoke in a voice loud enough to reach every corner of the precinct. "You hear that? He was going to give it back."

"Then why'd he run in the opposite direction when the peddler shouted at him to stop?" the officer asked.

The sergeant, towering over the scene behind his high desk like a judge on the bench, groaned and interrupted the argument. "If you want your Tommy not to get arrested, teach him not to pick things up off the sidewalk. Or maybe the reformatory will."

Tommy's mother dissolved into sobs. "He's a good boy."

As the officer led them away, the sergeant scowled at me. "You in the hat. What do you want?"

My heart thumped in my chest. *Should I salute?* I wasn't sure. "I'm here to work. Sir."

The man wiped his sleeve across his forehead. "Criminy! That's all we need. You want to become police commissioner, or did you have something else in mind?"

"You don't underst—"

"We're busy here, lady. If you've got a complaint, fine. If not—"

"My name is Louise Faulk. I was directed by Captain Percival Smith to report to this station to begin my job as a probationary policewoman."

He stared at me in disbelief, but slowly took in the brass buttons on my dress, which was partially obscured by my coat. "*You're* Faulk?"

"Yes, sir."

"Father in Heaven." He shouted for a nearby officer. "Hey, Jenks. Come look what downtown sent us. I didn't expect our newest police matron to arrive looking like a kid playing dress up."

A tall officer with a long face came over to inspect me. His dry smile made me bristle.

"What's the fashion this year, Jenks?" the sergeant asked him. "Feathers or fur?"

Jenks nodded at my hat brim. "Looks like this one hedged her bets."

"Very smart," observed the sergeant. "Did you ever see such a uniform? Must've been made in Paree!"

Heat washed over me. They were giving me the business, and if I hadn't already been so nervous I would've given some right back to them. I should have. Instead, I remained mute with discomfiture, which only provided my new colleagues with more amusement. A few more officers, catching wind of fun, joined in.

"She's prettier than the last few they sent us."

"Maybe she'll make better coffee."

"Got a better figure than Fiona and Martha, that's for sure."

One of the men leaned close enough to sniff my hair. "Smells better, too."

"Give 'er a pinch and see if she's softer than Fiona."

I hopped back. None of these men were going to touch me if I had anything to say about it. "Lay a hand on me and you just might lose it." The grinning faces around me froze, or collapsed. Perhaps I was overreacting, but I didn't care now. "I came here to do a job. You seem to think my being here is some kind of joke, but I took a test the same as all of you had to, and I made the second-highest score."

The men exchanged glances, and for a moment it seemed I'd impressed them into silence.

The sergeant scratched his sideburns. "Number two, huh?"

"Wonder what happened to number one?" another man asked.

"Probably got sent straight to the Eighth Precinct. They got new flush terlets in the jail cells this year, too."

Several men thought this was hilarious.

The sergeant finally put a stop to it all. "All right, Two." It took me a moment to register that Two meant me. "The Captain's not in—it's a little late for him—so you'll have to make your acquaintance of our big brass some other day. But you follow Officer Jenks and he'll get you set up. And the rest of you mind your p's and q's, and especially fingers. Officer Two here looks dangerous. I don't need any one-handed officers. You're all useless enough already."

His listeners hooted with laughter. Red-faced, I stalked after Jenks. It was not a promising beginning.

Jenks showed me the room where officers signed in, and rummaged through a drawer until he found a card for me to fill out with my address and vital statistics. A short statement agreeing to the terms of my probationary period was typed at the bottom, and I signed it. When I was done, Jenks handed me a badge. The whole procedure was far less ceremonious than graduation from my secretarial course had been. At least there I'd received a certificate and a handshake.

"You pin that on your uniform," he said, nodding at the badge, "but keep it with you even when you're not at the station and not in uniform. You're always a policeman. Well, policewoman. How old are you?"

"Twenty-one."

He shook his head. "Guess there's nothing to be done about that."

"I'll probably be getting older."

He snorted. "Sooner than you think, around this place. I should give you the nickel tour."

The ground floor contained the reception where Sergeant Donnelly held court, a few offices for the higher-ranking officers, other rooms for questioning suspects, and a meeting room. A small pantry had a small cook stove wedged in the back. "Here's where you make the coffee," Jenks told me. "Should have everything you need."

"*I* make coffee?"

"The sergeant likes having it available for the boys on their beats when they come in. It's hard for them, working all hours."

And to think, just a month ago I'd stood in the kitchenette at Van Hooten and McChesney, dreaming of the day when my job wouldn't involve being commanded to make coffee for my male coworkers.

We moved on then, but not far. "There's three floors up," he said, pointing to a staircase, "but those are the men's cells, dormitories for the officers between shifts, and extra rooms for the detectives." The policemen's schedule was a complicated grid of short and long shifts, rotations that often required officers to catch forty winks at the station instead of going home. "You women don't have to worry about that so much because the captain puts you on more regular shifts. He thinks it ain't right to keep lady officers sleeping at the station. When you do have two shifts in the same day, though, there's a cot downstairs for you."

He then showed me down to my new domain—*down* being the operative word. The female prisoners were kept in cells in the basement, and evidently policewomen were relegated to this area, too.

My duty was to look after the female prisoners in the cells and be on call when new arrestees arrived. "You gotta keep everyone in line," Jenks said as we walked. "Sergeant Donnelly doesn't like trouble, especially from women. Just 'cause they're females, don't think it's a cakewalk. Give me a cell full of thieving and murdering men over a pack of slatterns any day."

The room where the women were held was a cold, windowless place. At least, like the rest of the building, it was fairly new and clean.

Jenks leaned against the doorway and frowned at the cells with their floor-to-ceiling bars. "When you meet old Schultzie, you should ask him how this station used to be. He's been here since even before Clubber Williams in the wild old days, when it was anything goes. Back then, vagrants used to spend the nights down in the basement. That was before this new place was built. Now they got women down here, and running water, and beds with mattresses."

"Where do the vagrants go now?"

"They sleep on newspapers in the park, or along the waterfront. Or here, if we arrest them." He laughed dryly. "That's progress for you."

Several women launched themselves at the bars, rattling them to get our attention and shouting out requests. Wide, wild eyes stared at me as a cacophony of "Something to drink!" and "Hungry" and "When am I going to get out?" echoed around the room.

Jenks snarled at them. "Aw, behave! I brought you a nice new matron."

One of the figures reclining on a wood bench in the dim recess of a cell coughed out a laugh. "That's a matron? Looks like a kid."

I knew better now than to pipe up defensively. Jenks didn't give me a chance to, anyway. "She could be in diapers and she'd still be Officer Faulk to you."

Officer Faulk. My shoulders straightened. It was the first time I'd heard those words. So far I'd just been *Two, girlie,* or *Officer Two.*

One woman curled in a ball against a wall moaned. "I'm gonna be sick."

"Sure you are." Jenks leaned toward me and whispered loudly, "Don't let them fool you with their sob stories. They're none of them as innocent as they claim to be, and the ones crying sick or acting crazy are mostly just bucking for a chance to spend the night in a soft bed at Bellevue."

And how would you know that?

"Donnelly don't like it when the officers coddle the prisoners," he said.

"But they're not really prisoners, are they? Not in the true sense. They haven't been convicted of anything."

Jenks shook his head in disgust. "You'll learn."

He made learning sound like doom, but I was eager. "What next?" I asked.

"That's it."

I gaped at him. I'd expected there would be at least a bit more of an orientation period than this.

"Did you expect someone to hold your hand for ten hours?"

"Of course not." Although I had, actually.

"Then have at it. If you need something, give a shout. And if you're wanted upstairs, you'll hear that bell." He pointed to a round brass piece above one of the doors.

His exit caused a renewed flurry of rattling bars and shouts for help, water, food, a telephone call. They obviously thought I'd be an easier mark than Jenks. They weren't wrong. Unlike Jenks, I couldn't see all these women as guilty. True, a few hardened types looked like what they probably were—prostitutes still tricked out and painted for their nightly perambulations. Others I wasn't so sure about. One woman told me she'd been brought in for shoplifting.

"But I was only looking," she explained in a desperate voice. "I forgot I'd even picked up that bracelet."

"Sure," one of the prostitutes jeered at her. "That's why they call you Millie Pockets."

Millie Pockets stuck her tongue out at the woman, who in turn made a retort about what lewd acts Millie could perform with that tongue. Blushing, and kicking myself for blushing, I scolded the women the way my eighth-grade physical culture teacher had reproached us for singing risqué songs during recess.

"I'm gonna be sick," moaned the woman curled up in the corner.

I passed a glass of water to her. She did look green, but the liquor fumes coming off her told me she was drunk. I suspected she just needed to sleep it off.

As the night progressed, more women were brought in, mostly prostitutes picked up off the streets of the Tenderloin. These were the unfortunate women who didn't have the luxury of working in one of the numerous houses in the area, where a madam saw to it that they weren't caught—usually by paying the police to leave her establishment alone. My women were on their own, and though they sassed and groused, they bore their incarceration with an air of weary acceptance. Most had been here before and knew the ropes better than I did. A few even kept a deck of cards on their person, just in case of arrest, to guard against boredom. Most of the arresting officers let them keep their cards and cigarettes, they said. The basement air was blue with smoke, and the flutter of shuffling cards punctuated the hours.

The most troubled woman I dealt with that first night was named Cora—Crazy Cora, the others dubbed her. She arrived in a state of delirium tremens, seeing mice on the floor. There were probably rodents living in that building somewhere, but I never saw any that night. But to Crazy Cora, they were everywhere, and she mumbled fervent prayers that they wouldn't nibble away her toes before morning. On her side of the cell, it was just her and her invisible mice. The rest of the women formed a resentful huddle on the other side.

After hours of incoherent rambling, she calmed down somewhat. In fact, she became too quiet and slumped against the bars. The look of her inert body panicked me. I didn't want a prisoner to die, especially not on my first night on the job. When I moved closer to check on her, she grabbed my arm. "You've got to help me," she pleaded.

"I told you, there are no mice."

"No! Not that!" Her hand tightened on my arm. "I mean about all the repeating things."

I had no idea what she was talking about. I doubted she did, either. I tried to work my arm free from her grip, but her hold was tenacious.

"I keep going over all the things," she said. "Over and over."

I tried to unclaw her from my sleeve. "Why do you do that?"

"I don't know." She rocked forward, bracing her head between two bars as if she could squeeze her cranium into a vise. "It's my brain telling me to remember, so that it might all come out different."

"For God's sake, shut up," one of the prostitutes muttered. "My brain just wants some rest."

"I feel sick," my green-hued woman moaned.

Cora lowered her voice. "My brain won't let me forget."

"Forget what?" I asked.

"All the terrible things. Terrible," she repeated, still trying to stick her head between the bars. "But I keep going through it. The baby. The iron on the fire. I only stepped outside for a moment—just to talk to the neighbor." A keening wail came out of her, and for once it was the only sound in the room. The women who weren't asleep stared at Cora with eyes wide open. "Do you think I'll ever make it right, if I go over it and over it? It'll never turn out different, will it?"

I didn't know what to say. "I'm sorry."

She shook her head, speaking through a quiet stream of tears, "My brain says I got to repeat it all or I'll never learn. That's what it says—go over it all so I can see it clearly. See what I did." Another wail. "Oh, God! I'm so sorry!"

She sank to the ground, out of my reach.

I couldn't leave her alone. I just couldn't. I opened the cell, letting myself in and kneeling down beside her. "Cora, try to rest . . ."

She looked up at me with wild eyes, and in the next moment there was a sharp crack on the back of my head. I sank to the floor. My vision blurred, but I saw two of the prostitutes running out of the cell, slamming the door behind them. Then Crazy Cora dashed after them.

So much for trying to comfort the afflicted.

Across the cell, the moaning woman slumped against the wall let out a belch and finally released a nauseating spew of bile. As the vile stench reached my nostrils, serving as a stomach-turning sal volatile against my threatening unconsciousness, I groaned, less from disgust at the smell than at my own stupidity.

Thus far, my first night as a policewoman could not be deemed a great success.

CHAPTER 16

I dragged home as the rest of the city was stretching and yawning back to life. At six in the morning there weren't many people in the streets. Grocers and butchers in aprons as white as they'd appear all day were opening their doors as I passed. Trucks roared past, along with the occasional horse-drawn dray clopping by on its delivery route. I both admired and pitied the horses in town, beautiful working beasts being crowded out by ever-multiplying, smoke-spewing motor vehicles. A milkman carrying a basket rattling with glass bottles tipped his hat to me as I stopped to pat his horse's muzzle, but I could barely work up a smile in return. My head still ached from being sapped from behind, and my pride smarted from having allowed a jailbreak on my very first shift.

Granted, as escape attempts went, it hadn't been very successful. The two prostitutes were caught before they'd managed to sneak out of the building. Crazy Cora had been picked up an hour later stripping down to her shift and bust ruffle in front of the Metropolitan Life tower. Nevertheless, my new colleagues made hay from my bungle and had ribbed me over it mercilessly for the rest of my shift.

News of my ineptitude reached Fiona, the policewoman on the morning shift, even before we met.

"So you're Two," she said, unpinning her hat. She was a tall woman, thick set, with brown hair pulled back in a bun. She looked as if she'd been born to wear her sensible blue wool skirt and shirt, which, I couldn't help noticing, were of sturdier stuff than my uniform, which was already ripped in two places.

Fiona's nose wrinkled. I'd mopped the cell twice, but a lingering odor of sick clung to the area.

"It's been a long night," I said. "But I guess you heard."

Her expression softened a fraction. "The boys upstairs give you a hard time? They're a bunch of lugs, but most of them are okay when they're separated from the pack. It's when they're together that they act like hyenas."

"I'll mop again."

"Forget it," she said. "Go home and don't think about this place for twelve hours." She smiled. "And let me write down the name of a seamstress who'll make you up a uniform tough enough to withstand this place."

All through the night, I'd managed to hold myself together fairly well, but Fiona's kindness made me want to collapse at her feet in a puddle.

Her expression had approached a smile when she handed me the slip of paper. "Chin up," she said.

The words rattled me. That's what Muldoon had said. Now I knew why. He'd probably foreseen how I'd feel. He knew I'd envisioned myself doing the job of a male policeman—rubbing elbows with the community, using my wits to solve problems, doing my bit to make the city keep ticking along with some semblance of law and order. In reality I was consigned to a basement room, charged with minding what most would consider the dregs of the city's female population.

When I got home, I was thankful that Callie was still sound asleep. I crawled into my bed, ready to sink into oblivion. But first I had to battle the voice of Crazy Cora, telling me *I just have to go over and over it*. She was crazy—obviously—but the words spoke to me in a mad sort of way. I thought of Guy's murder, and all the people with opportunity and motive. What was I missing? An unsettling certainty that I'd heard or seen something crucial but failed to understand its significance gripped me.

How many days on the job before they started calling me Loony Louise?

"So how did it go?" Callie asked me that afternoon.

"Fine." I was too exhausted and too stubborn to admit that I was disappointed and demoralized. What would be the point of whining? I wasn't going to quit.

For the next few days, I did my time at the police station, then came home and slept even longer than I needed to. But when I woke, I was still tired. I felt isolated. I just couldn't confess to Callie—or Otto, or Aunt Irene, or anyone else who asked—that I'd started ticking off the minutes and the hours at work like a prisoner awaiting parole. My charges were the ones behind bars, but occasionally I wondered if I weren't the one who was really trapped. Most of them had a hope of being released by a judge in the morning, whereas I'd already been sentenced to stay at the Thirtieth Street Station for at least three months. In a jail, essentially. Even when I wasn't at work, I counted down my remaining hours of freedom until I had to go back to being Officer Two, precinct laughingstock.

Some of my colleagues were kind, like Officer Schultz. The old-timer had no intention of retiring but was too arthritic to walk a beat of more than three blocks' radius. Mostly he stayed at the station as a sort of doorman, sweeping up, cleaning spittoons, and telling stories.

My third night on the job, he approached me in the coffee cubby carrying a greasy cone of waxed paper in his old veined hand.

"Brought you a donut, Louise." He held it out to me, his face flushing in the dim light from the bare bulb high overhead. Droopy bags under his eyes gave him the air of a sweet old bloodhound. "A real one, from a place down on Flatbush near where I live. You only get sad excuses for donuts here in town now."

The gesture seemed so kind that I took the donut from him as if he were handing me a wax paper cone of gold. "Thank you, Officer Schultz."

"Call me Schultzie. I don't mind."

"Thank you, Schultzie. And thanks for reminding me I have a name other than Two."

"Just takes time to get used to the people around here." He laughed and added confidentially, "Well, I've been here thirty years and I admit I'm still not used to some of them."

"The trouble is, I spend most of my time in the basement."

He cast a glance at the stairway. "I don't envy you, and that's a fact. Walking the beat, there were some nights when I was ready to just hack my feet off rather than go another block. But even that was better than being cooped up down where you are."

As far as giving encouragement went, he'd missed the mark. Still, I appreciated the sympathy. "Thanks for the donut."

"Think nothing of it."

"Two!" Jenks's exclamation was a whip cracking through our moment of camaraderie. "I've been ringing and ringing for you. Then I decided to track you down. Now I stumble into this *Romeo and Juliet* scene between you and Schultzie."

"Donuts don't actually figure into *Romeo and Juliet,*" I said.

"Huh?" Jenks took a gander at the wax paper in my hand, then shot an irritated glance at Schultz. "You brought Two a Flatbush donut? And I thought I was your pal. I guess brotherhood doesn't count for much next to love's old sweet song."

From the set of Schultz's jaw, I guessed Jenks was one of those people it would take longer than thirty years to get used to.

"C'mon." Jenks jerked his long chin at me. "I need one of your girls."

He started walking, and I followed. "Which one?"

If he heard, he didn't let on. "You shouldn't encourage Schultz like that. He'll spend the whole night yakking at you and you'll never get anything done."

"I didn't send him a summons," I said defensively. "I was just in the coffee room, doing the sergeant's bidding, minding my own business. Unlike some I could mention."

Jenks's eyes narrowed on me. "Give a woman a job and suddenly she's a snippy britches."

Good thing we'd reached the basement, because I'd reached the end of my patience with Jenks. "Which woman did you want to see?" I asked.

"Gal called Mary McCarty. Two detectives upstairs want a word with her."

If they got even a single word, it would be a miracle. Mary, a girl of around eighteen, had been picked up for soliciting. After protesting her innocence, she hadn't said a word beyond giving her name and address. Her case seemed peculiar because she didn't dress at all like a girl walking the streets. Her clothes were quality, she wasn't painted up like a lady of the evening, and she didn't speak in gutter slang. She barely spoke at all.

"Why do they want her?" I asked.

He lowered his voice. "Her stepfather's a big noise. Leonard Cain."

The name hit me like a lightning bolt. All I could think of was his glowering at me on the train. I'd never imagined a man like him having family.

"Seems little Mary was out doing stepdaddy's work for him. Drumming up business, or making deliveries."

I thought of Mary's quiet, dignified demeanor as she sat in a cell with prostitutes and a pickpocket. "She doesn't look like a criminal to me."

"Oh, and you're an expert, are you?"

True, I'd only been on the job a few days, but even in that amount of time I'd come to recognize various stamps of guilt displayed by the hardened, the resigned, the unrepentant. Or the utter defeat of the vagrants and the intoxicated. Mary hadn't seemed hardened, defeated, or intoxicated. She just seemed . . . lost.

"Have the detectives located Mary's mother? Perhaps she could shed some light . . ."

"Cain's old lady came by and told us she's glad the kid's in jail. Says she's no-good baggage and oughta be locked up to teach her a lesson."

I frowned. "So much for motherly love."

He shrugged. "I always thought mothers were overrated myself."

"Sure," I said. "Who needs 'em?"

"Exactly."

Shaking my head, I led him over to the cell where Mary sat, hands in her lap, eyes on the floor. She didn't look up until I'd unlocked the steel door. "Detectives want to speak to you, Mary," I told her.

The girl trained her blue eyes first on me, then on Jenks, who was muscling me out of the way. Before he could grab her bodily, she stood. She had a slight, still-girlish frame, with red-blond hair and porcelain skin.

"Just follow Detective Jenks," I told her.

Mary hesitated, and Jenks sighed impatiently. "What's the matter? Is she a dummy?"

"No, she can speak." But why didn't she want to? If I'd been arrested wrongly, as she claimed to have been, I'd be arguing at the top of my lungs to get myself free.

Jenks sent me a disgusted look. "I don't mean can't she talk, I mean doesn't she have much going on upstairs." He tapped his own skull—surprisingly, there was no echo. "C'mon, girlie. You get another chance to tell your story."

As he steered Mary out of the cell, she stumbled alongside him, still mute but with a backward imploring gaze at me. I relocked the cell to the usual barbed remarks and complaints from the other women left behind.

"Don't let them push you around, Mary," one of the women called out.

Why would anyone push Mary around? Either she could help the detectives or she couldn't. But once Jenks had led her away, I thought about Cain's threats to me. Then I wondered again why a girl like Mary would appear to *want* to be in jail. Unless, as the detectives seemed to think, she was commanded to by her stepfather.

What were they hoping to learn from Mary? Could it have anything to do with Guy's death?

Maybe Muldoon was one of the detectives.

I waited a few minutes and then went upstairs. The interview was taking place in a room near the coffee cubby. A few officers were standing by the open door. Normally my appearance drew attention—the jailbreak still had my colleagues rolling in the aisles—but today all eyes were on the two detectives talking to Mary. Neither was Muldoon.

"Now's your chance, Mary. You tell us exactly what Cain had you doing, and we'll get the judge to go easy."

The detective who spoke was an older man, almost as tall and thin as Jenks, and his partner, spreading out over a chair turned the wrong way, was just as stout as his partner was lean. Physically they created quite a contrast, but they worked together like parts in a well-oiled machine.

"Go easy?" the stout one said. "What're you talking about? Any judge'd look at this sweet kid and just let her go. If she helped us."

The tall man leaned over Mary. "Hear that? *If* you help us. It's no good if you sit there clammed up like a . . ."

"Clam," the fat detective finished for him.

"Right. 'Cause you can sit there playing all dimply and innocent, but there's the question of what a girl like you was doing all alone on a street at night, approaching strange men."

"And if you don't say anything, there won't be a question left in anyone's mind."

"Certainly not a judge's."

"Straight-up solicitation."

Red splotched across Mary's cheeks, and her chin raised a notch. Pride finally forced her to speak. "I was asking directions."

The stout detective chuckled. "We've heard that before."

"It's the truth," she said.

"Directions where?"

"To a hotel."

The two detectives exchanged a long look, and the expressions on the faces of the cops around them were nothing less than gleeful. Indignant, I stepped forward—but a hand on my shoulder stopped me. I whipped around. Schultzie was shaking his head at me. *Let the detectives handle it,* those bloodhound eyes told me. Schultzie had decades more experience at this. Jaw clenched, I faced forward.

"Now, what's a pretty young girl like you want with a hotel when you've got a nice home to go to?"

Mary looked down at her hands. "I was running away."

"Where to?"

"Baltimore. I've got a girlfriend there."

"Thought you said you were going to a hotel."

"I missed the train. I was tired."

It sounded reasonable enough to me, but the detectives didn't think much of her story.

"All the way to Baltimore without luggage?"

"I checked it at the station."

"Where's the claim ticket, then?" He turned. "Did we find a claim ticket on her?"

Jenks stood at attention. "Not that I recall."

"It was in my purse," she said. "The officers took it after they brought me in."

The stout detective snapped his fingers but didn't look away from Mary. "Find it," he directed.

Jenks nudged the officer nearest him, and the man turned on his heel and darted off.

The thin detective began to pace in front of Mary. "That man you solicited—excuse me—*asked for directions.* Turns out he had a bag of heroin on him. He says you gave it to him."

She lifted her head. "He's lying. Heroin? Why would I want that?"

"You tell us."

"I've never seen it except in the cough syrup my mother gives me when I'm sick."

The detectives shared a smile at that. "Cough medicine, she says."

"Leonard Cain's daughter."

She stiffened. "Stepdaughter."

"What do you think pays for your nice clothes?"

Her mouth opened and closed like a beached fish, as if she were genuinely trying to figure that out.

"See, a nip of heroin every now and then's not bad," the seated detective explained. "Cough syrup, sure. Stuff's safe enough for kiddies. But others don't stop at a nip. They become fiends for the junk. Government's trying to put an end to crooks peddling the stuff around in large quantities, and not for medication."

This information cast an entirely different light on Guy's "business investment."

"Just tell us he put you up to it."

"Nice girl like you wouldn't get involved in all this sordid stuff. Not without his influence."

"He forced you to, didn't he?"

"And now he's not lifting a finger to help you. Why, he sent your own mother to tell us to *keep* you here."

Mary's face registered these last words with surprise. "Mama was here? She said that?"

"Sure she did."

Tears glistened in her eyes.

"Cain doesn't deserve your loyalty, Mary," said the fat man.

She stiffened, and her sadness turned into pure contempt. "I wouldn't lift a finger for him. You can lock him away forever, for all I care. But I didn't do what that man said. I was only asking directions."

The cop who'd been sent to look for the claim ticket came puffing back. "Not there," he said.

Mary's mouth dropped open. "That can't be."

"Did you lie to us, Mary?" the older detective asked.

"No! It was there. I saw them take it out of my purse."

"Maybe you *want* to go to jail."

The harangue went on for another half hour—thirty exhausting minutes of threats, insults, insinuations. When it was over, Mary looked numb. She'd never veered from her story. I practically had to drag her downstairs, and she seemed so forlorn that I took her aside toward the little washroom set aside for Fiona and me, out of sight of the others. I stowed my things in a little cabinet near there.

"Would you like a donut?" I asked her, remembering Schultz's offering to me.

Perhaps it was the donut, or being out of the presence of the men, but tension seemed to gush out of her. A tear spilled down her cheek. "I just wanted to go to Baltimore."

I sat her down on the cot provided for the policewomen. It was in a corridor, with nothing but a privacy curtain on one end. This was probably against a dozen rules, but I was playing a hunch. She wasn't saying why she'd run away from home, but my suspicions had been brewing since the detectives' harangue had begun.

I handed her the greasy waxed paper. "You're in trouble, aren't you?"

"The detectives say I'll go to jail."

"I'm not talking about the trouble the gorillas in suits up there were referring to. You've had other troubles, haven't you?"

Tears spilled faster. "I couldn't help being out tonight. Mama kicked me out—said the most horrible things about me." She looked at me, remembering I was the police. "I guess you know that, if she came here. She called me all sorts of names at home. But they aren't true."

"A man took advantage of you," I said.

Shock leapt into her eyes, and I knew I'd hit the nail on the head.

"It wasn't hard to guess." After her boarder attacked me, my aunt Sonja had wanted me gone, too. At least to Aunt Sonja "gone" hadn't meant to jail.

Her mouth tightened. " 'Took advantage'? That's a polite way of saying it, isn't it? He's a brute, and he used me like a beast would. Do you understand? He said I couldn't cause trouble that way."

I nodded, feeling sick.

"I told Mama, but she didn't believe me at first. Said I was fantasizing. *Fantasizing*—about that pig! Then she told me that if I were pregnant, that would be one thing." She shook her head. "I told her I couldn't be pregnant, but if I were I'd throw myself off the Brooklyn Bridge."

"Who was it?"

A bitter laugh tore out of her. "Are you a fool? It was Leonard Cain! Why else do you think my mother doesn't want me back? Why else would she turn against me and call me a whore to complete strangers? She'd rather I rot in jail than let the world know what kind of man she married."

I sank onto the cot next to her. Dear God. Her own stepfather.

She dashed tears off her cheeks with the back of her hand. "I should have left a year ago, only I was such an idiot. I hoped I was wrong about the way he looked at me. And I hoped Ma would protect me. Ha! She'd swap the happiness of both her daughters for that man."

"You have a sister?"

"I told him if he so much as laid a hand on Lena I'd kill him, and so help me, I will."

"You can't protect Lena from Baltimore," I pointed out.

"I'm going to send for her when I get there and find a job. I'll do anything . . ."

"But now you'll be in jail. Why didn't you tell the detectives what you just told me about Cain?"

"Would you have? My own mother didn't believe what I told her, and the policemen were already accusing me of passing a package of drugs to a man. But I swear I only stopped him on the street to ask directions."

I remembered the cold, menacing threat in Cain's eyes, and the way I'd instinctively recoiled from him. He was capable of what she said, I knew he was. "I believe you."

Mary sniffed. "That's fine, but I didn't see anyone asking your opinion upstairs."

I couldn't deny that. "The police want to catch your stepfather doing something illegal. What he did to you was a vile crime. When they hear you out, they'll be inclined to take your side."

"But Mr. Cain will deny it, and my mother will back him up."

"It's your word against his, but you have truth on your side, and his word is hopelessly tarnished. You heard the things the police suspect him of, and believe me, drugs are the tip of the iceberg." I thought about the gambling and all the murders he was rumored to have ordered. "The police will want to hear your story. Tell them."

"It'll be my word against his."

"But it might not be your word alone," I said. "If Cain brutalized you, he probably did the same to others. We could find these women and make your story more credible to a jury. Your testimony could put your stepfather behind bars for years and might save other girls. It might save Lena."

That, more than anything, broke the dam of her reluctance. "I'd kill him."

"You don't have to kill him. You just have to tell the truth."

After a little more cajoling, I convinced her to speak again to the detectives and explain the whole ugly story.

Upstairs, I let the sergeant know what I'd found out. His eyebrows shot up and he asked, incredulous, "You want I should call the detectives back for *that*?"

Anger rose in me. "Isn't rape still a crime?"

His fat chin jutted out at me, but after a moment's reflection he called Jenks over. "This better be the truth, Two. If it's not, your days are numbered."

He whispered to Jenks, who hurried out to do his master's bidding. No doubt that would involve rousting the detectives out of whatever all-night beanery they'd retired to.

I wanted to stay to hear the interview, but the sergeant put the kibosh on that. "You've got your real work to tend to."

Reluctantly, I left Mary in his charge and headed back downstairs. An hour dragged by, and I was fighting the mid-shift drowsies when I heard a scream. There was a commotion in one of the cells—a woman had tried to slash her wrists with a key she'd hidden beneath her skirts. Blood stained her dress and her wrists looked gruesome—God only knew how she'd managed to create so much damage with a brass key. The sergeant informed me that I would be escorting the prisoner to Bellevue. The cross-town errand stretched into a few hours.

By the time I got back, dawn was peeping over the city and my shift was almost over. As I entered the precinct, I was startled to see a distinguished, uniformed man with salt-and-pepper hair and a toothbrush mustache talking to Sergeant Donnelly, who nodded at me. "There she is now."

My heart sank into my heels. The stranger was wearing a captain's bars. This had to be the elusive McMartin. He and Donnelly had obviously been discussing me, which, according to my mind-set at the time, could only mean bad news. The sergeant had warned me that my days might be numbered, but I never dreamed that my hours might be, too.

I approached them and stood at attention while I was introduced to Captain McMartin.

"So, Faulk, there's been a stir here tonight. Sergeant Donnelly's been telling me you were responsible for getting Leonard Cain's stepdaughter to talk."

"I could see she was holding something back, sir."

"You *guessed* she was," Donnelly corrected with a glower.

"Saw, guessed . . . it makes no matter." McMartin clasped his hands behind his back. "However you divined the truth, you were able to dig down to the truth that two seasoned detectives couldn't coax out of her."

The word *coax* made it hard for me to keep my countenance. Their coaxing had looked like straight-up bullying to me.

I would gain nothing by criticizing two veteran detectives, however. And I couldn't toot my own horn when it was only my own hidden history that gave me insight into what Mary had been holding back. "It was a delicate matter," was all I said.

The captain nodded. "No doubt. Nevertheless, your success is a credit to you and this precinct. And, I daresay, your sex. Makes me think having these women around might not be such a bad idea after all. Eh, Donnelly?"

The sergeant turned a putrid shade of green. "Sir."

Relief flooded through me. I wasn't being fired. "Will a charge of rape be made against Leonard Cain?"

"Rape?" McMartin's forehead wrinkled. "No, but Mary's agreed to testify against him in the matter of the drugs. Selling that much raw heroin unlabeled is a clear violation of the Wiley Act of 1906. Shameful for a man to use an innocent young girl as a go-between in that dirty business."

I frowned, confused. "But he didn't. Mary was adamant. Cain raped her, but she knew nothing about the drugs."

"That's as may be, but it'd be a whole lot harder to make a charge of rape stick to Cain, especially when the mother denies it. Cases like that are always uncertain, especially if it goes before a jury. Never know which way the cat will jump."

I was astounded. "But the rape accusation is true, while the other—"

Donnelly pinched my arm. "The girl says the drug story's true."

Since when? "If she says that, it's only because she wants her stepfather in jail for something."

"That's what we all want," said McMartin. "And now, thanks to you, it's like Christmas coming a month early. We're all getting our wish. Mary's testimony should put Cain away for at least five years, so long as he doesn't get to the jury." He clapped me on the back. "Well done, Faulk."

I froze in bewilderment. Encouraging perjured testimony? It was hard to imagine a circumstance under which the jailing of Leonard Cain could be seen a moral wrong, but the NYPD had just managed it.

I balked at Sergeant Donnelly's warning glare. Clearly he thought I'd said enough.

"Where is Mary now?" If I could just talk to her . . .

"She's being taken downtown till we can figure out where to stash her until the trial. Her mother obviously won't have her back." The captain commended me again. "Keep up the good work, Officer Faulk."

I attempted a smile, as did the sergeant. The moment the captain was out the door, though, Donnelly rounded on me. "Don't go getting a swelled head, Two. Playing a lucky hunch doesn't make you a good cop."

As if I took pride in any of what had just transpired. "Tell me this," I said. "Did those drugs really have anything to do with Cain? Was there even a package of drugs at all?"

Donnelly frowned. "Cain's up to his ears in nasty business. Now we'll have him. That's what matters."

"More than truth?"

He shook his head. "Go home, Two. You'll think straighter after some shut-eye."

As I was leaving a short time later, I bumped into Schultzie on the stoop. "See you tomorrow," I said.

"Tonight, you mean."

I groaned. He was right. Sleeping during the day had turned my sense of days topsy-turvy. Tonight would seem like tomorrow after I managed to get some sleep. Which I fully intended to do.

I should have remembered the old saw about best-laid plans.

Chapter 17

When I arrived home, I almost slipped on a note someone had pushed under the door. It was from Abe Faber.

> *Louise,*
> *Ogden McChesney has requested a visit from you. He did not tell me why, although I believe my theory is once again proving true: the caged bird is looking outward. A positive development! I will be in court all day, but if you could find it in your heart, and schedule, to visit him, it could prove beneficial to his spirits, and therefore helpful to the prospect of mounting a successful defense.*
> *Yours sincerely,*
> *A. Faber*

Desire for sleep warred with curiosity. Why would Mr. McChesney want to see me?

I took a brief nap on the sofa and then changed clothes and left the flat again before nine o'clock.

This time Mr. McChesney and I were in an open visitors' room with a guard standing watch at the center of the long table provided. His gaze tracked our movements as if he expected to catch me slipping a weapon to the prisoner.

Mr. McChesney seemed to be shrinking by the day. His rough clothing drooped over his thinning frame.

"Aren't they feeding you?" I asked.

"Oh yes. The food is adequate. Your dear aunt even sent me a package through Mr. Faber. It contained a copy of *David Copperfield* and a bit of Bernice's lemon cake that I've always loved so."

"Novels and cake." I smiled. "Book people are easy to please."

He let out something approaching a laugh. Mr. Faber was right. Something had changed.

"Irene included a lovely note, too, urging me not to give up hope. She told me a man who'd asked for her hand as many times as I had couldn't be easily discouraged."

I was glad my aunt had reached out to him, but he couldn't have summoned me here just to tell me about that. "Have you remembered anything that might be helpful?"

He looked down at the table, then cleared his throat. "Not remembered, exactly, but I have an idea that might explain what happened to Guy."

I leaned toward him.

"The more I think on it, I do believe he might have taken his own life."

I remained perched forward, breath bated, until I realized that this was all he had to offer. It was the same idea, first put in my head by Jacob, that Muldoon had talked me out of weeks ago. "That seems unlikely."

"I don't see why," Mr. McChesney said. "Guy was always in some scrape or another. Perhaps he'd gotten himself in a particularly bad way—debts and so forth."

"But we know Cain paid him three thousand dollars before his death. It would be strange for a man to receive a large sum and then take his own life. The money would have given him hope."

"Whose word but Cain's do we have that Guy ever received the three thousand dollars?" he asked. "*I* never saw it."

"You said you didn't go into Guy's office."

He frowned. "Yes, that's true."

"Anyway, Muldoon told me that some of the ashes found on the first floor looked as if they might be the residue of bank notes.

Large ones. It gives credence to that part of Cain's story." Much as I would have liked to find the man culpable.

Mr. McChesney slumped in his chair. "I'm so alone with my thoughts here, Louise. All I do is go over everything. I guess I convinced myself that suicide made sense."

Crazy Cora syndrome. I sympathized.

"It would make sense if we could come up with an unsolvable problem that had been preying on Guy's mind—something for which three thousand dollars wouldn't have been enough. Think. Did you have any arguments with Guy over the financial straits the company was in?" I asked. "Could he have been depressed about that?"

"He didn't care about the company enough to argue. I was always frustrated with him when it came to the business. He would ask me about where we stood, and I would tell him that we stood very stubbornly in the red. And he would laugh at that. Laugh!" He shook his head. "As if it were all just a joke. Cyrus would have seen that the firm was put into the black, but Guy felt no responsibility for it. He was only there because it kept him from having to do something more taxing, like working at a job downtown. If we went under, as we were sure to do, one of his family connections would have found him a better sinecure in another business."

"So you never argued over the financial books," I said.

He chuckled. "The books? Heavens, no. He never even glimpsed at them."

"If we had evidence of Guy's seeing the hopelessness of Van Hooten and McChesney's financial position, it might have backed up the idea that he would've taken his own life in despair." I frowned in thought. "Not that it matters, I suppose, if all the financial records of the company went up in smoke." I remembered something then, and sucked in a breath. "Except they didn't, did they? You told Bob that you'd kept some at your flat."

His eyes widened in alarm. "When?"

"The morning of the fire. You told Bob to come see you at your flat to look them over and talk about the future of the company."

He waved a hand dismissively. "Those books were of no importance. I passed them along to someone."

"Who?"

"Someone I trusted."

"Was it Bob?" It would have made sense for him to entrust them to the accountant, and I'd suspected Bob was taking something out of the apartment when I'd bumped into him at Mr. McChesney's. Bob had denied the existence of the financial books, but I hadn't believed him.

"No, not Bob. You're looking in the wrong direction." He shook his head. "You should forget about those ledgers. There was nothing in them."

"Are you sure? If there's any trace of evidence, some hint at an aggrieved creditor who might have wanted to attack Guy . . ."

"There wasn't," he said. "I can assure you of that."

"Then why would it matter if I looked?"

He stared at me.

"There *is* something incriminating in those books, isn't there?" I asked.

"Nothing that incriminates me."

"Then why—?"

"Leave it alone." He stood up abruptly, so agitated that he almost lost his balance. He placed his palms on the table. "It was a mistake to ask you here. I only did so because I hoped you'd agree with me about Guy's committing suicide."

"Why would you care what I think? Why not tell the theory to Abe Faber directly?"

His gaze sought mine. "Irene told me that you were now a policewoman, and you know Detective Muldoon, don't you? I thought, since you might have access to evidence, and the ears of your colleagues . . ."

I would have given anything in that moment not to have heard him say that. He seemed to believe that by hook or by crook I could simply convince the detectives on the case that Guy committed suicide. That would be a very tidy situation for everyone—a solved case, no messy trial, no Ogden McChesney convicted of murder.

Yes, it would be very handy just to close cases by pointing the finger at a dead man, or picking the suspect who best suited everybody's ends. Wasn't that what had happened last night?

Cain needed a charge laid against him, and so they'd found someone who would make it. With my help.

Bernice's warnings about crooked cops echoed in my mind. That wasn't the kind of policewoman I wanted to be.

"I won't stop trying to find evidence to clear you of Guy's murder," I said. "But it would help if you cooperated. If you'd just tell me whom you gave the books to . . ."

"I don't want to be cleared at the expense of an innocent man's freedom."

"But if that man *isn't* innocent . . ."

He smiled sadly. "Goodbye, Louise. It was good of you to come."

I wanted to cry in frustration. He knew something. He could have told me exactly whom I was looking for, but he wouldn't. Why?

As I left the courthouse, his words stayed with me. "Someone I trusted," he'd said, when I'd asked him who had the remaining ledgers.

He'd ruled out Bob. So who could it be?

As an idea dawned on me, blood drained to my heels. Of course. I knew one person he trusted more than anyone.

Walter must have been taking the dogs out for their afternoon stroll, because Bernice answered the door. "Your aunt's upstairs. She's not feeling well."

"Then I'm doubly glad I came."

Hearing typing, I detoured to Aunt Irene's study. At my old post sat Miriam, perfectly at ease in her new surroundings. She glanced up.

"I was looking for my aunt," I said after we exchanged greetings.

"She's in bed with a cold. Could I take a message to her for you?"

The presumption rankled a bit. After all, she was my aunt. Why shouldn't I be able to witness her sniffles as well as a relative newcomer to the household?

It was my own insecurity bubbling up, of course. I felt shaky in my own job, so I was looking at Miriam as some kind of usurper. I took a breath. "You seem to have settled in."

She smiled. "Maybe a little more than I expected. I'm staying in the spare room while your aunt's ill—in case she needs something during the night."

Did Aunt Irene really need three people to see her through a head cold? "Doesn't Jackson miss you?"

Her smile evaporated. "He could use a little time by himself, I think."

I sank down into my aunt's velvet-covered reading chair. "He seemed troubled the last time I saw him. Has he still not found a job?"

She shook her head. "The best thing for him to do would be to go back home. To Alabama. He's never been happy here."

No, he never did seem to enjoy his life in this city. "Do you want to go home?"

"I like it here." She shifted in her chair and glanced away as she spoke. "I meant Jackson should go home alone."

"He wouldn't leave you."

It took longer than I would have thought necessary for her to answer. During the silence, it occurred to me that she might have already left him.

"His folks would welcome him back in the fold quick enough if I wasn't with him. He'd be back where he was meant to be."

"Where are any of us meant to be?" I asked. "I probably could have stayed in Altoona forever, but circumstances blew me here. I don't regret it."

"That's you. In Jackson's case, *I* was the circumstance. I never meant to make him unhappy, but I have."

"It wasn't all your doing, was it?" I asked. "It takes two to fall in love."

"And two to fall out of it."

"Maybe once Jackson finds work . . ."

She shook her head. "He hasn't been the same since that fire."

I understood what she meant, or thought I did. "I wasn't the same after my roommate's cousin was killed in our flat. Jackson might need time."

Her eyes looked on me dully, and I felt a rupture between us, as if I'd missed something important. "I'd better finish these pages," she said.

Perplexed at the abrupt dismissal, I went down the hall to my aunt's room. She was propped up in bed by a complicated network of pillows, with a carved lap desk in front of her. At the foot of the bed, the empty pillows for Dickens and Trollope confirmed my earlier hunch about Walter's whereabouts.

"Oh, Louise—it's kind of you to come see me." Her glance at the clock on her bedside table telegraphed that the visit was also inconvenient. "But my cold really isn't very serious."

"I actually came to discuss something related to the case. I've just been to see Mr. McChesney."

She glanced at me over her glasses and set down her pen. "You'd better pull up a chair."

I picked up the embroidered stool by her dressing table and settled it next to her bedside.

"Not too close," she instructed. "The last thing you want is to catch whatever I have." She blew her nose into a monogrammed linen handkerchief.

"Why are you working?" I said. "You should rest."

She wrinkled her nose. "How would bills be paid if I stopped working every time I felt a sniffle coming on?"

"Surely a day or two to get your strength back . . ."

"A day or two and I might lose my momentum." She patted the pages before her. "I'm awfully eager to get to the end of this one." A chuckle rattled in her chest. "It's my first mystery and I'm curious to see how it all turns out."

I could have told her—all I had to do was recite the events of four months ago—but I didn't want to interfere with her muse.

I cleared my throat. "Miriam says she's staying in the spare bedroom."

"She's such a help to me, I can't tell you."

I wondered if her helping might not be the slightest bit opportunistic. "Things don't seem to be going well between her and Jackson. I've noticed tension between them for a while, but I got the sense just now that she'd like to leave him permanently."

"That may be. I always find it advisable not to examine any marriage too closely unless you want reasons to stay single forever. When you're young you think being an old maid is the worst fate that can befall a woman, but from what I've witnessed, no one's more lonely than a person trapped in an unhappy marriage."

Neither possibility seemed especially happy to me.

"Now, tell me," Aunt Irene continued, "how was Ogden?"

"Your gifts lifted his spirits. He's showing a glimmer of wanting to cooperate with Abe Faber to clear himself of the murder charge."

"Good. I only wish there was more I could do for him."

"Perhaps there is."

Briefly, I recounted my conversation with Mr. McChesney. "So you see," I concluded, "I need to find the person with these ledgers."

"Yes."

"And since he said it was someone he trusted, I came here."

There was a delay before my meaning registered. She laughed. "Me? Pumpkin, you're barking up the wrong tree."

I tried not to let my disappointment show. "He trusts you."

"Yes, but even tending to my own books usually makes me want to weep. Ogden knows how I hate figuring—especially anytime there are irregularities. Why, just last year I had to go over my own books with him when I suspected a royalty shortf—"

Her words died, and her gaze fixed on the inkpot in its space on her lap desk.

"There was a shortfall?" I asked.

"Yes, for *Myrtle in Springtime*."

The novel Van Hooten and McChesney had published. After that, another company had offered her more money. Even though she'd written it almost two decades ago, Van Hooten and McChesney kept *Myrtle in Springtime* in print. It was one of their evergreens.

"I was only guessing, of course," she said. "But I consulted with Ogden, and a few months later I received a check from him, with his apologies."

"This was last year?"

She nodded.

"Did he say why the money hadn't been forthcoming?"

She sneezed. "It was an oversight, he said."

An oversight. "And this had never happened before?"

"No, not in all the years I knew Ogden. And I'm very thorough in my accounting, however much it pains me."

What had changed at Van Hooten and McChesney around that

time? Bob had been with the firm for eight years, and must have been an honest bookkeeper, or Mr. McChesney would have let him go. Of course, a year and a half ago was before I'd begun working there.

But it was just after Jackson had started.

I arrived at Jackson's flat without advance warning, hoping to catch him in an unguarded moment. I suppose I had in mind an ambush—that he'd be so startled by my perspicacity that a confession would gush out of him.

And then what? I didn't plan that far ahead.

It took a full minute for him to answer my knock. His eyes, which were bloodshot, widened at the sight of me.

"My old office mate. And now thief of my actual mate."

This was not how I'd intended the conversation to begin.

"I just saw Miriam. She said she was staying there until my aunt got better."

He didn't respond. How inebriated was he?

"Everyone at my aunt's is wild about Miriam."

He laughed and left me at the door, collapsing into the chair I assumed he'd only vacated at my knock. "Yes, she can be charming when she wants to be."

Invited or not, I went inside and took the matching chair opposite him.

"That's right," he said, "sit down. Might as well take advantage of our chairs while we've got 'em. In a week or so they'll have to be sold to a second-hand store."

"You still haven't been able to find work?"

He swirled some whiskey in a glass. "I was offered a job just yesterday—as a proofreader! Sixteen dollars a week."

That wasn't much. He'd probably been making twice that at Van Hooten and McChesney.

"It's not enough to live on," he said.

"Not even with Miriam working, too?"

His eyes were daggers. "She shouldn't have to work, and I shouldn't have to slave for peanuts, especially not for some third-rate publication run by cretins who attended third-rate schools."

"Well." I wasn't sure what to say to that, knowing that Jackson probably considered me lower than a third-rater.

"Why are you here?" he asked. "To gloat?"

"Of course not. I came to ask you a few questions."

He struggled to straighten up in his chair. "You already sound like a policeman. Should I be shaking in my boots?"

"This isn't really in the way of official police work. I was wondering if you could shed any light on something that happened soon after you started working for Van Hooten and McChesney."

He shifted slightly, curious in spite of himself.

"I believe the company had a little financial trouble around then," I said. "There might even have been a sudden shortfall in the books."

"I don't know anything about that."

"You never heard of any whiff of trouble, maybe some kind of discrepancy in the bookkeeping?"

"Are you trying to hint that someone stole from the company?"

"It's a possibility."

"And you think it was me? Sorry to disappoint you, but I never got any nearer to money at that place than my own pay envelope." When I didn't react, he asked, "Don't believe me? When did you ever see me involved in financial discussions with old man McChesney? I'll remind you—never. I was hired to be an editor, and my activities were limited to that sphere." His gaze narrowed on me. "What could possibly have made you think that I was cooking the books?"

I told him a little about my conversation with Mr. McChesney. "He said he gave the surviving ledgers to someone he trusted."

"And you thought of me?" He snorted. "The old man barely tolerated me. He considered me to be Guy's creature, and you know what he thought of Guy."

"Yes, but you would often be seen as the de facto head when both Guy and Mr. McChesney were out of the office."

"Only because I took charge. Someone had to, or that office would have been even more of a disaster than it was."

I acknowledged the truth in his words with a nod. "My aunt spoke of a missing payment from Van Hooten and McChesney around the time you started with the company. Or soon after."

"I can't explain that. I can only profess my innocence. Look at me. If I'm a criminal, then I'm the most unsuccessful one in town. I don't have a bean."

True. I doubted an accomplished thief or embezzler would be idly waiting to have his furniture sold out from under him.

"You shouldn't go around pointing fingers at people with no evidence," he said.

"I only want to piece together what we know. The timing made me curious, and Mr. McChesney said he didn't want to incriminate a person he trusted."

His expression soured. "If I'd stolen a dime from him, that old man wouldn't have covered for me. He never liked me."

That seemed an exaggeration. True, Mr. McChesney never voiced any appreciation for Jackson. "But he told me he would give you an excellent recommendation."

"Was that before or after he went to jail? Not much good to me now, is he?"

I frowned. The man invited antipathy. And now even his own wife had abandoned him. Given what I'd seen of how Jackson treated her, I couldn't blame her. Yet I wasn't entirely without pity for him.

"Until I was talking to Miriam tonight," I confessed to him, "I don't think I gave enough thought to what seeing Guy after the fire that morning must have done to you."

He stared at the carpet beneath his slippers, saying nothing.

"I'm sorry," I said. "I saw my roommate's cousin's body after she was murdered. I still have nightmares."

"Had it not been for your dentist appointment, you might have been the one who discovered what was left of Guy. More nightmares for you."

I'd almost forgotten about my fictitious dentist appointment. It seemed eons ago since I'd sneaked off to take the civil service exam. And now I was a policewoman.

"It's Bob you should be talking to, not me," Jackson said. "Ogden McChesney wouldn't lift a finger—or tell a fib—to cover for me. Only two people would he do that for. Bob's one."

"Who is the other?"

"You."

I drew back. "*I* didn't steal anything."

He laughed. "Of course not. You lack the imagination to be a criminal."

I stood. When I'd worked with Jackson, I'd disliked him. Now every time I ginned up a little sympathy for him, he managed to make me dislike him all over again. "If you'd ever put forth half an effort to be kind, you might make more friends," I said.

"Do you really believe it's as easy as that? Perhaps it is, for you. You have a knack for getting along. But I know who I am, and what people think of me. I've heard the jeers at my stiffness all my life. Do you think I wouldn't be different if I could, that *I* wouldn't be the kind of man whose company others enjoyed?" He slumped down. "I thought Guy was my friend. He gave me a job, at any rate. Then he treated me like his lackey. You don't think I heard him call me Old Baldy? And we were at Harvard together!" He shook his head. "Now he's dead, and hypocrite though he was, I've no one to replace him with. Even my own wife doesn't want to be around me."

"How was Guy a hypocrite?"

"He looked down his nose at my Negro wife, yet he was hiding a Jew bastard."

The thin crust of sympathy I had left for him crumbled to dust. "How did you find out about Guy's son?" Weeks ago, he'd said he didn't know much about the women Guy went with.

"Guy talked about him once after he had a few whiskies in him."

"Why didn't you tell me?"

"Why should I have? Guy told me about the boy in confidence." He shook his head. "Sharing a drink, you were his best friend. Then he'd sober up and become a Van Hooten again."

He emptied the last of the bottle into his glass. I certainly didn't want to stay to watch him drink it. I started for the door.

"Going off to arrest someone, Officer Faulk?"

I'd had about enough of his digs. "You've always underestimated me, Jackson." *And overestimated yourself.* "I *will* find out who killed Guy."

"Atta girl. Never say die." He lifted his glass. "Me? Saying die is what I do best. Someday I hope to take myself literally. I've been sitting here planning it all out."

I told myself to go, but I couldn't make my legs move. His words had frozen me. "What are you talking about?"

"My death."

"Jackson, you can't be serious."

"Why not? I've even got the place all picked out. Ever been to the waterfront? On the Hudson side, before you reach the steamship piers, a little farther down the island . . . that's where I'd do it. Pier Twenty-seven would be perfect. There was an accident there last year, a fire, and it's not repaired yet. Often it's deserted. It would be so easy." He smiled at me, and a shiver worked all the way to the marrow of my bones. "That's the great thing about never learning how to swim. One never need worry how to end one's life. You just step off into the water, into oblivion."

Was he really telling me he was going to drown himself? "Jackson, whatever problems you're having now, it doesn't mean things won't get better."

His brows rose into his long forehead. "My wife will return, I'll find a job, the bluebirds will sing again?"

"Sneer if you want, but all of those things might happen. They won't if you simply give up, though. You have to make an effort, and have faith that—"

"Thank you for those inspiring words, Pastor Louise."

I suppressed a growl of frustration. "Why did you tell me you would take your own life, if you didn't want me to encourage you not to?"

He shrugged. "It was just the drink talking."

Of all the maudlin, self-pitying displays, this took the cake.

"I'll go and let you to converse with your drink, then. You're obviously not going to listen to me." I left the flat, hoping with all my might that it would be for the last time. Sympathy had its limits, and mine for Jackson Beasley had just been reached.

But what if he meant what he said?

Poor Miriam.

By the time I got home, I felt dead on my feet and ready to catch a few hours of sleep—*catch* being the operative word. To a person working nights, daylight hours flitted by and sleep could prove elusive. Most days I'd barely managed to grab more than a few hours of solid sleep. To slumber during the day required a constant battle against street noise, slamming doors, and the Bleecker Blowers rehearsing their latest number.

When I woke up at five, I stumbled out to find Otto and Callie on the sofa. Seeing me, Otto sprang up. His self-conscious avoidance of my gaze alarmed me, as did Callie's gloomy expression.

"What's the matter?" I asked.

She waved her hand, not speaking. Otto took it as a signal to speak for her. He was dressed in a checked sport coat and a wildly striped silk tie and matching handkerchief. The Jolson influence.

"It's off with Teddy," he announced.

Callie hurled a pillow at him. "I didn't say it was *definitely* off."

"Yes, you did," he said. "Unless 'Teddy's dropped me' means something other than what I think it means."

"He's just mad, on account of Hugh."

I felt a sick gnawing in the pit of my stomach. "What did Hugh do?"

Her mouth tightened, and she fell silent again.

"Apparently he blames Teddy for taking you to the air park," Otto explained.

"And Teddy blames *me,*" she added.

"You'd think Hugh would be glad, if not grateful, that I'm trying to find out who killed his brother."

"He's sore that you accused *him,*" she said.

Otto nodded. "Being accused of fratricide doesn't sit well with some people."

"Well, I had to rule out the possibility," I said in my own defense. "Anyway, he convinced me I was on the wrong track, and managed to scare me half to death in the bargain. I don't know what he's bellyaching about." Hadn't complaining to Muldoon been enough for him?

"He says Teddy's taking you there was disloyal."

"Oh, for Pete's sake. Loyalty? Are they friends or members of some outfit like the Black Hand?"

"Exactly," Otto said. "What kind of weak-willed fool lets his friend pressure him to break off with his girl?"

Did Teddy really intend to make a split with Callie because of this? I felt terrible. "Maybe I could apologize to Hugh . . ."

She drew up. "Don't you dare. Hugh can go—fly an airplane. Teddy too. They're both lunatics, anyway."

"Finally," Otto said, "you've come to your senses."

Callie hopped off the sofa, her eyes red with tears. "Now look! I'll be all puffy for the run-through tonight." She ran to her bedroom and slammed the door.

I stumbled to the kitchenette to make coffee. Although I was awake now.

Otto tagged after me. "You think she still likes him?"

"I think she might love him."

He sank down on a step stool we kept by the kitchen door. It was a long moment before he spoke again. "Well, at least I have my music."

I put my hand on his shoulder. "You have more than that. And someday you'll be head over heels for somebody new."

"Sure." He didn't sound convinced.

"And maybe you'll get another song hit out of it. 'The one I love belongs to someone else'—what do you think of that?"

"I think you'd better stick to police work and leave the songwriting to the experts," he said. "Have you made any more progress in your investigation?"

After the disturbing end of my conversation with Jackson, I hadn't given much thought to what he'd told me about Bob, who surely had to be the one hiding the missing ledgers.

But even if Bob had done something illegal, and the secret was in the ledgers, what could that possibly have to do with Guy's death? Unless Guy had found out about the discrepancy and blackmailed Bob . . . In that case, Bob might have wanted to harm Guy.

The trouble was, I couldn't imagine Bob doing violence against anyone. And Mr. McChesney had said that Guy had no interest in the financial records of the company. So how could he have known enough about the missing money to blackmail anyone?

Mr. McChesney could be wrong about that, though. Just as my instinct that Bob couldn't be a thief might be wrong. Muldoon had warned me against relying solely on gut instinct.

The time I'd spoken to him about the company finances, Bob hadn't said much. But he'd certainly acted suspiciously that morning coming off the elevator at Mr. McChesney's. I'd bet money he'd been hiding those ledgers under his coat. But if he hadn't wanted to answer general questions weeks ago, he wasn't likely to open up to me now that I actually suspected *him*.

I could do something drastic like show up with my badge, but that would be taking a risk. If he complained to anyone at the department, I'd be done for. I was already lucky that Muldoon had quashed Hugh Van Hooten's complaint. I was just a probationer. Any infraction would be excuse enough for the NYPD to give me the heave-ho.

I looked at Otto. Coffee wasn't all that was percolating. So was a plan.

"I don't like that look in your eye," he said.

"You visited the office and met all my coworkers, didn't you? Including Bob?"

"Yes—I remember him." He looked even more nervous. "What do you want me to do?"

"Relax. I can't use you. I need someone Bob's never seen."

It was time to call on my master of disguise.

CHAPTER 18

"I'm not really conversant in legal lingo," Walter warned as we approached Bob's street. He was dressed in a gray suit, black coat, and bowler hat. Wire spectacles and a thin mustache completed his look. He'd wanted to wear a putty nose, but I thought that would be going overboard.

"Bob isn't either. You'll do fine. Just speak plainly to him, but be firm."

"Plain but firm," he repeated.

I assumed if Bob kept the ledgers anywhere, it would be at home, so the plan was to ambush him there. Or, rather, Walter would do the ambushing. I would wait nearby.

For this mission, Aunt Irene had lent Walter a calf-skin briefcase, given to her by Mr. McChesney. It seemed apt that it would be part of his disguise as the assistant to Mr. McChesney's attorney.

"Tell him the ledgers are vital to Ogden McChesney's defense, and if you don't get them, the police will certainly come back for them."

"Is that true?"

"No," I admitted, "but try to make it sound true."

Walter turned on 103rd Street while I waited on Lexington Avenue, pacing up and down the block. Had we missed Bob? I checked my bracelet watch. After ten. If he had already started at a new job, he might have left for work already.

This was a nice neighborhood, more recently built up than neighborhoods downtown, with bright four- and five-story brick buildings lining the avenue, which rose on an incline here. On a cross street I even spotted a couple of wood buildings from the days when this was the hinterlands. Now, their bright white clapboards seemed to mark them as doomed for demolition. Even the signs and awnings looked newer here, and there weren't so many pawnshops and second-hand stores. I shaded my eyes and looked in the window of what appeared to be a small department store, with tidy glass-front counters and attentive clerks as well groomed as the customers.

At the watch counter, a clerk pulled out a pocket model for a matron with a baby buggy. The woman deliberated as if she had all the time in the world, and asked to look at several more. The clerk, who obviously *didn't* have all the time in the world, strained to keep his patience, especially when there was another customer at an adjacent counter impatient for his attention. Finally, he left the matron to debate the matter of the watch to herself.

When he turned away, the woman took one of the watches and slipped it into her baby carriage. Thinking again, she chose another and cached it away, too. Then she turned to go.

I blinked, not quite believing what I'd seen. Bold as brass, the woman pushed her buggy toward the front exit, bestowing a smile on the doorman posted there. The man clearly hadn't seen her take the items, and the watch clerk was still preoccupied. I debated what to do. Wait till she came out and tackle her? Follow her and hope I came across a policeman?

You're a policeman, jinglebrain.

I patted my satchel, which had my badge inside it. "You're always a policeman," Jenks had told me. This was why.

I reached the door just as the woman was coming out, still smiling grandly at the doorman. Her smile died when she found her buggy blocked by me.

"Excuse me." Her tone was so imperious, I wanted to laugh. "I need to get by."

"I'm sure you do," I said. "And quickly, am I right?"

The haughty look on her face dissolved into doubt.

The doorman wedged closer to see what the problem was. He scowled at me. "See here, miss. You need to step aside and let this lady pass."

"You wouldn't want me to do that," I said.

The woman's throat clutched in annoyance. "Of all the—"

"Sir, this woman just stole from your store." I dug my badge out of my purse and held it up for their inspection. "I'm Officer Faulk, New York City Police. Ma'am, I witnessed you take at least two watches from the counter and put them into your baby carriage."

By this time, a small crowd had gathered, both from inside the store and around me on the sidewalk. The woman played to her audience, sputtering indignantly. "That's outrageous! I did nothing of the kind. I'm a customer here." She turned to the doorman. "Are you going to allow me to be harassed by this, this person?"

The watch counter clerk attempted to poke his nose out the door. "What's going on?"

The doorman pointed at me. "Lady says she's a policeman."

"She's a lunatic," the thief insisted.

"She stole two watches from your counter," I told the clerk.

His brows rose, but then he took several steps back to check his counter. When he turned back, his forehead was lined. "We'd better get Mr. Griswald."

Cornered, the woman burst into tears. "But I need to go home and feed my baby," she wailed. "Wait till my husband finds out how you treated me."

The men exchanged worried glances, and I lost patience. "For Pete's sake. She's lying. Look in the perambulator if you don't believe me. I'll bet she doesn't even have a baby."

To prove my point, I yanked the yellow blanket from the bed of the buggy, revealing a plump, bald baby in a woolen footie suit. I would have been embarrassed had there not also been two gold watches nestled next to him. Also a silver gravy boat, and two very finely carved ivory hair combs, as well as a fox stole with the price tag still attached to the tail.

The crowd gasped.

"Fetch a policeman," the watch clerk instructed his coworker.

The doorman looked at me, and I held up my badge again.

The watch clerk stared at it, his face a mask of indecision. "Fetch a real policeman, just in case," he told the doorman. Then he spoke to the thief and me. "You ladies come with me. Mr. Griswald needs to hear about this."

Remembering Walter, I hesitated. How long would this take?

The clerk's brow arched. "Unless you aren't really the police?"

My chin lifted. "I am." I followed the clerk to a back office, where a round man in a tight gray suit—Mr. Griswald, I presumed—gaped at the amount of merchandise the woman had attempted to make off with.

The clerk perceived his own difficulty now. "I don't know how it happened," he said. "I only turned back for a moment to help another customer . . ." He looked down at the beady eyes of the fox head in the buggy. "We don't even carry furs."

"Laemmle does, down the street," Griswald said. "That's his tag."

The woman continued to weep. "I'm just a poor widow."

"Five minutes ago you threatened to send for your husband," I reminded her.

She inhaled on a sob. "M-my child is s-s-starving."

Our gazes were drawn to the baby, who appeared to be the opposite of starving. Also, he conducted himself with an eerie calm that made me suspect he was an experience-hardened diapered accomplice.

To be honest, I was relieved when a policeman arrived. Though I had several days of station work under my belt, I'd never arrested anyone on my own. I wasn't even sure where the nearest precinct was. The beat cop who came, Officer Healy, seemed as astonished as everyone else at my badge. "For the love of Christmas." He scratched his head. "Good thing you kept your eyes open, darlin'."

"Officer Faulk," I corrected him. "Nineteenth Precinct. I just happened to be looking through the window."

"Glad you were," Griswald said. "And Mr. Laemmle will be, too. And who knows how many others."

A better idea of how many others was revealed when the woman was instructed to sit down and she clanked into a chair. Her coat's lining was a veritable cupboard containing more silver, bracelets, and other trinkets, as well as nine silk scarves. "They were on a discount table," she said in her own defense.

Officer Healy and I escorted her to the Twenty-ninth Precinct on 104th, where the captain in charge shook my hand and slapped Healy on the back, joking to the other cops about his new partner. Healy was good-natured and took the ribbing in stride. "You mugs could only dream of having such a pretty helper," he told his colleagues, winking at me.

I extricated myself as soon as I could and hurried back to the intersection where Walter and I were supposed to meet. To my relief, he was there, practically hopping in agitation. "Where've you been?" His mustache hung slightly askew. "I looked all over for you."

I explained about catching the shoplifter; then it was his turn. "I didn't get the ledgers. He said Mr. McChesney destroyed them, but I didn't believe him."

I didn't either. Mr. McChesney would simply have told me if he had destroyed them.

Maybe Jackson's hunch about Bob was correct.

"Also, I'm not sure he believed me when I said I worked for Mr. Faber," Walter said. "He kept staring at me—looking into my eyes. 'I know you,' he said. And the worst part is, he may be right."

My heart skipped a beat. "How?"

"He came to one of our Thursday nights. With Mr. McChesney."

I sucked in a breath. "I didn't remember."

"It was before you moved here. Maybe a couple of years ago. I knew at once I'd seen him before, but by then it was too late to back out."

"I wonder if he'll remember where he saw you." I felt uneasy. "Maybe the disguise was enough to throw him off the scent."

"I should have kept the nose," Walter grumbled.

And we still had no ledgers. The whole exercise had been a failure, except to make Bob's behavior seem more suspicious. "You really think he was lying?" I asked.

"Oh yes." Walter pushed his mustache back in place. "Guilt was written all over his face. He's hiding something."

But was it murder he was hiding?

I went home to catch a quick nap before going to the station house for my last night shift of the week. I would have the next day off and the following night; then Sunday morning I'd begin the early shift Fiona had been working.

Callie was home on lunch break, putting on a brave front but exuding gloom with every sigh. Mere days remained before *Broadway Frolics* opened. She should have been buzzing with anticipation. Instead, she was perched in the uncomfortable chair, hunched over a stocking with a darning needle. I hadn't seen her darn anything since our leanest days at the Martha Washington Hotel, where we'd met.

I edged onto the arm of the sofa. "I'm so sorry about Teddy."

"It wasn't your fault." The words came out so quickly, I was fairly certain she did blame me.

"No, Otto was right. I didn't come right out and accuse Hugh of being a murderer, but I certainly implied it."

She dropped her hands in irritation. "I wish you had called him a murderer outright. Why not? Poisoner's just the name for him. He poisoned Teddy against me."

"Teddy'll come to his senses, or he's not worth having."

"You got the second part right. Why should I want some man-child who lets his best friend lead him around by his apron strings?"

I imagined Hugh in an Old Mother Hubbard getup with a miniature Teddy clinging to him. It might have been funny if Callie hadn't been so miserable.

"You know what I almost did?" she asked, not waiting for a response. "I almost threw myself at Otto."

"Oh no."

"I said almost. Luckily I got wise to myself. I can't just hurl myself at the nearest thing in pants every time my heart feels a little empty. I did that last summer, and poor Otto looked like a sad calf for weeks when I realized my mistake."

Judging from the way he'd spoken the other night, there were still a few moos left in him.

"I just need to take myself out of the swim," she said. "Last summer I got Ethel murdered, and you were almost killed, too. And I made Otto unhappy."

I wasn't sure Otto's bruised ego and my near death were on par, but I understood what she meant. "You've had an unlucky streak,"

I said, "but your luck's bound to change. You're going to be a sensation in your show."

The corners of her mouth were just beginning to tilt upward when a crash of breaking glass sounded behind me. Gasping, Callie tackled me a fraction of a second before a missile whizzed past my head over the back of the sofa. We were both facedown against the worn velvet upholstery when whatever had sailed through our window landed with a *thunk* against the wall behind us. Something solid dropped to the wood floor, along with a confetti of plaster chips.

Callie's terrorized glance met mine and we slowly lifted up to peer over the sofa's back. I was afraid we'd see a bomb or some incendiary that crazy anarchists were reported to lob through windows. Instead, what lay on the floor was only a fat brick.

"There's a note attached." Callie got up and hurried over to it. She untied the twine holding the piece of paper in place and unfolded it. After a quick perusal, she said, "I think it's for you." She turned the page around so I could read the block letters written in red paint: *YOU WERE WARNED!!!*

A gnawing began in my stomach. I didn't have to ask who'd arranged this delivery. Cain. "On the train back from Philly, Leonard Cain warned me to stay out of his business. Last night, I convinced his stepdaughter to testify against him."

Callie's eyes were saucers. "So now he's going after you? Why? Did he see you at the police station?"

I bit my lip. "No, he didn't see me. He wasn't there." The gnawing intensified.

"That crook must have henchmen posted outside police stations," she said.

"Or inside."

The notion of a gangland plant in our precinct made me sink back onto the couch. I wasn't overly fond of any of the men I worked with—I hadn't known any of them even a week. But the idea of one of them being crooked wrenched something inside of me. Especially when I remembered Captain McMartin had never been at the station at night, until last night.

A pounding on the door made us jump. "You girls in there—open up!"

It was Wally.

"The unlucky streak continues," Callie muttered.

Wally had heard the glass breaking, and a neighbor boy had seen a man running down the street, away from our building. The chubby kid, cap in hand, stood next to our landlady's son. They were both breathing heavily.

"He was a short fellow, dark, in a gray coat," the boy told us breathlessly. "I shouted 'Hey!' and ran after him, but he was like Jim Thorpe. You want I should go to the police?"

"I am the police," I said.

Man and boy gaped at me. To convince Wally, I had to produce both my badge and my official letter signed and sealed by the police commissioner.

"If you're the police, why're people throwing bricks through my windows?" Wally demanded.

I was not going to go into the investigation of Leonard Cain with Wally. In fact, I wasn't sure whom to tell. It was a matter for the police . . . but which police? If Cain's spy was someone in my precinct, I needed to be careful. There was only one person I knew I could trust.

"Don't blame Louise," Callie said. "It was Leonar—"

"People bear all kinds of grudges," I interrupted, sending Callie a visual cue that I wanted to avoid Cain's name.

"Ma's not going to like this," Wally grumbled. "And she ain't gonna pay for that window."

The next hour was consumed with bickering about who bore responsibility for paying for the window's repair. I finally agreed to pay, if Wally would at least board over the broken pane until I could get new glass. Not one to shy away from a bargain, Wally tacked some wood over the hole so we wouldn't freeze.

When he was gone and the flat was finally empty again, I stretched, exhausted. "I need to get a little shut-eye before the nightly grind starts again."

"You're going to *sleep*?" Callie asked. "I don't think I'm going to be able to sleep ever again. What if Cain decides to lob a bomb into our window next time?"

It was a worry, but I tried to calm her fears and my own. "Taking out an entire apartment building wouldn't be his style."

"You're right. His style is assassinating people on quiet streets when they least expect it. Aren't you scared?"

I yawned. "I'll be more scared after I sleep."

"Sure, toddle off to bed." She shook her head. "And if I don't see you again before you wake up for work tonight, it was nice knowing you."

I didn't see her again. When I got up, the stocking she'd been darning was wadded into a ball with the needle stabbed through its heart. Nearby, on the table, lay a note.

Gone to buy new stockings. Then rehearsal.
—C
P.S. Be careful!

I dressed in the mended uniform Myrna had made for me—the last time, perhaps, I would have to wear it. I'd taken Fiona's advice and ordered a sturdier outfit from the seamstress she recommended, who said it would be ready tomorrow afternoon. Tomorrow. I was so looking forward to having an entire day and night off, I could taste it. A full twenty-four hours of rest and freedom. Of course, I would have to get up very early on Sunday, so it wouldn't make sense to sleep too much during the day.

For all my bravado in front of Callie, Cain's brick wasn't far from my mind as I made my way to work. Several times I felt my heart leap as footsteps sounded behind me, and on a streetcar I sized at least three men up as potential assassins. It was a relief to approach the precinct, where I was fairly certain I wouldn't be killed.

I'd just turned onto Thirtieth Street when someone grabbed my arm. I lurched around, ready to take a swing at my attacker. Instead of a Cain thug, though, Bob's face, twisted with anger, loomed close to mine. "I thought you were my friend!"

I tried to shrug him off. When that didn't work, I gave him a swat. "I am, but I won't be if you don't let go of my arm."

He didn't let go. "You sent a spy after me. Why?"

"Because I knew you wouldn't be honest with me. You were hiding something the last time I saw you. I'm not sure you told the truth today, either."

He laughed sharply. "*You're* one to talk! You dressed up your aunt's butler."

Walter was right—he'd been recognized.

"The glued-on mustache was a tip-off," Bob said. "After he left, I finally remembered seeing him serving drinks. I telephoned your aunt's house to find out where you were working."

"And my aunt told you?"

"No, the man did. He didn't recognize my voice." He sneered. "Some spy."

Poor Walter. He'd be crushed. Almost as crushed as my arm. I'd always sized Bob up as a weakling, but I hadn't imagined him in the throes of anger. His grip was strong, and his uncharacteristic rage alarmed me. I'd looked into the face of a man driven to desperation before, and I recognized the signs now in Bob's bespectacled eyes.

"If you swear you don't have the ledgers, you don't have them," I said, keeping my voice measured. "I just needed to make sure."

"Of what?" he barked. "That I was a thief? He said he wouldn't tell!"

"Who said? Guy?"

"Guy?" He shook his head. "What does Guy have to do with any of this? Ogden McChesney was the one who gave me his promise."

"Promise of what?" I asked.

"That he wouldn't tell anyone I'd taken money from the company. And now here you are. The police. And *he* told you!"

So Jackson had been correct. "If Mr. McChesney knew you stole from the company, why did he keep you on?"

"Because it was just once." He thought again and backtracked. "Well, three times. Janet had just had the twins, and one of them was in the hospital. I needed money, and I had nowhere to turn, no one to ask for help. You have no idea what it feels like to be under that kind of pressure and have no one to turn to. And no one at the office would have found out, except that your aunt called Ogden about missing a check. And then . . ." Tears filled his eyes. "I confessed to Ogden right away. And I paid it all back. Every penny."

"That's fine," I said.

"Then why would he do this to me? Why are you persecuting me?" He took my other arm then and shook me like a rag doll. "Why won't you leave me alone? He said I'd never go to jail!"

"Bob, listen. It wasn't Mr. McChesney who told me about you."

"I don't believe you. No one else knew!"

"I guessed, and so did Jackson."

"Is this blackmail?" With every word he grew more hysterical and gave me a firmer shake. "Is that what you want?"

"I only want to help Mr. McChesney. He didn't kill Guy."

"And you think *I* did?" His eyes snapped open wider. "You want to send *me* to jail?" He shook me again. "I can't go to jail. I have children!"

My teeth rattled. I didn't hear the voice shouting behind me, or realize what was happening until Schultz appeared behind Bob and spun him around.

"Hold it right there, fella!" Schultz said. "That's a police officer you're assaulting."

It could only have been the uniform that momentarily cowed Bob in front of the world's oldest policeman. "I can't go to prison!" he cried again.

Schultz puffed out his chest and drew up to his full height, which was still several inches below Bob's chin. "We'll see about that."

Bob looked like a cornered animal. This could escalate into something very bad. "It's okay, Schultz," I said.

"Not on my watch, it's not," Schultz insisted. "This man can't go around assaulting girls in the street, especially not police girls."

"I didn't assault anybody!" Bob shouted.

Schultz turned as red in the face as Bob. "I saw you, fella!"

I stepped between the men just as Bob lashed out. His swinging fist hit the side of my eye, knocking me sideways.

I stumbled and then looked up through one squinted eye. Schultz was vibrating in outrage. "That's it! You're coming to the station, bub!"

Oh God. I did not want this. "I'm fine," I lied, still reeling. Bob's shaking me and that punch had left my brain feeling as if it were coming unglued from my skull.

With his other arm, Schultz steadied me.

"Bob and I used to work together," I explained.

He glared at Bob, whose glasses were askew and whose teeth were chattering with nerves. Yet his throwing that punch seemed to have subdued him finally. "I'm sorry, Louise," he said, tears in his eyes. "I never meant to hurt you."

Schultz's gray brows met in consternation. "So that's how it is. Couldn't leave her alone, could you?"

Bob's eyes widened in offense at the implied salacious spin on his words. "I'm a married man," he protested.

Schultz made a sound of disgust. "They usually are."

CHAPTER 19

Bob was in trouble, but it soon became clear that I was, too. Intimidated by the blue uniforms and brass buttons that descended on him after Schultz marched him into the precinct, Bob spilled the short, sad history of his career as an embezzler. The police heard about his twins, the pneumonia that afflicted the smallest boy, the doctor bills. He admitted stealing. "It was five hundred dollars—$446.63, to be exact—and I repaid every penny. Just ask Ogden McChesney. He's in one of your jails, so it shouldn't be hard to talk to him."

The sergeant and Jenks exchanged glances. "McChesney's the geezer who burned down a building and killed his partner," Jenks said.

"You were part of that?" Donnelly asked Bob.

"No." He pointed at me. "She was trying to prove I was mixed up in it. That's why she was harassing me and sending her aunt's butler to pretend to be working for Ogden McChesney's attorney."

As soon as the words left his lips, I winced.

Eyebrows shot up and two surprised faces swung toward me. Never mind for the moment the implied police harassment indicated in Bob's words. In unison, Jenks and Donnelly exclaimed, "Your aunt's *butler*?"

If my job survived the night, which was starting to look unlikely, I'd never live that down.

"I was trying to find out if he took the money," I said.

Donnelly squinted. "He admits he did."

"*Now* he does," I said.

"I told Ogden McChesney about it," Bob said. "I confessed everything to him last year and paid the money back. There was no reason to send someone in disguise to my house. Unless she was trying to blackmail me, or frame me."

The accusatory looks that the gathered policemen had first focused on Bob were now aimed at me. I'd made a mess of this entire situation, and now I did my best to talk my way out of it. Finally, Bob was taken to a room by himself to await questioning by detectives more knowledgeable about the McChesney case, while I was sent downstairs to work. Not without a warning, however.

"I'll have to mention this situation to Captain McMartin, Two," Donnelly said. "Might even require a review by a deputy commissioner."

My heart sank. "Yes, sir."

"Police harassment, complaints from the public . . . These aren't things the brass like to hear about. Especially not from a probationer who's already allowed a jailbreak on her watch."

During her first week, he didn't have to add.

Having convinced Mary McCarty to testify against Cain might not work in my favor, either. There was someone in this station reporting to Cain who would be glad to see me gone.

I stumped downstairs with the suspicion that this might be my last night on the job. The only one who looked more down in the mouth than me was Schultz.

"I never guessed I was going to get you in the soup," he said.

"I know."

"I just saw that mug attacking and thought, 'Schultzie, my boy, you've gotta do something.' That's the trouble with lightning reflexes. Years of training—can't turn 'em off."

"You did the right thing," I said.

He didn't appear convinced. "I'll see if I can scare up something for that eye of yours. You're going to have a lulu of a shiner."

I'd forgotten about my eye, but the moment he mentioned it, the dull ache reasserted itself. It was difficult opening my left eye beyond a squint. The women waiting for me in the cells thought it was hilarious.

"Who walloped you?" one asked.

I shrugged off the question.

Another laughed. "You look like my ma used to the morning after my pa's payday. You married?"

"No."

"Of course she's not married," a woman sitting on the bench in the back of the cell scoffed. "Lady cops don't get married. What kind of man would marry a cop?"

The first woman sized me up through the bars. "If the pay's regular, somebody would."

My self-confidence sank another degree. The pay was only regular if you managed to stay employed. And alive. In my case, both contingencies now looked doubtful.

My imminent dismissal made me strangely sentimental about the job I'd struggled to endure all week. The taunts of the prisoners and the tedium of the hours suddenly didn't bother me. Even making coffee and scrubbing up seemed like worthy work. Who would be looking after all this when I was gone?

Around midnight, my bell clanged, summoning me to the sergeant's desk. Was this it? Were they going to tell me to go home even before my shift ended?

Upstairs, Donnelly jerked his head toward a back room used for interrogations. "Detective wants to talk to you."

For some reason, I hadn't expected Muldoon. They'd even said they wanted to find a detective familiar with the McChesney case. Maybe I'd pushed him so thoroughly out of my mind because I just didn't want to face him. He'd have every right to say *I told you so.*

His expression darkened when he saw my face.

"What happened to you?"

"I walked into a fist."

He muttered under his breath. "Have you seen a doctor?"

"I'll be fine." I attempted a smile, but even crinkling my eye that little bit smarted. "Good thing Bob Sanders hasn't been pushing anything heavier than pencils for the past decade."

"This isn't funny, Louise. He's saying you might have been trying to blackmail him."

"Then he's all wet. I never asked him for money. I just wanted to find out the truth, and I did." I sat down. "The hard way."

"Why didn't you tell me about Bob's embezzling?"

Wasn't anyone listening to me? "I didn't know for sure he'd embezzled anything until two hours ago. I didn't even suspect until this morning."

Muldoon sank into the chair opposite mine, crossed his arms, and blew out a breath. "So let me guess . . . You thought this Bob character's embezzling had been discovered by Guy, who then blackmailed him. Which in turn made Bob murder Guy."

"Okay, so I was on the wrong track."

"Why? It sounds plausible."

"Not when you consider how much Guy needed and how little Bob has. Guy was a gambler, not a nickel-and-dimer." I shrugged. "Besides, even if Bob were being blackmailed, I can see now that he wouldn't kill Guy. That's not the kind of man he is."

Muldoon's gaze homed in on my left eye.

"His swinging at me wasn't intentional," I said. "He was cornered, and frightened."

"You're sure making a lot of excuses for someone you took pains to bring in."

"I didn't bring him in. He followed me, and Schultz did the rest."

He contemplated the situation, and me. "Now do you believe in McChesney's guilt?"

"That he murdered Guy? No."

He looked tired. I wondered what shift he was supposed to be working and how long it had been since he'd slept.

"I hope you'll let Bob go now," I said. "He has a family."

His abrupt laugh made me jump. "So I've heard. Repeatedly. Also, he paid back every penny."

"I owe him an apology," I said.

"He hit you." Before I could respond, he said, "I know, I know. It was a mistake. But even putting your black eye aside, the man stole from the company he worked for. He should have been arrested when McChesney discovered the theft."

"Mr. McChesney's very kind. He did what he could to put me off Bob's scent."

"I can't figure McChesney out. He forgives robbery and then commits arson and insurance fraud. He's either soft in the head or just plain crackers."

"Neither makes him a killer."

"Neither clears him, either."

And so we came full circle, right to the same frustrating impasse we'd started from. "We never do seem to agree, do we?" I said.

His expression didn't soften, but the tension in his eyes shifted from irritation to a guarded friendliness. "We never do."

I laughed.

"What's so funny?"

"There. We just agreed."

He didn't smile. "I don't know how much I can help you now, Louise. I'll put in a word, but—"

"But I'm a probationer." I stood. "Thanks, but I know I've made a hash of things. My first week hasn't exactly been a blaze of glory. Not that the jailbreak was all my fault—"

"Jailbreak?"

I waved a hand. "That's what they're calling it around here, but nobody escaped for very long. Still, it looked bad. And if I were a more prudent person, I would've dropped my private investigation as you advised me to a dozen times. But I can't let Mr. McChesney face possible death for something he didn't do."

"Maybe it's a good thing you discovered the job's drawbacks so early. There will always be people you want to help. You can't save people from themselves."

I nodded because the advice sounded wise. I wasn't sure they were words I could live by, though. Maybe *I* wasn't wise.

"There's another drawback I discovered today." I told him about the brick, the message, and my near certainty that someone in the precinct had reported the events surrounding Mary McCarty's arrest to Cain. "Otherwise, Cain couldn't have known I was involved in his arrest at all."

Muldoon looked thunderous. "Why didn't you tell me this right away?"

"Because we were talking about Bob."

"I mean this afternoon. Louise, the man is dangerous."

"If he wanted to kill me, he's had plenty of opportunity. I haven't been hiding. The brick was just meant to scare me."

"You don't seem scared enough, in my opinion."

"Oh, I am. And I'm worried about which colleague of mine here is reporting to him."

He scratched his chin. "You didn't tell McMartin or Donnelly about the brick?"

I shook my head.

"Maybe that's for the best. For now."

A chill went through me. I pointed out the coincidence of McMartin's making a rare evening trip to the station house the night Mary McCarty was brought in. "You think he's Cain's spy?"

"Impossible to say." He considered for a moment. "Internal inquiries are a long game. We shouldn't tip our hand by telling too much too soon, Louise."

That *we* comforted me. "I should probably go back to work. If I am going to lose my job after a week, I don't want to be remembered as a shirker."

"No one could ever think that."

Though I was ready to go, something in his expression made me hesitate. "I'm sure I'll see you again, because of Mr. McChesney," I said. "Maybe the next time I won't be a policewoman anymore. But you never liked me much as a civilian, either."

"I've always liked you, Louise." The words, blurted out, created a strange current in the air. For a moment we hung suspended in each other's gazes, raw and surprised. The wall clock ticked off one second, then two.

Muldoon shook his head, then added, "When you're not annoying the hell out of me."

Which was almost never.

I smiled, in spite of the eye. "Good night, Detective."

"Good night, Officer Faulk."

After our conversation, the night snailed along. Busy work kept me awake. I swept, mopped, and dusted every square inch of area I was responsible for. Maybe I'd be remembered as the most bungling probationary policewoman in the history of the NYPD, but at least no one would be able to add sloppiness to the list of my failings.

At the end of my shift, Fiona came in, dropped her bag on our bench, and stared around the place. "Looks like you've been busy. Nice job." Taking in my face, she lowered her voice. "That's quite a shiner you got. I heard about the trouble last night."

I nodded. "I was wondering if I should wait for Captain McMartin to come in before I go."

"Did anyone tell you to?"

"No, but I thought he might want to tell me not to come back."

"Of all the . . ." She let out a sound that was half laugh, half irritated bark. "What do you think this is, finishing school? You don't wait to be asked 'not to come back.' If they want to fire you, they'll give you a date for a hearing and they'll lay out in detail all the reasons you didn't make the grade. Until then, try not to be such a dumb cluck. Keep your head down and show up when and where you're told."

After this speech I almost felt I should salute, but she didn't even wait for acknowledgment. She caught sight of one of the women sitting behind bars. "Is that you, Mollie? What are you doing in the cage? Back in the badger game?"

A week ago, the question would have seemed like Greek to me. Now I knew that Mollie was a specialist in luring well-to-do tourists to their hotel rooms and getting in a compromising position so her "boyfriend" could burst in and shake the poor tourist down for blackmail money.

"Some cop was pretending to be the mayor of South Bend." Mollie sounded resentful, as if the cop's trapping her was as underhanded as her scam. "You can't believe a word nobody tells you anymore."

I took Fiona's advice and left the station without asking for a verdict on my future.

I felt too wound up to want to be alone, but it was early for visiting my aunt, and Callie would still be asleep for a few hours yet. I knew only one person sure to be up at this hour.

One reason for Otto's continuing to be an early riser might have been the situation of his apartment facing Union Square. The street noise of the waking city was loud there even at seven, which was the time I arrived. A piano rag grew louder as I walked up the stairs to his flat.

He answered on my second knock, bundled in sweaters to fight off the arctic blast that greeted me. My appearing on his doorstep didn't surprise him. In fact, he barely looked at me. "Oh, good, it's you." Without preamble, he waved me in and accepted the small sack of bagels I'd brought him. "I was just thinking that I needed a girl."

He didn't wait for my reaction, only hurried back to his piano bench.

"Anyone else might take that the wrong way," I said, shivering.

He was already biting into a bagel and frowning at the music in front of him. "This is no time to act dippy, Louise. I need your help."

There was an old ladder-back chair next to his Spartan table, and I dragged it over to the piano. I left my coat on.

"Have you noticed it's a little frigid in here?"

He nodded. "I bought a new suit, so I'm economizing. Al laughed at my old one—said it looked like a summer camp for moths."

"So you spent all your money buying a suit to impress your new pal and now you can't afford heat?"

"As soon as I get this song done, I'll be in clover again. Al needs a novelty number for his new show."

"The tune I heard when I was coming up the stairs sounded good to me," I said.

"The tune's all right, but I don't have the lyric. It needs a hook. He wants it to be about a girl making excuses to a man to sneak out to see another beau. What would a girl say?"

I shrugged. "Visiting a sick aunt? Washing her hair?"

He tried it out. " 'She's always visiting Aunt Mildred.' " He frowned. " 'She's always washing her hair.' "

"Hard to imagine Al Jolson capering down the center stage of the Winter Garden singing about shampoo," I said.

Otto chewed and thought some more. "What was the last lie you told?"

Sadly, there had been quite a few recently, but I mentioned the first one that popped into my head. "I said I was going to the dentist when I wasn't."

I remembered the twinge of guilt I'd felt about the fib when I'd slipped the note under Guy's door to let him know I wouldn't be in until the following afternoon. He'd been talking to Cain, but I hadn't wanted to wait for that meeting to end. Little did I know I'd never see Guy again, or that the investigation into his death would end up jeopardizing the very job I was taking the test for.

While I was wrapped up in my own thoughts, Otto muttered to himself. Then, as if struck by a bolt from the blue, he spun around on his piano bench in excitement. "Louise! I take back everything I said. You're a genius with lyrics!"

"Because I lied about going to the dentist?"

"Exactly."

He took up a pencil and began scribbling on the music in front of him.

"I guess if Irving Berlin can make a hit out of 'Snooky-Ookems,' all bets are off," I joked.

"What?" He already seemed to have forgotten I was there. "Oh yes. And thanks for the bagels. I was starving. You must be a mind reader."

I stood up. When Otto failed to defend his songwriting hero, he was well and truly distracted. "I'm going home."

"Oh!" Abashed, he got up, too. "I'm sorry, Louise. It's just that Al wants this song. Was there something you wanted to talk about?"

"Not really."

He looked into my face for the first time, and his eyes bugged. "Holy cats! What happened to your eye?"

"Accident at work."

"It looks like somebody punched you."

I looped my bag over my shoulder. "I should probably go home, put a compress on it, and get some sleep."

He trailed me to the door. "I'm sorry I've been preoccupied this morning. I'm so glad you came by, but this song . . ." He held the door for me. "What if I came by your flat later? Before your shift?"

"I'm off tonight." *Maybe off forever.*

"Even better. We can have supper." He frowned. "Except I forgot. No money."

I put my hand on his arm. "Go write your lyrics before your muse skiddoos. I'll cook something for us to eat tonight, and we can talk more then."

The rest of the way home, uneasiness nagged at me. Every time I thought of the fib I'd told about the dentist, I felt a qualm. Why? In my mind's eye, I saw myself pushing the note under Guy's office door and slipping out, leaving him and Cain alone in an otherwise empty building. But what was so odd about that?

At home, I was still too keyed up to sleep, so I did a few household chores, taking the clothes we couldn't wash out ourselves to the laundry and then dusting and sweeping out the living room. Because of Callie's love of knickknacks, dusting took the longest. Usually wiping off every souvenir trinket, slightly damaged bit of decorative china, and novelty gewgaw left me cursing her magpie ways, but this morning the Toby jugs, ashtrays, and whatnots didn't bother me. I was glad for the mindless activity. All the while, I was careful not to disturb Callie sleeping behind her closed bedroom door. Performing household chores silently was one skill I'd perfected in the past month.

Finally, when my mind was as tired as the rest of me, I collapsed on my bed in the clothes I was wearing, too dog-tired to do more than kick off my shoes.

As I drifted off to sleep, I forgot about everything. The trouble at the precinct, Guy, Mr. McChesney in jail, even the supper with Otto that I'd promised to make. My mind became a restorative blank, right up to the moment a heavy pounding on the apartment door jolted me back awake and drove me out of bed. Was a Cain henchman about to bust down my door? The apartment was dark except for one lamp Callie must have left on. I grabbed the nearest weapon I could lay hands on—a brass doorstop in the shape of a duck. It felt comfortably heavy in my hands as I approached the door, which was almost bending with the force of each new knock.

"Who is it?" I asked.

"Miriam. I need your help."

CHAPTER 20

I opened the door, and Miriam whisked inside. She leaned against the hallway wall, sucking in shuddering breaths. She eyed the brass duck warily and then noticed my eye. "Did Jackson do that to you?"

The question threw me. She thought Jackson had hit me? I shook my head and put down the duck. "No, of course not. What's wrong?"

"He's lost his mind. I told him I was leaving him. I think he's going to do something terrible."

Something terrible like hit *me*? That didn't make sense.

I shut the door and took her arm. "Come sit down and tell me exactly what he said." I turned on some lights and nodded toward the sofa. She gratefully went over to it and sank down, wiping her hands on the coat she hadn't taken off. "When did you see Jackson?" I asked.

"This evening. I shouldn't have gone back to the apartment, but I needed some more of my things. When he saw me packing clothes, he started raving. He called me a"—she swallowed—"a name he never used to call me, or even use in my hearing. If he had, I'd have left him before tonight."

"Was he drinking?"

"When isn't he drinking now? Ever since the fire."

I nodded. "Guy's death hit him hard."

An incredulous sound caught in her throat. "Anger and jealousy, that's what hit him. It's been eating him alive since we came north. That kind of bitterness is like termites—it just kept boring into him till there was nothing solid left of the old Jackson I knew at home. But ever since the fire, he's turned all that bitterness on me."

He hadn't treated her well before the fire, either. Not acknowledging your own wife wasn't love. But maybe she didn't realize how invisible she'd been to the rest of us.

"And then I thought he was going to come to blows with a man at the apartment tonight," she continued.

"What man?" My mind immediately conjured up my old nemesis. "Ford Fitzsimmons?"

"No, it was"—she frowned in thought—"Bob. That was the name. He came by when I was packing up my things. They talked. Yelled, sometimes. I was right in the next room."

"What were they saying?"

"It was all about you. Something about you bothering Bob, and some money Bob had stolen and paid back, and how Jackson shouldn't have told you about him."

I'd mentioned Jackson to Bob outside the precinct, I remembered now. I shouldn't have done that.

"That man, Bob, told Jackson, 'She's police now, and she'll do anything to get McChesney off.' " Miriam frowned. "Then, as Jackson was pushing him out the door, Bob said, 'You'll be next.' "

"Next?" I wondered aloud. "Next to what?"

"He meant you'd be after Jackson next, 'cause you were making up all sorts of things to tell the police so you could free your old boss."

"I didn't make anything up."

She shrugged. "The man didn't seem in his right mind."

It no longer took a stretch of imagination to envision Bob going off his hinges.

Miriam continued. "After he left, I came out of the bedroom with my suitcase and told Jackson that I didn't want anything more from him, and he wasn't to pester me at your aunt's. I need that job."

"Aunt Irene wouldn't hold Jackson's rudeness against you."

"I don't think she'll have to. When I was at the door, Jackson said, 'This is goodbye forever, Miriam. You won't see me after tonight. No one will.' So I asked where he was going. And he said, 'If you really want to know, ask Louise. This is the end.' "

Cold flooded through me.

"Then he tore out of the house, and I went back across the park to your aunt's. I was shaken, so I explained all that had happened, and she told me to come here right away."

I crossed the room to get my coat. "Jackson didn't say anything else—just 'Ask Louise'?"

"And 'This is the end.' "

Jackson had told me his darkest fears, but not his own wife?

The urge to run to help my old coworker gripped me, but tendrils of suspicion held me back. Something didn't fit . . .

But I couldn't do nothing.

I crossed to the table and scrawled a note, then folded it. "I'm going to look for Jackson," I said. "If he is where I think he is, I need to hurry."

Miriam stood. "I should go with you. He's unpredictable." She narrowed her eyes on my face. "And it looks like you've already been through enough today."

She didn't know the half of it. I jabbed a pin through my hat to secure it. "Don't worry about that. I need you to—"

Another knock at the door startled us. Miriam's eyes went wide, and my own heart skipped a few beats before it dawned on me who it was. I opened the door.

A big bouquet of chrysanthemums breezed across the threshold, followed by Otto. "Louise, you're a wonder. If you hadn't—" He noticed my coat and hat, and Miriam. Joy melted into worry. "What's going on?"

"I'm meeting someone, and I need you to take a message to Muldoon." Belatedly, I introduced him to Miriam and handed him the note. "Give that to him."

Otto shook his head. "How on earth am I going to find Detective Muldoon?"

"I don't know. He may be at his precinct, or headquarters downtown. Try the precinct first. You remember where it is."

Of course he did. He'd spent an entire day there last summer.

"But where will you be?" he asked.

"Pier Twenty-seven."

Otto dropped his bouquet in the umbrella stand. "What's down there? Shouldn't I go with you?"

"No—I need to go alone. But I can't stay there with Jackson too long. If you can't find Muldoon, bring anybody in a uniform."

Otto, bug-eyed with panic, dug in his heels. "I knew there would be trouble if you started investigating again."

I propelled him toward the door. "There'll be less trouble if you find Muldoon. So hurry."

"I'll go with you," Miriam assured Otto. Her gaze sought mine. "I think I understand what's going on."

"I hope you'll explain it to me," Otto grumbled.

All three of us hustled out the door and parted ways outside the building. They headed toward Sixth Avenue, and I hurried in the direction of the river.

Apprehension vibrated through me. A puzzle that had been niggling at the back of my mind for weeks was slotting into place. Maybe Crazy Cora was right—go over the past enough, it all did eventually become clear. For weeks I'd looked at the scant evidence from the fire, but of all the clues, the one I'd studied least was the one that I myself had left: a note telling Guy of a fabricated trip to the dentist.

The waterfront seemed a lot like the Bowery with a nautical theme. I skimmed past men grouped outside taverns—some of which looked like blind pigs that served liquor with no license. West Street, facing the river, contained a hodgepodge of new warehouses and old brick buildings in various stages of dilapidation. Refuse from the day's trade littered the cobblestones, including old fruit and grain that had jostled off loading carts. A feast for rats. Streetlights put out a feeble gleam, but between each there were long puddles of darkness. Maybe that was for the best. The air smelled of fish, a nearby tannery, and the Hudson, which was both a mighty river and, in places, an open sewer.

No wonder swells lived on Fifth Avenue, I thought. It was as far as a person could get from the two rivers and their attendant seedy saloons and riffraff.

And yet . . . The sound of water lapping against piers and the hulls of boats had a mesmerizing quality. From the dockside I spied barges and tugboats passing, plus a few crafts that appeared to be floating homes, with laundry lines of shirts, linens, and long johns flapping like flags. There were larger boats, too—one a sailing vessel with a towering mast. Ships and ferries let out lowing hoots that I rarely noticed a few blocks over. And then there were the piers, man-made peninsulas jutting out scores of yards over the river. Even empty, they seemed to be awaiting activity, adventure. Despite everything, it didn't surprise me that certain people were drawn here. There was something romantic about the gleam of the fat harvest moon on the river.

I approached Pier Twenty-seven and stopped, eyeing the empty slip to see if I could spy Jackson there. He'd chosen his spot well: of all places I'd passed so far, it seemed the most forsaken. Fire had deprived the pier of its cover, and now the area was open with only a few vertical braces remaining, awaiting restoration. The half-demolished walkway of the pier had ropes across it, blocking pedestrians, and a sign warned DANGER: KEEP OUT. Across the street was an old warehouse and an empty lot, where a few lumps indicated men passed out. A desolate place. If one came across it in a moment of despair, the lure of oblivion the river offered would be hard to resist.

Where was Jackson? Maybe he'd given up waiting.

Perhaps I was wrong, and he'd actually jumped. "This is the end," he'd told Miriam.

But I doubted it. As I looked out over the deserted pier, I suspected this was less a mission of mercy than an ambush. Or perhaps it was one bitter man's idea of a practical joke. I hiked up my skirt and picked my way over a rope barrier and down a step onto the lowered wooden planks of the pier. My footsteps echoed, and the cold breeze off the Hudson gave me a forlorn feeling. If Jackson were wise, he'd be out of the city by now. Flee, that's what I'd do if I were him. A man could head west, or north to Canada, change his name, and perhaps never be tracked down.

I turned to go and Jackson was there, between me and the sidewalk. He had on a dark overcoat and the same bowler hat I'd seen him wear to work for months. In fact, he looked more like his regular self than he'd seemed since the fire.

"So you came," he said. "Took you long enough."

"Miriam had to find me."

"And to convince you to come?"

"I was ready to do that right away."

I didn't like the way he blocked the walkway and my route of escape. The longer he stood, the more his calm manner unsettled me. He was composed, almost casual, with a sort of heedless slouch to his stance.

"She told me you were distraught," I said.

"And you came to beg me not to jump." He shook his head. "Don't play innocent, Louise. I know you're not. You've known all along that Ogden McChesney didn't kill Guy. You realized today it wasn't Bob. You even sent him to threaten me."

"Bob acted on his own—because he was furious with me." I tilted my head so that my eye would be more visible in the moonlight. "He gave me this."

He seemed genuinely surprised. "So all that righteous anger was real?" He chuckled. "Strange that you could have made Bob, of all people, so angry."

"I had the wrong end of the stick."

"But now you've got the right one."

I swallowed. "I think so."

"What tipped you off?"

"You did. Twice, you mentioned my going to the dentist the morning of the fire."

"So?"

"I never went to the dentist, or had any intention to. That was a lie. I slipped a note under Guy's door right before I left, while he was talking with Cain. Everyone else had gone home. So there was no way you could've seen that note unless you went into Guy's office after Cain left."

He considered this, then shrugged. "Maybe I did. What of it?"

"You never told the police you were in Guy's office after Cain left, and you said the building was in flames when you arrived the next morning. So you couldn't have seen my note then—it would have been ash." I'd worked this out on my way over, but saying it aloud made my voice dry. I'd always thought of Jackson as a bore, an office martinet, but never a murderer. "How long did you wait that night to kill him?"

He looked toward the river. "I'd been hiding upstairs, in the top floor storage room, where we kept all the old titles. It seemed forever before I heard Cain leave—I'd started to worry Guy would go back to the club with him."

"I'm surprised he didn't."

"No, Guy had started staying later since his Jewess had flown the love nest. All his money problems and his guilt over his bastard son had begun to prey on his mind, making it less enticing to go home and face old Mrs. Van Hooten and play the favorite son. He'd cried into his whiskey glass over it all with me a few times. That's why I thought it was a good bet he'd stay late that night. Not working, mind you. Just moping. Maybe he did have a shred of conscience in him somewhere."

"Not enough to make him marry Myrna, or acknowledge his own son." I tried to use my dislike of Guy to keep Jackson talking. His confession was bittersweet vindication to me—I'd been right that Mr. McChesney hadn't killed Guy. Unfortunately, there was no way Jackson would tell me of his guilt if he thought I would leave the waterfront alive. I needed to stall for time. "Guy was a scoundrel. You did—well, never mind."

White teeth flashed. "Go ahead, say it. I did the right thing. That's what you meant, wasn't it?" He sneered at my faint sound of denial. "Of course it was the right thing. Oh, I could tell you stories about Guy. He was always a callous bastard."

"He was your friend."

"So-called. I always clung to the idea of his being my friend. Back in college, he introduced me to a set I never would have been allowed into, and by hook or by crook I got him through Harvard. That was my purpose. I was too naïve then to realize I was being used. I'd never been good at attracting friends. Don't know why. So I let myself be a sort of glorified friend-tutor. Of course, after university he had no use for me."

"Until you came to New York last year and looked him up. He helped you, gave you a job."

The control in his expression snapped. "You see? That's what everyone thought! Wasn't I lucky to know Guy Van Hooten? I was Guy's pity hire."

"Not at all." Who did he think "everyone" was? Jackson was hardly a man people around the office spent much time gossiping about.

"But who did all the work around that place?" he said, as if I hadn't spoken at all. "While Guy drank his life away and the old man malingered and fretted, and the others loafed upstairs, who was it who kept the wheels turning? *You* saw. I ran that company. But I wasn't even given my own office—I had to share a room with the secretary and the office boy. And who did old man McChesney turn to after the fire?" He almost spat the name. "Bob."

"You had killed Guy," I reminded him.

"McChesney didn't know that! And what about *him*? An arsonist who showed up and played the victim. Edwin Booth couldn't have acted it better."

"You were pretty impressive yourself. Your shock at Guy's death had me fooled."

My flattery hit its mark. "You noticed that, did you? Well, I can't claim much credit for that. The fire's what threw me. Just imagine the night I'd gone through—triumph at having seen Guy die by my own hand. Then, once I got home, frantic worry beset me. What had I done? How many clues had I left behind? I'd cleared away our glasses and thrown the poison into a trash can in the park. But the police have all sorts of detection methods now, don't they?

"I barely slept a wink. When I finally marched off to work, I imagined there would be a Black Maria waiting to cart me off when I arrived. But as I approached the building—flames! Beautiful tongues of fire erasing my crime entirely. It was hard to hide my jubilation. *That* was acting."

His excitement at his own luck sickened me. "Bravo, then."

"In the beginning I was sorry *you* weren't there first. That would have made it seem more like a normal day. But I'd seen the note about the dentist and I knew you'd be late, so I was able to sit back and savor the sight of that fire as long as I dared without drawing suspicion."

And in so doing, how many lives had he endangered? If the fire had spread, delay could have been fatal for the neighboring buildings.

From the gleam in his eye, he didn't care. He wouldn't have minded if ten people had died, or a hundred. Covering his crime was the important thing. His own hide was all that mattered.

He'd reached the end of his narrative—which might also mean the beginning of the end for me. I'd hoped Muldoon would arrive or that some means of escape would occur to me. But none of the options I could think of seemed likely to succeed. I could run . . . or take to the river. Jackson could probably outrun me, but he couldn't swim.

Yet that water looked dark and cold.

"When you went down to Guy," I said, backtracking, "after Cain left . . . How did you do it?"

"How did I get Guy to drink cyanide, you mean?"

At my nod, his lips turned up. "Like getting fish to swim. 'Mix me a drink, General,' he said. He called me General back in our Boston days, when I'd made him do his assignments. Which mostly meant I sat and watched while he copied what I'd written, you understand. Yet he dared to have contempt for me."

"And so you poisoned his drink." I tilted my head. "Your apartment building has mice. Is that what gave you the idea?"

"You do pay attention occasionally. I might have put too much in. Guy was violently sick." The memory caused a shudder. "Revolting, but my biggest fear was that he'd purge all the poison. Apparently not." His lips turned up in a smile. "It's given me some comfort these past weeks to remember Guy died like a rat."

"And a man who kills his own friend . . . What is he?"

It was too much. Jackson took a step forward. "Weren't you listening? He was *never* my friend. He used me, and others, too. He treated women abominably and tossed them aside like soiled handkerchiefs. You think Myrna Cohen was an exception? I assure you, she wasn't. He had nothing but contempt for all women. If Edith Van Hooten hadn't controlled the family purse strings, he would have walked away from his own mother. He had no sense of loyalty, or duty."

"Guy might have been all the things you say. I don't know much more about him than what you've told me. But I do know he was human, and a human can change. It's rare, I know—but we all have that potential. Guy, in the end, might've decided to turn over a new leaf and own up to his responsibilities."

"Are we discussing Guy or a novel?" He laughed. "In the last chapter, will stern old Edith Van Hooten take in the half-caste Jew grandson to her bosom?"

Every time he spoke of Myrna's child, I hated him a little more. Pretending became impossible. "You're despicable."

"And you're pathetic, with your silly pretensions at trying to be a detective. Do you realize how enjoyable it was to feed you little tidbits that I knew would send you chasing off down blind alleys? You were like an untrained coonhound bounding after every jackrabbit." He shook his head, mocking me. "Yet you take yourself for a clever person. Even now you think you'll talk me out of killing you."

At least now I was certain of his intention. I lifted my chin. "Did you bring poison with you?" I couldn't resist taunting him back. "The poison confused us, you know. My aunt calls it the woman's weapon."

In response, his hands came out of his pockets. The blade in his right hand glinted in the moonlight.

Every cell in my body froze. A memory from the summer flashed through me. Blood. Callie's cousin's lifeless body sprawled facedown on a bed. A butcher knife in her back. A horrible way to die.

I was not going to die that way. Not if I could help it.

"You're not that kind of killer, Jackson." I swallowed. I hoped he wasn't at least. "You could have knifed Guy in the back, but you didn't."

"I had time then. I need to get rid of you quickly."

"You won't get away with it. Miriam knows I went looking for you."

"She won't talk. Her kind doesn't get involved with the police."

That's all he knew. "Someone else knows I'm here, too." I smiled with a confidence fabricated from thin air.

His eyes shifted in doubt. "Where is this person, then?"

"Fetching the police."

He gave that statement a fraction of a moment's thought. "Then I'd better hurry."

Jackson wasn't a man in peak physical condition, but he struck faster than I imagined him capable of. Ever since I'd glimpsed the knife, I'd been poised to run, trying to anticipate how best to dart past him. But he saw my dilemma at once and feinted to the left, then caught me as I made a dash for it. As he grabbed my arm, spinning me back in the direction of the water, I screamed. But who would hear me? The lumps in the empty lot scores of yards away? Streetwalkers?

I didn't expect rescue, but I wasn't going down without a fight. I twisted and kicked, escaping his grasp and breaking into a run—the wrong way. The only choice was to scramble farther out on the pier, but I didn't care. I stumbled away, yelling myself hoarse, until my head jerked back in blinding pain. The bastard ripped off my hat and grabbed my hair.

"Shut up!"

Standing behind me, he had his right arm crooked around my neck. Steel punctured my left cheek. A little lower, one swipe of the blade, and my throat would be cut.

Jackson's hairy wrist pushed my chin back so I was pinned against him. He wasn't wearing a glove—he'd probably known he'd be wielding the knife. He'd planned this. Planned my death. I searched frantically for a way out—fast—but all I saw was water, and those distant barges with the long johns flapping at me like a goodbye.

I had one weapon, one chance. I took it. I opened my mouth and bit down as hard as I could on the soft pad of Jackson's thumb.

Years spent around my uncle the butcher had familiarized me with the sound of an animal in pain. Jackson's cry reached a hog-being-slaughtered pitch, but I waited for the sound of the knife's clattering to the planks at our feet before I unclamped my teeth from his hand. I lunged for the knife, but he kicked it away. It went spinning off the edge of the pier. The sickening taste of his blood in my mouth didn't stop me running. The end of the pier had a rope strung across it, the flimsiest of barriers. I hiked my skirts above my knees and scrambled over it. There was a good twenty-foot drop to the water lapping below. Jackson, cursing and bending over his clutched hand, followed me.

"You bitch! You bit off my thumb!"

I doubted it. "I don't care if your whole hand comes off. Go complain to someone at Bellevue."

"As soon as we're through."

"Your knife is gone," I pointed out.

"Drowning will work as well."

"Then you'll die. I can swim and you can't. You told me so yourself."

"And you, like an idiot, took me at my word."

Frustration roiled through me. I *had* believed him, and now here I was, perched on the edge of a pier over a cold, filthy river. My gaze scanned the world beyond his shoulder—dry land—and I saw a flash of figures running down the sidewalk beneath a streetlamp. My heart rose, and I lifted my hand to signal them. Only the briefest of cries escaped my throat before Jackson's hand hit my chest.

The shock of it knocked the air out of me, and instead of hailing my rescuers, I found myself wheeling my arms as I pitched backward off the pier, toward the black water below.

I dropped like a stone. It was a long way down, yet there seemed to be no time to catch my breath. Freezing river water swallowed me, and I inhaled too late. Cold, murky liquid filled my nostrils, my lungs. My breathing passages were smothering in liquid, and trying to cough it out only made things worse. Meanwhile, all the wool, cotton, and leather on my body pulled me down with the efficiency of a dropped anchor. I was a good swimmer, but I was used to feeling buoyant in the water, floating along in a bathing costume of the lightest wool, not heading straight for the bottom like a boulder.

I could die. The idea startled me almost as much as the iciness of the water and my inability to breathe. My drowned body would wash up somewhere, and what then? Otto and Miriam wouldn't know what had happened. Several would mourn me—Callie, Otto, Aunt Irene, Walter, maybe even Bernice. Muldoon would shake his head over how I'd mucked this up. And the NYPD would record the death of the most disaster-prone and shortest-lived probationer in its history.

I would never again look into the face of the son I'd given up.

Frustration brought me back to myself. I wasn't dead yet. Hard as it was, I forced myself to kick.

At the same time, something exploded next to me. I panicked, then realized it was a man in the water, sinking like I was. Muldoon? I continued to kick for my life.

It seemed like an eternity, but I finally broke the surface and simultaneously inhaled and hacked up the liquid that had been trapped in my lungs. It was a struggle not to sink again. And then my waterlogged companion bobbed up, too. I looked over and groaned in irritation. It was Jackson.

Almost before I could react, he lunged and grabbed my neck, forcing me down again. This time I was able to inhale a breath that was half air, half Hudson.

My limbs, benumbed with cold, had trouble obeying my commands. Yet I kicked out, and one kick landed right where I aimed, at Jackson's middle. For a moment, I was free, and I surfaced again, gulping and paddling my arms to get away.

Above, a figure on the pier looked down. "Louise! Are you okay?"

Muldoon was stripping off his coat.

"I've got her," Jackson called back, a split second before his hands landed on my shoulders and shoved. I went under again.

I struggled, but felt myself being held under and pulled farther out. Jackson was stronger than he looked, and he was counting on my already weakened state to make it easy to finish me off. And Muldoon had been so close. So close.

I stilled my breath, wanting to hang on for as long as I could.

The hands holding me under suddenly let go. At first I thought perhaps Jackson had thought he'd killed me already. When I bobbed up to the surface, however, the water was churning. Muldoon, hair glistening wet and all askew but jaw set as ever, was throttling Jackson, who attempted to box him through the water. I was treading water, trying to find a way to help. Finally, I managed to pull myself around Jackson's back and grabbed his heavy coat collar, which I yanked down until his upper arms were slightly straitjacketed. Enough to allow Muldoon to get hold of him.

"You're caught, Beasley," he said.

Callie came around to my way of thinking, and sooner than I would have thought possible. Later in the day, after she'd gone to her show's final dress rehearsal before the big Broadway opening, there was a knock on my door. I padded across the room in my slippers, girding myself for an encounter with Wally. We still hadn't fixed the window.

But it wasn't Wally at my door. It was Hugh Van Hooten, his mouth tensed in an impatient frown, battered hat twisting in his hand. When his gaze reached my face, he exclaimed, "Great God. You look horrible."

"Thanks."

"Sorry," he said. "That probably sounded rude. But your face really is something out of Edgar Allan Poe."

"You should have stopped at sorry," I told him. "Would you like to come in, or do you prefer insulting me from the chill of the hallway?"

"In, I think." He strolled past me, heading straight for the parlor, taking it all in as critically as if he were a potential buyer. "This place isn't as bad inside as the looks of the house would lead you to think. A little cramped, though. I have a closet wider than this parlor." He frowned at Callie's curio shelf. "That kind of thing is totally useless."

I'd been on the verge of offering him something to drink, but thought better of it.

Not that Hugh noticed. He plopped himself down on the sofa, crossed his spidery legs, and let out a sigh. "Of course you know why I'm here."

"I don't have the foggiest idea."

His lips twisted like a man swallowing a sour pickle. "Obviously, I came to thank you. For finding out who killed Guy. It's been an awful business—very hard on my mother especially. And quite a distraction for me."

"It's good that you'll no longer be distracted, then."

"Yes." He sighed, as if the worst bit of his visit was yet to come. "Also, I wanted to apologize."

The last words came out so fast, I almost missed them. "You're apologizing to *me*?"

"Who else?"

"Callie."

He blinked. "What has she to do with anything?"

"You busted up her relationship with Teddy."

He sputtered at the accusation. "That's the most idiotic thing I've ever heard."

"Didn't you tell Teddy not to bring Callie to the air park again?"

"Yes, but so what? Women don't belong around airplanes. Besides, it's not as if I give Teddy orders. I'm not his father."

"He looks up to you. Heaven only knows why, but your opinion is gold to him."

"I see." He frowned. "I'd been wondering why he was moping around like a sad puppy."

"You never asked him?"

"Didn't seem any of my business."

"Well, now it is. So you can tell Teddy that he should call on Callie, who is wonderful and who, incidentally, would be an excellent pilot, no matter what you think of women flyers."

I half expected him to retract his apology and storm out. Instead, he studied me for a moment the way he might inspect a misfiring piston. "You're really quite interesting for a girl. I hadn't noticed that."

"There's no call to overwhelm me with flowery compliments."

If he heard my sarcasm, he didn't acknowledge it. "Well, girls are usually such nuisances. Only a fraction of them seem inclined to use their brains. And they always cause problems."

"Like Myrna?"

"Well, yes." He frowned. "There's no helping her."

"Yes, there is." I leaned forward. "Tell your mother she has a grandson. That's all you have to do."

He barked out a laugh. "All! All Odysseus had to do was face the Cyclops."

"Nice way to talk about your mother."

"You've never crossed her."

"No, but I saw how much she loved her children."

"Guy, you mean." He sighed. "Well, you could be right. I suppose if you can jump into an icy river to catch Guy's killer, I could have a heart-to-heart with Mother about Guy's illegitimate child."

Personally, I would rather jump into the Hudson again, but saying so wasn't going to help my argument. "You won't regret trying."

"I might, but as you say, it may help. I called Guy a coward for not telling her. I've been no better than a coward myself."

He left soon after this, exiting the apartment as abruptly as he'd appeared. The whole encounter was so brief and so strange, I doubted anything would come of it. But that very night I was awakened from a deep sleep by Callie, who lifted me in a hug before I was fully awake.

"You're a miracle worker, Louise."

I blinked back exhaustion. "I am?"

"Teddy came backstage after the show tonight with the biggest bunch of flowers you've ever seen. He was all apologies. He said Hugh told him he was a fool if he turned his back on me just because he said so, which he now insists he never did. Poor Teddy was so flustered. But he said Hugh's change of heart must have been on your account, because Hugh said that if I'm half as smart as you, I'm golden."

"Then you're platinum, because you're a hundred times better."

"That's what Teddy said. But he was wondering if maybe you and Hugh . . ."

I was so sleepy it took a moment to catch her drift. I laughed. "No."

"What a shame." Callie sighed. "We could have all gone flying together."

That wasn't the end of my good deeds, however. Callie later reported that Myrna and son had been asked to Thanksgiving dinner at the Van Hootens. No telling how that would turn out, but the invitation alone indicated the old lady must have thawed a little.

Now it seemed that only my own future was uncertain.

The department had given me a week's leave. At the end of that time, after Thanksgiving, I was supposed to report back and find out if I had any future with the NYPD. Yes, I'd caught a criminal, but as Muldoon had warned, the brass didn't appreciate probationers acting as detectives. And there was still the matter of the jailbreak and the unseemly behavior regarding poor Bob.

I remained on pins and needles, even as I tried to catch up on sleep and revel in Callie's success. Her show opened to solid reviews, with a few special mentions for her. I pinned the newspaper clippings all over the house, and Otto and I went to the show three times.

Thanksgiving's being on Thursday gave my aunt an excuse to turn her Thursday evening into an all-day extravaganza. At noon, the dining room was packed with her friends, who were treated to a feast cooked up by Bernice, me, and Miriam.

The holiday inevitably carried with it wistful thoughts of family members who were missing in my life. Was Calvin Longworth enjoying his first taste of turkey, I wondered? Did his parents realize how much they had to be thankful for? Even memories of my Altoona family carried sadness, and nostalgia. It had been almost a year and a half now since I'd seen Aunt Sonja, my uncles Dolph and Luddie, and my young cousins. A hundred times I pictured the table they'd be sitting around: the meticulously polished silver, the wedding crystal, and Aunt Sonja's best Meissen china. Did they ever wonder about me? I was tempted to write them and tell them about my success in settling in New York and finding a career . . .

Except that I didn't want to brag about being a policewoman if I was about to be pitched out of the department.

Though Aunt Irene's nearest and dearest friends came in and out all day, my own friends were not there. Callie was spending the day with Teddy. I wondered what his family would make of his bringing a showgirl home for Thanksgiving. Otto was also conspicuously absent. At the last minute, he'd sent a message that he had to work but would be stopping by in the evening with a surprise. Not having him there to joke with about Altoona probably added to my melancholy, which I tried not to show.

The one person I knew sympathized with me was Miriam. However well she was fitting in with Aunt Irene's household, she didn't disguise the sadness in her eyes when our gazes met that day. I knew she didn't regret Jackson's being caught, or the end of her marriage. If anything, she was relieved to know that he was locked away. But she was also far from home on this day that seemed to be all about home and families.

In the evening, I served hors d'oeuvres and drinks to visitors who crowded into the parlor. I watched the door, expecting each newcomer to be Otto. Once when I looked up, Muldoon was strolling in. The last time I'd seen him was Saturday night, after we'd both been fished out of the river, although he'd sent over a fruit basket to the flat. He nodded to me and then went to greet Aunt Irene, who effused over him like a long-lost friend.

I threaded my way over to him, offering him my drinks tray by way of greeting.

His lips turned down slightly. Champagne wasn't his beverage, I guessed.

"We have everything." I tilted my head toward Walter tending the ornate bar across the room.

"No, thanks. I only came by because I wanted to talk to you." He studied my face. "Your eye's better."

It was at the yellow stage, which Aunt Irene had helped me cover with makeup. The thin red mark across my cheek was still visible, although the doctor who'd looked at it swore it wouldn't leave much of a scar. Muldoon's gaze took in the red gash. His grim expression made my heart sink.

"I'm out," I guessed. Of the police department, I meant.

"Why would you think that?"

"Because of the way you're looking at me. You might as well be hooded and carrying a scythe."

He gestured toward the dining room. "Why don't we go in there and have a talk."

The dining room was mostly empty. I led the way. When we were both seated, I decided a little liquid courage wouldn't go amiss. I belted down half a glass of champagne.

"All right," I said. "You can tell me. I can take it."

"You're not going to lose your job," he said. "The Van Hootens made a big fuss about your discovering Guy's killer and helping to catch him."

"They did?" Yes, Hugh had thanked me in person, but I was still shocked. And Muldoon's mentioning *Van Hootens* in the plural made it seem as if Edith Van Hooten must have said a word on my behalf, too.

He nodded. "What's more, two merchants from Lexington Avenue contacted downtown, saying that you should get a commendation for catching a shoplifter."

"But what about the attempted jailbreak?"

He shrugged. "A killer and a thief off the street more than cancel out that little episode. From what I've heard, you'll be able to finish out your probationary period."

"Have you discovered who Cain's spy is?"

He shook his head. "That will take a longer investigation. I know it's hopeless to tell you to be careful, but you need to keep your eyes open."

I could feel myself sitting taller. "And *that's* what you came to tell me?"

"Mostly."

Happiness surged through me, along with the desire to club him with an empty champagne bottle. "Why didn't you come out and say so right away? You didn't have to scare me half to death."

He looked as if I'd lost my mind. "What did I say to scare you?"

"It was how you looked."

"I can't help the way I look," he said.

"Yes, you can. It's called a smile. I seem to recall you have a very handsome one when you choose to employ it."

Two lines deepened in his brow, and he looked more serious than ever.

I laughed. "Here—a little bubbly might help you to remember the mechanics of it." I pushed a glass toward him, and he took it.

"Louise, I—"

All at once, the entire room seemed to suck in its breath. Everyone turned toward the door.

I stood up halfway, then thumped back down again as excited murmurs went through the room in a wave. Otto had come in with Al Jolson. The entertainer fed off the guests' adulation, and his always wide smile grew wider. He went to my aunt, going down on his knee and kissing her hand as if she were royalty. Aunt Irene fluttered both at the attention and at the coup of having landed such an illustrious guest. "I hope you'll entertain us a little, Mr. Jolson."

"Friends call me Al," he corrected.

"That's what Al and I have been up to most of the day," Otto said. "We've been working out a song for him to add to his new show when he takes it on tour." He turned to Jolson. "Should we try it out?"

"No time like the present, kid."

They headed to the piano, and the rest of the room pivoted to follow them, like a school of fish.

I had a hard time looking away, too, but something Muldoon had been saying bubbled back into my mind. I touched the sleeve of his jacket. "What did you mean by *mostly*?"

He glanced back at me. "What?"

"You said that the news about my job was 'mostly' what you came here for. What else?"

"To check on how you were and to see what kind of day you'd had." His voice lowered and tentatively, he put his hand over mine. "I thought maybe you'd be missing your home."

"Oh." My eyes felt hot, and for a moment I tried to gulp past a knot in my throat. How had he known?

"Louise . . ."

I shook my head. "It's nothing. I have been thinking of home today, and feeling a little sad. That's probably because Aunt Irene and I visited Mr. McChesney early this morning. It was awful. I felt so good about catching Jackson, but Mr. McChesney's still going to be in jail for a long time."

He nodded.

"So it feels bittersweet now. Not the victory I'd expected."

"Welcome to police work," he said.

The piano launched into an up-tempo number and Jolson started belting out a song. *My song,* I realized.

Otto caught my eye, briefly, and then returned his adoring gaze to his new idol. Jolson was playing the small crowd much as he did dancing up and down the apron of the Winter Garden, singing in his manic patter about a girl who'd strung him along with increasingly feeble excuses, ending with the line, "She didn't really go to the dentist."

The crowd laughed, and by the third chorus we were all singing along. I glanced over at Muldoon, who was looking at me, his lips turned up in a smile.